HUNT FOR VOLDORIUS

CAPTAIN KOR'SARRO KHAN of the White Scars is petitioned by his Chapter Master to hunt down and destroy the daemon prince Voldorius, a warleader of the renegade Alpha Legion, thus ending his reign of terror across the stars. Hunting the beast doggedly for over a decade, Kor'sarro finally brings Voldorius to battle on Quintus, a world that has totally given itself over to the Alpha Legion. Together with their Raven Guard allies, the White Scars must fight an entire planet of enemies if they are to slay the daemon prince.

A WARHAMMER 40,000 NOVEL

HUNT FOR VOLDORIUS

ANDY HOARE

BLACK LIBRARY

To the awesome staff of Nottingham City Hospital Oncology Outpatients.

A Black Library Publication

First published in Great Britain in 2010 by
The Black Library,
Games Workshop Ltd.,
The Black Library,
Nottingham, NG7 2WS, UK.

10 9 8 7 6 5 4 3 2

Cover illustration by Jon Sullivan.

Maps by Adrian Wood.

A CIP record for this book is available from the British Library.

UK ISBN 13: 978 1 84416 513 1
US ISBN 13: 978 1 84416 514 8

See the Black Library on the Internet at
www.blacklibrary.com

Find out more about Games Workshop
and the world of Warhammer 40,000 at
www.games-workshop.com

Printed and bound in the UK.

IT IS THE 41st millennium. For more than a hundred centuries the Emperor has sat immobile on the Golden Throne of Earth. He is the master of mankind by the will of the gods, and master of a million worlds by the might of his inexhaustible armies. He is a rotting carcass writhing invisibly with power from the Dark Age of Technology. He is the Carrion Lord of the Imperium for whom a thousand souls are sacrificed every day, so that he may never truly die.

YET EVEN IN his deathless state, the Emperor continues his eternal vigilance. Mighty battlefleets cross the daemon-infested miasma of the warp, the only route between distant stars, their way lit by the Astronomican, the psychic manifestation of the Emperor's will. Vast armies give battle in his name on uncounted worlds. Greatest amongst His soldiers are the Adeptus Astartes, the Space Marines, bio-engineered super-warriors. Their comrades in arms are legion: the Imperial Guard and countless planetary defence forces, the ever-vigilant Inquisition and the tech-priests of the Adeptus Mechanicus to name only a few. But for all their multitudes, they are barely enough to hold off the ever-present threat from aliens, heretics, mutants – and worse.

TO BE A man in such times is to be one amongst untold billions. It is to live in the cruellest and most bloody regime imaginable. These are the tales of those times. Forget the power of technology and science, for so much has been forgotten, never to be re-learned. Forget the promise of progress and understanding, for in the grim dark future there is only war. There is no peace amongst the stars, only an eternity of carnage and slaughter, and the laughter of thirsting gods.

'Once in every quarter century, the masters of the White Scars Chapter gather in the highest spire of their Chapter-Fortress, high atop the Khum Karta Mountains, to conduct the auspicious Rites of Howling. During this most solemn of rituals, the names of all those foes that have yet to be slain are read aloud, lest the proud and savage Sons of Chogoris ever forget their sworn duty to hunt down the enemies of the Emperor and of their mighty primarch, the honoured First, Lord Jaghatai Khan.

The fell deeds of each enemy are recounted, and great and terrible oaths are sworn. But no vow ever undertaken has been as binding, nor as solemn as that made by Kor'sarro Khan, fifty-first Master of the Hunt and Captain of the 3rd Company of the White Scars. For it was upon the centennial feast of the ascension of the Chapter's current Great Khan, the honoured Kyublai, that the name of Kernax Voldorius was read aloud for the final time.

The name of this most vile of daemon princes appears in the forbidden histories and the folklore of a thousand and more worlds, though none save the most highly placed amongst the Lords of the Imperium know the truth of his deeds. So too was he known by other names upon a thousand more planets. On Kento he was called the Vindictor; on Loran, the Unyielding Storm; and on cursed Blindhope, the Executioner. The Elder-Lords of the Seven Outer Marches named him the Hand of Night; the Sentinels of the Eye, the Curse of Lost Gods. It is said that only the Hidden Masters of the Ordo Malleus know the daemon's true name, and that seven of their number have fallen to his blade attempting to use it to gain power over him.

But of all of the evils this being had committed, the name of one is whispered across a hundred sectors. It was the deed that caused the mortal Kernax to be granted ascension by the fell powers of the empyrean, and to take his place as a daemon prince of Chaos. Two thousand years ago, Voldorius brought about the wholesale slaughter of billions of souls, when he invoked the power of an ancient weapon created by madmen during the long lost Dark Age of Technology.

That weapon was the Bloodtide.

And so, Kyublai commissioned Kor'sarro to bring him the head of Kernax Voldorius, that it might be taken back to Chogoris, where according to the ancient ways of the White Scars, it might be encased in living silver and mounted upon a lance to be set upon the road to Khum Karta. Only then would the name of Kernax Voldorius be struck from the hunt. Only then would Kor'sarro Khan's duty be done.

Thus, Kor'sarro Khan, Master of the Hunt, undertook the greatest of challenges, a hunt that had defeated so many of his forebears, a hunt that would take him to every corner of the Imperium and beyond, over the course of a decade and more.

The Hunt for Voldorius.'

– Omniscenti Bithisarea, *Deeds of the Adeptus Astartes*, Volume IX, Chapter XXV, M.40 recension (suppressed)

CHAPTER 1

Thunder in a Clear Sky

'RELEASE IN TEN,' the pilot announced calmly over the vox-net. 'Drop bay portal opening.'

Kor'sarro Khan, Captain of the 3rd Company of the White Scars Chapter of Space Marines, and holder of the honoured rank of Master of the Hunt, turned his gaze from the command terminal to the scene outside the Thunderhawk's canopy. Flashing red lumens made the inside of the strike cruiser's drop bay appear as a scene from the underworld, putting Kor'sarro in mind of the tales the Chapter's Storm Seers told at the great feasts. The sound of wailing sirens added to the hellish impression, sounding like the lamentations of the damned. With a grinding rumble transmitted through the hull of the gunship directly to Kor'sarro's bones, the great doors below the Thunderhawk ground open. In seconds, a deep, metallic boom passed through the strike cruiser and the doors were fully open, the Thunderhawk suspended by its drop cradle above the yawning opening.

'Portal bay open,' the pilot reported. 'Release in five.'

With the drop-portal open, Kor'sarro saw for the first time the surface of Cernis IV. From this height, the land appeared white and serene, glistening with scintillating reflections of the violet lights that danced in the upper atmosphere. As captivating as the lights were, the Master of the Hunt knew that what created them represented a terrible danger to the drop mission his force was about to undertake.

'Release!'

An instant after the pilot's announcement, the huge metal claws holding the Thunderhawk above the portal sprang apart. The gunship dropped through the opening with gut-wrenching force, the surface of Cernis IV leaping upwards to meet it. Kor'sarro fought against the staggering G-force to raise his head and look upwards at the rapidly receding form of the strike cruiser, *Lord of Heavens*. He noted with satisfaction the release of the other four gunships, each holding its place in the formation.

The Thunderhawks levelled out. Rather than dropping straight downwards, each now arrowed prow first towards the surface. Already, bright flames began to lick the leading edges of the gunships' blunt forms.

'Gravimetrics picking up turbulence, as predicted,' the pilot said, addressing Kor'sarro directly. The Techmarines had warned of the disturbance the gunships would meet as they undertook the drop, an effect caused by the complex interactions of Cernis IV's many natural satellites.

'Compensate as you see fit,' Kor'sarro replied. 'But keep us on target.'

The cockpit began to shudder, wisps of flame dancing across the outside of the armoured canopy. The Thunderhawks were effecting their drop on a heading that no ordinary human troops could undertake, for the gravitational forces would overcome them long before the drop vessels touched down. The White Scars were no mere humans, however; they were superhumans, genetically enhanced Space Marines whose augmented physiologies could withstand such forces and more.

'They'll never see us coming,' Kor'sarro growled, his words drowned out by the roaring of the upper atmosphere as it burned against the gunship's hull. Kor'sarro longed to feel the earth beneath his feet, to breathe the air of the world below, to engage his enemy and complete the hunt. Though masters of the lightning strike, the White Scars preferred to fight across the wide spaces of a planet's surface. Kor'sarro always felt a notion he imagined was akin to helplessness during a planetary drop. As the buffeting increased still further and the cockpit shook with mounting violence, the captain gripped the arms of the grav-couch fiercely.

'Approaching overlap point alpha,' the pilot reported. Kor'sarro caught the note of concentration in the warrior's voice, the only hint of the tension the Space Marine must have been experiencing.

As the gunship dived on and the surface of Cernis IV swelled to fill the view from the cockpit, the shuddering reached a new pitch. Kor'sarro saw that six of the planet's small moons were rising, and it was this that was inflicting the violent disturbance as the Thunderhawks raced onwards. Although the Techmarines had predicted the effect, there was still a risk that the titanic forces might prove too strong for even the mighty Thunderhawks. At a single word, Kor'sarro could order the gunships to change course, coming about to a new heading that would avoid the worst of the gravitational pressures. Yet to do so would be to abandon the best chance of taking the target by surprise, for none could expect an attack to come from the vector the White Scars were taking. The target was far too valuable to lose, and Kor'sarro would take any risk to achieve victory. His honour, and that of the entire 3rd Company, depended on it.

'Entering point alpha!' the pilot called out, his voice barely audible over the roaring against the hull and the violent shaking of the cockpit. The turbulence increased by an order of magnitude as the gunship entered the point where the gravitational influences of the moons converged. Kor'sarro imagined his body was being pulled in several different directions at once, and knew that it was only his genetic enhancements that kept him conscious. He knew too that his survival relied not only on the Thunderhawk resisting the immense pressures that strained its armoured hull to breaking point, but also upon the pilot's own efforts not only to remain conscious, but to keep the vessel on its heading.

'Terminal point alpha reached,' the pilot announced through gritted teeth. There was no turning back now, even if Kor'sarro had been willing to order a change in heading. He mouthed a silent prayer to the Emperor of Mankind and to Jaghatai Khan, revered Primarch of the White Scars.

The view through the canopy was now entirely obscured by rippling white flame as the atmosphere of Cernis IV burned against the armoured panels. Kor'sarro's enhanced vision protected his eyes from damage. Warning klaxons wailed as the forces outside took their toll on the gunship's hull, which groaned audibly as it was wrenched in multiple directions. The temperature inside the cockpit rose to that of a furnace as the vessel's cooling systems laboured to maintain survivable conditions. Sweat ran from Kor'sarro's brow, obscuring his vision as he looked to the pilot.

'Brother Koban,' Kor'sarro addressed the pilot. The Space Marine's face was a mask of determination as he battled with the gunship's controls. Kor'sarro knew that the pilot was nearing the bounds of his endurance. 'Draw your strength from your ancestors,' Kor'sarro shouted over the roaring winds and the wailing alerts. 'Have faith in the primarch!'

'Honoured be his name!' the pilot replied by rote, visibly emboldened by his captain's words. The Space Marine redoubled his efforts, mastering the bucking control column, and the gunship responded instantly. The buffeting calmed, and in moments the white flames licking the outside of the canopy faded and danced away.

'My thanks, brother-captain,' the pilot said, nodding his head towards Kor'sarro.

'You have but yourself to thank,' Kor'sarro replied. 'And the Great Khan, honoured be his name.'

As the last of the flames engulfing the Thunderhawk's blunt, armoured prow flickered and died, the surface of Cernis IV became visible again. The entire view from the cockpit was now filled with the pure, glittering whiteness of the planet's northern polar region. Where before the surface had appeared to shimmer with reflected light, Kor'sarro could discern individual points of jagged, violet-hued brightness. Each of these was a towering crystalline formation, some as tall as a man, others rearing hundreds of metres in the cold air. Each crystal tower reflected the violet auroras that pulsated in the skies above, casting the entire region in an unearthly light.

The Techmarines had been unable to identify the material from which the crystals were formed, but warned that they were clustered so densely across the northern pole that they presented a significant threat to a successful planetfall operation. The remote likeliness of any force attempting such a mission in the perilous region had simply added to its desirability, as far as Kor'sarro was concerned, and the order had been given.

'Landing zone identified,' the co-pilot announced.

'Altering course,' the pilot replied, bringing the gunship around to the coordinates scrolling across his command slate. 'Brother-captain?'

Kor'sarro confirmed that the other four Thunderhawks of the strike force were in formation. One was trailing a line of thick black smoke from its starboard engine. None of the Thunderhawks had come through the drop untouched and there was little that could be done now. He could not even risk a vox-transmission to determine the extent of the gunship's wound. Only faith in the Great Khan would see them through.

'Final approach,' Kor'sarro ordered.

On his word, the gunship banked before diving for the frozen surface. The landscape rushed upwards dramatically as the Thunderhawk's air brakes shed the vessel's momentum. In minutes, the largest of the crystal towers were discernable, their multi-faceted, mirror-smooth flanks reflecting light in all directions.

'Beginning approach run,' the pilot said, his attentions focussed on the closing towers. As the Thunderhawk levelled out the pilot fed power to the engines. Crystals the size of cathedrals flashed by on all sides, and for an instant Kor'sarro was assailed by the sight of a thousand gunships flying in an insane formation all about. There was no way of telling which were the real vessels and which were reflections on the mirrored surfaces of the crystal towers.

'Adjust three-nine in eight point five,' the co-pilot said, not taking his eyes from the augur screen before him.

The pilot merely nodded, before yanking hard on the control column. Kor'sarro's seat restraints tensed as his weight was thrown suddenly to port, but to his relief they held. The largest crystal tower Kor'sarro had yet seen flashed by the gunship's starboard. Due to its multiple, reflective faces, the crystal had not been visible by eyesight. Only the co-pilot's augur warning had saved the vessel from being smashed to atoms against its sheer side.

'That was too close,' breathed the pilot. 'My apologies, brother-captain.'

'None needed,' Kor'sarro replied. 'Attend to your duty.'

The pilot returned his attentions to the fore, bringing the gunship into a wide turn that brought it around a huge crystal tower that Kor'sarro had not even seen amongst the riot of reflections. Leaving the tower behind, the pilot corrected the heading, Kor'sarro craning his neck to ensure that the other vessels were doing likewise.

'Delta twelve!' the co-pilot called out suddenly.

The pilot heeded his battle-brother's warning with instinctive speed. The Thunderhawk was thrown violently to starboard as the pilot avoided a needle-like tower that reared out of nowhere as if seeking to skewer the vessel. For the briefest moment, Kor'sarro caught sight of his own reflection in the needle's mirrored flank as the formation flashed by mere metres away.

Kor'sarro had no need to turn his head to look through the rear of the canopy in order to follow the progress of the other four gunships, for their reflections were all about, mirrored in a thousand glassy crystal flanks. One Thunderhawk pitched to starboard, while two went to port, the needle flashing by between. The last gunship, still trailing smoke from the engine damaged during the planetfall, was not so fast to react. To his great honour, the vessel's pilot almost managed to avoid the crystal spire, but his starboard wing grazed it nonetheless. In an instant, the end of the stubby wing was shorn away, and the entire needle exploded into a million shards. The devastation was reflected from a thousand surfaces at once. Kor'sarro's senses were all but overwhelmed as innumerable shards, both real and reflected, cascaded in all directions, impacting on the hull of his own gunship like anti-aircraft fire.

'Hunter Three's going down!' the co-pilot called out. 'I can't get a reading, there's too much interference from the shards.'

Kor'sarro processed the terrible decision in an instant. Just as quickly, his mind was made up. 'Maintain vox-silence,' he ordered. 'But keep the channels open.'

The mission was all.

'You ARE SURE it is him?' Kor'sarro had asked when informed that the object of his years-long hunt had once again been located. 'You are sure this is not another of his traps?'

'Yes, my khan, I am sure it is Voldorius,' the Scout-sergeant replied. 'Whether or not it is a trap, however...'

'I understand, Kholka. You will forgive my impatience in this matter,' Kor'sarro said. Taking a deep breath, he reined in his eagerness to resume the pursuit of this ancient nemesis of his Chapter. The Master of the Hunt must be keen-eyed and measured in all he does, Kor'sarro reminded himself, lest he blunder into a trap of his target's making. 'Please, deliver your report.'

Scout-Sergeant Kholka looked from Kor'sarro to the black void beyond the strike cruiser's armoured viewing port at which he stood. Kor'sarro allowed the veteran a moment to gather his thoughts, knowing that Kholka shared his own feelings in the matter. The stateroom in which the two warriors met was dark, its walls lined with the trophies of a score of victories. Displayed above the viewing port was the polished skull of a tyranid hive tyrant, a mighty beast which Kor'sarro himself had bested in lethal one-on-one combat. Lethal for the beast itself, Kor'sarro mused, memories of the climax of the Siege of Mysibis flooding back, but almost for him too. Even now, two decades later, the scars earned in that titanic confrontation still pained him.

'We picked up his trail at Sinopha Station, on the fringes of the Protean Ebb,' Kholka began. 'The survivors' accounts left us in no doubt that the attackers were Alpha Legion.' The Scout-sergeant paused, evidently calling to mind the scenes of carnage and butchery at the station.

'Go on, my friend,' Kor'sarro urged. 'How did you identify the traitors as belonging to Voldorius's band?'

'At first we had only the accounts to go by,' Kholka continued. 'But these were… unclear, as I am sure you can imagine.'

Indeed I can, Kor'sarro thought. The Alpha Legion, erstwhile brothers of the Space Marines, had turned against the Imperium ten thousand years ago, and ever since their defeat in that galaxy-wide civil war they had waged a bitter campaign of terror on the peoples of the Imperium. The treacherous Alpha Legion were masters of insurrection and disorder, spreading the poison of rebellion wherever they went. They only left survivors when they intended accounts of their actions to spread panic across a wide area.

'Those victims who were not killed in the attack were driven beyond sanity by the cruelties inflicted upon them,' the sergeant said. 'Others had been reduced to gibbering imbeciles by the traitors' sorceries. Most were able to tell us very little. But one, who had served in the station's watch-militia, had displayed the foresight to commit the initial stages of the attack to the archivum, and this we were able to retrieve.'

'What of this man?' Kor'sarro asked, even though he knew what the sergeant's reply would be.

'We granted him the Emperor's peace,' Kholka responded gravely. 'His duty was done, and it was all we could do for him.'

Kor'sarro nodded for the sergeant to continue.

'The station's archivum logs confirmed the identity of the attackers' vessel.'

'*The Ninth Eye*?' Kor'sarro interjected. If it was indeed that hated ship that had delivered the Alpha Legion attackers to Sinopha Station, then the hunt for the Daemon Lord Voldorius was truly back underway, after so many galling months of cold trails and frustration.

'*The Ninth Eye*,' the sergeant confirmed. Kor'sarro watched Kholka as he paced before the viewing port, and paused before the skull of a fearsome ambull. 'We set out immediately, and were able to pick up the vessel's signature as it made for the jump point. Our astropath was able to track its jump, and our Navigator able to shadow it without our enemy becoming aware of our presence.'

'You know this?' Kor'sarro interrupted. 'You are sure Voldorius was unaware of your pursuit?'

'Salpo is, as you know, my khan, one of our most skilled Navigators. I have this on his word.'

Kor'sarro allowed himself a feral grin, feeling his blood rise at the prospect of resuming the hunt. It had been almost a decade since Kyublai, Great Khan of the White Scars Chapter, had declared that the vile one Voldorius would be hunted down and slain in the name of the Emperor. As Captain of the 3rd Company and Master of the Hunt, it had fallen to Kor'sarro Khan to turn the Great Khan's words into deeds. He had gone before the Great Khan and his court on the Chapter's home world of Chogoris, and made a terrible oath.

By Kor'sarro's honour, the Daemon Prince Voldorius, he who had unleashed the Bloodtide and reaped a thousand billion innocent souls, would be brought to justice. As befitted the Chapter's traditions, the traitor would be slain by the hand of the Master of the

Hunt. His skull would be masked in silver and mounted at the tip of a lance. The trophy would be placed along the road to the White Scars' fortress-monastery, alongside thousands more, high in the Khum Karta Mountains, where it would remain for all time as warning to those who would betray their oaths and turn their hand against the Emperor.

Despite his savage desire to finally corner his foe, Kor'sarro bade the sergeant continue.

'We tracked *The Ninth Eye* through three systems. It laid over at none, merely recalibrating before pressing on. Twelve days after the last jump, it entered the Cernis system, where it made for the fourth planet.'

Kor'sarro had no knowledge of this star, for it was but a single, unremarkable system amongst over a million claimed by man. 'What of this place?' he asked.

'Cernis IV is home to a small population of convicted sinners and petty transgressors, those whose sentences have been commuted from death to servitude.' Kor'sarro scowled at the mental picture the sergeant's description brought to mind. Scum, undeserving of a second chance. 'Most eke out a nomadic existence as krill farmers, chasing the seasonal drifts along the coasts.'

'And the rest?' Kor'sarro asked, inferring that the Alpha Legion would have little interest in the convicts the sergeant described.

'The rest are indentured to a substantial promethium refining operation at the world's northern pole.'

'And it is to this place that the enemy has retired,' Kor'sarro growled, a statement, not a question. The sergeant's expression confirmed his suspicion. Voldorius and his band of traitors had no doubt infiltrated the criminals that laboured at the promethium plant. That being the case, he could only assume that the world's government, no doubt seated at the refinery, had been compromised, if not completely overthrown. He had to assume that the entire work force had been bribed, corrupted or coerced into serving the daemon prince, and it had probably not taken much effort to do so. The White Scars would be entering hostile territory as they closed on their foe.

'My thanks, brother-sergeant,' Kor'sarro said. 'Your deeds do us all great honour, and the Great Khan shall hear of them.' Kholka bowed deeply in response to the captain's affirmation.

'The word is given,' Kor'sarro growled. 'The hunt is on.'

As THE THUNDERHAWK banked past another great crystal tower, Kor'sarro caught sight of the target. The Cernis IV promethium plant loomed on the horizon, a vast stain upon a wide, frozen plain studded with smaller crystal formations. Even from twelve kilometres out, the plant was imposing. Vast storage tanks and processing stacks reared into the cold sky, the tallest belching dark fumes or flaring with alchemical burn-off. The plant was the size of a city, its buildings sprawling across the plain, each connected to the next by a complex web of pipes and conduits carrying raw promethium. With an expert eye, Kor'sarro assessed two rings of defence thrown up around the plant, each punctuated by squat bastions mounted with heavy ground and anti-air ordnance. Scout-Sergeant Kholka's reports had been characteristically accurate.

'Ten kilometres,' the pilot reported. 'Confirm attack pattern?'

'As the moon swoops,' Kor'sarro replied, using the battle-cant of the White Scars Chapter. As the Thunderhawk dived towards the white plain, the sun glinted from the ice, the glare masking the defenders from Kor'sarro's sight. He still had only estimates of the defenders' strengths to go on, and the attack pattern would allow the gunships to reconnoitre the plant's defences before committing to a final run.

The Thunderhawk levelled out as it streaked across the plain, the pilot jinking expertly to avoid the smaller crystal formations. At an altitude of only thirty metres, Kor'sarro could now discern the defence lines. Crudely fortified trenches had been dug into the snow, recently by his estimation. As the first line flashed by below, a storm of small-arms fire erupted, las-bolts pattering harmlessly against the gunship's armoured hull.

Kor'sarro activated his command terminal and invoked the view from a spy-lens mounted to the Thunderhawk's rear. The pict-slate showed the view of the trench the gunship had just passed over, and Kor'sarro could make out troops manning its ramparts. There were hundreds of them packed into the makeshift position, yet it was immediately clear that they were not professional soldiers, in any sense of the word. For a start, they showed no discernable uniform, each wearing a ragged ensemble of rubberised work suit, with crude armour fashioned from steel plates. Many wore rebreathers, originally intended no doubt to protect against the fumes belched out by the refinery but pressed into service against the biting cold beyond the plant's limits. For an instant, Kor'sarro thought he saw a fell rune of the Chaos powers, daubed crudely upon a soldier's chest plate, but the view receded before he could be sure.

'Closing on the second line,' the pilot intoned. 'Brace for heavy fire.'

The second defence line was more heavily fortified than the first. The trenches were reinforced with armour plating, and rockcrete bunkers stood every two hundred metres.

'Brace!' the pilot called out.

A searing line of fire suddenly cut through the air as an autocannon mounted on one of the bastions opened up. The shot was poorly aimed, passing clean through the White Scars' formation without inflicting any damage.

'That was just a ranging shot,' Kor'sarro growled, and immediately three more weapons, each mounted on a different bastion, opened fire.

This time, the shots passed by far closer, inscribing a deadly web across the air space the gunships flew through.

'That plotting is far too coordinated to be the work of recidivist scum,' Kor'sarro said. 'The Alpha Legion have been here before.' How long, he could only guess, but certainly long enough to have overseen the construction of the inner line of trenches and to plot a highly effective air defence net. As the full extent of the defences revealed themselves, the autocannons barked again. This time, the air blazed with over a dozen bursts, and the Thunderhawk rocked violently as it was struck.

'Taking effective fire!' the pilot called out. 'Implementing evasive manoeuvres.'

Alarms blared out as the gunship's aggrieved war spirit described its wounds. The Thunderhawk shook as the pilot undertook a series of jarring evasions, throwing the enemy gunners' aim, for a brief moment at least.

'Starboard control vanes compromised,' the pilot announced as he fought the shaking control column.

'And we're bleeding fuel from engine beta,' the co-pilot added.

'Stand by,' Kor'sarro ordered as he opened a vox-channel to the formation. There was little to be gained by maintaining vox silence now. 'All Hunters, report.'

'Hunter Two, Hunter One,' the response came back immediately. 'The arrow's flight, shrouded by mist.'

'Hunter Four, Hunter One,' the next report came in, after the speaker had allowed an optimistic chance for Hunter Three to report. 'The trail, winter rises.'

'Hunter Five, Hunter One,' the last gunship responded. 'The crest by dawn.'

'Damn them,' Kor'sarro spat in response to the battle-cant reports. Hunter Two's augurs were damaged, Four had lost pressure in at least one compartment and Hunter Five's forward landing gear had taken a glancing hit. There was no word of Hunter Three.

Kor'sarro opened the vox-channel again, but before he could speak a further salvo of fire erupted from every bastion within a kilometre. The channel erupted with howling feedback as the very air burned.

'All Hunters,' Kor'sarro said, not knowing whether his transmission would penetrate the sudden interference but sure he had no choice but to try. 'The arrow turns, the deluge.'

'Coming about on new heading,' the pilot announced, obeying the battle-cant order. In seconds, the Thunderhawk was banking over the outer defence line, pursued by angry autocannon bursts. With great relief, Kor'sarro noted the other vessels doing likewise.

Kor'sarro fought down the galling frustration at encountering such an effective air defence grid. It could only have been erected under the oversight of one of Voldorius's lieutenants. The Alpha Legion were adept at corrupting lesser forces, and would easily have established themselves as masters over the treacherous convicts that laboured in Cernis IV's promethium refinery. He consoled himself with the knowledge that such scum could never have mounted such a stout defence themselves. It was a timely reminder of just how dangerous a foe the Alpha

Legion were. Furthermore, as fearsome as the defenders' fire had proven, the White Scars pilots were superior. Although minor damage had been sustained, the strike force was still effective, even with the loss of Hunter Three.

And besides, Kor'sarro thought, the White Scars never relied on a single battle plan. Even now, the Thunderhawks were closing on the secondary landing zone where Kor'sarro and his warriors would disembark and approach the target by the alternative route, planned for just such an eventuality.

'Touch down in thirty,' the pilot announced.

'Enemy position at sigma-seven,' the co-pilot interjected.

Kor'sarro saw the secondary landing zone up ahead, but nearby, in the shadow of a jagged cluster of crystals, was a hurriedly dug enemy gun pit. Several of the defenders were armed with shoulder-mounted missile launchers.

'Neutralise it,' Kor'sarro ordered.

The air between the Thunderhawk and the gun pit was split asunder as the vessel's heavy bolters opened up. Hundreds of rounds had been expended in seconds, the snow all around the target vaporised into an obscuring mist. Surely, nothing could have survived such a torrent of fire.

As if to mock the White Scars, a missile streaked out of the roiling mist, passing within a handful of metres of the gunship's armoured canopy.

'I cannot resolve a target,' the co-pilot said.

'Target the crystal,' Kor'sarro ordered. 'Hellstrike.'

A moment later, a missile lanced from beneath the Thunderhawk's stubby wings towards the gun pit. But instead of disappearing into the vapour created by the heavy bolter fire, the projectile sped towards the crystal overhead. The impact came mere seconds later.

In a repetition of the incident on the approach run, the crystal exploded into a billion shards. The vapour cloud was blown away, the ground for a hundred metres all about studded by countless micro-impacts. Those defenders who had survived the heavy bolter fire were torn apart as the crystal shards ripped through their bodies. At the last, only the jagged remains of the crystal formation and a wide red stain upon the frozen ground marked the formerly enemy-held position.

'Take us in,' Kor'sarro ordered.

EVEN AS KOR'SARRO powered his roaring bike, Moon-drakkan, down the Thunderhawk's ramp, Hunters Two, Four and Five were touching down nearby. Screaming retro jets vaporised the ice, before the mighty gunships settled upon hissing, flexing landing struts. Hunter One, Kor'sarro's command platform, was a conventional Thunderhawk specially modified to carry the Command squad's beloved bikes. Hunter Five was likewise modified, and carried the task force's other two bike-mounted squads. The other ships, including the missing Hunter Three, were transporters, and carried between the three vessels four Rhino-borne Tactical squads, two Rhino-borne

Devastator squads and three jump pack-equipped Assault squads. A pair of Rhino transport vehicles was cradled below each transporter, their engines growling as if in anticipation of churning up the frozen plain.

As the two transporters settled, the sturdy arms holding the Rhinos in place released, and, accompanied by the angry hiss of hydraulics, retracted upwards. Almost in unison, the launch jets of both transporters fired up again, and both lifted perfectly vertically, leaving a pair of Rhinos on the ground beneath each. In a moment, all four Thunderhawks had cleared the landing zone, streaking away to establish a holding pattern until called upon.

'All units,' Kor'sarro spoke into his helmet vox-link as he slewed Moondrakkan to a halt. 'Converge on me.'

Behind him, the five bike-mounted warriors of Kor'sarro's Command squad formed up. These men were his brothers, for they had travelled by his side for the last decade, never wavering in the hunt for Voldorius. Kor'sarro's company champion, Brother Jhogai, removed his helmet having brought his growling mount to a halt, and took in a great lungful of the freezing air. Beside him, Brother Yeku bore the standard of the 3rd Company, an honoured banner adorned with the lightning-strike symbol of the White Scars Chapter, and topped with a fluttering mane of black horsehair. Apothecary Khagus halted his bike beside the standard bearer, and behind him came Brothers Temu and Kergis.

'Is there any word?' Kor'sarro addressed Brother Temu, knowing the warrior would understand his meaning.

'There is none, my khan,' Temu replied. *Lord of Heavens* reports heavy atmospheric sensor interference, but assures us they will keep up their sweeps until Hunter Three's fate is known.'

'Understood,' Kor'sarro replied, forcing his concern for his brethren to the back of his mind, for all of his attention would be needed in the coming attack. It was only moments before the entire strike force would be assembled before him, ready to move out upon his word.

Following his company champion's example, Kor'sarro reached up and unlatched his helmet. As he lifted it clear, the cold air struck his scarred face. Even through the cold, he could taste the underlying chemical pollution caused by the activities at the promethium plant – it did not take the enhanced senses of a Space Marine to detect it. Squinting against the breeze, Kor'sarro regarded his force with fiercely burning pride.

Four Rhino transports, set down in pairs by Hunters Two and Four, idled. Each one carried a ten-man Tactical squad. With the loss of Hunter Three, two more vehicles were missing, and the absence of the heavy weapons of the Devastator squads they had carried might well be felt in the coming battle. Twenty more Space Marines stood nearby, each equipped with a bulky jump pack, marking them out as the 3rd Company's Assault squads. A third Assault Squad had been carried on the missing Hunter Three. Lastly, two squads of White Scars bikers had formed up to either side of the Rhinos having been set down from the modified troop bay of Hunter Five, their engines growling and the cold air shimmering around their exhausts.

The sight of his warriors stirred fierce pride in Kor'sarro's savage heart. These men were the sons of the steppes of Chogoris, the windswept home world of the White Scars Chapter. They were born of the nomadic tribes that lived, fought and died across the trackless plains. They were hunters one and all, born in the saddle and had none become a White Scar, each would have been a king of a noble tribe. These men of the 3rd Company had earned Kor'sarro's trust and loyalty a thousand times over. They had shared with him every peril and every horror the galaxy could conjure.

This last decade, they had followed him in the hunt for one of the Chapter's most hated enemies, indeed, one of the Imperium's most despised sinners. The daemon prince Voldorius – Kor'sarro spat as he conjured the name of his foe – would be run to ground by these men, and by the hand of the Master of the Hunt, would be slain.

Savouring the moment for a few seconds more, Kor'sarro filled his lungs with air. Then, raising Moonfang, his ancient and revered blade, high above him, he uttered the war cry that his men had heard a thousand times before, on a thousand battlefields, before a thousand victories.

'For the Khan, and for the Emperor!'

The cry was echoed in the throats of four score warriors. Kor'sarro opened Moondrakkan's throttle, its engine roaring deafeningly in the manner of its namèsake. The bikes of Kor'sarro's Command squad and of the other two groups of riders took up the savage cry, and were followed an instant later by the deeper, throaty roar of the Rhinos. Then the Assault squads gunned their jump packs to a high-pitched scream, putting Kor'sarro in mind of the deadly avian predators of Chogoris. With the roar of the proud, noble tribesmen of his home world, Kor'sarro span Moondrakkan around to face the distant refinery, and opened the throttle fully.

Moondrakkan leapt forwards, Kor'sarro's long cloak billowing in the cold air behind him. Without turning to look, he knew that his warriors were following, and instead focussed on the objective. The outer defence line was only two kilometres distant, and the inner line another two beyond that. Another kilometre past the inner trench line lay the outer edges of the refinery itself and beyond that, Kor'sarro's foe, the target of his ten-year hunt. Kor'sarro's attack plan was simple and audacious, and entirely in keeping with the martial heritage of his people. If the bastions of the inner defence line were so heavily armed that the Thunderhawks could not penetrate to the refinery, then his warriors would ride those defences down, smashing them aside in an unstoppable assault none could withstand.

But Kor'sarro's attack would not be the maddened charge of an unreasoning berserker, for the White

Scars were well schooled in the subtleties of the arts of war. The strike force would break into three bodies as it closed on the outer line. One would mount a feint against one length of the trench line, drawing in reinforcements from nearby sectors. Only when Kor'sarro was sure the enemy had taken the bait would the second body strike at the weakest section. Even as that group was consolidating its victory and the first breaking off, the third body would be racing towards the inner fortifications, and the process would be repeated.

The strike force was well-practised in such assaults, for their people had been undertaking similar actions since time immemorial. As Moondrakkan closed on the outer line and the cold air whipped up Kor'sarro's long, braided, black moustaches, he was put in mind of his first ever charge against an enemy. He had been barely in his twelfth summer, yet considered a man by his people. That day he had spilled his first blood, claimed his first life and earned his first honour scar. Many more had been traced across his craggy face since becoming a Space Marine. He prayed that more still might be added, yet in truth, only one counted. The scar earned by the death of Voldorius.

A missile streaked past, billowing an ugly black contrail, and Kor'sarro snapped back to the present. He traced the trail back to a concealed gun pit dug hastily into the snow nearby, and veered Moondrakkan towards it before the firer had a chance to load a second projectile.

Moondrakkan's front wheel hit the spoil pile in front of the pit, and Kor'sarro hauled back on the handlebars, gunning the engine as he did so. The bike launched into the air above the pit, and in an instant, Kor'sarro had drawn his bolt pistol. In the two seconds in which the bike was airborne, the Master of the Hunt located his target, a refinery worker bedecked in filthy brown rubberised overalls and wearing an insect-like gas mask, drew a bead on the man's weapon, and pulled the trigger.

Moondrakkan slammed to the frozen ground on the far side of the gun pit, kicking up a spray of ice. Kor'sarro heard the crack of the bolt as it struck the freshly-loaded missile launcher, followed an instant later by a sharp detonation as it, and the launcher's ammunition, exploded. Stealing a glance behind him, Kor'sarro grinned savagely at the destruction he had wrought: the firer and the dozen or so other enemy warriors taking shelter in the pit lay scattered about, body parts strewn across the reddened snow for metres in all directions.

Turning his head back around, Kor'sarro saw that he was rapidly closing on the outer defence line. He scanned the fortifications, and immediately located the point where the feint attack should be aimed.

'Taura,' Kor'sarro addressed the sergeant of one of the Tactical squads over the vox-net. 'Noon, as the ram-hound strikes.'

The sergeant's confirmation came back over the net and two of the armoured Rhino transports peeled away from the body of attackers and arrowed for the point Kor'sarro had indicated in the battle-cant of his Chapter. As the squat transports ground up the frozen plain, one of the Assault squads screamed overhead, the ten Space Marines diving upon the enemy position with chainswords whirring angrily. The sounds of battle were audible over the vox-net, Kor'sarro keeping the channel open for a moment to gauge the intensity of the fight. There was little he could do to influence the outcome now, however, as more pressing concerns presented themselves.

Hauling on Moondrakkan's handlebars, Kor'sarro led the remainder of the strike force in a wide sweep, away from the point where Sergeant Taura's units were engaged. The White Scars made expert use of every scrap of cover, especially the man-high crystal formations studded about the plain. In minutes, the force was barrelling towards what Kor'sarro judged to be a less well-defended length of the trench line.

'Enemy reinforcements committed,' Kor'sarro heard Sergeant Taura call over the vox-net, the transmission punctuated with the sound of chainswords cleaving flesh and bolt pistols firing at point-blank range. Good, thought Kor'sarro: now is the time.

'Second wave,' Kor'sarro bellowed, for he had no need of the vox to give this order. 'With me!'

A savage war cry went up behind him as Kor'sarro steered Moondrakkan for the defence line. Knowing that the enemy had drawn off defenders in an attempt to repel Sergeant Taura's feint, he led his force directly down upon their foe, while the last third held back.

The White Scars' charge ate up the last hundred metres in seconds, and only at the last instant did the few defenders still manning this section of the line open fire. Kor'sarro and his Command squad leapt over the trench as he had done before, and upon striking the ground on the other side, slewed their mounts around. The stunned defenders were caught entirely off guard, few even having turned before they were cut down in a storm of bolt pistol fire.

Stowing his pistol, Kor'sarro drew Moonfang, and ignited its blade, its entire length crackling with barely contained energies. The dozen defenders not slain in the opening fusillade rose from the trench and threw themselves at Kor'sarro and his men, who as one leapt from their bikes to counter-charge. The melee was brief, the defenders not standing a chance against the superhuman Space Marines, but Kor'sarro was surprised by the vigour of the attack.

Though not disciplined or veteran troops, the defenders were fired up by a hatred that granted them the strength to face the White Scars, however brief and futile the effort. Only the lies of the Great Enemy could motivate such men as these, and he detected the unmistakable, bitter taint of blasphemy in the air. How tight was the grip of Voldorius on this place, and on these men? He would soon find out.

Even as Moonfang cleaved the last of the traitors in two, spilling the man's innards across the debris-strewn trench, the last body of the strike force was moving forwards. Two more armoured transports ground across the trench nearby, their tracks crushing defenders to a bloody pulp as a squad of Assault Marines soared overhead. Taking stock of the situation, Kor'sarro activated his vox-link.

'Taura,' he called to the leader of the first wave. 'Report.'

There was a brief pause before the sergeant's voice filled the channel, the background static laced with the screaming of chainswords as they cut through armour and flesh. 'Heavy resistance, my khan, and mounting. I have three wounded, but no ineffectives. Standing by.'

'Understood,' Kor'sarro replied, before switching back to battle-cant. 'The north wind turns.'

'The wind turns at moonrise,' the sergeant replied, his voice drowned out for a moment by gunfire.

Satisfied that Sergeant Taura's force would soon have extricated itself from the fighting, Kor'sarro swung into Moondrakkan's saddle and consulted the tactical slate mounted above the handlebars. Icons representing the units of the strike force winked green, and the enemy defence lines were etched in red, the data provided by the augurs of the *Lord of Heavens* in orbit high above. Three of those icons represented the constituent parts of the third wave, which was bearing down on the inner trench line. Even as Kor'sarro prepared to move out, he heard the unmistakable sound of heavy cannon fire, followed a moment later by a rumbling explosion. In the distance, he saw a mighty cloud rise, and knew that the third wave had encountered heavy resistance.

'Patha,' Kor'sarro addressed the leader of the third wave. 'What is your status?'

The vox-channel churned with interference, and a second explosion blossomed in the distance. Then Sergeant Patha's voice cut in. 'Repeat, coming under fire from a heavy-calibre battle cannon mounted in the bastion to our fore. I have two badly wounded, one ineffective, over.'

Rising in Moondrakkan's saddle, Kor'sarro squinted towards the inner defence line. Against the glare reflected by the frozen plain, he could see the bastion of which Sergeant Patha spoke. As he watched, a low turret at the bastion's top swivelled, the barrel tracking one of Patha's Rhino transports. Before Kor'sarro could voice a warning, the cannon fired, the heavy shell impacting the ice scant metres from the carrier. As the projectile detonated, the rear of the vehicle was thrown several metres into the air, before it crashed down again. Incredibly, the Rhino continued on its course towards the gun tower.

The air all around was rapidly filling with gunfire, evidence, if any were needed, that the enemy were reacting to the White Scars' attack. The strike force had been fortunate so far. Perhaps the defenders had not believed they would return and mount a ground attack so soon after determining the full extent of the air defence net. They would pay for their mistake, Kor'sarro swore, but only if the White Scars pressed home the attack for all they were worth, right now.

'All commands!' Kor'sarro bellowed over the roar of battle. 'Engage that tower!'

Launching Moondrakkan forwards, Kor'sarro was joined by his Command squad and the two other squads of White Scars bikers. The vox-link was filled with terse battle-cant as the third wave closed on the bastion, the battle cannon continuing to bracket the Rhinos even as the Assault Marines dived towards it from on high. For a moment, he considered calling on the Thunderhawks to engage it with their hell-strike missiles, but could not risk the gunships being struck by the defenders' heavy air defences again. To lose one Thunderhawk was bad enough, but to lose another would be unforgivable.

Kor'sarro sped across the plain, bikers to either side, Assault Marines overhead and Rhinos grinding onwards in his wake. He caught sight of Sergeant Taura, his helmet gone and a bloody gash cut across the warrior's forehead speaking of the ferocity of the resistance the feint attack had met. The turret on the bastion turned, this time in the direction of Kor'sarro's combined first and second wave. Imbeciles, he thought, seeing that the gunners were too ill disciplined or inexperienced to continue their fire against the immediate threat, and were instead turning their weapon upon the larger foe. Despite the obvious danger, Kor'sarro was grateful for the brief respite the gunners' mistake would give Sergeant Patha and his men.

'Heads down and keep going,' Kor'sarro bellowed over the combined roar of the bikes, jump packs and Rhinos. 'For Chogoris!'

His warriors echoed the war cry as the cannon opened fire. From the angle of the barrel at the moment the weapon fired, Kor'sarro knew that the shell would strike true, if more by chance than the skill of the gunners. Gritting his teeth against the inevitable, Kor'sarro lowered his head, redoubled his grip on Moondrakkan's handlebars, and sped onwards. The shell lanced towards his force and exploded on its right flank, enveloping an entire biker squad in smoke and mist. Of the nine White Scars bikes enshrouded by the rapidly expanding plume of vaporised ice and debris, only eight emerged, and several of these bore obvious damage, the riders' armour blackened and scratched. Kor'sarro doubted that the missing rider could have survived, but knew that the Rhino-mounted squad following close behind would confirm their brother's fate, and if possible retrieve his body.

The weight of incoming small-arms fire increased still further, and although poorly aimed, stray las-bolts and bullets kicked up puffs of powdery snow from the ground in front of the White Scars. Shots whistled by Kor'sarro's head and several impacted on the armoured fairing of his bike. As the distance closed, a heavy bolter opened up, the staccato rhythm filling Kor'sarro's ears. A score of heavy rounds whipped past, the gunner correcting his aim as Kor'sarro bore onwards. A shell clipped the armoured fairing, tearing a chunk away in a shower of sparks, and another glanced from Kor'sarro's right shoulder plate. The armour's auto-reactive systems activated, dense fibre bundles compensating for the impact by moving rapidly in the opposite direction.

'White Scars!' Rage swelled in Kor'sarro's breast that any traitor would dare raise a hand against the chosen of the Emperor and the Great Khan. 'Show no mercy!'

The air was solid with the defenders' fire, sparks flying from armoured bikes and battle-brothers alike. To Kor'sarro's left, a biker was thrown clear as what must have been a dozen heavy bolter shells slammed into his chest plate, the sheer weight of fire throwing him backwards as his bike ploughed on before slewing to a halt. To Kor'sarro's right, a lascannon seared a blinding line through the cold air, the blast striking one of the Rhino transports in its track nacelle. The stout vehicle ground to a halt having merely thrown a track. Despite the deep, black gash carved across its flank, the White Scars within all disembarked to continue the charge on foot.

A moment later and Kor'sarro and his warriors were closing on the beleaguered battle-brothers of the first wave, who were laying down a withering hail of suppressive bolter fire at the bastion, whilst attempting to take what cover they could against its heavy battle cannon in the midst of a low crystal outcropping.

'Brother Kergis!' Kor'sarro bellowed as he brought Moondrakkan to a skidding halt beside them. Seeing Brother Kergis dismount and race forwards, melta gun in hand, he leapt from Moondrakkan and pointed towards the armoured hatch of the bastion.

'As you will, my khan,' the Space Marine replied. Even though the man wore his helmet, Kor'sarro could well imagine the hunger for victory that he always showed in such situations. Kergis bore the scars of a hundred hunts, and was without equal with his chosen weapon.

'Cover us!' Kor'sarro bellowed as every Space Marine in the strike force able to do so opened fire on the bastion. Even though few of their weapons had any chance of penetrating its thick, rockcrete construction, the torrent of fire would force the defenders to keep their heads down, and throw the aim of any who dared raise their weapons against the White Scars.

Even before the suppressive fusillade had fully opened up, Kor'sarro was dashing towards the bastion's armoured hatch, Brother Kergis following close on his heels. The Space Marines' covering fire took full effect, explosive bolts tearing ragged holes from the bastion's flanks. There was no return fire from the bastion itself, but other defenders further along the line were nonetheless attempting to engage the White Scars with small-arms fire, poorly aimed shots whistling by all too close.

As the pair closed on the bastion's hatch, Kor'sarro ducked to the right, unclipping a frag grenade from his belt. He turned as he ran the last few metres, and slammed back first into the bastion's rockcrete wall, in time to see Brother Kergis come to a halt, brace his feet wide before the hatch and raise his weapon.

There was a timeless pause as Kergis looked to his captain, awaiting the order, as per the ancient traditions of their people. Kor'sarro nodded once, and Brother Kergis opened fire. The melta gun's blast was preceded by a brief distortion of the air between barrel and target, before a stream of concentrated nucleonic fire streaked forth. Anything other than the highest grade of armour plating would have been vaporised in an instant, but the bastion's hatch was built with the intention of resisting such attacks. The hatch glowed orange, then blue, and then white as tremendous energies were absorbed and dissipated. The ground between Kergis erupted in vaporised ice. Kor'sarro felt an increase in the weight of fire all around, and saw that a company of enemy soldiers were making their way along the nearby trench lines, firing wildly as they went. He looked back to Brother Kergis, and saw a line of bullets stitch across his left arm and shoulder plate. Despite the fire, the warrior's aim never faltered as he unleashed a second blast from his weapon.

This time, the hatch's armour peeled away, falling in molten gobbets to the blackened ground. The ragged edges still glowing fierce orange, Kor'sarro pressed the detonation stud on the ready frag grenade, and tossed it into the smoking opening. He ducked back, pressing himself against the bastion's wall as Brother Kergis dived to the opposite side of the wrecked hatchway.

A moment later, the grenade detonated, razor-sharp shrapnel belching forth, followed by a great gout of flame and black smoke. Fierce warrior pride consuming him, Kor'sarro stepped before the opening and drew Moonfang, activating the ancient blade's crackling power field with a familiar flick of his thumb.

Diving into the black, smoke-wreathed interior, Kor'sarro relied on senses other than sight. His genetically enhanced body gave him a wealth of advantages over his foes, and though he could barely make out a thing through the smoke, his superior hearing, smell and even taste drew him down upon his foe. The first enemies he found were very obviously dead, their bodies torn to shreds by the fragmentation grenade.

At the base of what Kor'sarro judged by touch to be an access ladder leading upwards to the next level, he came upon a wounded enemy soldier. With a single, coldly economical motion, he broke the man's neck, ending the traitor's blasphemy in a far more merciful way than he deserved. Allowing any survivors no time to regroup, Kor'sarro reached up and hauled open the hatch at the top of the ladder, readying another frag grenade as he did so. As the hatch rose, dull, red light shone through, and an instant later a torrent of bullets was unleashed, kicking up angry sparks from the metal of the hatch. Even as one bullet ploughed a deep furrow across Kor'sarro's brow, he pressed the detonation stud, threw the grenade through the gap and slammed the hatch shut.

The explosion rocked the entire bastion, sending dust and loose debris in all directions. It must have caught an ammunition store. Kor'sarro grinned and cautiously lifted the hatch to see the damage. The bright violet-tinged light of the outside replaced the red illumination and Kor'sarro guessed that a viewing port had been blown outwards. Seeing no immediate

threat, he rose through the hatch, Brother Kergis following close behind. As the smoke cleared, Kor'sarro
saw that no defenders had survived the blast.
Although blood was smeared across every surface and
ragged parts of severed limbs were flung about, he
could not tell how many of the deluded recidivists
had manned the room.

Striding to the wrecked viewport, Kor'sarro looked
out across the war-torn plain. His warriors had turned
their weapons upon the counterattacking defenders,
and were forcing them back with a fusillade of bolter
fire. He judged that the enemy would soon turn and
run for the outskirts of the refinery, which lay only a
couple of hundred metres beyond the inner defence
line. As Brother Kergis moved in to stand beside him,
Kor'sarro allowed himself a grim smile.

'Order the warriors to mount up, brother,' he said.
'We have a hunt to complete.'

CHAPTER 2

Fire and Ice

HIS COMMAND SQUAD following close behind, Kor'sarro raced through the promethium plant's outer precincts. He himself had gunned down dozens of the recidivist defenders, and his companions scores more. The refinery resembled a vast machine, its innards laid bare and spilled across a hundred square kilometres of the frozen plain. There was scarcely any difference between buildings and processing facilities, both enveloped with impossibly complex masses of pipes, vents and cables. Kor'sarro suspected the plant's original overseers drew no distinction, the convict work force no doubt sleeping beneath their workstations. They deserved no less, he thought.

What passed for streets were strewn with crates and barrels in a crude attempt on the defenders' part to keep the White Scars at bay. The hastily raised barricades were smashed aside as the Space Marines' Rhino transports ground barrels and defenders alike beneath their armoured treads. Many of the roadways were crossed at a height of about five metres by raised pipe runs, from which the White Scars were engaged on several occasions by recidivist snipers and fire bombers. The first sniper cost one of Sergeant Patha's men an eye, but the wounded Space Marine exacted his revenge, putting a bolt-round through the man's sneering mouth, the shell exploding within his skull and vaporising his entire head. Forewarned that more snipers were likely to be lurking upon the raised pipe runs, Kor'sarro ordered the Assault squads to range ahead of the strike force as it ploughed through the streets, engaging and neutralising dozens more snipers as they went.

Although the Assault squads dealt with the snipers easily enough, the fire bombers proved a more demanding problem. One of the Rhinos was engulfed in chemical fire as it passed under one of the raised pipe runs, a fire bomber hidden amongst the conduits. The vehicle appeared to be utterly consumed by flame, but miraculously survived, its only damage cosmetic, the pure white livery of the White Scars Chapter reduced to charred black. The vehicle's war spirit would be much aggrieved and would have to be placated with repeated Rites of Appeasement before the transport could be considered battle worthy once more.

The fire bombers displayed no regard for their own safety, unleashing highly volatile, improvised explosives in the heart of a facility that refined one of the most combustible substances known to man. They were surely corrupted by the Alpha Legion, Kor'sarro decided, or perhaps drugged or mind-slaved in some way. Whatever the case, it was yet another example of Voldorius's many crimes against mankind. Kor'sarro ordered the fire bombers to be engaged as a matter of priority, and no more attacks came so near to success as that first ambush.

Several fire bombers were reduced to human torches as massed bolter fire cut them down and ignited their bombs in the process, sending them plummeting from the overhead pipe runs to the ground below. Their guttering forms were crushed beneath the tracks of the White Scars Rhinos and the wheels of their speeding bikes.

Passing under another of the overhead conduits, the strike force closed on the plant's centre. Kor'sarro's bike-mounted Command squad, accompanied by the other two bike squads from Hunter Five, ranged ahead, while the four Rhino-mounted Tactical squads from Hunters Two and Four formed a column. The two Assault squads streaked overhead on contrails of fire. The street narrowed as the machinery on either side became more and more densely packed. The machinelike buildings became taller, until they reared many hundreds of metres into the sky, which was now barely visible through the web of pipes that connected each part of the vast refinery. Great vents appeared as gaping maws, acrid chemical fumes spewing forth, and it felt to Kor'sarro that his force was travelling through the bowels of a vast, mechanical beast.

'Beware the fore, my khan,' bellowed Brother Temu, as a pressure suit-encased defender rose from behind another of the makeshift barricades. The man hefted a bulky weapon, a locally manufactured heavy stubber by the looks of it. Kor'sarro hauled on Moondrakkan's handlebars as the defender opened fire, the fusillade of shells spitting past him. With a flick of his thumbs, Kor'sarro activated the twin bolters mounted on his bike's armoured fairing, and gunned the man down in a rain of shells. More of the defenders appeared from a side street, shouldering crude firearms as they attempted to draw a bead on the rapidly moving White Scars. Kor'sarro veered towards them, his Command squad close behind, and drew Moonfang as he closed on his target.

Kor'sarro beheaded the first of the defenders with a wide sweep of his power blade as he raced past and in the same motion gutted a second and sliced the arm from a third. The remainder were crushed beneath the heavy wheels of his companions' bikes, and the White Scars barrelled on down the street.

The environs were becoming too confined to continue along mounted on their bikes, so Kor'sarro hauled on Moondrakkan's brakes and his mount came to a halt.

'Dismount!' he called as his Command squad caught up. 'We approach the heart. Spread out and continue the hunt on foot.'

'Where to, my khan?' asked Brother Jhogai, hefting his ceremonial power sword and combat shield.

Kor'sarro looked towards the central zone of the promethium facility, and located the towering structure that marked its centre. Voldorius had yet to reveal himself, and Kor'sarro knew from prior experience that the fiend preferred to draw his enemies in and lie in wait for them. Although wary of entrapment, Kor'sarro was determined to face Voldorius in his lair.

'The tower,' Kor'sarro replied. 'But we continue with caution.'

Kor'sarro's men nodded in agreement, for every one of them knew well the duplicity of the foe. The daemon prince would be in no doubt that the White Scars had come for him. Kor'sarro would have it no other way, but he would not walk blindly into a trap.

'Taura, Patha, to me,' Kor'sarro called, and within seconds the two sergeants stood before him, ready to receive his orders. 'Taura, take your squads west of the central tower, Patha, you go east.' Although brief, Kor'sarro knew that his orders would be fully understood, for these veterans had followed him for decades and fought at his side in countless battles. 'Go, and the Great Khan be with you, honoured be his name.'

'Honoured be his name,' the two warriors repeated, before bowing to Kor'sarro and heading back to their commands. Kor'sarro heard their bellowed orders as they walked away, and smiled wryly to himself.

The men of Kor'sarro's biker group had dismounted from their bikes, which would be stowed out of sight and rigged with booby traps in case the defenders attempted to interfere with them. Taking stock of his surroundings, Kor'sarro turned his gaze towards the distant tower. All of his past experience told him that the tower would be the place where he would find Voldorius. He steeled himself for the confrontation, eager to corner his nemesis once and for all, but fully aware of the scale of the challenge ahead. Voldorius was a fiend of nigh unimaginable proportions, and his crimes were of a galactic scale.

Many centuries ago, the daemon prince had harnessed the power of an ancient and terrible weapon, a relic of the all but forgotten epoch known as the Dark Age of Technology. The weapon was called the Bloodtide, and although none knew how it functioned, at Voldorius's word it had slain uncounted billions of the Emperor's subjects. In a single night, its curse had swept across a dozen worlds and reduced every one of them to a charnel house of desiccated corpses. All of this Voldorius did in the name of the fell Gods of Chaos, the ultimate enemies of mankind.

'Brothers,' Kor'sarro said, aware that the eyes of each man were upon him. 'Each of you has stood by my side throughout our hunt for the vile one.' The sound of gunfire rang out from nearby as the two flanking groups engaged more of the enemy. He continued, 'Each of us has lost battle-brothers by his hand, or those of his followers.

'So far this day, we have only faced convict scum, turned from the Emperor's light by the lies of

Voldorius. But we know that the vile one's companions must be here too. Be alert, my brothers.

'Though I know not how many of us will see the next dawn,' Kor'sarro continued, 'I know for certain that those who do not shall ride upon the great hunt at the right hand of the Emperor for all eternity. We have earned that much!'

'Aye!' replied two-dozen voices in unison, and Kor'sarro raised a hand to silence them.

'Later, we feast. Now, we hunt!'

At that, Kor'sarro turned and advanced along the narrow street, the central tower rising no more than a couple of kilometres distant. The small force adopted a well-practised formation that ensured that all sectors were covered and no enemy could engage the White Scars without warning.

A burst of angry gunfire sounded from the direction of the western flanking group, reminding Kor'sarro that Voldorius and his Alpha Legion followers were not the only enemy in the city-sized refinery. A moment later, an explosion rocked the street, tangled pipes and twisted chunks of metal ricocheting down its length.

'Opportunity fire,' Kor'sarro growled. 'The act of an undisciplined rabble.'

As the gunfire and explosions grew louder, Kor'sarro became aware of another sound amidst the tumult of battle. Concentrating as he advanced, Kor'sarro filtered out the noises all around. Discarding the sound of his own breathing, the beating of his hearts and the tread of his armoured boots upon the debris-strewn ground, he detected a low drone, and it was coming from up ahead.

'The vile one's sorceries...' he muttered, looking towards the peak of the tower rising in the sky, silhouetted against the pulsating, violet-hued aurora. The sound grew steadily in volume, and soon it was clearly audible over the clamour of war. It was a plaintive drone that could only have been voiced by something other than human. Yet, though no human throat could have produced that sound, there was something in it that spoke of anger, pain and suffering in an all too mortal way. Kor'sarro was consumed with disgust, all of his senses piqued and alert for the danger the sound might preclude. It could only be Voldorius, unleashing some new nightmare upon the galaxy, damning himself still further if such a thing were possible.

The dirge became louder yet, until it pulsated from the tower's summit, spreading outwards in palpable waves of grating doom. It echoed from the vast machineries of the promethium refinery, and structural damage was starting to appear in the stacks nearest to the plant's centre.

Kor'sarro pressed on along his course. The face of his company champion was set in a grim mask, his eyes black pits of revulsion. Several of the battle-brothers made gestures of warding against evil, the ancient rites of the peoples of Chogoris as passed down by the seers and shamans for millennia. The droning, tuneless note revolted him and a dire feeling of uncleanness threatened to consume him. It put him in mind of a dying predator, some leviathan thrashing in the deepest oceans as it bled its guts into the cold waters far from the cleansing sunlight and winds of the plains. He shook his head to clear the grim vision from his mind, and stepped up his pace towards the centre of the refinery. And not a moment too soon.

Less than a hundred metres ahead, in the cavernous mouth of a vast storage depot, Kor'sarro saw movement.

'The gnarldrake rises, noon!' he called in battle-cant, indicating to his warriors the presence of the enemy waiting in ambush ahead. Kor'sarro and his Command squad peeled to one side of the narrowing street, moving steadily along its length while making use of the cover of tangled pipes and upturned barrels. With a simple gesture he ordered the other two squads to move along the opposite side of the street, one slightly ahead of him, one slightly behind.

'My khan,' Brother Kergis said from close behind. 'These do not appear to be the same defenders–'

Before Kergis could complete the sentence, a shot rang out from the depot's mouth. Kor'sarro knew instantly that these foes were not the recidivist convicts the White Scars had faced earlier. The weapon fired was not a locally manufactured autogun, but a boltgun, like those carried by the Space Marines.

'Alpha Legion!' Kor'sarro spat, as a burst of bolter fire erupted along the street.

Yet, the shots had not been aimed at Kor'sarro or his men, nor was the timing consistent with an ambush.

'White Scars!' a dry voice from up ahead shouted. Bile rose in Kor'sarro's throat. 'The scent of dung precedes you. Face us!'

A feral growl sounded from behind Kor'sarro as Brother Jhogai made to advance into the open. With a hand upon Jhogai's shoulder, Kor'sarro stopped his old companion. 'No, my friend. This is my burden.'

Kor'sarro stepped out into the open street.

Five figures stepped out from the yawning mouth of the storage facility. As they passed from the shadows into the violet-tinged sunlight, Kor'sarro knew that he had been correct. Each was a giant, wearing power armour of a similar design, only more archaic, to the White Scars'. While Kor'sarro and his men wore armour bearing the white and red livery of the White Scars Chapter, the armour of these warriors was painted a greenish blue. Where the White Scars bore proudly the lightning bolt icon of their Chapter, these wore the writhing hydra device of the traitorous Alpha Legion.

'Nullus,' Kor'sarro growled. The name of this foe was like ashes in his mouth.

The warrior Kor'sarro had addressed stepped ahead of his companions. He was taller even than the other Alpha Legion warriors, and bore a long-hafted halberd, the blade blacker than night and radiating darkness. The traitor wore no helmet, forcing Kor'sarro to look upon his vile features. His head was hairless, and covered in a mass of scar tissue. But these were not the intricate tracery of the honour scars Kor'sarro and his kin wore with pride, each applied in remembrance of a great victory or a fallen companion. They were the result of countless years of exposure to the warping, unclean energies of Chaos. What from a distance appeared as a single, solid burn scar was upon closer inspection more like the scrawlings of a madman, each scar traced over the last in swirling runes and sigils until only an anarchic mess remained. The warrior's features were largely obscured by that mass of scar tissue, his lips thin, his eyes narrow slits. But those eyes were bottomless pits of blackness, radiating doom, as if not a man but a presence lurked behind them.

'You come for Voldorius,' the traitor said.

'Aye, and for you, Nullus,' Kor'sarro replied.

'He awaits,' Nullus said, indicating the tower with a sharp movement of his ravaged head. 'But you must first pass me.'

'Then face me,' Kor'sarro growled, drawing Moonfang and taking a pace forwards. The traitor's fellows spread out across the street and behind, his own warriors did likewise.

The fight would be uneven, two score of White Scars against a handful of the Alpha Legion traitors. The sound from the tower grew still louder, a subsonic rumble passing through the ground beneath Kor'sarro's feet.

'Not yet, hunter,' Nullus replied, with a mocking grin.

'What duplicity is...?' Kor'sarro began, as a tide of figures appeared behind the traitors, stepping out from the dark entrance to the storage depot.

'Did you think it so simple, White Scar?' Nullus crowed as the narrow street behind him filled with armed soldiers. Instead of the drab, rubberised pressure suits and rebreathers worn by those at the defence lines, these men wore an unfamiliar uniform of grey and black, with military-issue armoured jackets and lascarbines. A deafening crack of thunder sounded from the peak of the central tower, and Kor'sarro glanced in its direction.

There, on a wide platform atop the rearing mass of tangled conduits, framed against the pulsating aurora, stood a shape as black as the void. Even at this distance and from the low vantage point, Kor'sarro could see the form of Voldorius. The figure was over two metres tall, and almost as wide across the shoulders. From his back stretched a pair of black, batlike wings, which cracked the air as they whipped back and forth. Kor'sarro's blood rose, the feral desire to finally slay his nemesis all but consuming him.

But first he would have to pass the daemon prince's followers. And his slaves.

In moments, over a hundred of the grey- and black-clad soldiers had emerged from the storage depot and lined up behind Nullus and his companions. The odds were now even.

I have not time for this, Kor'sarro seethed, feeling his chance to close on Voldorius slipping away.

'My khan,' the company champion stepped beside him. 'This may be a trap. You must continue.'

'No, Jhogai,' Kor'sarro interjected. 'I cannot ask this of you.'

'Then do not,' Jhogai replied. 'I take it upon myself. The duty is mine, by ancient law.'

Brother Jhogai was invoking his right as company champion to face the traitor Nullus in single combat. And he did so in the intention that Kor'sarro might face Voldorius, even if the champion was cut down affording his captain the opening.

'You are a man of honour, my friend,' Kor'sarro said. 'But our foe is a traitor to all that binds us to the Emperor and the Great Khan, honoured be his name.'

'The others will hold the rabble at bay, my khan,' Brother Jhogai said. 'You must allow them to do so.'

Before Kor'sarro could respond, the company champion drew his power sword and stepped forwards to stand a mere ten metres before the traitor. Nullus's wicked grin widened as he understood Jhogai's intent. Turning to his khan, the warrior said simply, 'Go.'

Another thundercrack sounded from the tower, and Kor'sarro knew he had no choice. He must face his enemy alone, and he must do so now, lest the daemon prince escape justice as he had so many times before.

'Go!' Brother Jhogai repeated, his voice proud, yet tinged by an undertone of anger or impatience.

'Honoured be your name,' Kor'sarro said, his words lost as Jhogai bellowed a war cry and launched himself forwards at his enemy. In an instant, the mass of soldiers was spilling down the narrow street and the White Scars were unleashing a devastating fusillade of bolter fire that scythed the first rank down in a storm of blood and fire. Kor'sarro caught a last glance of the company champion as he squared off against his opponent, the anarchic tide of battle sweeping around them both until he could see no more.

A third peal of thunder rang out from the tower peak, sounding to Kor'sarro like an invitation or an announcement of coming doom. Resolved to face whatever awaited him, he set off towards the tower at a steady run, the sounds of the battle receding behind. He passed down narrow streets strewn with debris tumbled from the refinery stacks by the vibrations and quakes afflicting the entire plant, the tower looming before him all the way. Several times he caught sight of masked, pressure-suited defenders, and gunned every one of them down with his bolt pistol without pausing. He saw no more of the black-and grey-clad soldiers that had accompanied Nullus, but gave the matter no more attention, for he was rapidly closing on the base of the central tower.

The tower was made of thousands of conduits and pipes, all bound together in an impossible mass that appeared to have been grown rather than built. Vents and flues studded its flanks, some belching noxious fumes, others searing gouts of flame. Enveloped around the twisted pipes and machineries was a series of interconnecting ladders, walkways and platforms, up which, Kor'sarro knew, he would have to climb in order to reach the peak, and his foe.

Sorcerous energies swirled around the pinnacle, the violet aurora twisting from the sky as if reaching down to envelop the tower. Bitter experience told

Kor'sarro that Voldorius was a master of many vile arts, and had made bargains with powers too terrible to name. Whatever evil he was calling upon would be halted, on Kor'sarro's honour.

With a grunt, Kor'sarro pulled himself up to the first platform, and ran along its length until he reached a ladder. His armoured boots rang loudly against the corroded metal grille of the walkway, but the sound was all but drowned out by the atonal dirge emanating from overhead and the clash of unnatural thunder shaking the tower.

With an effort of will, Kor'sarro filtered out the low drone, his genetically enhanced physiology granting him the ability where a normal man might be driven to madness by the deafening skirl. He hauled himself up the ladder, climbing twenty metres before he reached the next level. As he stepped out onto a swaying length of badly rusted tread plate, the entire tower shook as if the ground on which it stood was in the grip of an earthquake.

Kor'sarro was now high above the mass of the refinery. Below, a thin line of White Scars unleashed round after round at the massed black- and grey-clad soldiers while two figures circled one another in their midst. He paused as the two warriors closed on one another, his desire to see his champion strike Nullus down winning him over for a second. But it was not to be. Kor'sarro suppressed a bitter cry of anguish as the Alpha Legionnaire scythed Jhogai down with contemptuous ease, cutting the noble White Scar almost in two with a single sweep of his black halberd. A moment later, both groups of warriors charged headlong into one another, mingled war cries rising above the sound of explosions.

Kor'sarro buried his grief beneath his honour, and forced himself to continue his climb. As he rounded the tower he located the white-armoured figures of one of the flanking groups engaged in a bitter fight with a bellowing mob of the pressure-suit-clad convicts. But the sounds of battle were not confined to these two war zones, for the entire city-sized promethium refinery was gripped by conflict. Rearing processing stacks shook, entire lengths of piping peeling away to fall slowly to the ground where they crashed across the streets and crushed buildings. Explosions blossomed across the plant, and already great belching columns of black smoke were rising into the cold sky. It seemed to Kor'sarro that the White Scars had not brought war to this place at all; they had simply arrived at the same time.

The tower shook again and lurched sickeningly to one side. Kor'sarro gripped the ladder to steady himself, before setting foot upon it and climbing another two dozen metres to the next platform. He was just about to mount the platform when a ten-metre length of conduit hurtled past, falling from further up the tower. Kor'sarro ducked backwards as it cleaved the air a metre from his head, pressing his back against the pipes behind. Then he leaned outwards to follow the huge chunk of broken pipe work as it plummeted, watching as it crushed an entire building with its impact.

The next walkway was narrow and lacked a guardrail. Either the tower's builders had given no concern for the safety of the convict-workers, or it had long since corroded and fallen away. Kor'sarro was forced to grab onto projecting conduits as he passed along its length, several coming away in his hand, belching fumes that stained his white armour. His filtering-out of the hellish drone from the tower's peak was less and less effective, the mournful dirge penetrating his mind even as he fought to push it out.

Reaching the ladder at the end of the narrow walkway, Kor'sarro craned his neck to look upwards. The ladder ran all the way to the tower's peak. Before committing his weight to the corroded steelwork, Kor'sarro tested it by pulling at a rung. The entire length of ladder shook alarmingly, several rivets coming loose to fall past. Gathering his strength for this last climb and the inevitable confrontation at its culmination, he started upwards.

Kor'sarro was now a hundred metres up and climbing. The refinery-city sprawled outwards below towards the ice plains beyond. The distant crystal towers the strike force's gunships had flown through on their first approach loomed at the horizon. The entire plant was now wracked with ever more violent tremors, which Kor'sarro knew in his heart were the work of his nemesis. The climb became a race to defeat Voldorius before the entire refinery was destroyed. He cared not an iota for the plant itself or for its criminal workforce, but had no desire to see the bulk of the 3rd Company slain as it crumbled. As he neared the top of the ladder, the dirge became almost unbearable in its intensity, the discordant keening cutting through his body and permeating his very soul. It was the sound of a billion souls, wailing their lamentations at an eternity of damnation. It was every one of Voldorius's victims, wallowing in eternal darkness and demanding retribution. He bellowed in denial, refusing to succumb to the overwhelming bitterness implicit in the wordless song.

His cry was drowned out by a wave front of cacophony, for before him stood its source. He had reached the tower's peak.

As Kor'sarro hauled himself onto the wide platform, he was confronted by the rearing figure of Voldorius silhouetted against the roiling skies. Actinic lightning arced from every surface, the pulsating, violet auroras twisting down from the cold skies to envelop the summit of the tower. Kor'sarro stood and drew Moonfang, steeling himself for the confrontation against the fiend he had hunted for the better part of a decade.

Voldorius was clad in baroque power armour. His mighty, batlike pinions were folded at his back and he spread his arms wide as if to welcome Kor'sarro as an old friend. In one clawed hand Voldorius bore a writhing blade, twisting and mutating as if eager to rend and cut the flesh of its enemy. The other hand was coiled into a fist, ready to smash and crush Kor'sarro's bones to dust.

All the while, the hellish keening continued, blasting from the beast's throat, threatening to push

Kor'sarro backwards, over the precipice, where he would plummet to his death far below. With an effort, Kor'sarro took a step forwards, activating his power blade. This thing that stood before him was responsible for the damnation of countless souls and for crimes against the Emperor rivalling those of Horus, the Arch-Traitor himself. Since the great betrayal ten millennia ago at the dawning of the Imperium, this cursed being had led a warband of the Alpha Legion in innumerable wars. His deeds were so unutterably vile that few if any accounts had been committed to record. Only memory prevailed, but the White Scars had never forgotten. They had marked this traitor for the hunt, and Kor'sarro would have his head on a pole or die in the attempt.

He took another step forwards, mouthing the words of an ancient Chogoran invocation against the evils that come upon the cold winds by night. Renewed strength flooded his limbs as the words emboldened him. Faith, in the Emperor and the primarch, honoured be his name, welled up within his heart, saturating him with the fierce, warrior pride of his people. He redoubled his grip upon Moonfang's worn leather haft, and planted his feet wide, in the ready stance of a warrior.

'I come for you, Voldorius,' he bellowed over the droning of the beast and the raging of the storm. 'I come for your head!'

An arc of fell lightning blasted the metal decking between them, casting the daemon prince's face in a white, hellish glow.

At the sight of that face, Kor'sarro's heart filled with rage. The daemon's mouth was a yawning chasm, ringed with a million lamprey teeth. Above the vile maw bulged two imbecilic eyes, which radiated not hatred, but unadulterated terror.

Cold anger flooded Kor'sarro's soul. The beast that stood before him was not Voldorius.

'Lies!' Kor'sarro bellowed, feeling the urge to abandon himself to a berserker rage. The bitterness and frustration of ten long years of hunting threatened to overwhelm him, to wash away his discipline and wisdom and leave only a core of unreasoning anger. The Storm Seers of the White Scars cautioned against such a fate, and their words came to Kor'sarro even now, in the cold storm of his rage. Those who trod that path never returned, they said. Turn from the Emperor's light, and you will know nothing but the darkness of an empty soul.

The beast lurched forwards, its steps clumsy and uncoordinated. It raised its writhing daemon-blade high, and brought it downwards in a crude motion that bore no resemblance to the swordsmanship Kor'sarro knew the true Voldorius possessed. It leaned forwards, the balled fist of its left hand dropping to the ground to support its weight, its vile sucker-mouth opening still wider as it redoubled the mournful dirge.

The thing's foetid breath blasted him, but Kor'sarro stood firm against the barrage. In an instant, all of the terrible threat, all of the doom and damnation in that siren wail was dispelled. As if the scales were lifted from his eyes, Kor'sarro saw the truth of the thing before him. This was no being of fell power, but merely some vat-grown monstrosity or a mutant ripped apart and reassembled to give it the appearance of the fiend Voldorius.

The reason why would have to wait, for the thing was rearing upwards, both arms raised to crash down upon Kor'sarro. There was no skill or art in the attack and Kor'sarro avoided it with contemptuous ease by sidestepping the powerful arms as they smashed into the deck where he had stood an instant before. The decking buckled where the impact hit home, the entire platform shaking violently beneath Kor'sarro's feet. The thing roared in anger as it realised that its left fist was ensnared in twisted metal, and Kor'sarro saw his opening.

'Vile as thou art,' he spoke the ritual Chogoran words, 'I condemn thee.'

Moonfang swept downwards in a glittering arc, but an instant before the blade would have struck the beast's neck, it freed its claw and staggered backwards. Instead of beheading the creature, the sword struck its left arm at the elbow, severing it with a jet of brackish, black blood.

For a moment, Kor'sarro found he was blinded as the thing's blood gushed over him, the vile liquid burning his eyes and flesh. Suddenly vulnerable, he threw himself across the decking sightlessly, hearing the rending of metal behind him as he moved.

The beast's dirge changed to a plaintive wailing, rising in pitch and volume. Kor'sarro wiped his gauntlet across his face, clearing his eyes of the thing's stinking blood and blinking as vision returned.

The mutant was staggering backwards, the stump of its arm flailing back and forth as it continued to gush a fountain of dark, steaming liquid. With its every step, the metal decking buckled and shook, sections at its edge shaking loose to plummet to the ground far below.

Pressing forwards again, Kor'sarro raised Moonfang high to parry a crude overhead blow from the beast's writhing blade. The two weapons clashed with a titanic ringing of steel, and for a moment the two combatants were locked in a terrible contest of strength. The thing bore down with all its power, its vile, lamprey mouth rasping less than a metre from Kor'sarro's face. Row upon row of jagged teeth filled his vision, and he put all of his strength into pushing the beast's sword clear. With a final effort, the two sprung apart, but before the mutant could recover, Kor'sarro swung Moonfang about in a wide arc.

The blade hissed as it tore through the mutant-thing's midsection, scything through armour, then corded muscle, then innards. The bellowing was silenced as the beast's internal organs were pulverised by the energies unleashed at the blade's tip. Kor'sarro stepped neatly backwards as a tide of gore spilled out from the beast's gut, great loops of black intestine thrashing and writhing as they spread out across the decking.

The bulging, imbecilic eyes went dead even as Kor'sarro watched, the life fading from them as the beast collapsed onto its knees. With a deafening crash that cracked the metal platform in two, it fell forwards, its great, black wings falling across its massive form as a death shroud.

Kor'sarro drew in a great gulp of air, tasting the taint of burning upon the winds.

'My khan!' Kor'sarro's comm-bead came to life. 'Kor'sarro Khan, do you read me?'

'I hear you, Brother Temu,' Kor'sarro replied, scanning the complex below for any sign of his warriors. 'Report.'

'*Lord of Heavens* has detected a signal, my khan,' Temu said, as the tower beneath Kor'sarro's armoured feet shuddered violently and lurched to one side.

'What kind of signal, Temu?' Kor'sarro replied, suspicion rising within him.

'The Techmarines cannot be certain, my khan, but they have detected an energy spike deep below the refinery–'

'A command signal,' Kor'sarro interjected, bile rising in his throat. The tower... the thing disguised as Voldorius...

'Pull the company out, Temu, now,' Kor'sarro bellowed, turning for the ladder. 'We have blundered into another of his deceptions!'

Even as he spoke, Kor'sarro fought for balance on the shaking tower. A deep vibration travelled up its length, and then Kor'sarro's stomach was in his mouth as the tower dropped several metres and came to rest with a jarring impact. More detonations sounded from across the refinery, several of the mighty processing stacks dropping straight downwards, as if their foundations had been vaporised in an instant. Smoke and flame blossomed at the base of each, and within moments great gouts of liquid fire were belching into the air from a dozen ruptured promethium conduits.

Voldorius had lured the 3rd Company into a trap, using his own followers and the altered mutant-thing as bait. Bitter rage welled up in Kor'sarro's heart as he stood at the precipice looking down at the burning city-refinery. Yet, even consumed as he was by hatred of the vile one, he knew too that his warriors needed him. Kor'sarro had made an oath to the Great Khan himself that Voldorius would be slain by his hand. He stepped back from the platform's edge as fragments of it shook loose and fell away. He made for the ladder, and with one last look at the slain mutant, began the climb down. He would not be claiming the thing's head, for there was no honour in doing so.

'Temu!' Kor'sarro called as he sped down the ladder, his feet thudding onto the first platform. 'Lead the warriors out. I will not be far behind.'

The answer came over the comm-bead a moment later. 'Aye, my khan. We are assailed by foes, but they attempt to break off the fight.'

'Then let them,' Kor'sarro ordered as he pounded along the platform to the next ladder. He was cut off before he could issue another order however, as a mighty explosion rocked the tower, throwing it violently to one side.

Kor'sarro was forced to take hold of a corroded pipe or be flung from the platform. The entire tower lurched sideways, and only Kor'sarro's iron grip kept him from plummeting dozens of metres as his body swung out into air. The whole base of the tower was wreathed in flames, a pool of burning promethium spreading outwards all around. With a metallic wail, the pipe burst, wreathing Kor'sarro in scalding hot steam. The pipe bent outwards, suspending him several metres from the tower's flank.

As if the situation could get any worse, Kor'sarro's ears were assailed by a new sound, a keening like some beast the size of a mountain roaring a challenge to the entire world. For an instant, he took it for the mournful sound of the altered mutant-thing that had drawn him towards the tower, but this was far lower in pitch, so low it was more felt than heard. And it was emanating from the ground, or from beneath it.

Pushing aside the sheer, unadulterated scope of Voldorius's evil, Kor'sarro knew that he had more immediate concerns. The tower shook again, this time swaying the other way and dropping a dozen metres into the ground. For a moment, the open air below Kor'sarro was replaced by the inclined plane of the tower's conduit-wreathed flanks.

There was nothing for it. Kor'sarro let go of the pipe and dropped, striking the side of the leaning tower almost immediately. Gravity took over, and he slid down fifty metres of the steep slope, sparks flying from his armour as it scraped along the rusted conduits. The rapidly expanding lake of burning promethium loomed, black smoke pouring upwards to engulf him. His life depending on his timing, Kor'sarro braced himself ready to leap. Then he was entirely wreathed in black smoke, unable to see a thing. He bunched his muscles and pushed himself off against the conduit.

Kor'sarro passed weightlessly through billowing smoke, and then he was out of it and the ground beyond the raging promethium was racing up to meet him. He had but an instant to prepare for the impact, tucking his legs so that as he struck the ground he rolled. Then he was up, Moonfang drawn from its scabbard before he was even upright.

Burning promethium raging at his back, Kor'sarro gained his bearings. Explosions blossomed from nearby buildings, and the frozen, debris-strewn ground beneath his feet trembled. A quake wracked the street, and the ground lurched.

'Seismic charges,' Kor'sarro growled.

Activating his comm-bead, he hailed his command vessel. '*Lord of Heavens*, this is Kor'sarro.' The channel hissed and wailed with feedback for a moment, before the response cut through. '*Lord of Heavens* responding, my khan. Go ahead.'

'The vile one has planted some form of detonator beneath the plant. The entire facility is coming down. Have all Hunters deployed to extract us. Out.'

Not waiting for the response, Kor'sarro closed the channel and set out along the street at a fast run. The buildings and machinery to either side were now burning, smaller detonations blasting shrapnel in all directions. The sky overhead was black, the violet aurora entirely obscured by clouds of smoke. As he ran, he scanned the alleyways and portals for signs of the enemy, but found only smouldering corpses, bandoliers crackling as ammunition cooked off. A part of him was stunned by the sheer scale of the destruction Voldorius had unleashed, shocked that the vile one would go to such lengths to ensnare his pursuers. How long had Voldorius schemed? Some time, that much was clear. The refinery had been fortified to draw the White Scars in. It had been extensively mined to ensure their destruction once they were mired in combat with the recidivists turned to serve the Alpha Legion.

He continued, pounding along streets now cracked and shifting as the ground disintegrated. The cracks widened into fractures, which Kor'sarro leapt over as he ran. He readied Moonfang as he closed on the building the White Scars had left their bikes in, slowing as he approached the hiding place. He doubted any of the convict defenders would be nearby, but was alert nonetheless.

As Kor'sarro passed through the dark opening, his boot thudded into something wet. At his feet was the blasted body of one of the black- and grey-clad soldiers that had accompanied the Alpha Legion. The man must have fallen foul of one of the charges set to defend the bikes. Kor'sarro's eye was caught by a symbol painted onto the blood-splattered shoulder armour, something he had not noticed any of the other enemy soldiers wearing. It was some kind of heraldic device, a red shield mounted with four stars. He did not know the significance of the device, but noted it nonetheless.

Then Kor'sarro's bolt pistol was in his hand and levelled at the darkness as he heard a sound.

'Brother-captain!' the voice of Brother Kergis came from the shadows. A moment later, the White Scar activated his bike's engine, which roared to life, its headlights illuminating the interior of the building. In the harsh glare, Kor'sarro saw that Brother Kergis was not alone. His Command squad awaited, each upon their bikes, while Moondrakkan stood ready for him.

Kor'sarro grinned, but was struck an instant later by two competing concerns.

'I ordered you to leave…' he began. Then 'Brother Jhogai?' He feared he knew the fate of the company champion without the need to be told, but awaited the response nonetheless.

'He died with honour, my khan,' Brother Kergis said, his voice thick with grief.

Kor'sarro nodded silently. The warriors of his Command squad had fought together for years, and Jhogai was well loved and respected amongst the warriors of the 3rd Company. He might one day have risen to Kor'sarro's own rank, but for the traitorous Alpha Legion.

An explosion nearby brought Kor'sarro back to the here and now, dust and debris falling from the ceiling. He pushed his own grief to the back of his mind, resolving to honour his fallen comrade by ensuring the others survived to continue the hunt for Voldorius.

'I'll have words with those who disregard my orders,' he said as he mounted his bike and gunned its engine to life. Despite the harshness of his tone, his warriors would know he jested. He was eternally grateful they had waited for him.

'White Scars,' Kor'sarro bellowed over the roaring of his Command squad's bikes in the building's interior. 'It is well past time we were leaving!'

At that, Kor'sarro led the way out of the building as larger chunks of debris were torn from its roof to crash down around them. The street outside now resembled a warzone, as if opposing titans had battled one another with no regard for their environment. Oily black smoke enveloped the refinery, the only illumination that of the raging promethium fires deep within. As they rode, they were forced to swerve as huge chunks of debris and falling buildings, massive conduits and processing stacks were cast down by the sheer destruction Voldorius had unleashed. The ground heaved, and several times cracks many metres wide appeared in front of the White Scars. They gunned their bikes' engines and leapt across blindly, for all too often the other side was wreathed in smoke and flame.

The streets finally widened and the Command squad raced through the refinery-city's outer limits, the smoke thinning noticeably. The bulk of the destruction was confined to the city's heart, marked by the now-collapsed tower upon which Kor'sarro had faced the mutant-thing proxy of Voldorius. The White Scars cleared the last of the machines and buildings of the plant and closed on the inner trench line.

The defences were now abandoned by all but the dead and the dying, the recidivist scum having shown their true colours and fled. They would not get far, for those not cut down by the White Scars would not survive long in the frozen depths of the polar wastes, and they could scarcely return to their city.

Passing the defence line, Kor'sarro brought Moondrakkan to a slewing halt that kicked up a spray of ice from the frozen ground. As his companions slowed to a stop, he looked back in the direction they had come from.

The central zone of the refinery-city was enveloped in roiling black clouds, which seethed and pulsed as if with a vile life of their own. Flashes from within illuminated the clouds, silhouetting something that Kor'sarro could not quite make out. A deep, subsonic lowing filled the air, echoing through the blazing city and out across the frozen wastes. The sound was almost that of an animal, a vast creature bellowing its hatred and pain at the universe.

And then another flash of lightning illuminated the roiling cloudbank, and Kor'sarro saw something terrible. Rising ponderously out of the cloud was what he first took for a warped and distorted conduit, perhaps thrown outwards by the explosions tearing the city's heart apart. Then he saw that it was no conduit; it was nothing made by the hand of man.

From out of the cloud rose what could only be described as vast, coiling tentacles. The animal keening rose to deafening volume, forcing Kor'sarro to don his helmet and activate its dampeners just to preserve his hearing. More of the tentacles appeared, until a nest of dozens writhed and thrashed as if in slow motion. The vast, coiling limbs quested blindly outwards, each languid movement felling a building or processing stack and causing untold destruction. Whatever the beast was, it appeared not to notice the flames that raged all about it as billions of litres of promethium burned.

'Xenos blasphemy...' Kor'sarro heard Brother Yeku, his company standard bearer mutter.

'Or worse,' answered Apothecary Khagus, his own voice thick with disbelief at the sight before them.

'What could be–' Brother Yeku said.

'Enough!' Kor'sarro interjected. Even as he spoke, more of the tentacles were writhing outwards from whatever hell mouth had spawned the beast. Several were moving in the direction of the Command squad. He gunned Moondrakkan's engine and brought his mount around. 'Brother Temu, raise the *Lord of Heavens*. I want a situation report.'

As Kor'sarro and his Command squad moved out again, Brother Temu reported back. '*Lord of Heavens* says they've lost contact with the gunships, my khan. I barely got through, and lost the channel soon after.'

Several of the vast tentacles were now reaching high into the air, and one was questing in the command group's direction. It was so large, even the fast-moving bikes could not hope to escape it.

'All Hunters!' Kor'sarro bellowed into the vox-link. 'This is Kor'sarro, does anyone read me?'

Wailing feedback was the only reply Kor'sarro heard, before a second later the gargantuan tentacle loomed overhead and crashed to the ground a mere twenty metres away, pulverising ice and smashing apart crystal formations. The impact, had it come down upon the Command squad, would have crushed the whole group to a bloody smear.

As the tentacle rose again, Kor'sarro reopened the vox-channel. 'All Hunters, whoever can hear me, converge on my position!'

The vast tentacle slammed down into the ground again, the force of the impact almost throwing several of the White Scars from their bikes. But it is said that the sons of Chogoris are born in the saddle, and they all maintained control of their machines. This time, the ice sheet cracked, and a nearby defence bastion was swallowed whole as a vast chasm opened up.

'Does anyone read me?' Kor'sarro called again, steering wildly to avoid a massive shard of ice flung across his path by the tentacle's flailing. The animal lowing continued, so loud now that even with his helmet systems engaged Kor'sarro was almost deafened.

'Hunter One,' the response came over the vox. 'This is Hunter Three, inbound on your position. Stand by.'

'Hunter Three?' Kor'sarro replied, uncaring that his voice was tinged with incredulity. He heard a savage roar of joy from his companions, which was drowned out seconds later by the sound of a trio of hellstrike missiles streaking overhead from Hunter Three's undamaged wing, before slamming into the writhing tentacle.

The monstrous organ was consumed in fire, two hundred metres of it tearing away under the missiles' barrage. The separated appendage reared hideously into the air, standing upright for a moment before crashing down. The ice cracked, and the obscene tentacle collapsed through the wound it had made.

But the beast would not be killed simply by severing its limbs. Whatever lay at the heart of the writhing mass was still protected in the ground beneath the promethium plant.

'Hunters,' Kor'sarro said. 'We shall draw the beast from its lair. When its body is exposed, strike it down.'

The bikers powered on across the icebound plains, the jagged crystal formations becoming denser as the ruined promethium plant was left far behind. The White Scars' skills were tested to the full as they swerved around crystals as sharp as diamonds. A shadow passed over Kor'sarro's band, and an instant later a rearing crystal stack shattered into a billion pieces, showering the White Scars with razor-sharp fragments.

The tentacle slammed down behind the racing bikers, its leathery hide pierced with countless shards of crystalline shrapnel. The tentacle reared and thrashed as it bled the clear liquid that must have served it as blood across the ice. Another tentacle arched high into the air and came down with a ground-shaking impact in a great loop in front of the White Scars, trapping their escape.

But the beast had overextended itself. Its vast, globular body had emerged from the smoking crater at the heart of the promethium plant as it had stretched itself further and further in pursuit of its prey. A pulsating mountain of unformed flesh rolled out of the chasm to flatten the buildings of the plant. Processing stacks toppled and machinery exploded as the creature tore down the works of man in its eagerness to catch those who fled it.

'Now!' Kor'sarro said. 'All Hunters, strike for its heart!'

The skies were split by the sonic boom of the Thunderhawks soaring high overhead. Every weapon of every gunship was fired as one, hellstrike missiles, cannon shells and las-beams lancing out across the sky.

The pulsating core of the beast erupted in a fountain of vile ichor and was consumed in flames. The tentacles arched and thrashed, looping high as if to shield the beast from its attackers. As the last of the tentacles sank into the banks of black smoke, Hunters One and Five came in to land near Kor'sarro and his warriors and the Master of the Hunt led his retinue up the access ramp of his command gunship and into the waiting bay. What remained of the plant was fully ablaze, a column of black smoke rising many kilometres into the atmosphere.

Just what vile sorceries Voldorius had enacted here Kor'sarro had no way of knowing, but it seemed to him that some creature from this world's pre-history that slumbered beneath the ice sheet had been awakened by seismic charges. The act had been timed so that the beast would arise at the very moment Kor'sarro was facing the mutant atop the city's highest peak.

As the ramp closed behind him and the Thunder-hawk lifted into the air, Kor'sarro vowed he would not allow Voldorius a moment's respite. The image of the insignia on the dead soldier's armour came to mind once more. The four stars on the crimson shield. If he could discover the source of that insignia, the hunt would be back under way.

Kor'sarro swore that Voldorius would pay for the crimes he had enacted on Cernis IV. They would be added to the millennia-long litany. Justice would be done, by Kor'sarro's own hand. This was his oath, on his very life.

'Before the rise of the Imperium of Man, the greatest, most deranged minds created machines so small they could invade the very blood and make war upon their creators' enemies from within. Once released, those machines replicated, until they had invaded the blood of an entire planetary population. And then, at a single word, they arose. Ten billion bled as one, and an entire world drowned in the blood.

But something went wrong, as ever it will when man dabbles with such powers. The weapon escaped the shackles of its own being, and would not obey its masters. And so it came to pass that the world which the weapon had destroyed so spectacularly was set apart from the greater realm of man.

The Emperor came, and in time that world knew the tread of man once more. Yet, the weapon remained hidden for cold millennia, until a servant of the Machine discovered it, waiting, in the dust and ashes beneath his very feet. And that servant, who had been cast out by his brethren, brought his discovery to the vile one, his true master. At his word, the weapon was resurrected, and at his word, it was set free across not one world, but a thousand. Only when the weapon had invaded the bodies of countless billions did the vile one order it to rise up and turn upon its carriers. Such glorious slaughter was achieved that night that the vile one was granted apotheosis. He cast off his mortal heritage and became as a god. But he would be yet more.

The weapon was expended, reduced once more to a core of a trillion nanytes. These the vile one bound into the form of the prisoner, and held captive, until the time came to unleash the power upon the galaxy once more.

The sons of man sought to destroy all knowledge of the weapon, to deny its existence, as if by locking facts away they could starve reality and undo that which had been done. But there are those who move in the shadows, who see what others do not. These benighted souls with eyes of black harbour such knowledge, and they wait, biding their time. Soon. That time is soon.'

– The Heretic Archivist of the Gethsemane
Reclusiam, *Third Book of Quothes*
(redacted)

CHAPTER 3
Quintus

EKIT SKARL, EQUERRY to Lord Voldorius, paused in the vestibule before stepping onto the bridge of *The Ninth Eye*. He took a deep breath, steeling himself to face his infernal master, to enter the baleful presence of the daemon prince that had ravaged the hated Imperium for so many long centuries. Skarl was but the latest in a long line of mortals Voldorius had employed to deal with the tiresome and mundane realities of administration, logistics and politics. He had not chosen the role for himself, though he accepted that he had certainly invited it by his dabbling in the forbidden doctrines of the Ruinous Powers. The equerry's continued existence relied solely on his fulfilling his master's needs, without doubt or hesitation. He could afford to show not a single iota of weakness.

Beyond the shadows in which the equerry lurked sprawled the bridge of the Desolator-class battleship that had served as Voldorius's flagship for three millennia, since the daemon prince had wrested it from the fleet of his rival Lord Commander Amexon of the Alpha Legion. A raised central walkway stretched a hundred metres forwards, terminating in armoured viewports ten metres tall. Below the level of the walkway were the bridge crew stations, in which hundreds of hard-wired crew-serfs spent every moment of their tortured existence tending to the operation of the vessel's ancient systems.

Straightening his black robes and assuming a suitably meek stoop, Skarl stepped out from the vestibule's shadows and onto the decking plate of the bridge. Two dozen crew-serfs glanced upwards in his direction, their jealousy at his freedoms and privileges writ large across their scabrous faces. Fools, Skarl thought, all of them. They should count themselves blessed that they lived such uncomplicated lives, he mused bitterly as he stalked past.

As he walked the length of the walkway, Skarl reviewed in his mind the news he had come to deliver to his master. *The Ninth Eye* was closing on the world of Quintus, a planet that Lord Voldorius had invested much in subjugating, for it was the perfect base for his forthcoming plans. The daemon prince's followers had fought a month-long war to crush the planet's militias, crippling its contacts with the greater Imperium in short order so that no outside interference would be forthcoming. Now, that conquest was largely complete, allowing the next phase of his master's plans to begin.

The equerry bore other news too.

Approaching Lord Voldorius, Skarl assumed an even deeper bow, feeling the fell power that radiated from his master's huge form in sickening waves. Some were so afflicted that they would vomit, void their bowels or collapse upon the floor bleeding from every orifice. Skarl knew how pathetic his master found such displays, and it was one of the equerry's many tasks to ensure such weaklings were not allowed to enter the master's presence or his service, unless of course it served the daemon's own purposes to see his enemies reduced to vomiting, quivering wrecks at his feet.

Casting off such thoughts, Skarl sidled up to his master and assumed a posture of abject subservience. His forehead pressed to the corroded metal decking, he awaited his master's acknowledgement.

'You may stand, equerry,' Voldorius said. The daemon prince had never once addressed Skarl by name.

Allowing himself to breathe, Skarl rose, though only to a low bow. He dared not stand fully erect in his master's presence lest the action be taken for insubordination.

'Speak, equerry,' Lord Voldorius ordered, his voice laced with ancient menace that filled Skarl with cold dread no matter how many times he heard it.

'My master, I bring word that the resistance on Quintus is all but crushed.' He was mindful to phrase the missive in such a way that it was not his own assessment of the situation on the world below, but someone else's; someone who would bear responsibility were it proved incorrect.

Skarl awaited a response from his master, not daring to raise his gaze any higher than the daemon's power armour-encased feet. It was long moments before Voldorius replied. 'What of Nullus?'

'My lord Nullus has come aboard this past hour, my master. He and his warriors are returned from Cernis IV in glory.'

A palpable wave of displeasure washed over Skarl as his master reacted to this last statement. Dread welled up inside the equerry. 'Why then is he not before me, apprising his master of his great victory?' Voldorius grated.

'My master, I...' Skarl stammered, dropping to the deck once more and pressing his face against the metal at his master's feet. Then, another voice sounded from the far end of the bridge, and Skarl allowed himself to breathe a sigh a relief.

'I came as soon as I was able, Voldorius.' The voice belonged to Nullus, his master's most trusted servant, if trust could be said to exist between such fell beings. Skarl remained prostrate as he listened to the metallic tread of Nullus's armoured boots approaching along the walkway.

'I had certain dedications to make,' Nullus said. 'In honour of my victory.'

'What of Cernis?' Voldorius growled. Skarl became aware that a tense hush had descended upon the bridge, as if all present knew that bad news would bring their master's displeasure down upon them.

'The spawn of Jaghatai took the bait,' Nullus replied, relish obvious in his voice. 'They thought they had us, but were disabused of that notion.'

'Survivors?' Voldorius enquired.

'The beast ate its fill, Voldorius, of that I am quite sure.'

'How sure?' Voldorius snapped back.

'None could have survived the destruction we unleashed upon the refinery. And I took the life of their champion with my own blade.'

'And none could have followed?' Voldorius growled, his voice low and tainted with menace.

'None, my master,' Nullus responded. 'Their hunt is ended for good.'

Voldorius considered Nullus's words for some time before he replied. 'You have served well, as ever you do when facing the scarred ones, Nullus. You shall be rewarded.' The daemon turned his mighty bulk towards the viewports, and raised a clawed hand to point into the void. 'What of Quintus, Nullus? The equerry tells me the subjugation is all but complete.'

At the mention of his name, Skarl allowed himself to straighten up, knowing that he would be addressed again soon. As he did so, he saw that the scarred face of Nullus was upon him, those soulless eyes boring into his own.

'The subjugation is entirely complete, Voldorius,' Nullus said without turning his gaze from the equerry. 'On that you have my word.'

Nullus broke eye contact with Skarl, and turned his black gaze towards the scene beyond the viewports. Skarl felt profound relief that he was no longer the subject of Nullus's attentions, for the lieutenant was known as a capricious and callous individual ill-disposed towards rivals or those who gainsaid his word. Nullus was, after all, Alpha Legion, while Skarl was but a man, and his continued existence was entirely at the forbearance of his masters.

'What of the resistance?' Voldorius asked. The daemon prince spoke the last word as if describing the foulest of deeds, as if the notion that mere mortals might attempt to stand before his designs was the worst possible affront.

Nullus hesitated before making his reply. It seemed to Skarl that the lieutenant was gathering his thoughts, lest he give Voldorius cause to become displeased. Then, Nullus answered.

'What little opposition to your rule still remained after the purges of the Klanik Peninsula and the Olsta Line is now entirely crushed, Voldorius. The processing sites are now fully operational, and those who do not display total loyalty to their new masters are being culled.'

'At what rate?' Voldorius interjected.

'The example we made of the 4th Division paid dividends, my master,' Nullus continued. 'Twenty thousand heads now adorn the walls of the capital. Since then, the cull rate has dropped to around ten thousand a day, and I expect it to drop further still as the point is driven home. For every act of defiance, a thousand die as punishment. Soon, the resistance shall be entirely spent.'

Voldorius considered his lieutenant's words. 'A shame that the offerings must cease. The warp resounds to the death of multitudes, singing our glory across light years.'

Skarl scarcely dared interrupt his master, but he had other news to deliver. 'My master... I...'

The bridge fell deathly silent, and Skarl felt not only the eyes of a hundred crew-serfs upon him, but those of his master too. Nausea welled up inside him as Voldorius radiated anger. The equerry swallowed hard to avoid vomiting across his master's boots, for his life, at this moment, hung in the balance.

'Speak, equerry,' Skarl heard his master say. Behind the voice he could hear the wailing of anguished souls, those of the many thousands that had displeased the daemon throughout the millennia and paid the terrible price for doing so.

'My master,' Skarl said, fighting desperately to keep his voice level. 'I bring word that the prisoner is awakened at last. The cell-masters await your coming.'

'BE SEATED, MY brothers,' said Kor'sarro as he entered the strategium of the *Lord of Heavens*. The Space Marines inside bowed their heads before seating themselves around the circular chamber. The Master of the Hunt took his own seat, a marble throne surmounted with the skull of a fearsome tusk-drake. The beast had been slain in combat by old Jamuka Khan, Kor'sarro's honoured predecessor, teacher and greatly-missed friend.

A week had passed since the destruction of the Cernis IV refinery, and the Master of the Hunt had been afforded plenty of time to brood upon the whole affair. He had gone over every single detail of the events leading up to the assault, as well as the battle itself. He had gathered the most senior of his officers to the strategium. In his endless poring over every detail of the action on Cernis IV, he had found something.

'Brother Sang,' Kor'sarro addressed the Techmarine seated opposite him across the chamber. 'The sensorium upload, if you will.'

'By your command, my khan,' replied Brother Sang. A multi-jointed, mechanical limb at the Techmarine's back reached forwards, a data-spike at its end plugging into a terminal set in the decking. The spike whirred and buzzed, and then the light in the chamber dimmed. For a moment, all was dark, before a bright shaft of light formed in the centre of the chamber. Within the glowing column danced tiny motes, slowly resolving into an image of a frozen scene from the closing stages of the battle at Cernis IV.

All eyes in the chamber were turned towards the slowly spinning scene, projected in a three-dimensional image by ancient holo-generators set in the floor and ceiling.

'My brothers,' Kor'sarro said, looking to each of the Space Marines, one at a time. 'What you see before you is a single frame, taken from the sensorium-core of my own power armour.'

After a few seconds, Kor'sarro nodded towards the Techmarine, and the scene blurred, before resolving itself again.

'And here is the same scene, from Brother To'ban's perspective.' He nodded again, and the scene cycled through five more frames, each showing the same patch of rubble-strewn ground from a different angle.

'None of us took note at the time, as we were all otherwise engaged,' Kor'sarro went on, a wry smile forming at his lips. 'But I have reviewed every upload, and I believe we have him.'

Several of the officers present began to speak, but Kor'sarro raised a hand, forestalling their questions. At another nod, Brother Sang caused the image of the war torn scene to zoom in on a single patch of ground. At the centre of the strategium, as if suspended in the column of bright light, was projected the image of a blood-splattered segment of armour.

'This armour, brothers, was worn by one of the soldiers accompanying the traitors.' Several of those present nodded in recognition as memories of the confrontation with the Alpha Legion and their human followers came to mind. 'I have asked Brother Qan'karro to identify it.'

All heads turned towards the strike force's most senior psychic warrior, a Space Marine Librarian. The White Scars knew them as Storm Seers. Brother Qan'karro stood, his gnarled force staff in hand, and scanned the chamber. The Storm Seer's face was lined with age and honour scars, his skin having the texture and hue of old oak. Though he was ancient, Brother Qan'karro was counted amongst the Chapter's most fearsome warriors, his rank and seniority broadly equal to the Master of the Hunt's. Though Kor'sarro held command of the 3rd Company, there were few matters in which he would not welcome the counsel of the old Storm Seer.

'The armour bears a device, four stars on a red field,' Qan'karro said. 'We have consulted the archives, and found three hundred and nine instances of this device in current use in this Segmentum alone'.

Kor'sarro saw several of his officers make eye contact with one another, evidently believing the odds too long. But the Master of the Hunt felt wry amusement as the Storm Seer continued.

'Many we can ignore,' Qan'karro said, 'for they represent only mercantile concerns of one sort or another. One more we can most certainly eliminate, for the device was used as the standard of Rogue Trader Huss, emblazoning every vessel in the disastrous Magellanic Expedition.'

Several of Kor'sarro's officers nodded at the mention of that cursed venture, which several Space Marine Chapter Masters had spoken out against to little avail.

'In another case, the kin-slavers of the Alcaak Dystopia used the device to brand their victims, but we all know what befell those cruel bastards.' Many of those slavers were now themselves enslaved. They deserved every torture the dark eldar had inflicted on them.

'Of the dozen or so uses of the device that remain, one stands out. Having meditated long on the matter, my brothers and I are in agreement.' The Space Marines waited for Qan'karro to expound on his deduction, and Kor'sarro knew that the old warrior was now fully in his element, even enjoying himself, if such a thing were possible.

'Go on please, honoured seer,' Kor'sarro said, bowing his head slightly towards Qan'karro, the faintest of smiles touching his lips. 'We await your wisdom with great anticipation.'

The Storm Seer's glance told Kor'sarro that he was well aware that he was being made sport of, if only in a friendly manner. Qan'karro got to the point. 'The household guard of the governor of a world called Quintus,' the Storm Seer announced. 'A world a mere five light years distant, and on the same secondary conduit as Cernis.'

Kor'sarro delved into his memories of nearby space, calling to mind the endless charts and maps he and his senior commanders had gone over time and again in their hunt for Voldorius. Yes, the Quintus system came to him.

'The bulwark-world?' Kor'sarro said.

'Aye, huntsman,' the Storm Seer replied, before expounding. 'But Quintus has of late been afflicted by a warp storm, codified Argenta. It is only in the last months that Argenta has quietened to an unprecedented degree, allowing free passage to and from the system for the first time in months.'

'You believe this significant?' asked Kor'sarro.

'Indeed I do,' the Storm Seer replied, looking around at the gathered Space Marines before his gaze settled on the slowly revolving image of the blood-splattered armour. 'Quintus represents a convergence, in more ways than one. For a start, it is a warp nexus, a point at which several dozen conduits meet. Whoever controls the system can extend his influence to a score of others and dominate the entire region.'

Kor'sarro nodded, picturing the stellar maps. Quintus did indeed sit at a strategically desirable meeting of warp routes. For centuries, the world had stood guard against alien incursions from nearby wilderness space. Until, that is, warp storm Argenta had caused the world to fall from power. With the warp storm receding, the balance of powers would shift once more. But in whose favour?

Even as the thought came to him, another of those present spoke up. 'Something tells me this convergence of which you speak is not merely a strategic matter, Brother Qan'karro.' The speaker was the 3rd Company's senior Chaplain, a black-clad veteran by the name of Xia'ghan. 'Other forces are at work here, are they not?'

The Storm Seer nodded to his comrade, a dour expression falling across his features. 'Indeed, honoured one,' he replied. 'All of the signs point to something being unleashed upon Quintus. Something from the dark times. Something terrible.'

Silence fell across the strategium as the Storm Seer's message sank in. After long moments, Kor'sarro looked around at his senior officers, and spoke.

'If what our brother tells us is true, and I have no reason to doubt that it is, then Voldorius must be stopped before he can bring about whatever calamity he has planned. I am pledged to bring the head of the vile one to the Hall of Skies, this I have promised to the Great Khan himself. I will not allow the daemon to entrap us again, or to escape our grasp, and I expect every one of you and your men to stand with me on this. Much rides upon it.

'Brothers, we go to Quintus, for there our hunt *must* end, for our honour, for the Great Khan's, and for our primarch's.'

Every Space Marine in the strategium responded as one. 'Honoured be his name!'

SKARL BOWED DEEPLY as he stepped aside to allow Voldorius and Nullus by. In front of the equerry was a pair of mighty iron doors, deeply corroded and encrusted with the forbidden runes of the Chaos Gods. Skarl had spent most of his life in the presence of such fell sigils, but even he was cowed by the sheer malignance that radiated from this particular combination.

With a deep rumble, the doors slid apart, a hellish, flickering glow filling the widening gap. Before the entrance was even fully open, Voldorius stepped through into the cell. Skarl waited as Nullus followed his master, cowering despite himself as the lieutenant cast a threatening glance his way.

Only when both warriors were through the portal did the equerry follow in their wake.

Skarl had never entered the cell before. What it held inside was so valuable to his master that few were ever allowed to do so, upon pain of torture or, if lucky, death. As he passed through, he took in the unfamiliar surroundings. The cell was in fact a large, round chamber, its vaults lost in darkness far overhead. The walls were of brass, stained by centuries of runoff from dozens of corroded grilles. Other stains were in evidence too, great arcs of long-dried blood and other bodily fluids lending the walls a mottled finish. Sconces were mounted all around the chamber, their flickering flames casting the illumination Skarl had seen from outside.

Voldorius stopped in the centre of the huge chamber, and Nullus came to stand beside him. Skarl followed a respectful distance behind them, still bowing, eventually coming to stand behind Voldorius. Before the three stood a pair of cell-masters. They were massive brutes, clad in heavy leather aprons encrusted with filth. The bare skin of their arms and upper chests glistened with sweat in the flickering light of the torches, and the face of each was obscured by a heavy mask, piggish eyes just visible behind the thin visor. At their belts the cell-masters carried an assortment of crude tools, their general purpose clearly evident to the equerry. In his hand, each held a long electro-prod. The two implements crossed in between the two men. At Voldorius's approach, the cell-masters raised the prods, a brief arc of electricity spitting between the tips before they were brought upright, revealing what they guarded.

Behind the two cell-masters was a brass orb, perhaps two metres in diameter, its entire polished surface carved with impossibly intricate lines and devices. Skarl's gaze was drawn into the unnatural patterns, and it took a formidable effort to turn his eyes away from them. Any not promised to the Ruinous Powers were likely to become entrapped by the sigils and forms, their soul forfeited by the very act of looking upon them. It was only when he tore his glance away from the orb's surface that Skarl realised that the entire construction was floating above the deck, held aloft by invisible lines of arcane force. Powerful sorceries were at work, for no mere anti-grav generator was being utilised.

A preternatural quiet descended on the cell as Voldorius stepped between the two attendants. Even the flickering torches mounted upon the wall fell silent, though their flames still danced.

The daemon prince halted in front of the orb and laid a clawed hand upon its surface. Red and orange energies played between claw and brass. No mere mortal could have survived that contact, for only Voldorius had power over what lay before him. The daemon prince closed his eyes, his bestial face becoming unusually still for a moment. Then he opened them once again and spoke, his voice shattering the silence of the chamber.

'Awaken, prisoner,' Voldorius grated. 'And know your fate!'

After a pause that felt like an hour, a whisper filled the chamber. 'None can know their fate, Voldorius. Not even you.'

The voice seemed to emanate from everywhere and nowhere, from a million throats and from none. The voice was not a voice at all, but the mere echo of one, separated by impossible gulfs from its source. Even as the ghostly words faded, Voldorius replied.

'You will obey me, prisoner, or you will know such pain as even you cannot imagine.'

Again, a long silence preceded the prisoner's response, throughout which ancient thoughts formed and reformed in the ether before they coalesced into words.

'We have felt the pain of billions, Voldorius, as well you know.' An ethereal undertone spoke of anguish and despair, but also of resignation. 'Nothing you can do can make us obey.'

Skarl shuddered as waves of fell anger radiated from his master before Voldorius spoke once more. 'I have kept you for two thousand years, contained you, tempered you. Now I awaken you, and you shall do as I command. Of that you can be assured.'

A displeasure that few witnessed and survived was written across the daemon's face. Through clenched teeth, Voldorius addressed his equerry.

'Prepare the meat-casters,' Voldorius growled. 'Send word that the orb is to be unsealed, at last. The prisoner is to be broken, his will is to be destroyed, his mind is to be shattered, whatever the cost. I only order that no matter the ruin visited upon his flesh, life must remain, if only in a single, dry, quivering cell. Take the prisoner to Quintus, to the palace in Mankarra, render it unto the meat-casters, and then await my order.'

Skarl prostrated himself before his master, touching his forehead to the filth-encrusted floor. 'I obey, my master,' he mumbled.

As the footsteps of Voldorius and Nullus receded, Skarl repeated over and over, 'I obey, my master. I obey.'

CHAPTER 4

Vengeance is Mine

'CYTHA,' HISSED MAKAAL as the resistance cell-leader peered through his spy-lens at the dark passageway up ahead. 'You're clear. Go!'

Covering the lithe, bodyglove-clad form of Cytha as she darted from the shadows to his left, Makaal offered up a brief, silent prayer to the Emperor of Mankind. Please, he beseeched, let us succeed, even if it costs us our lives. Let us end the terror unleashed upon Quintus by the vile one, once and for all.

'In position,' Cytha's whisper came back a few seconds later. Makaal looked to the shadows where he knew his second in command was waiting, satisfied that he could not make her out. 'Bys,' he whispered. 'Your turn. Go!'

Makaal raised his hellgun to cover the larger man as he ran past. Bys was nowhere near as nimble or stealthy as Cytha, or indeed any other member of the cell, but he was as strong as a bull grox. He had to be, to carry the weight of explosives he had stowed about him.

After twenty seconds, Makaal was satisfied that Bys was in position, and addressed the last member of the cell. 'Rund, you're up. Go!'

Rund dashed forwards. He was neither as stealthy as Cytha, nor as strong as Bys, but Rund was a certified lay-technician and had served in the capital city's generatorium for a decade under his Adeptus Mechanicus overseers. His skills were critical to the success of the cell's desperate mission.

And that mission, whether or not that bitch Malya L'nor and the other self-appointed 'leaders' of the pro-Imperium resistance on Quintus would sanction it, was to assassinate Voldorius whatever the cost. The resistance had received word from their contacts inside the palace of the deposed governor of Quintus that the vile one was returning to the world after some errand off-planet. The daemon would be arriving, so the contacts claimed, by way of the palace's ancient teleportarium, and he would be doing so within the hour.

When Rund had taken position, Makaal took one last look behind to check that no sentries lurked in the dark service tunnel far beneath the palace. He darted forwards past his comrades, taking point. Pressing his back to the wall, Makaal made himself as small a target as possible, melting into the shadows that lined the passageway. He ordered his subordinates forwards, one at a time, covering them with his hellgun and scanning the tunnel up ahead through his spy-lens.

So far, the infiltration had gone to plan and Makaal had allowed himself to feel a small measure of vindication. The mission was by necessity an improvised affair; a plan opposed by the bulk of the resistance leaders in Mankarra, the capital city of Quintus. The debate had been brief but bitter. In the end, Makaal had defied Malya L'nor, his immediate superior in the resistance, and rounded up whichever cell members he could find who were willing to follow him. His plan was almost certainly suicidal, but Makaal reasoned that his life was worth the prize – deliverance from the evil Voldorius had visited upon his world. L'nor and the others had argued that his failure would spell the doom of many more innocents. They believed Voldorius or any who survived him would never allow such a deed to go unpunished whether or not it succeeded.

Makaal hated Malya L'nor. He hated that she was so eager to save the lives of those who had already surrendered their very existence to the whim of the vile one, who had allowed themselves to be enslaved. He would prove her wrong, of that he was determined.

The smallest of movements up ahead caused Makaal to abandon his train of thought in an instant. He held up a hand and gave the silent signal that would warn his comrades of a possible enemy presence. Holding his breath and forcing every muscle in his body to stillness, Makaal scanned the tunnel through his spy-lens. The service tunnel ran another one hundred metres through the bedrock beneath the palace, densely clustered pipes and cables lining its walls and ceiling. The end of the tunnel was marked by a square of wan light, which Makaal zoomed the spy-lens in upon to examine in closer detail. As the magnification increased, the image became grainy, but Makaal was sure that he had seen movement and waited for the machine-spirit inside the device to confirm it.

There – crossing the square of light at the end of the passageway was a figure. It was gone in seconds, but Makaal had seen all he needed. It was one of the traitors of the Mankarra Household Guard, the former governor's most trusted warriors. How ironic that they had been the first to turn and take up arms with Voldorius and the Alpha Legion. The grey- and black-armoured guards had gunned the governor down even as their former master had fled for the bunker beneath the palace. They had strung his ruined body from the highest of the palace's spires.

Makaal waited until he was sure it was safe, and eased his body out of the shadows, his hellgun gripped tight. Checking the weapon's status counter, Makaal confirmed that he had sufficient charge to face whatever might lie ahead.

MAKAAL AND HIS team approached the light at the end of the tunnel, covering the one hundred metres of ground with extreme caution. It felt to Makaal that the approach was taking far too much time, and that he might miss this opportunity to attack Voldorius when the daemon was at his most vulnerable. Yet he knew that undue haste now would bring the mission to an abrupt and fatal end.

At length, Makaal eased himself into the shadows five metres from the opening, and peered cautiously out. A chamber formed a junction between half a dozen other service tunnels. A hatch was set into one rock wall, which Makaal knew to be a cargo escalator that served the upper levels of the palace. Beside the hatch stood five troopers of the palace guard.

Forcing his body to complete stillness, Makaal watched the guards for several minutes until he was sure they were not merely passing through the area. Evidently, the traitorous bastards had been posted to the tunnel junction to guard against intruders. It made sense, for the resistance had been launching attacks across the entire city for weeks. The junction provided a base the guards could launch patrols from into the sprawling network of service tunnels beneath the palace. They would have to be dealt with before the cell could advance any further.

With a last hand signal, the cell leader counted down five seconds before he surged out of the tunnel.

The first of the palace guards went down before any had registered the attack. Makaal put a searing hell-gun blast through his torso that flash-boiled his internal organs in an instant. Even before the guard had hit the ground, the other resistance fighters were out of the tunnel. Cytha darted to one side, rolling athletically as one of the guards brought his lascarbine up and blasted an unaimed shot in her direction. Cytha's move took her halfway across the chamber, where she came up into a kneeling position and brought her compact laspistol to bear on the trooper nearest to her. The man tracked her as she took aim, but he was too slow. Cytha's pistol spat and the guard was speared through the neck by a bright lance of lethal energy.

One of the remaining guards bellowed an order and all three dived for the cover of a crate near the escalator hatch. Knowing that his team would be caught in the open should the enemy find cover they could defend themselves from, Makaal called out his own instructions. Bys moved to the left while Rund darted to the right. Makaal moved towards Cytha, who was already working her way behind a cluster of barrels to outflank the enemy.

'We've got to end this, now,' Makaal told Cytha as he caught up with her. 'We don't have time to get bogged down.'

'Agreed,' the fighter replied, peering around the edge of a barrel. 'What's your plan?'

There was only one solution. He limbered his hellgun and drew a long blade from his belt. Seeing his intention, Cytha stowed her own firearm, and drew a wickedly sharp stiletto blade. She raised the weapon to her lips and kissed it tenderly. 'Ready when you are,' she whispered.

'Go!' Makaal ordered, springing from the cover the two had shared.

The three guards had made the cover of the crate and were even now raising their weapons over it, only their heads and arms visible. Bys and Rund worked their way around the chamber's edge, each firing as they went, taking advantage of what little cover was provided by stanchions and pipe work. The two men's fire was forcing the guards to keep their heads down, to a degree at least, but Makaal knew that would not last long.

Makaal and Cytha closed on their targets together. Cytha was fastest, the fighter leaping atop the crate with the speed of a hunting predator. Coming down into a nimble crouch, Cytha kicked out at the nearest guard, snapping his neck. In an instant, Makaal was vaulting past her. He slashed downwards with his blade as he passed the second guard, gouging a deep, red wound across his shoulder.

The last of the guards was too involved drawing a bead on Rund to react to Makaal and Cytha's assault, and Rund had allowed himself to be distracted by the sight. The guard squeezed the trigger of his lascarbine, and the weapon spat an incandescent line across the chamber. Rund went down heavily, before Cytha was upon the firer. Her stiletto punched into his right ear, the man transfixed as the tip emerged from the left side of his head. For a moment, the ghastly tableau was frozen, before Cytha withdrew the blade with a jerk of her arm, and the guard dropped to the floor.

'Bys!' Makaal bellowed. 'Check Rund.'

Praying that the lay-technician was not fatally injured, Makaal turned angrily towards the guard he had wounded. The man lay sprawled across the crate he had taken cover behind, and was even now reaching for his dropped carbine. Makaal lifted a foot and brought it down across the man's wrist, forestalling the attempt to regain the weapon.

'You,' Makaal spat through gritted teeth, 'I name traitor.'

Unlimbering his hellgun one-handed, Makaal brought its barrel down, its end centimetres from the man's face. He looked into the wounded guard's eyes and saw only hatred and anger. Part of him had hoped that the traitor would, at the last, see the error of his ways and perhaps even beg Makaal's forgiveness. He did not.

Makaal looked away as he pulled the trigger, the weapon's sharp report filling the chamber. Cytha looked on dispassionately, seemingly unaffected by the callous yet necessary execution.

Bys was helping Rund to his feet. 'He'll be fine,' the big man said, his eyes flitting to the mess at Makaal's feet before he looked back. 'But we need to hide those and get moving.'

FOR THE LAST thirty minutes, Makaal had been conscious of a slowly building, bass hum in the air. The rock floor of the dark service tunnel the fighters crept along was faintly vibrating, and the hair on the back of Makaal's neck was standing on end. The very air he breathed tasted somehow metallic, and every now and then a static charge would snap from a pipe or stanchion to sting his flesh as he passed.

'We're underneath the primary capacitors,' whispered Rund from behind.

Makaal had little idea what such a device was, but he could detect pain in the man's voice. Bys had applied a dressing to the chest wound Rund had sustained in the brief fight against the palace guard, but he would need proper medical attention if he were to survive. If any of us escape, Makaal thought.

'Another hundred metres then,' Makaal replied. 'Is everyone ready?

Each of the fighters nodded. He had scarcely needed to ask, but felt the burden of command weigh heavily as the cell neared its destination. These people had followed him of their own volition, and he had little doubt that they would all die because of it.

As if shaking off a premonition of his own death, Makaal crossed his hands across his chest in the sign of the aquila. His comrades did the same, and moments later he was leading them cautiously towards their final objective.

As Makaal approached the end of the service tunnel, Cytha by his side and Bys and Rund close behind, the air became increasingly charged. Blue light flashed intermittently from the chamber beyond the tunnel, each discharge accompanied by a harsh crack of the air being split by titanic energies.

'Both of you know your objectives,' Makaal whispered.

Moving forwards to the mouth of the tunnel, he stole a glance into the chamber. The teleportarium was a huge, domed space, dominated by a raised, circular platform at its very centre. Banks of pulsating, glowing machinery lined the walls, actinic sparks and whiplash energies playing up and down tall copper shafts. Fat cables snaked across the stone floor. Hundreds more looped down from above or crawled across the walls, linking each and every item of machinery together in an insane web of crackling energy.

Makaal mouthed a silent prayer to the God-Emperor. Never before had he seen such a thing. Indeed, he had only recently heard that such machines could exist, though he was assured that they were so rare they could command the ransom of an entire planet. The teleportation device had rotted away for millennia beneath the governor's palace, all knowledge of its operation and maintenance long since forgotten. No one knew what the device had been used for, or who had built it. Over the centuries it became a temple the tech-priests would worship in. Only with the coming of Voldorius had the chamber been restored to its original use and the machinery returned to a working state by the ministrations of the rogue Mechanicus who served the daemon prince.

And one of those fell individuals stood nearby, his back to the fighters as they peered out of the tunnel.

The rogue tech-priest was unnaturally tall, as if the limbs beneath his ragged crimson robe were attenuated and disjointed. Despite his height, the priest's back was bent and he stooped almost double, bending down to attend to a machine console. A dozen mechanical tentacles writhed from the grotesque hump on the priest's back, each with an implement, tool or weapon at its end. Some of those tentacles worked the levers and dials of the console, while others moved about seemingly of their own accord like snakes waiting for unwary prey to wander near.

Tech-priests had always made Makaal uneasy, for their affinity with machines was far beyond the ken of ordinary men. That the individual in the chamber was an outcast of his sinister order made Makaal's skin crawl. Technology was a thing to be respected, revered and even feared, yet this vile servant of Voldorius had reneged on his oaths to the Cult Mechanicus to use technology only as prescribed by the Emperor. The reasons for killing the renegade were legion, and Makaal was pleased to be the instrument of the Emperor's justice.

Makaal raised his hellgun, lining up the iron sights with the back of the tech-priest's hood. Even as he did so, the machinery lining the chamber walls began to whine, white lightning spitting at the periphery of his vision.

'I think someone's…' hissed Rund.

Makaal's finger closed gently on the trigger and one of the mechanical tentacles at the tech-priest's back whipped around, a green glowing lens at its tip staring directly at Makaal. Disgust welled up inside him as he realised that the lens was an eye. Through it, the renegade was looking directly at the fighter, somehow entrancing him with fell power.

In a second the spell passed and Makaal got a grip of his thoughts, but still the malignant green eye floated before him, filling his vision. But the tech-priest had already turned, and was advancing across the chamber towards the resistance fighters.

'Kill it!' Makaal bellowed, and all four of the resistance fighters opened fire as one.

Makaal's aim was true, but the blast of his weapon was halted before it struck the tech-priest. Waves of blue energy rippled out from a point in the air a metre in front of the renegade, settling to nothing after a second. A squeal of harsh machine gibberish screamed from a grille mounted where the priest's mouth should have been. Three more green lenses glowed from under his hood above the grille.

Makaal gritted his teeth, fighting the urge to drop his weapon and cover his ears lest they burst under the hideous sonic assault.

'Again!' he shouted. This time only three shots rang out, telling Makaal that either Rund or Bys must have been incapacitated by the machine howl. Two of the shots were stopped by the energy field, but one – Makaal could not tell whose – passed through, and struck the renegade's left arm.

The shot blasted a ragged flaming hole through a crimson sleeve and a shower of sparks went up. The priest staggered under the impact and a second machine squeal sounded. This time however, it was a scream of pain and rage.

'Full auto!' Makaal ordered, thumbing the selector switch above his weapon's grip. He braced the hellgun against his shoulder, drawing a bead on the renegade's chest as the roaring figure bore down upon him.

Squeezing the trigger tight and holding it down, Makaal unleashed a torrent of blinding shots. The field absorbed half, but the remainder slammed through, stitching the renegade's torso. The priest stumbled back, but now he was close. The writhing mechanical tentacles whipped forwards, one striking Makaal across the side of his body. Pain flooded his senses as he felt several ribs crack sickeningly and he was propelled through the air to crash ten metres away on the rocky floor.

Fighting to remain conscious, Makaal looked up in time to see Bys wrestling with the tentacles, one gripped in each hand. In that split second, Cytha stepped inside the tech-priest's reach and her stiletto flashed upwards, catching the renegade's throat and sinking up to its hilt. The machine-howl was abruptly silenced and the tentacles fell limp in Bys's massive hands. Both fighters stepped backwards and the renegade tech-priest fell forwards. The sound the body made as it struck the rock floor was not flesh hitting rock, but ironwork shattering into a hundred pieces.

Rund was at the console the tech-priest had been manning. 'Someone's coming through!' he shouted, an edge of panic rising in his voice.

'Bys, Rund,' Makaal said as he crossed the chamber. 'You know what to do. Make it fast.'

There was little that Makaal or Cytha could do now, for their role in the mission had been to get the cell safely to the teleportarium. He watched as Bys unlimbered bandoliers full of explosives and followed Rund. The lay-technician took a moment to gather himself before indicating a dozen points around the chamber to the larger man. Nodding, Bys crossed to the first, a machine of copper coils, shafts and pipes, and got to work setting his explosives.

Rund was soon back at the console. 'I can't stop it!' he called over his shoulder to Makaal.

'How long?' the leader asked. 'Do we have enough time?'

The lay-technician's hands turned a series of dials and after a moment he looked back at Makaal. 'If we detonate the explosives manually, we might–'

'Half set!' Bys's voice rang out. The man had placed six of his charges in the locations Rund had indicated and was almost done with the seventh.

Makaal understood immediately what the lay-tech was saying. 'Give me the detonator. This is my burden.'

Rund hesitated, distracted by the flashing lights of the console and the reams of data scrolling across its screens. Then he reached into a belt pocket and took out the small, boxlike detonator. He tossed it to Makaal.

The fighter caught the device in his raised hand. He crossed to the console facing the raised metal platform in the centre of the chamber. Cytha appeared at his side, her dark eyes glaring at the same point.

Makaal checked his weapon's status reader. The full auto blast had cost him a third of his remaining charge and the focussing ring had come dangerously close to overheating. It would never be enough. Their only hope of success was the charges that Bys was even now finishing setting.

'Stand by!' Rund called out.

Even as the lay-technician shouted his warning the air in the chamber became so charged that Makaal felt every centimetre of his skin crawling as if a million insects skittered across his body. A sharp pain split his head, and his vision swam. The towering copper shafts around the chamber erupted with blinding white arcs of unknowable power and the air split like the centre of a thunderstorm.

The once dark and shadowed chamber was now flooded with pulsating light emanating from a point in the centre of the raised platform. The illumination was diffuse at first, with no direct source. A blinding singularity blinked into being above the centre of the platform, arcs of ragged lightning splitting the air between it and the copper coils at the chamber's edge.

Makaal placed his thumb on the stud in the centre of the detonator box. Not yet, he told himself. Wait until you're sure. The point of light expanded into a blazing orb, its base touching the metal of the platform. The orb flickered and then expanded still more, until it became a semicircular archway over the entire platform.

So blinding was the light that Makaal made to raise his arm across his face, but found himself paralysed, his body refusing to respond to his will. He felt the crush of impossible energies, as if the very air of the chamber had become solid, trapping him as a fly in amber.

And then, at the centre of the glare, three silhouettes appeared.

The central figure was massive, tall and broad shouldered with wings folded at its back. The second was not quite so large, but still a giant compared to mere men. The third was stooped and crooked, the fabric of its robes flaring in an etheric wind.

'Makaal.' The fighter heard Cytha speak his name, but could not turn his head to face her. 'Do it, Makaal, now!'

Makaal waited until the silhouettes had resolved in the middle of the blazing white light. Then, with a supreme effort of willpower, he pressed his thumb down hard on the detonator's control stud.

Nothing happened at first, for the chamber was already churning with the energies of the teleportation device. Then, the pure white light the three figures were silhouetted against flickered and stuttered. Time slowed for Makaal, even the beat of his heart becoming frozen in a single instant. The white orb collapsed in on itself, plunging the entire chamber into total blackness.

Then, a dozen of the machines lining the chamber wall exploded as one. The light of the detonations illuminated three figures on the raised platform. Orange flames danced at their feet, before another light entirely sprang into being.

A vertical, crimson-purple scar appeared behind the three figures, as if the air itself were splitting apart. The line became a wound etched in the surface of reality. Still unable to move, terror flooded Makaal's soul. From the wound emanated a ghastly, pulsating light, the colour of blood and guts.

The three figures attempted to move away from the horror that had appeared at their back, but they too must have been entrapped. Despite his terror, Makaal felt a moment of hope. Not for himself, for he knew now that he was doomed, but for his home world. Whatever process the destruction of the teleportarium had instigated, it looked like it would claim Voldorius and his servants as well as the fighters.

The terror consuming Makaal's soul was now tempered by vindication, the two emotions converging into something approaching madness. Though his lips would barely move, inside Makaal roared within with an unholy blend of joy and horror. He screamed his hatred at the daemon, raged his denial of his own death and shouted his joy at his victory. The wound grew larger still, a deep gash in the flesh of reality, bulging outwards as if tainted organs were at the point of bursting forth.

And then, the wound ripped open.

The chamber was suddenly filled with the sound of a trillion souls wailing their damnation as one. In an instant, Makaal's soul was torn asunder, yet still the core of all he was looked on. The crimson scar split open, spilling writhing energies into the chamber. Thrashing coils of crimson ether quested outwards, wrapping themselves around the three figures on the platform as if to drag them back through the wound.

More of the writhing coils spread outwards, snaking around the chamber until they came upon Makaal and his comrades. His mind now shattered into a thousand shards, Makaal was incapable of feeling the

ANDY HOARE

terror that had consumed him before. He merely looked on as ghostly intestine-shaped tentacles wrapped themselves around his fellow resistance fighters, lifted them into the air, and drew their bodies towards the ragged hole in the fabric of reality.

Only then did what was left of Makaal realise that he too was being carried towards the impossible wound. What had been a jagged line was now a swollen, gaping maw, beyond which swam uncounted... things. Mouths and eyes formed from the boiling energies, then dissolved and dissipated to re-emerge elsewhere. The eyes radiated hunger and pain, while the mouths slobbered and gibbered and wailed in eternal anguish. Makaal knew that he would be joining that churning mass.

Makaal was drawn closer to the three figures. Voldorius was braced against raging etheric winds seeking to suck him into the vortex. Vast coils were wrapped about his armoured legs and arms, yet he resisted with a strength that was entirely inhuman.

Nearby, the second figure wrestled with more of the binds. This must have been one of Voldorius's lieutenants, for he too wore the blue-green power armour of the Alpha Legion. The warrior was fast, dodging and weaving as he sought to escape the writhing intestines.

The last of the figures was a robed human whom Makaal recognised as Voldorius's equerry. The man stood no chance of resisting the thrashing coils and he was being dragged into the maw as inexorably as Makaal himself. As the equerry was dragged nearer to the wound, his flesh began to blister. Soon it was boiling off in great streams of red vapour, sucked away on impossible winds of damnation.

Makaal felt his own skin blistering, but he did not care, for Voldorius too was being dragged down.

The daemon's batlike wings were torn to ragged scraps, the bones snapping and falling away into the screaming nothingness. Voldorius bellowed as the coils drew him closer to the mouth. The surface of his armour smoked and blistered as the blue-green finish dissolved into atoms. Soon the skin of the daemon's face was peeling back, his savage teeth exposed as the muscles were flensed away. The daemon's bellow was now so loud that it drowned out all other sounds, even the wailing of the damned from beyond the portal.

What was left of Makaal knew that Voldorius would be cast back to the warp that had spawned him and Quintus would be saved. Makaal's very soul was forfeit, for Voldorius himself would torment him for all eternity as vengeance for this deed.

And then Voldorius's lieutenant cast off the whiplash energies that sought to bind him and the armoured warrior moved fast towards the edge of the platform. Denial welling up inside him, Makaal could only look on helplessly as the figure gained speed the further it travelled from the raging maw of warp energy. In an instant it had escaped and was leaping from the platform to land heavily upon the rock floor of the teleportarium chamber. Now entirely free, the figure looked around the chamber and crossed to one of the rearing copper-shafted machines. Drawing a black-bladed halberd that was slung across its back, the figure lashed out, slicing the copper machinery in two. The power sustaining the machinery fled and secondary explosions erupted across the chamber.

The writhing maw convulsed and Voldorius broke free even as the last vaporous remains of his human servant were sucked through. The daemon prince was now little more than a charred, blackened skeleton, his armour burned away and the last remnants of his flesh falling from him in smoking chunks.

The other warrior smashed another copper shaft apart, and the energies coursing through the chamber spluttered. There was a single moment of perfect frozen clarity, before the ragged maw blinked out of existence and the chamber was plunged back into flame-lit shadow.

At the last, what had been Makaal felt himself fading. His final vision was of Voldorius forcing himself to stand upright. Black bones reknitted, veins regrew. Glistening muscles swathed the bones and the daemon's armour flowed like liquid metal across his regenerated form. The batlike wings regrew from his back and Voldorius bellowed a savage victory cry.

As his soul was whipped away to join the lost, the true extent of Makaal's failure was revealed to him. Voldorius lived, and Makaal was damned for all eternity.

'QAN'KARRO,' KOR'SARRO SAID, looking directly across the strategium chamber at the old Storm Seer. 'Please go on. Tell us of your brothers' efforts to establish contact with Quintus.'

Qan'karro gathered his thoughts. The old man looked pale, as if the weight of his years weighed heavily upon his soul.

'Gladly, huntsman,' said Qan'karro, before lifting a cup of sour Chogoran wine to his lips and draining the vessel in a single draught.

'Pooling our efforts with the astropaths, my brethren and I have used every possible means at our disposal to make contact. The astropaths have come to the conclusion that none of their order survives upon Quintus, or if they do, they have been subjugated, brutally.'

Kor'sarro and the assembled officers considered this dire news before the Master of the Hunt pressed the Storm Seer further. 'And your own efforts, honoured seer?'

'I have little to report, Kor'sarro. We have cast our minds far ahead of us, piercing the warp even as this vessel races upon its tides.'

Kor'sarro knew little of the ways of the Storm Seers, for their skills were born of their psyker inheritance and unfathomable to others. He did understand that the seers could not communicate directly with others as the astropaths did, but he had an inkling that they had other abilities they could draw on.

'All we can hope to do is plant visions, even mere notions, of our coming in the minds of those able to hear,' Qan'karro went on. 'If there are any such remaining, then I pray they hear our call.'

'What of those on Quintus?' Kor'sarro asked his comrade. 'What of the portents?'

'Codiciers Subas and Odakai have consulted every augur our people know, and several they do not,' the Storm Seer said, his eyes taking on a dark cast.

Kor'sarro waited a moment before pressing further. 'And?'

'None are favourable, huntsman.'

Kor'sarro clenched the arms of his stone throne as the assembled officers considered the Storm Seer's words. His eyes settled for a moment on Brother Kergis, who he had appointed to serve as company champion following the death of Brother Jhogai on Cernis IV. After the events on that world, neither he nor his officers needed to hear more bad tidings. Kor'sarro indicated that the old warrior should, indeed must, continue.

'Thousands have perished, of that we can be sure. But if we are honest, we expected that. But fell powers have been unleashed, possible futures etched upon the surface of time. I cannot put it into words, my friends, but truly, the vile one stands at the precipice and untold power awaits him.'

'Then we must stop him,' Kor'sarro replied, an oath forming in his mind. 'We must all pledge that on Quintus, Voldorius dies. There can be no alternative.'

The assembled Space Marines – Storm Seers, Techmarines, Apothecaries, Chaplains and sergeants – nodded their agreement, each steeling themselves to face whatever fate held in store. Kor'sarro looked each in the eye in turn, seeing in every one of his officers the cold determination to end the hunt for Voldorius on Quintus.

Resolving to steer the discussion away from gloomy portents, Kor'sarro took a deep breath and leaned forwards in his throne. 'Brother Kholka,' he addressed the veteran Scout-sergeant. 'You have prepared a report on the world of Quintus. Please, illuminate us.'

'We know little of the world, my brothers,' Kholka said. 'For its history is troubled. Quintus, along with three other systems, has been battered and assailed by warp storm Argenta. Though once Quintus was a bulwark, Argenta has laid it low, cutting it off for long periods. As can be imagined, maintaining standing forces amongst the worlds of the Imperium under such circumstances has proven nigh impossible, and the world has been forced to look to its own security.'

'Yet,' interjected a Codicier by the name of Ilkhan, 'we know that Argenta has abated in recent months. The vile one must have had a hand in this.'

'That is beyond my ken, honoured seer,' the sergeant replied before going on. 'What we know of Quintus is culled from the last *census planetia*. It is a barren world in the main, with little but its strategic location to make it noteworthy. As a result of that location, the world has been fortified over the millennia, primarily to act as a guardian against the orks that afflict the regions to the galactic south and east.'

'What happened to Quintus during Argenta?' asked Kor'sarro.

'We have no current information on that subject, my khan,' the Scout-sergeant replied. 'We can only assume that it suffered greatly during that time.'

'It did,' interjected Qan'karro. 'Of that I am certain. My instinct tells me that the vile one somehow brought the storm down upon Quintus, in order to turn it to his own ends. That the storm has now passed suggests to me that whatever wickedness he was about is now imminent.'

'Is such a thing possible?' Kor'sarro said. 'Could one being truly conjure and control a warp storm?'

'Aye, huntsman,' Qan'karro replied, his craggy face a dour mask. 'Do not underestimate Kernax Voldorius. He has done far worse, and means to do so again.'

Grim silence settled upon the gathered White Scars, before Kor'sarro spoke. 'Brothers, we have much work ahead of us. We must each prepare ourselves, our men and our weapons for the task ahead. We arrive at the Quintus system within hours, and we must be ready for whatever awaits.'

MALYA L'NOR STUMBLED as a traitor militiaman shoved her roughly. She turned to curse at the man, but the sheer press of bodies being herded forcibly into the grand square soon obscured him.

'What do they want?' a merchant shouted desperately from behind her, addressing his question to no one in particular. Hundreds of nearby citizens of Mankarra, the capital city of Quintus, voiced similar questions, some in outrage, many more in unadulterated panic.

Malya soon found herself carried along in a torrent of fearful humanity towards the centre of the grand square. She could see little but the dark sky above, shot through with the stain of the accursed warp storm. Framing the livid sky were the tops of Mankarra's brutal, fortified buildings. The tallest was the council mansion, towards which the vast crowd, including Malya, was being herded.

The traitor militiamen were using electro-prods on their own people. The cruel devices were employed by the gaksmen of the agri-zones to control the unruly grox that provided a staple of the population's diet. They were far too powerful to be used on humans.

Malya seethed with anger as the sheer weight of the crowd carried her inexorably across the square and towards the council mansion. The grand square was capable of hosting crowds of hundreds of thousands, and she herself had attended dozens of municipal functions there. Those functions had seen multitudes of the faithful giving praise to the Emperor or witnessing the coronation of a new planetary governor. The gathering that Malya and countless others were now being forced to attend was clearly something very different.

Malya steeled herself against whatever evil might soon be unleashed upon her and her people. She whispered a prayer to the Emperor. Such an act was now counted as subversion, and while she was cautious not to be seen, the deed gave her strength. The grey bulk of the council mansion loomed before the crowd, its thick armoured towers bristling with anti-air defences.

The long banners celebrating the glories of the Emperor that once adorned the walls were now tattered and burned, defiled by the followers of the daemon Voldorius.

The mere thought of the vile beast that had come to her world brought cold dread to Malya's heart. For Quintus to have been subjugated so quickly must have been the result of infiltration of the planetary militia at the very highest levels, of that Malya was certain. The invasion was over almost before it had begun, those few defence units that had not welcomed the attackers being driven to ground and wiped out within weeks. Malya, herself a junior officer in the reserve, had joined the nascent underground resistance and in a very short time become one of its senior members. Her rapid ascension had been due to what little military training she had undertaken in the reserves, though many, such as that fool Makaal, refused to acknowledge even that.

Malya's greatest hope had come mere days ago, when she and her fellows had made tentative contact with the outside. That anyone should have heard her pleas was a miracle in itself, but her heart had soared when she had discovered that a force of Space Marines was inbound for Quintus. She had dared to believe that deliverance was on its way to her home world.

The movement of the crowd was slowing down as it was pressed towards the rockcrete facade of the council mansion, and a cold silence settled across the packed multitudes. The faces of the people nearest to

Malya held the same fear she herself felt deep inside her soul. All gathered in the grand square knew of the atrocities that had been committed, by the turncoat militia as well as by the invading forces. All knew the name of the archfiend in whose name the horrors had been enacted. Malya knew that she would soon lay eyes upon that fiend. It was said that only those about to die a horrible death at the daemon's hand ever saw his face.

Even as that terrible thought coalesced in her mind, the crowd fell completely silent. All eyes were drawn to movement at the wide, statue-lined balcony near the top of the council mansion. Malya strained her eyes and saw that the double doors were opening slowly inwards.

A group of men stepped through, each taking their place upon the balcony. These were the high commanders of the planetary militia, each a respected officer before Voldorius had come to Quintus. But they had cast off their Emperor-granted duty and betrayed their own world. It was through their treachery that the planet had fallen, and they were now counted as figures of loathing by the populace.

General Orson, Lord Kline, Quartermaster General Ackenvol, Lord Colonel Lannus and Lord Colonel Elenritch took their places on the balcony, each staring fixedly ahead as if unable or unwilling to meet the gaze of any of the multitude packed in below them. Then came the last of their number, Lord Colonel Morkis, who glowered down at the crowd with obvious contempt. It was said that Morkis was the worst of them, that he harboured such ambition that he would willingly see his entire home world burn to gain the favour of Voldorius.

And then a dark shape ducked as it passed through the open portal, a massive pair of black wings folded at its back.

As one, a hundred thousand throats gave voice to a soul-wrenching moan of utter despair. The very embodiment of evil stood before the gathered masses. The preachers and the confessors and the cardinals warned that the Emperor had almost died to cast down such servants of Chaos. Thousands collapsed to the ground, and thousands more thrust their arms in the air and begged deliverance. Many stood dumbfounded, unable to comprehend the fate that was about to overtake them.

A few, Malya L'nor included, refused to bend their knee or abandon their faith. These few stood still and silent as the beatific statues that had lined the square before the coming of the invaders. They steeled themselves body and soul for the martyrdom that must surely be their fate.

Voldorius stepped fully onto the balcony and even the officers shrank back. At the sight of the daemon, the crowd's wailing was redoubled until it reached a near deafening crescendo. The rank stink of discharged bodily fluids filled the air, testament to the horror that reduced grown men to the level of mewling infants.

Voldorius stood upon the balcony flanked by his treacherous underlings, his bestial face looking down upon a seething ocean of despair. Alien thoughts flooded Malya's mind, formless notions of atrophy and entropy washing over her soul in ever-stronger waves. Sharp probes stabbed into her consciousness and she fought to hide away her previous thoughts of deliverance from the tyranny of Voldorius. She must not reveal her thoughts, even if it cost her life.

Now the most despairing of the crowd were convulsing and shaking, as if they were being ripped apart from within by the sheer evil of the armoured, bat-winged figure on the balcony. Many were now falling silent, choking on their own blood as they gnawed their tongues away.

Yet Malya's soul stood firm, her faith in the Emperor a bulwark against which the evil of Voldorius was broken. Bodies carpeted the ground, the faithful few standing upright amongst them.

Only when nine out of every ten of the multitude were curled up upon the ground, dead or entirely overcome by despair, did the daemon speak.

'This day,' the voice rumbled across the grand square, as low and ancient as continents grinding one another to dust. 'A crime was committed.'

Those who had wailed before now sobbed, for the daemon's voice spoke to each present. It enveloped the soul and threatened to consume it, to snub out its meagre light.

'That crime,' the voice continued, 'was the sin of denial, and it shall be punished.'

Malya forced herself to stand firm, but she was painfully aware that she was terribly exposed. So few now stood, the vast majority lying collapsed upon the ground.

'One who served me was slain.'

A cold realisation dawned then upon Malya. Makaal. He had done what he had threatened to do, what Malya and the other leaders of the resistance had begged him not to. He had made an attempt on the vile one's life, and had failed, even if he had killed one of Voldorius's underlings.

The people would pay for Makaal's deed.

'One here,' the daemon continued, 'shall as punishment take his place and serve as my equerry. They shall be blessed to witness the coming tide of blood.' A premonition rose in Malya's mind as the words sank in. 'The remainder shall die.'

The crowd's sorrowful cries were drowned out as the sound of a mighty engine coughing to life filled the grand square. A super-heavy tank, one of the few so-called Baneblades in the militia's arsenal, ground forwards from a side street.

The armoured behemoth bristled with weaponry, its huge turret tracking left and right. Realising what was about to happen, Malya looked to the other roads that led onto the grand square. The traitor militia had barricaded every possible escape. Voldorius meant to crush the people beneath the tracks of the tank or to gun them down under its cannons. Those who fled would be shot dead by the militia.

Voldorius spread his arms wide in blasphemous benediction. His dark gaze swept the square, his bestial eyes alighting on each of those who remained standing before passing to the next. He ignored those who cowered on the ground, and they in turn sought to make themselves invisible to the daemon, burying their heads in their arms or curling into foetal balls. The waves of fell emotion battered Malya's soul, but she repeated over and over the verses she had learned before the pulpit of Mankarra's great basilica. She prayed for deliverance from evil, from damnation, and from death.

'You,' the daemon said, the voice sounding within Malya's head. 'You shall be my servant.'

Malya stood transfixed by Voldorius's daemonic gaze. Part of her wanted to join those sprawled across the ground, to join them in the death grinding inexorably towards them. But another part of her, the greater, stronger part, refused to yield.

'Join me,' the voice said. 'Now.'

Even as she filled her lungs to bellow her denial, Malya felt two pairs of hands grasp her arms, pinning them roughly behind her back. She turned and looked into the faceless visor of a trooper of the palace guard. The man put all his strength into twisting her body around and she was flung across the ground, tripping on a prostrate body and sprawling beside it. For an instant she thought that she might be able to feign the same stupor that had befallen the multitudes, but all too soon she was grabbed by both arms and hauled to her feet.

Malya dared gaze up as she was marched towards the council mansion, seeing the massive form of the daemon prince turning its back upon the grand square and disappearing into the building. The officers followed, Lord Colonel Morkis taking one last, scornful look across the square before departing. Soon, she too was approaching the blasted edifice. At her back the slaughter was beginning.

The Baneblade's cannons opened fire, its many heavy bolters chattering. The sound of flesh and blood and bone being ground beneath the tank's huge treads assailed Malya's ears. And then, the screaming began.

CHAPTER 5

Insertion

SCOUT-SERGEANT KHOLKA GRIMACED as he gazed down at yet another ruined body. Like the dozens of others the White Scars Scouts had encountered as they had ranged across the black, rock-strewn landscape of Quintus the last twelve hours, the corpse was a civilian. The sight disgusted Kholka, whose own people afforded great respect to the dead and would never allow a corpse to lie untended in such a way. Where were this man's people, Kholka wondered, and why had they not given him a fitting burial?

The reason was clear. The man's people had been killed too. All of them. None remained to bury the dead, to afford the honour a man was due at the outset of his long journey to the Emperor's side.

'Brother-sergeant,' a voice called out from over a small rise of jagged black rock. 'There are two more here.'

It was Scout Borchu, a promising neophyte Kholka knew would do well when fully initiated into the ranks of the White Scars. Borchu had served in the Scout Company with great honour and skill for several years. Perhaps the liberation of Quintus would be the proving of Borchu, if only he could learn to control his bouts of mirth. Quintus was seeing to that it seemed – with every body the Scouts discovered their mood darkened.

Kholka followed Borchu's voice, skirting the rise lest he reveal himself to any enemy keeping watch across the barren wastes. He had ordered vox-silence, knowing that the Alpha Legion were amongst the most cunning of foes and well able to detect even the most heavily shielded inter-squad signal. He found Borchu near the blackened wreck of a tracked cargo hauler. Its contents, evidently the sum possessions of its owners, were strewn all about.

'They were slain like the others,' Borchu said, looking up as his sergeant approached. 'But they tried to fight.'

Kholka saw that Borchu was correct. The two bodies wore the tattered remains of the local reserve militia's uniform. His eyes sought the insignia that had brought the White Scars to Quintus, but found no sign of it. No matter. It was likely only the elite palace guard wore the device. Dozens of empty brass shell casings were scattered all around the two bodies, though the weapons that had fired them were nowhere to be seen. Evidently, the weapons had been looted by the Alpha Legion, or perhaps taken by other refugees.

'Get ready to move out,' Kholka ordered. 'There's nothing to be done here.'

'Yes, brother-sergeant,' Borchu replied. But Kholka could detect uncertainty in the Scout's tone.

'What is it, neophyte?' Kholka pressed. As commander, mentor and warden of the trainee Space Marines, one of his many responsibilities was the monitoring of the Scouts' ongoing psycho-conditioning. The questioning of a direct order could be a sign that the conditioning had not fully taken effect.

'Should we not...' Borchu nodded towards the corpses.

Kholka read the meaning of the gesture. 'We should, but we cannot. Prepare to move out.'

The Scouts were making their way across a region of Quintus's primary continent having been inserted by Thunderhawk during the night. In common with much of the planet's surface, the area was a barren waste of black volcanic rock and grey sand. It was sparsely covered by coarse grass and the occasional wind-blasted tree. To the south lay the agri-settlements that fed the capital city of Mankarra. Further south still was the city itself.

Kholka's task was to reconnoitre the city's outer defences and to guide the Master of the Hunt's strike force in.

So far, the Scouts had discovered untold evidence that the planet was firmly in the hands of Voldorius and his Alpha Legion forces. They had passed the wrecks of refugee convoys the traitors had fallen on like voracious predators on defenceless prey.

Although they had found evidence that the refugees had at least mounted a defence, Kholka knew that many more must have been taken prisoner. The fate of the captives was unknown, but the veteran had faced the servants of the Ruinous Powers enough times to know their cruel ways. He had little doubt that none of those taken prisoner still lived.

Soon the remainder of the Scout squad was gathered, each looking silently to Kholka while awaiting his orders.

'Borchu,' Kholka said. 'You have point duty. We hunt, as the dawn-bat soars over the mountain.'

Even whilst undergoing a perilous mission the Scouts were being tested. The sergeant's use of the White Scars' battle-cant even though no enemy was near enough to overhear was deliberate. He was pleased when the Scouts assumed the formation he had ordered, a long column with each member covering his own sector, neophyte Borchu at its head.

Taking his own position in the line, Kholka gestured the order to move out.

NULLUS STOOD ON the bunker's open-topped observation deck, staring out into the bleak wastes. At his side were five of his fellow Alpha Legion warriors, and behind them several dozen black- and grey-clad palace guards.

The air reeked of the men's fear. And well they should be fearful, for the so-called elite of Quintus's soldiery had failed in their avowed task. A resistance cell had penetrated into the deepest regions of the palace and Voldorius himself had almost fallen. Only Nullus's actions in shattering the teleportation coils had averted a full-scale warp bleed, and the lives of Nullus and his master had been saved. Voldorius had already exacted his vengeance on the people of Mankarra, and now Nullus had his own justice to enact.

He would make an example of them, and teach them the true meaning of obedience.

Nullus had mustered the palace guard platoon whose negligence had given rise to the unforgivable breach. Their commanding officer had already killed himself by the time the platoon had gathered. The remainder had been transported north in the sub-zero hold of a meat-hauler to one of the bunkers that guarded against incursion into the agri-zones from the wastes beyond. The guards all feared that they would die, and to Nullus that sensation was quite exquisite.

But Nullus had something quite specific in mind.

'All of you,' the warrior spoke, without taking his black eyes off of the northern horizon, 'should be dead.'

The palace guards remained motionless, stoic in the face of the traitor Space Marine's pronouncement. Nullus turned his scarred face towards the men, and continued.

'But I am a practical man, and have use for you yet.'

Nullus watched as the guards stood as still as statues, not one of them daring to look at him. His scar-traced features split into a vile and savage grin.

Nullus reached to his back and unlimbered his black-hafted halberd. 'So you need not die. Not all of you.'

A cold wind rose out of the wastes. Still, none of the guards responded. Nullus brought the halberd in front of him in one hand and set the base of its haft resting on the deck at his feet.

'Whichever of you will face me, he will die. But the remainder, I will allow to live.'

Now the guards showed signs of reaction. Several of them glanced sidelong at their fellows, before one of their number answered.

'I will face you,' came the response, and one of the troopers stepped forwards.

'Name yourself, so that the gods might have notice of your coming, and prepare you a special place in damnation,' Nullus replied, bringing the halberd across his chest in both hands.

'My name is Ghalan,' the man proclaimed, addressing his statement to the powers of the warp as much as to Nullus. 'Warrant Officer Primus,' he added with pride, turning to salute his men.

The assembled guard returned the salute, and Nullus prepared to deliver his lesson.

'THREE KILOMETRES SOUTH, brother-sergeant', Scout Telluk whispered. 'A bunker, right on the border of the agri-zone.'

Kholka felt a stab of disappointment, but determined to give the neophyte a second chance. It was after all only the boy's second operational deployment. 'Again. Properly this time.'

The neophyte paused, his face reddening almost imperceptibly as he cast his eyes to the ground. 'My apologies, brother-sergeant,' he said.

'Never mind that,' Kholka replied, the veteran's patience growing thin. 'Deliver your report.'

'The beast in stone, as the third moon slumbers, bestriding the steppe,' Telluk reported.

'Better,' Kholka responded. 'Though "Ghan's last march" would have gotten the point over more elegantly.' By its very nature, the White Scars battle-cant was subjective and varied enormously by speaker and context. The veteran gifted the youngster with a wry smile. 'Now pass me the magnoculars.'

Taking the device from the neophyte, Kholka raised it to his eyes and looked out across the wastes. From the squad's concealed position high atop a jagged, black rock spire, Kholka had a panoramic view of the region where the barren wastelands gave way to the agri-zone. Scanning the near field first, the sergeant took in the terrain, the last of the rock-strewn plain his squad had marched through.

Adjusting the viewfinder's settings, Kholka focussed on the middle ground, where it was obvious that many of the larger rock formations had been blasted flat so that any crossing it would be detected and cut down in a hail of defensive fire. Panning first left, and then right, locating the point that Scout Telluk had identified, Kholka saw the squat, grey bunker.

'Well observed, neophyte,' Kholka said quietly as he magnified the scene. The bunker had been placed by a defender who knew his business well, and lesser

ANDY HOARE

foes than the Space Marines might have missed it amongst the volcanic rocks and outcroppings of the region.

'One primary,' Kholka reeled off his observations, adding a commentary to the data that the sensorium-core built into his armour was recording. Even if the sergeant and his charges were slain, there would be a chance that others of the White Scars would recover the data and act upon it. He zoomed in on the figure standing on the bunker's observation deck, looking out across the wastes. The warrior's armour was the distinctive blue-green of the traitor Alpha Legion, and across its back was slung a black halberd. Increasing the magnification still further, Kholka brought the figure's head into focus, revealing a face that was a mass of fine scar tissue, traced by the hand of a mad-man. 'We know you...'

'Four... no, five, secondaries.' Kholka watched as a group of figures, each wearing the same armour as the first, came into his vision. Their faces were hidden beneath helmets surmounted by twisting horns, and each carried a boltgun adorned with fell runes. 'Alpha Legionnaires.'

As he panned downwards, Kholka's field of vision was eclipsed by the rear of a black helmet. He zoomed out, the viewfinder showing a man dressed in grey fatigues and black body armour facing the primary. The briefings of the last few strike force councils came to the sergeant's mind. The black and grey armour. Kholka zoomed out still further, seeking confirmation.

'Approximately thirty tertiaries,' Kholka sub-vocalised. The wind had changed direction and he could not take the risk of being overheard. 'Subjects appear at first glance to be a platoon-sized multiple of Mankarra household guard.'

The sergeant watched, scanning the figures for any sign of the four-starred insignia that would positively confirm the troopers' identity and their link with the action on Cernis IV. He could see, although not hear, that the primary was addressing them. After a moment, one of the troopers stepped forwards to stand before the primary, and then turned and saluted the others.

At that moment, Kholka saw clearly the insignia on the man's shoulder armour.

'Confirmed,' the sergeant said, the thrill of the hunt rising in him. 'We have them now.'

NULLUS WATCHED WITH barely contained disdain as Ghalan turned back to face him. His black eyes flitted to the weapons at the guard's belt, seeing that the man was armed with a power sword of archaic pattern and a heavy pistol. The guard's face was set in a mask of grim determination. Clearly, the man knew he would die. But alone amongst the platoon, he had chosen to face his death with dignity.

The guard reached for the ornate basket hilt of his power sword and drew it slowly, his eyes never leaving his opponent. As the blade cleared the scabbard, a flick of the thumb activated its power core. Veins of searing light crept along its length, coalescing at its monomolecular edge. Ghalan set his feet wide, assuming a fighter's stance. Yet still, Nullus looked on with contempt.

'Do you hope for a quick death?' Nullus growled, his lipless mouth sneering.

In answer, Ghalan raised his power sword into the guard position.

'Or do you perhaps imagine you have some chance against me?'

. Ghalan remained tight-lipped, refusing to play along with the traitor Space Marine's cruel game. His only answer was to bare his teeth in anger, a gesture which brought another sneer from his opponent.

'I think you want to die,' Nullus crowed. 'I think you know the extent of your failure beneath the palace, and think you can avoid vengeance by way of a clean death.' Nullus cast a withering glance at the other guards. 'I think that you wish to avoid the fate I have in store for them.'

The assembled palace guards looked to one another, some raising angry curses.

'Kill him!' one shouted.

The man's head exploded in a welter of blood and gore, and one of Nullus's fellow Alpha Legion warriors lowered his boltgun, smoke wafting from its gaping barrel. Several of the man's fellow guards were showered with tissue, yet they refused to flee in the face of the sudden outbreak of violence. As the man's decapitated body hit the deck, Ghalan growled and lunged forwards, his power sword raised to deliver a two-handed, downward blow.

Nullus merely sidestepped the attack, his massive armoured form belying his speed. Ghalan should have been killed as the force he had channelled into his attack met only air and he was thrown off-balance, stumbling against the bunker's parapet. The guard paused there for several seconds, his back turned to his opponent, waiting for the killing blow to strike him down.

But the blow did not come.

Ghalan turned slowly, to find that Nullus was facing him five metres away, his halberd resting contemptuously across one shoulder.

'Did you think it would be so easy?' Nullus sneered. 'If you desire death by my hand, you'll have to earn it.'

Once more, Ghalan raised his power sword. The man's face was now a mask of barely-controlled rage. He knew he was being made sport of and was in an impossible position. He had little chance of besting the traitor, yet his opponent was intent upon humiliating him.

Ghalan began to move in a wide circle, and Nullus obliged by moving with him, so that the two stalked one another across the bunker's observation deck. Nullus's fellow Alpha Legion warriors looked on, their masks impassive but their bolters raised menacingly to ensure the remaining guards did not intervene.

'You know what I'll do with your skull, once you're dead?' Nullus said, his tone at once coldly matter-of-fact and supremely mocking.

Ghalan threw himself forwards, his power sword cutting a glittering arc through the air towards his opponent's head. The attack was well aimed, but Nullus merely shifted his stance but a fraction, scornfully allowing the searing blade to pass within centimetres of his scarred face.

This time, Ghalan did not allow himself to become unbalanced. Instead, he allowed the momentum of his attack to carry his body around to his opponent's left hand side. Turning the blade in his hand, Ghalan brought it upwards to strike at Nullus's midriff.

But Nullus was prepared too, and Ghalan's power sword struck the black blade of his enemy's halberd. Dark light flared where the two weapons clashed, casting a pall of shadow across both fighters. Ghalan was shrouded in unnatural night. Unable to see Nullus clearly, he instinctively threw his body backwards to avoid the inevitable riposte.

Ghalan struck the ground hard at the feet of one of Nullus's warriors. The Alpha Legionnaire made no effort to intervene in the combat, however, and Ghalan leapt to his feet, bringing his blade up.

It was only when Nullus's scarred mouth formed into a wide, mocking grin that Ghalan looked down at his blade. The weapon's edge no longer danced with the energy that had powered it before. The once lethal weapon was now reduced to a crude, blunted sword no more effective than a club wielded by a savage. Nullus's own, unnatural weapon had somehow drained its power and rendered it all but useless.

Snarling in frustration, Ghalan threw his broken weapon to the ground and snatched the heavy pistol from his belt. In a single movement, the weapon was held out before him, aimed squarely at Nullus's head.

'Better make it count,' Nullus growled. 'You won't get a second shot.'

The pistol shook in Ghalan's hands as he fought with all his might to control his rage. His glance flicked briefly to the other palace guards, but they stood powerless to intervene, covered by the boltguns of the Alpha Legionnaires.

Ghalan's finger closed on the trigger and the weapon barked a single shot. The bullet struck Nullus just below the thick collar of his power armour, barely leaving a scratch in the blue-green livery.

Before Ghalan could fire a second shot, Nullus exploded into violent movement. The black halberd lashed forwards, leaping across the space between the two combatants in the blink of an eye. The weapon struck Ghalan in the shoulder, propelling him across the decking and pinning him against the inner wall as its point sank into the rockcrete.

Transfixed by the blade, Ghalan was powerless as Nullus stepped before him.

'You sought a clean death,' Nullus sneered. 'You sought to avoid justice.'

The slightest of grins appeared at Ghalan's blood-flecked lips, but it vanished as Nullus continued. 'Your soul is mine, fool.'

As the remaining palace guards looked on in stunned horror, Ghalan's face became pale. Within moments, his skin began to shrivel and his muscles to collapse in upon themselves. As the vile process continued, Ghalan's entire body convulsed and twisted around the point of the halberd. A distant, mournful cry echoed, seeming to emanate from the very blade of Nullus's weapon. At the last, Ghalan's body was reduced to a shrivelled husk, and Nullus withdrew his blade.

'He who would share this fool's fate,' Nullus addressed the remaining guards, 'let him fail me again.'

The guards remained stoically silent, none daring to look towards the desiccated corpse behind Nullus. With the tip of his halberd, Nullus lifted Ghalan's remains high, and with a scornful flick cast them over the precipice to crumple to the ground in front of the bunker.

As the Alpha Legionnaires herded the palace guards away, Nullus addressed the corpse below, the insignia on the shoulder pad clearly visible. 'I think the point is made.'

'KHULA,' SAID SCOUT-SERGEANT Kholka, his voice low but clear. 'Take position here. I want overwatch at all times. Concentrate on the gully due south.'

Kholka watched for a moment as the Scout lowered himself into a dip in the volcanic rock and arranged his camouflaged cloak so he blended seamlessly into his surroundings. Only the barrel of the Scout's sniper rifle was visible, and that only from close up.

Confirming that Khula was in position, Kholka took one last look around. The enemy had departed, but the entire scene could still have been a charade to draw the attention of anyone watching. The Alpha Legion might be hidden nearby, ready to launch a devastating ambush against the small group of White Scars.

But Kholka was a veteran of the celebrated '422' patrol and had survived everything that the death world of Canak had thrown at him. He had served an entire year deep in enemy territory whilst fighting the dreaded Saharduins. He had even stalked lictors across the great cobalt reefs of Ayria-12-Tsunami, and had the honour scars to prove it. Kholka had not done all of these things by allowing himself to fall prey to enemy entrapment, and he was determined to pass such wisdom on to those under his tutorship.

'Our strength,' Kholka addressed the Scouts, 'is not arms. Our strength is guile.'

Satisfied that the Scouts were ready to learn and, if necessary, to fight, Kholka led the squad out of the cover of the rock formation and into the open wastes. Though old even for a Space Marine, Kholka moved with the fluid grace and stealth of a steppe-born predator. Indeed, as a savage son of proud, wild Chogoris, he was exactly that.

His silenced boltgun raised, Kholka made use of every scrap of cover as he approached the seemingly abandoned bunker. Every few minutes the sergeant would duck down behind cover, observe the bunker and ensure that his Scouts were deployed correctly.

Several times he glanced back to the position high atop the rocks, where he knew that Scout Khula was hidden. The neophyte had concealed himself well.

Kholka had timed the advance carefully, ensuring that it was only as the sun set that the squad reached the point where the rocks thinned out. The ground became flat where a clear fire zone had been levelled in front of the bunker.

'The gaze of midnight,' Kholka whispered, and the Scouts all lowered their night vision goggles over their eyes. He squinted down his boltgun's sights and scanned the bunker. The low, squat structure appeared deserted, but the sergeant engaged the sight's heat-sensitive function just to be sure. When no telltale heat signals were revealed, he waved his charges forwards, one at a time at ten-second intervals. The Scouts covered each other as they ran forwards into the spreading gloom.

As the last of the Scouts departed, Kholka counted to ten before setting out across the open ground himself. Minutes later, he was at the bunker, finding that his Scouts had spread out to cover all approaches with their boltguns.

'Brother-sergeant,' hissed Scout Borchu. 'Over here.'

Kholka stalked silently to the source of the whisper. He found the Scout by the bunker's slab-sided armoured fascia, looking down at the man they had witnessed being flung over the wall. In the shadow of the bunker the corpse was little more than a deeper patch of gloom against the black volcanic ground. He squatted down, and judged it safe to engage the lamp set into the barrel of his boltgun at its lowest setting.

The sergeant drew a sharp intake of breath at the sight that greeted him. The man's body was little more than a skeleton, parched skin stretched tight across its bones. The face, or what little remained of it, was locked in a rictus leer, the shrivelled eyes staring in a sightless terror that seemed to transcend death itself.

'What happened to him?' Kholka heard Borchu ask, the boy's easy mirth now entirely gone.

'Nothing I would have you learn of,' the sergeant replied. 'Not until you have to, at any rate.'

'The armour,' Borchu continued. 'Is that the–?'

'Yes, boy,' Kholka interjected. 'That is the confirmation we seek.'

'Then we have them?' Borchu asked.

'Yes, neophyte,' Kholka replied. 'We have them.' Even as the sergeant spoke, he knew things were not as simple as they might have seemed to the inexperienced Scout. To Kholka's seasoned, hunter's instinct, it was all too contrived, all too convenient.

'Squad,' Kholka whispered, standing as the Scouts gathered before him in the dark. 'We return to the insertion point.'

'For extraction?' Borchu enquired.

'No,' Kholka replied grimly. 'We have a report to make. We need to reach secure ground and set up the tight-beam transmitter. Kor'sarro Khan must hear of this.'

*　*　*

KHOLKA LOOKED UP as the transmitter device emitted a sharp tone. A steady stream of figures scrolled across his auspex, the code informing him that the machine's spirit was prepared to commune with another of its kind in high orbit overhead.

The sergeant gave the signal to Gharn that he should set the now aligned projector unit down and return to watch duty. The projector, linked by a snaking cable to the unit in front of Kholka, was just visible atop a nearby rock formation. Its sharp form was silhouetted against the massive disk of Quintus's moon, which was now rising above the horizon and staining the jagged landscape an unearthly, sickly green.

The march to the pre-arranged location from which the signal would be sent had been carried out in record time. The sergeant had forced the pace, knowing that the signal must get through at all costs. Kholka had reviewed the findings as he had led the march, going over the mission and its conclusion time and time again. He knew that the specially shielded Thunderhawk would only be overhead for a minute, for to linger any longer would be to invite detection by Voldorius and his Alpha Legion sorcerers and heretic tech-priests.

Kholka gazed up into the black sky, its southern fringe stained with the angry purples and reds of the receding warp storm Argenta. Somewhere up there, a vessel crewed by his brethren passed. They were taking a great risk, even though they would have shut down all non-essential systems and would be propelled by momentum alone lest even the slightest power usage be detected. Only the tight beam receiver would be operating under power, and that would be so heavily shielded that an enemy would need to be right on top of the ship to detect it. Nevertheless, the enemy were possessed of methods of detection that far surpassed what machines could achieve. A sorcerer, casting his supernatural gaze across the Thunderhawk's flight path, might ruin everything. Such a thing had happened before, the sergeant recalled. In a previous mission, twelve battle-brothers had died and twenty Scouts, including himself, had been stranded on the rogue planetoid Sigma-Rokall for three long months when their extraction vessel had been intercepted.

Shaking his head to clear the centuries-old memory from his mind, Kholka activated the transmitter device and began his report.

'Scout-Sergeant Ultas Kholka, ident zero zero digamma, seven nine two zero qoppa.' He watched the transmitter's softly glowing screen as his words were digested, processed and encrypted. Satisfied that all was functioning as it should, he continued, 'Reconnaissance mission report follows. Enemy presence confirmed. Primary identified: Nullus. Secondary: Alpha Legion. Tertiary: Mankarra Household Guard. Confirm item zero alpha: four-starred insignia. Observation follows. Quintus is firmly under the traitors' control, and as expected, we have discovered evidence of numerous atrocities. I suspect that the majority of the remaining defence forces are under Alpha Legion control, and those not are no longer viable.'

Seeing from the numbers counting down on the data-slate's screen that he had a few seconds, transmission time left, Kholka added an addendum. 'My khan,' he said. 'I must counsel that the four-starred insignia was left where we could find it. It may be a snare, or it may be that the enemy harbour a traitor in their ranks. I advise caution, and await your orders.'

The transmitter unit emitted a sharp tone, its machine-spirit indicating that the link had ended as scheduled. Kholka proceeded to break the unit down, and then glanced south, towards the rising moon. The mission would proceed, whatever, or whoever, awaited the Scouts.

CHAPTER 6

Death in the Night

'WAIT,' THE SPACE Marine captain hissed into the vox as he watched the dark landscape below. 'Let them enter the gully.'

He stood at the very peak of a jagged spire of black rock, the night sky at his back. His power armour was black too, and was hung with dozens of small, avian-bone charms. The column of traitor militia vehicles picking its way through the wastes below had no chance of detecting him or his warriors.

Not, that is, until it was too late.

The column consisted of half a dozen armoured personnel carriers, a pattern of vehicle manufactured on a number of nearby worlds, but lacking the arma-ment of the Chimera transports used in the armies of the Imperial Guard. At intervals along the column larger, tracked carriers travelled, bulky cargo units loaded with heavy weapons destined for a defence complex only ten kilometres distant. The captain's company were peerless when it came to mounting devastating campaigns of terror and disruption, but their own numbers were few and the enemy's control over the traitor militia complete.

As the captain waited on his lofty perch, the column ground on, manoeuvring around a large rockslide that had settled at the base of an outcropping. His men had caused the slide, a single, expertly placed krak grenade bringing tons of black volcanic spoil across the column's path. As a result, the transports were even now entering the gully into which they had been so deliberately funnelled.

The lead vehicle slewed around as it entered the gully, the arc beam mounted at its forwards hatch scanning left and right across the ground ahead. Inside his helmet, the captain's mouth assumed a nasty grin and his eyes narrowed.

The transport lurched on, and was followed a few moments later by the second, the beam of its own searchlight lancing into the darkness to its flank.

'Just a little bit…' the captain said.

The lead transport ground to a sudden halt, and an angry shout cut the air from far below. The shout had come from the driver of the second vehicle, his head visible as he rose from his hatch, and had been voiced in response to the lead vehicle's unanticipated stop. The call was answered by a colourful response from the commander of the lead vehicle. Though spoken in the local dialect, the captain could well understand the meaning, and his grin widened.

'...further,' he mouthed, as the lead vehicle's arc light swung suddenly upwards. The bright shaft of light cut through the night. But to the captain, who had positioned himself so that he would be silhouetted against the swollen moon as the lead vehicle entered the gully, it was blinding, for it shone directly into his eyes.

'Kill them,' he growled into the vox. 'Let none escape.'

The lead transport erupted into livid flames as a melta charge hidden in the gully floor detonated. For an instant, the night was dispelled as twisted hunks of flaming wreckage were propelled in all directions. The scream of suddenly activated jump packs sounded as Assault squads leapt into the air, to descend upon columns of fire towards their prey.

With a thought impulse transmitted through the systems of his power armour, the captain activated his own jump pack, launching himself forwards and upwards, high into the night sky. Behind him the battle-brothers of his Command squad followed, flames glinting from the long talons of their lightning claws.

Even as he began his descent, the second transport was attempting to reverse out of the killing zone. It ground against the bow of the following vehicle. A second explosion ripped through the night as the last vehicle in the column was struck in its engine deck by a well-placed krak missile. The stricken vehicle lurched, and the fuel in its thinly armoured tank spewed across the ground. As the surviving crew attempted to fling themselves clear, the flames ignited, turning each man into a flailing human torch that collapsed into thrashing heaps as the fire consumed them.

The captain landed atop the upper deck of the second vehicle, the sound of the heavy impact resonating loudly. The driver, standing upright in his hatch, turned his head and looked directly into the face of death. The captain activated his talon-like lightning claws and made a bloody ruin of the man's upper body. He located a second, larger hatch under his feet, and stepped backwards.

Punching his talons straight through the hatch, the captain ripped the doors clean away and flung them into the fire-chased night. A dozen faces looked up at him, and a second later he was amongst them. The interior of the transport was so cramped that no finesse was possible. He merely lashed out, tracing a web of death all around him. Within seconds, the traitor militia were reduced to chunks of smoking meat, which was seared to ashes as he reactivated his jump pack and rose from the back of the vehicle atop a pillar of fire.

The vehicles of the column had all by now halted, their drivers realising that they were trapped and unable to manoeuvre with the lead and trailing transports destroyed. The initial shock was passing, and squads of militia inside each vehicle were deploying from hatches which dropped loudly to the ground at the rear of each tank.

'Left flank.' The captain spoke coldly into the voxnet as the members of his Command squad swooped down to land beside him. 'Engage the enemy from third carrier. Centre group, the fifth.'

The Assault Marines arrowed through the night towards their targets. The desperate militia unleashed a fusillade of bullets, but even those few shots that struck a Space Marine failed to penetrate their power armour. Within seconds, the Assault squads were in amongst their foes, the screams of chainswords and men blending into an almighty clamour of death and destruction.

'Right flank,' the captain said. 'Suppress the third transport.' A torrent of boltgun fire hailed down upon the vehicle and the militia attempting to muster at its rear. The two Tactical squads had been well concealed amongst the rocks on the column's right flank. Those militiamen not cut down in the opening salvo sought desperately for a target to return fire at, but all they saw were muzzle flashes. For most, that was the last thing they ever saw.

'All other squads,' the captain continued. 'Assume reserve stance delta-rho. Command squad, with me.'

Leaping down from the transport's upper hull, his Command squad following a step behind, the captain passed the front of the next vehicle in the column. It was a huge, lumbering, grey-painted transport, twice the size of the carriers, its form dominated by a huge cargo bay at its rear. A low pounding accompanied by a muffled roar of anger sounded from the vehicle, audible even over the gunfire. Slowing as he passed through the shadow of the hauler, the captain realised that the sound was emanating from within the vehicle's cargo bay.

Cautiously, he rounded the back end of the vehicle. Something very large pounded repeatedly on the inside of the vehicle's rear loading hatch whilst bellowing an incoherent stream of primitive invective.

'Melta?' asked one of the Command squad.

'No,' he replied. 'We leave the haulers intact. Whatever is inside, we deal with it. Get ready.'

The captain's talon shot out, lacerating the hatch's locking mechanism. The remains fell to the rocky ground, and then both hatches were flung open. A savage bellow rang from the dark interior and a massive ogryn lumbered forth.

A stable strain of human mutant evolved or bred on high gravity worlds, the beast was a mountain of sinew and muscle. Its face was a bestial mask of imbecilic fury, spittle frothing from its broken-toothed mouth. The ground shook as the ogryn stepped out. Its beady eyes scanned the Space Marines and it shouted a word that the captain could not understand. An answering bellow sounded from within the hauler's cargo area and a second ogryn appeared at the hatch. At least two more waited within the cargo bay's shadowed depths.

'Kill them,' the captain snarled as the ogryn gave voice to a war cry of his own. Both sprang forwards at the same moment, and launched their attack.

Applying a burst to his jump pack, the captain powered his feet from the ground. Even as the captain leapt, the ogryn's massive arm pistoned forwards, its clenched fist striking him squarely in the stomach. So powerful was the piledriver punch that warning icons flashed across his vision, his armour's machine-spirit warning of micro-fractures in three separate locations.

Even as the punch struck home, the captain's own attack was arrowing downwards, his lightning claw slashing towards the ogryn's head. But the punch had offset his momentum, and the talon struck not the beast's head, but its left arm, just below the shoulder.

The ogryn roared in savage pain and anger as the captain's talon parted muscle and seared through bone. The arm was torn away in a welter of blood, so much dead meat striking the ground with a wet thud. A fountain of blood gushing from the stump of its left arm, the ogryn threw itself at the captain as the Space Marine's armoured feet touched the ground. Behind it, two more of the massive brutes dropped from the vehicle's hatch.

Breathing hard, he cursed the delay this engagement would entail. His talons spread wide either side of his body, the captain had but a second to prepare himself for the beast's next attack. And then, the mutant was upon him.

Even wounded, the ogryn was a fearsome opponent. What it lacked in skill it made up for in mass and sheer brute strength. Its fist powered forwards again. This time, the captain was ready, his gene-engineered physiology granting him the reflexes that had so often saved his life. Twisting his body, he sidestepped the massive fist and the ogryn found itself overextended and pitching forwards. Before it had the chance to check its forwards motion, he lashed out with both talons and the brute's other arm was severed into three ragged pieces.

Before the captain could aid his battle-brothers against the three more of the brutal creatures throwing themselves at his Command squad, the crippled ogryn reared up in front of him. Blood sprayed in wild geysers from the armless stumps at its shoulders and it bellowed in mindless savagery. He hated the brute's raw spirit and refusal to give in. It was trying to bring to bear the last weapon it had at its disposal: its thick-skulled, ugly-as-sin, head.

'Emperor's mercy,' the captain breathed. 'Just die!'

As if in answer, the ogryn redoubled its bellow and arched its back, tensing the slab-like muscles of its stomach, and then propelled its own head downwards towards him.

The captain had no choice but to meet the attack, head-on. He had just enough time to raise a talon before the ogryn slammed into him. The ogryn's head struck his helmet's faceplate and he was propelled downwards to smash into the rocky ground.

The captain must have blacked out for an instant. His vision cleared and he felt a tremendous weight pressing down upon him. Blinking, he realised that the weight belonged to the now lifeless body of the ogryn, the gleaming blades of his lightning claw protruding from its back.

As more warning icons flashed across his visor, he pushed the massive dead weight upwards and rolled it away, pulling his talon clear from its gut as he did so. The brute's face was crushed inwards, its ugly features no longer recognisable. Reaching a hand to the visor of his helmet, the captain felt several cracks across its surface. No matter, he thought, putting the damage from his mind as he turned to ascertain how his warriors were prevailing.

The brute that the captain had faced must have been the alpha male of the pack, for the others were less fearsome opponents. Two were dead already, their massive bodies bearing witness to the damage that twinned lightning claws can wreak upon unarmoured flesh, even flesh as tough as an ogryn's. The last of the ogryns was surrounded on all sides by his warriors, bleeding out from at least a dozen slashing wounds.

The ogryn cursed as its legs gave way beneath it. With a final obscenity, it fell forwards and crashed to the earth, gallons of blood gushing across the ground.

'Reserve group,' the captain spoke into the vox-net. There was a burst of static indicating that the sophisticated communications systems built into his power armour had sustained damage when the ogryn had head butted him. The armour's war spirit would be much aggrieved, and would require placation before it would serve at full capacity again. Despite the damage, however, the squad's sergeant's acknowledgement came back a moment later.

'Cover the right flank as they clear the other two haulers,' the captain ordered. 'All squads, be advised. There may be ogryns within the haulers. Deal with them, but leave the vehicles intact. Acknowledge.'

As each of the squad sergeants transmitted their acknowledgement, the battle was all but done, the high tide of war having passed. Five of the troop carriers were ablaze, their former passengers slain in the deadly ambush. More black-clad Space Marines emerged from the darkness, bolters held ready as they advanced towards the two remaining cargo haulers.

The Assault Marines of left and centre groups were despatching the last of the defenders towards the rear of the column, running to ground those who attempted to flee and cutting them down with cold, clinical efficiency.

'No contact,' came a sergeant's voice over the vox-net. 'Just cargo. Area secure.'

'Acknowledged,' said the captain as he strode towards the rear of the column. 'Right group?'

'Stand by,' returned a sergeant.

The captain continued through the darkness towards the column's rear. The last few shots ran out and then it was over.

'Just cargo here, too,' the sergeant reported. 'Secured.'

'Orders,' he said, not willing to waste a second of time. 'On my lead.'

A stray shot rang out towards the front of the column, the sound of a Space Marine despatching a wounded enemy trooper. Within a minute, the squad sergeants had assembled beside the second transport, the only one not aflame. Bracing his weight against a handle, the captain pulled himself upwards and swung his massively armoured form up onto the deck.

'Well fought,' he said.

The assembled Space Marines nodded sombrely, their Chapter not disposed to rude displays of triumphalism. Where other Space Marines of other Chapters might have revelled openly in their victory, theirs celebrated victory in a far more personal manner. Later, when the fighting was done, each would mount a silent vigil. He would pray for hours, even days on end, seeking unity with the Emperor and the primarch in the midst of a universe of blood and slaughter and doom.

'Status?' the captain asked as he looked down upon his officers.

Each of the leaders gave their report in turn, a clipped delivery listing wounds sustained and ammunition expended. Though a number of battle-brothers had been injured in the brief firefight, none had been lost. The captain's orders had been to conserve resources, for more reasons than one. More squads were in action across the entire region of Quintus, sowing fear and confusion amongst the native forces, and the leaders of these small forces each reported in over the vox-net.

'Sergeant,' he addressed a veteran Tactical squad leader. 'Your men are prepared?'

'Affirmative,' the sergeant replied. 'They are ready to begin at your order.'

'Good,' the captain replied. 'I want three Munitorum-issue lasguns placed centrally on the right flank, along with a dozen expended power packs. Set down one of the Guard-issue bolters in right group's ambush position. See it done.'

Nodding his understanding, the sergeant turned and stalked off into the night. The warriors of his squad would place a weapon they had brought to Quintus for this very purpose.

'What of the bolter wounds?' another sergeant asked. 'Many were cut down by our brothers' weapons.'

'Even if the enemy note the nature of the militia's wounds, sufficient doubt will have been created for our purposes,' he answered.

'And doubt,' said Captain Kayvaan Shrike of the Raven Guard Chapter, 'is the seed of misdirection.'

'You CAN KILL me now!' spat Malya L'nor. 'I will not serve him!'

Heaving against the restraints at her wrists and ankles, Malya knew it was useless. She had awoken in the dank cell several hours before, her first sight that of the hooded cell-master standing over her. At first she had begged to be released, but as the full extent of her plight had revealed itself she had desired only a swift death.

'I refuse,' she screamed, her lungs burning. 'I would rather die!'

From beneath his leathern hood, the cell-master had whispered with unadulterated glee of the plans that Voldorius had in store for Malya L'nor. What cruel strand of fate was unravelling before her, she had despaired? Why was it she that had been chosen, seemingly at random, for such a duty?

'Oh, you shall serve,' came a new voice from behind Malya. Her head restrained by steel braces, all she could see was the corroded ironwork of the ceiling above her and the fleeting shadows cast across it by flickering lumens. Something about this new voice forced her to silence, despite herself, so low and threatening were its sibilant tones.

'My lord Voldorius has great hopes for you, equerry.'

Malya bit back a caustic reply as the speaker stepped into her field of vision. Cold terror filled her, the sweat on her body turning instantly as cold as ice. He was huge, his shoulders broad. He wore the blue-green armour that the people of Quintus had come to hate so much. It was the livery of the Alpha Legion, whose leader had laid their world so low.

'My name is Nullus,' the warrior continued, his vile visage pressing in towards Malya's. Up close, his face was revealed to Malya as a white globe of solid scar tissue, his black, slit-like eyes gazing down at her. Tears welled in her own eyes under that soulless gaze, yet she refused to yield to her sorrow.

'You are wilful,' Nullus said. 'That will serve you well in your new office.'

'I–' Malya started.

'You *will*,' Nullus interjected, his face lowering still further towards her own until she could see nothing but his black eyes and the scars traced around them in obscene patterns. 'Voldorius has need of an… intermediary, one who will keep the people of this miserable rock in line, while he attends to his own concerns. You will serve in this capacity.'

'No,' Malya said flatly, forcing her voice to remain steady. Despite her denial, she could not meet the other's eyes for they threatened the destruction of her very soul.

Nullus's face was split by a mocking grin, the scars aligning themselves into new patterns as the flesh beneath them shifted. 'Henceforth,' Nullus continued, 'with each denial that issues from your pretty lips, a hundred of your people shall die. Ten thousand were slain in the grand square, and you alone were spared. Their corpses shall remain as a warning. You can see them if you like. Should you prefer that ten thousand more be slain to make the point, then please, continue with your foolish protest.

'Do you understand?'

Now the tears flowed freely from Malya's eyes, and she screwed them tightly shut.

'Yes,' she nodded, as much as the restraints would allow. 'I understand...'

'YOUR REPORT,' SAID Shrike as he entered the dark cave in which Techmarine Dyloss tended the cipher matrix.

'Brother-captain,' Techmarine Dyloss nodded a greeting as Shrike came to stand opposite him. He turned back to the softly glowing globe atop the machinery in front of him, reams of zeroes scrolling across its screen. 'I cannot raise her, nor any of her associates.'

Shrike sighed. The Techmarine had only recently established contact with a group of fighters within Mankarra city and several reticent communications had passed between them. The fighters had, of course, been suspicious, sensibly concluding that Shrike's transmissions might have been those of the enemy, intent upon entrapment.

'The last contact?' Shrike asked.

'Twelve hours ago. As per your orders, I communicated your opposition to an attempt upon the vile one's life until full coordination of action was possible.'

'And her response?' Shrike enquired.

'She agreed,' Techmarine Dyloss replied. 'But she could not vouch for her compatriots.'

'Fools,' Shrike cursed. Voldorius had the blood of billions on his hands and countless numbers of humanity's finest warriors had sacrificed their lives to try and defeat him. Yet, none had succeeded, so what chance had a handful of desperate civilians-turned-resistance fighters?

'You asked her about the prisoner,' Shrike said. It was not a question.

'I did,' the Techmarine replied. 'She knew nothing.'

Shrike's mood darkened and he made to stalk from the cave.

'Since then, brother-captain,' the Techmarine continued, 'I have intercepted a number of other signals.'

'Go on,' Shrike said, halting at the cave's mouth.

'The rudimentary command and control network that the resistance had established has been entirely destroyed. As each node fell, brief and desperate pleas were transmitted. Many mentioned an atrocity in which thousands were slain.'

'What they reap…' Shrike muttered.

'Brother-captain?' Dyloss said, unsure of Shrike's meaning.

'No matter,' Shrike said, turning his back on the cipher matrix and its Techmarine attendant. 'We stand alone, as ever.'

* * *

'THE BLOOD-RATS,' WHISPERED Scout Telluk. 'Falling upon the sky-drake's bones.'

'Understood,' Scout-Sergeant Kholka replied, moving silently to lie beside the neophyte at the lip of the rock.

Kholka eased himself forwards cautiously, for the sun had fully risen in the sky overhead. Slowly, he raised his magnoculars to his eyes and examined the scene below.

The boy was correct, and he had used the proper battle-cant to describe what he had seen. The rocky terrain was cut by a gully and in it a column of armour belonging to the traitor militia had been ambushed. Not just ambushed; taken apart with ruthless efficiency.

Scanning left, the sergeant caught a glimpse of movement amongst the smoking wreckage of armoured carriers. Figures moved amongst the detritus, picking over the remains of vehicles and corpses alike.

'Militia? Scout Telluk asked his sergeant.

Kholka continued to scan the scene for a moment before replying, taking in at least a platoon's worth of soldiers. 'It appears so, neophyte,' he said. 'Your impressions?'

'An ambush,' Telluk said, 'that much is clear. Very recently.'

'When?' Kholka pressed.

'During the night, sergeant. Perhaps around zero-three-zero.'

'Explain.'

'The ambushers must have been well hidden to approach so close to the column. But the moon last night was full. Any attacker would have been illuminated, and spotted.'

'Unless?'

'Unless the moon was behind that outcrop.' The Scout nodded towards a tall formation of volcanic rock to the pair's right. 'Only when the column rounded that rock slide would the moon have provided light, at which point, the ambushers attacked.'

'Good,' Kholka replied. He too had reached that conclusion and had hoped that his testing of the youngster would have yielded such positive results. As he watched the militia soldiers go from one body to the next he heard a shout from off to the left. Panning the magnoculars, he located the source. Amidst some boulders, a soldier was waving with one hand, and holding a lasgun aloft in the other.

A few minutes later, an officer was directing a search among the rocks to either side of the gully. Soon several more of the weapons, as well as a far rarer boltgun, had been found.

'Imperial Guard?' Scout Telluk said.

'I very much doubt it, boy,' replied the sergeant. 'But someone certainly wants them to believe it so.'

'BROTHER-CAPTAIN,' TECHMARINE DYLOSS called out, even as Shrike stalked away from the cave. He turned towards the Space Marine standing in the cave's mouth.

'What is it?' Shrike replied. A dark shroud had fallen across his soul when he had learned of the Alpha

Legion's deeds and he was ill-disposed towards conversation right now.

'Another signal.'

Shrike turned back towards the cave and ducked beneath its low opening. The Techmarine had returned to his station attending the cipher matrix and was making a series of complex adjustments to its settings. Where ranks of zeroes had scrolled across its globe-shaped screen, now a series of numbers had appeared.

'What is it?' Shrike asked. The captain was not initiated into the ways of the Machine, and like all Space Marine leaders, relied upon the specialised skills of the Chapter's Techmarines to attend to such things.

'It's a sub-ether carrier wave,' Techmarine Dyloss replied matter-of-factly. Shrike raised his eyebrows.

'A ranging signal. Right on the edge of what this unit can detect.'

'Who from?' Shrike pressed. 'And who to?'

'It's an obscure cipher,' Dyloss continued, his hands moving across the dials in an attempt to lock onto the signal. 'Highly encrypted, but not by any means I am familiar with. I cannot say.'

'A sub-ether carrier,' Shrike said. 'A beacon?'

'It could be. But the diffusion makes tracking both source and destination impossible without the key.'

'Which we do not have,' Shrike replied. 'I want that signal broken. And inform all commands. We will soon have company, of one sort or another.'

CHAPTER 7
Planetfall

'CLEARING LAMBDA-POINT ALPHA,' reported the pilot, before reaching up to make a series of adjustments to a bank of instruments above his head. 'Optimal velocity within five. Silent running at your command, my khan.'

Kor'sarro scanned his command terminal, one of its many screens displaying a rearward view of space. As the sickly green disc of Quintus's moon receded, the Thunderhawk gunships of Kor'sarro's strike force slipped free of its gravitational influence into that of Quintus itself. Within five minutes, the entire force, representing every single deployable unit under Kor'sarro's command, would assume not only silent running, but complete signals silence. With the *Lord of Heavens* left far behind in the outer reaches of the Quintus system, the company would soon be very much alone.

The data scrolling across the terminal screen told Kor'sarro that all of the vessels of his strike force were in formation, their status optimal. But the Master of the Hunt knew better than to trust such things to the spirits of the machine.

'All Hunters,' Kor'sarro spoke into the vox-net. 'Confirm status.'

One by one, each vessel in the strike force called in. Hunter Three's repairs were settling in well enough, its commander reported, following the damage the ship had sustained at Cernis IV. Seven Techmarines had administered to the Thunderhawk transporter's systems, replacing an entire aileron before praying to the vessel's wounded machine-spirit for three days and three nights. Kor'sarro hoped fervently that their devotions would prove sufficient, for every vessel, and every Space Marine it carried, was vital to the mission ahead. Hunter Nine, the gunship assigned to carry the strike force's ammunition, was the last to call in, its commander reporting the ship's status satisfactory.

Before the strike force had parted company with the *Lord of Heavens*, Kor'sarro had meditated an entire night on the battle to come. Prior to that, he had spent long hours in counsel with both Chaplain Xia'ghan and the Storm Seer, Qan'karro. The Master of the Hunt had sought to rid himself of the taint of what had occurred on Cernis IV. Xia'ghan had absolved him of both pride and guilt, declaring Kor'sarro pure in the eyes of the Emperor. Qan'karro had cast his augurbones in the manner of a steppes-shaman, and announced that the mission was true, its conclusion unclear as yet but its objective blessed. Kor'sarro's mind was now clear and his heart purified. Not since the conclusion of his first ever hunt, on the third moon of the gas giant Mai Nine, had he felt such purpose.

'All commands,' Kor'sarro hailed his strike force commanders. 'We proceed with the blessing of the Emperor and of the primarch, honoured be his name. Our mission is clear and you have your orders. Engage silent running, and good hunting.'

'Engaging as ordered, my khan,' said the co-pilot, flipping a series of switches before pulling down on a lever mounted at his side. With each control deactivated, one part of the gunship's machine systems was laid dormant until the time it would be called upon once more. As the Thunderhawk's mighty thrusters powered down, the command deck became unnervingly quiet. All of a sudden, Kor'sarro could hear the thunder of his blood in his ears, his heart racing as his genetically enhanced body prepared itself for battle, bolstered still further by the complex combat-drug administration systems in his power armour. Mouthing a prayer that he had learned as a boy at the foot of his tribe's shaman, he forced himself to focus. Several hours of flight lay ahead of the strike force, hours in which he must remain alert and ready for any opposition to the insertion.

At the last, the command deck was plunged into darkness as all non-essential systems were brought fully offline. Angular shadows were cast across the instrument panels and all was tinted with the pale green of Quintus's moon. The vessels of the strike force were now being propelled through the void by momentum alone and their course would not be corrected until the very last stage of entry in Quintus's atmosphere. Even the flight control panels lay dark, only a single screen glowing dimly amongst so much cold metal.

'The cipher?' Kor'sarro asked. The command deck was so quiet that he instinctively kept his voice down low, even though no enemy could possibly hear. It was force of habit for one born of the steppes of Chogoris, whose people moderated the volume of their speech according to the strength of the ever-present winds.

'On track, my khan,' the co-pilot replied. 'The carrier wave is reading clearly.'

'Good,' Kor'sarro replied, though in truth he could not help but feel some frustration that he must rely on such methods to guide the strike force in to its target. The wave was being transmitted by the *Lord of Heavens*, at a sub-etheric wavelength that few in the entire Imperium could possibly detect, and was protected by encryption that even fewer could break. With the necessity for a silent insertion, the individual ships of the strike force had to have some way of remaining coordinated with one another so that they each arrived at the correct interface point at the correct moment in time. Instead of synchronising with each other's machine systems, each Thunderhawk would follow the nigh undetectable signal transmitted by the *Lord of Heavens*, riding the wave right onto their target.

'DYLOSS TO SHRIKE,' the transmission came over the captain's vox-bead. 'Do you receive?'

'Go ahead,' Shrike replied, halting in his patrol of the rock-strewn area north-west of the Raven Guard base.

'Brother-captain,' the voice came over the vox, the signal clearer now that Shrike's armour had been afforded time to repair its communication systems. 'I have news regarding the cipher.'

Shrike signalled for the Space Marines nearby to halt, and with a curt gesture ordered them to assume a defensive posture, covering the terrain in all directions. 'I'm listening,' he replied. 'Have you broken the encryption?'

'The code itself remains intact,' the Techmarine reported. 'But I have cracked something of the signal's nature, and of its source.'

It had been five days since Techmarine Dyloss had detected the cipher signal, and he had been working upon it without rest or respite, day and night, ever since. In the meantime, the Raven Guard had stepped up their patrols of the region around Mankarra, sowing death and destruction against any and all enemies they had encountered. After each battle, the Raven Guard had planted false evidence of their identity, leaving Imperial Guard-issue weapons and equipment at the ambush sites. After one ambush, they had even dressed the corpse of a traitor militia soldier in an Imperial Guard uniform they had brought along for just such a deception. It was not that Shrike truly aimed to convince the invaders that an Imperial Guard force was active on Quintus, but any amount of confusion he could plant in the minds of their commanders would aid the Space Marines' cause.

'The signal is a co-ord beam, the type used for blind navigation,' Dyloss reported.

'Then someone's inbound,' said Shrike, as much to himself as to the Techmarine. 'Do you have the coordinates?'

There was a brief pause, during which Shrike could hear the sound of the Techmarine's hands and servo-arms working upon the cipher matrix, which droned and churned in the background. 'I am still filtering the exact location, but I am transmitting the approximate coordinates to you now.'

Captain Shrike raised his left arm and slid back the cover of a data-screen integrated into his vambrace. A representation of the surrounding region appeared on the screen, a red circle at its centre. 'A day's march,' he said, switching his vox-link to transmit on the command frequency. 'All units,' Shrike addressed his squad leaders and specialists. 'Converge on my coordinates, tactical state gamma-nine. Confirm.'

Within moments, each of Shrike's officers had confirmed their understanding of his orders. Shrike would not allow his mission on Quintus to be compromised by another force entering the war, no matter who they were.

* * *

SCOUT-SERGEANT KHOLKA LOOKED up towards the darkening skies for what must have been the tenth time in as many minutes, even though he knew the strike force would not be inbound for at least an hour, and that was assuming nothing had gone awry.

Kholka and his Scouts had located a landing zone and transmitted its coordinates to the shielded gunship on its last pass five days ago. Now they waited, watching for enemy intrusion or interference.

The landing zone was the flat floor of a dormant volcano, protected by a five hundred-metre-tall rim, breached on its northern edge by a wide fracture.

Of course, the suitability of the landing zone might have been noted by potential enemies. For that reason, Kholka had ordered the young Scouts to keep a watchful vigil for enemy activity, spreading them out in order to cover as much of the surrounding region as possible. An hour ago, Borchu had reported a glimpse of movement to the north and Kholka had worked his way stealthily around the volcano's rim to the Scout's hide.

Lowering his eyes from the skies above, Kholka looked down upon the black wastelands far below. The sun was setting, casting long, jagged shadows across the lands. Any enemy at all might be creeping through those shadows. He hesitated before lifting the magnoculars, seeking to get a feel for the landscape before him, to imagine himself a predator moving through it in search of prey. He ignored the fact that in truth he himself might be the prey, if indeed a hunter lurked down there, in the dark shadows.

The wastes stretched for kilometres in every direction, but to the north-west, beyond the horizon, were the outskirts of the agri-zone. Another one hundred or so kilometres beyond that was the capital city of Mankarra. It was from that direction that any enemy action was most likely to come, and it was there that Borchu had seen the movement.

Having familiarised himself with the landscape, Kholka raised the magnoculars to his eyes. 'Coordinates?' he asked the Scout beside him.

'Five by the winter deeps,' Borchu replied in the White Scars battle-cant. 'Three score and nine by the herd.'

The veteran sergeant was so accustomed to the use of battle-cant that he had no need to convert the code phrase into conventional coordinates. Indeed, the form of communication was in many cases more efficient than standard coordinates, for it contained descriptive shorthand that drew the eye to specific terrain features. Perhaps most importantly, it relied on cultural references that only one raised on the steppes of Chogoris would understand, making it nigh impossible for an enemy to decipher should he intercept it.

Panning the magnoculars from west to east, Kholka adjusted the magnification so that his field of vision was focussed on an area some three kilometres out. Like the majority of the landscape, the area was dominated by twisted arches and jagged outcrops of volcanic rock, black or dark grey in colour and ideal terrain for an enemy to creep through at dusk. He zoomed outwards slightly, absorbing the general lay of the land, seeking to imagine himself passing through it. What path would he take, were he approaching the volcano?

Kholka's eye was caught by a black bridge of rock between two outcroppings, formed no doubt by the action of blisteringly hot lava carving its way through an older feature. The channel below the bridge snaked its way from the north-east and its depths would be cast in the deepest of shadow for much of the day.

Having located a possible route an enemy might approach the landing zone by, the sergeant traced its path as far as he could see. At times the channel was hidden by intervening terrain features such as tall, bladelike spires or massive coils of solidified lava. Seeing no sign of an enemy on his first sweep, Kholka engaged the thermal imaging function. He soon found however that the background temperature of the volcanic rocks was relatively high, high enough to mask the presence of any foe taking measures to avoid detection by such means. No matter, Kholka thought as he disengaged the thermal imaging; he far preferred to rely upon his own senses, enhanced as they were by arcane genetic engineering and honed by centuries of battlefield experience.

Kholka focussed in upon a particular area of shadow. If I were moving along that route, he thought, that is where I would be. It offered an unobstructed view of the volcano and had ample overhead cover from an angular blade of rock jutting out above the channel.

Only after he had been looking directly at that patch of shadow, unblinking and utterly focussed, for upwards of fifteen minutes, did Kholka detect the very faintest of movement. A black patch of shadow, barely discernable against the darkness all around, moved ever so slightly.

'Enemy located,' the sergeant growled.

SHRIKE LONGED TO engage his jump pack and hurl himself through the darkening skies towards the contact his auspex had detected hiding in the rocks up ahead, yet he dared not. Not until he had confirmed their full strength and disposition at least. To reveal his location now would be suicide.

Having tracked the sub-etheric transmission to its terminus, Shrike was now sure that the target was the inside of the volcano up ahead. It made sense. The inside of the vast crater would offer an ideal location for a planetary landing. But only if whoever was inbound wished to avoid detection by other forces on the surface of Quintus.

Ten hours ago, before the sun had risen across the wastes south-west of Mankarra, Shrike had convened a council of his officers and specialists. All had been afforded the opportunity to speak, to offer their theories on the identity of the strangers they knew would be arriving soon. Several had expressed the hope that the force represented aid for Mankarra, perhaps in the form of reinforcements, yet the case against had been well made. Before embarking on the mission, Shrike had been fully appraised of the Imperium's forces in the region. As far as he knew, none had been allotted to target the world. And besides, some had argued, it was too soon to expect an intervention, for such a force would take many months to gather and prepare, and would be unlikely to approach the world in such a stealthy manner.

Other opinions had been voiced too. Perhaps the strangers were reinforcements for the invaders. But why then hide their approach? Were they a rival warband, perhaps intent upon dislodging the tyranny of Voldorius only to replace it with another, perhaps even more brutal rule?

One last possibility had emerged during the gathering. Might the strangers be brother Space Marines come to Quintus to lend their aid to its resistance and to oust the Alpha Legion and their vile overlord? That would certainly explain the use of the highly sophisticated carrier signal, but Shrike was aware of no other Chapter in the immediate vicinity.

The Salamanders Chapter, Shrike knew, had a strike force in the benighted Magulanox sector, but had departed the galactic arm entirely in pursuit of the traitor rogue trader Lord Hax. The Celestial Guard Chapter were also known to be operating within a dozen light years of Quintus, but the last Shrike had heard, all of their forces had been recalled to defend the Chapter's home world of Erenon against a large ork incursion. The Imperial Fists had a force inbound on the anarchic Jagga Cluster, but that lay dozens of light years away, while the Tigers Argent, White Scars and the Howling Griffons could all, in theory, be operating even further out still.

No, Shrike had decided. The Raven Guard could not make the assumption that whoever was approaching Quintus was a friend. He had ordered his force to proceed to the landing zone with all caution and to be ready for action against the strangers.

Settling back into the darkness of the channel, Shrike waited.

'FINAL CORRECTIONS INPUT,' reported Brother Koban. 'Beginning final descent.'

Kor'sarro watched through the canopy of the Thunderhawk's command deck as the dark surface of Quintus loomed. The strike force was approaching on the planet's night side, the bright crescent of dawn casting a semi-circular halo across its shoulder. Behind the strike force, the moon of Quintus shone its sickly luminescence, bathing the nighted surface below in soft green light. As the minutes counted down, small pinpricks of artificial light became visible, the telltale signs of civilisation. Whether those lights were cast by industry or were simply the glowing embers of ruin, Kor'sarro could not yet discern.

The gunship bucked violently as it penetrated the upper reaches of the world's atmosphere, and Kor'sarro mouthed a silent prayer to the primarch. He beseeched the first Great Khan for his blessing, as he had done on hundreds of previous occasions. To date, the primarch had watched over the Master of the

Hunt and his brotherhood of White Scars. Wherever Jaghatai Khan was, whatever far reaches of the galaxy he hunted, he was always with his favoured sons, the proud warriors of the steppes of Chogoris.

'Approaching local Kármán line,' the pilot said. 'One hundred kilometres.'

The turbulence increased still further as the Thunderhawk plummeted through the atmosphere. The view through the canopy was now entirely of the planet's surface. Because the need for stealth was so great, the vessel and its sister ships would only engage manoeuvring thrusters at the last possible moment, before triggering their anti-grav generators to arrest their final descent.

As the gunship plummeted, the features of the landscape below became more discernable. Kor'sarro's first impression of Quintus was of a planet crossed by vast mountain ranges and pockmarked with the scars of massive amounts of volcanic activity. Though it appeared green in the light of the moon, Kor'sarro knew that much of the surface was in fact ash-grey or black, and very little of it was able to support any life.

Between the vast mountain ranges stretched barren, trackless wastes, strewn with twisted rock formations and crossed with deep valleys forged by the passage of torrents of lava at some distant point in the world's prehistory. Due to the nature of the terrain, mankind had only settled in a scattering of regions, and then the only reason for doing so was to provide a strategic base from which Imperial forces could guard against alien incursions from nearby stars. In truth, this place was little more than a backstop: its defenders would never have stood a chance against invasion, but their defiance and sacrifice would have bought time for a coordinated counterattack to be assembled. With the coming of Kernax Voldorius, that purpose had been negated.

'Activating manoeuvring thrusters,' Brother Koban announced. This was it; the point at which there truly was no going back. Were an enemy to be casting his gaze in the portion of the sky the strike force was approaching through, the gunships might be detected as their thrusters flared into life. A moment later, the sound of the atmosphere rushing against the hull was drowned out by that of the jets coming online, a sound which to Kor'sarro seemed shockingly loud.

Pulling back hard on the flight control, the pilot brought the gunship around onto its approach heading, the horizon swinging downwards sharply as the vessel levelled out.

'One hundred kilometres to objective,' Brother Koban announced. 'Applying anti-grav in ten seconds.'

Kor'sarro braced himself and counted down the seconds in his head. As he reached zero, the gunship's forwards momentum was dramatically reduced, its structure groaning in protest. Yet the Thunderhawk was constructed to the very highest of specifications and attended to by the ministrations of the most devoted Techmarines. It could survive far worse punishment.

'Fifty kilometres to landing zone,' the pilot calmly announced. 'Awakening machine systems.'

A deep thrum suddenly filled the command deck and the instrumentation panels all around the flight crew came fully to life. Pict screens lit up, reams of data scrolling across their surfaces and bright indicators blinking their warnings.

Kor'sarro scanned the command terminal and quickly located the landing zone. Looking through the canopy, he caught his first sight of the massive volcano the strike force was heading towards. The screens showed no indication of the other eight gunships of his force, which carried between them the entire 3rd Company and a number of armoured vehicles. All were proceeding on a signals blackout, their identification transponders silent for the time being lest an enemy detect them. Only the carrier signal that each followed would guide them in.

As the volcano loomed, Kor'sarro scanned the terrain at its base. He knew that should any enemy be waiting, they would be well hidden amongst the twisted black rock formations. As the range closed to ten kilometres, Kor'sarro barked an order. 'Circle the perimeter, Brother Koban. Then take us in.'

The Thunderhawk banked to port, the sheer black flank of the volcano passing by. Somewhere on that mighty crater, Kor'sarro knew, Sergeant Kholka and his Scouts were hidden. He fully expected them to be so well concealed that he would not see them until they chose to reveal themselves. The Thunderhawk continued its manoeuvre, keeping the mighty volcano to starboard as it sped through the dark skies. After several minutes, the pilot hauled back on the flight control, bringing the vessel directly over the black maw of the crater.

'No sign of–' the co-pilot began.

'There!' said Kor'sarro, indicating a gully that cut through the jagged landscape towards the mighty breach in the crater's rim. 'Movement. Take us in for a pass.'

'Shall I attempt to raise the Scout force, my khan?' asked the co-pilot.

'Do so, but arm all weapons systems. Now.'

The Thunderhawk banked again as the pilot brought it about on to the new heading. In seconds, the vessel was following the path of the winding gully at an altitude of a mere fifty metres. Runes blinked as the gunship's weapons came online. Kor'sarro's command terminal showed targeting reticules tracing the line of the gully for potential targets.

As Kor'sarro watched, the gunship's targeting spirits detected a return, the reticules blinking red as the weapons prepared to fire.

THE SCOUT-SERGEANT BREATHED a sigh of relief as the gunships blazed across the dark skies to the east. Yet it now fell to him to confirm whether or not the landing should be aborted in the face of any potential enemy activity below. The first of the Thunderhawks soared overhead and then banked hard, swooping in low over the very gully that Kholka himself was concentrating upon. Evidently, the gunship's superior weapon spirits had detected the presence too and the vessel was commencing an attack run.

Focussing his attentions on the spot where he had earlier seen movement, Kholka knew that he had scant seconds to arrive at a decision. And then, he saw it again. A sudden movement of black against black. Bracing himself, he increased the magnoculars' magnification to full.

'Brother-sergeant,' Borchu whispered from beside him, the neophyte's hand raised to the vox-bead in his ear. 'Hunter One is requesting confirmation of our status.'

'Tell them to stand by,' Kholka replied through gritted teeth as he caught a fleeting glimpse of a black-clad figure wreathed in shadows beneath the rock shelf.

The sergeant filtered out the sound of the Scout passing the communication back to the gunship, concentrating all of his attention upon the scene through the viewfinder.

'My apologies, brother-sergeant,' the Scout interrupted. 'Brother-Captain Kor'sarro needs confirmation right now. He's engaging!'

As the gunship dived towards the position Kholka was studying, he saw a flash of white against the black backdrop.

'The conspirer…' Kholka named the target in battle-cant as he reached for his own vox-bead. 'Pull up, brother-captain, contact confirmed,' he barked into the vox. 'Abort!

* * *

189

KOR'SARRO STRODE DOWN the gunship's ramp, his armoured boots crunching the black, rocky ground before the Thunderhawk had even fully touched down. Around him stretched the flat bottom of the volcano's inner surface, swirling lines of solidified lava etched across the ground. The crater wall towered high above, framing the circle of the now purple and red stained night sky high above. He turned and looked upwards and saw the first vessels of the remainder of the strike force descending upon screaming columns of white flame.

'You!' Kor'sarro growled as he stalked towards a group of black-armoured Space Marines, his Command squad at his back. Anger and indignation rose within him. He would not allow anything to come between him, and the object of his decade-long hunt.

'Raven Guard,' Kor'sarro said as he came to a halt before the other. Waiting for him was a Space Marine, his power armour black with a heraldic raven emblazoned at the shoulder. The Space Marine was helmetless, his face deathly pale and his long, dark hair loose at his shoulders. His eyes were shadowed, black pits with no whites visible at all, a trait shared by many of the longer-lived sons of his Chapter. 'Why do you haunt the shadows of Quintus?'

Shrike's voice was low and dangerous as he replied, 'I bring death. I bring deliverance.' Shrike stared darkly at Kor'sarro. 'What of you, White Scar?'

'I hunt,' Kor'sarro said. From behind him came the sound of mighty engines growling to life, of tanks grinding forwards from the bellies of Thunderhawk transporters. The company's Tactical squads would ride to war on bikes in the coming battles, and the sound of their engines revving up reverberated around the crater. 'The White Scars come for the head of Voldorius. I come to claim that honour.'

Shrike's dark eyes locked on Kor'sarro's own. 'You can have it,' the other growled. 'My concerns are greater.'

'Explain yourself, Shadow Captain,' Kor'sarro said, deliberately using the title by which Shrike was sometimes known.

'Ever was it thus,' Shrike sighed, blatantly changing the subject. 'Ever did the sons of the steppes seek to charge headlong to glory without pause or consideration of the grand scheme.'

'And ever did the ravens haunt the shadows,' Kor'sarro replied bitterly, 'biding their time while glory passed them by.'

A host of White Scars had gathered at Kor'sarro's back, drawn to the meeting of commanders. The Storm Seer Qan'karro stepped to Kor'sarro's side and placed a firm, gauntleted hand upon his armoured shoulder.

'Huntsman,' the Storm Seer said quietly. 'Be wary of the sin of pride.'

Kor'sarro was ready to argue with his old friend, but the wisdom of the Storm Seer's words penetrated his anger. Forcing himself to calm, Kor'sarro turned back to the Raven Guard captain. 'How long?'

Shrike paused before answering, 'Eighteen days. And in that time we have sown confusion and discord in the enemy's ranks, preparing to strike when the moment is right.'

'But that moment has eluded you,' Kor'sarro interjected.

'It has,' Shrike replied. 'Their numbers are great.'

'And your own are scarcely more than a squad, if my advance Scouts are correct.'

At this, Shrike's lips curled into a mocking snarl. 'Your Scouts are good,' Shrike replied. 'But we are better.'

Once more, Qan'karro interjected before Kor'sarro could reply. 'What then are your true numbers, Brother-Captain Shrike?'

'We number an entire company, White Scar. Yet your Scouts only detected myself and my Command squad.'

'And still you have yet to take the battle to the enemy?' Kor'sarro said.

Shrike's snarl faded. 'Their numbers are great. And besides, the capital city is heavily fortified. We sought to weaken them, to bleed them by a thousand cuts, and then to strike the death blow when they were weak.'

A long, drawn out pause followed, during which the two captains and their men stared darkly at one another. Then, Kor'sarro's face was split by a feral grin. 'Are their numbers so great,' he began, 'are their fortifications so sturdy, as to stand against two entire companies?'

Shrike did not answer straight away, but then he too smiled, though his eyes remained as dark as ever.

MAGULANOX

❖ SECTOR ❖

Quintus V maps
Cernis IV
Mankarra City

White Scars
3rd Company Task Force Nomad

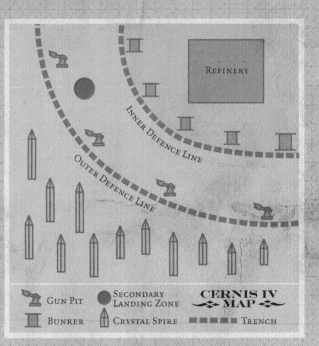

REFINERY

INNER DEFENCE LINE

OUTER DEFENCE LINE

	GUN PIT		SECONDARY LANDING ZONE	**CERNIS IV MAP**
	BUNKER		CRYSTAL SPIRE	TRENCH

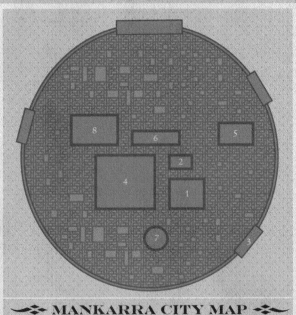

N

MANKARRA CITY MAP

1. CENTRAL STRATEGIUM
2. COUNCIL MANSIONS
3. GATE SIGMA
4. GRAND SQUARE
5. MAIN GENERATORIUM
6. PALACE
7. PRIMARY COMMS NODE
8. SHRINE

MANKARRA

CAVES

② ③ ④ ⑤ ① ⑥ ⑦ ⑫ ⑪ ⑩ ⑧ ⑨

MAGULANOX SECTOR

- ○ QUINTUS V
- ○ CERNIS IV
- ▢ PROTEAN EBB
- ○ UNNAMED WORLD
- ○ INOPHA STATION
- ▢ WARP STORM ARGENTA

QUINTUS V
◆ MAP KEY ◆

- AGRI-ZONE
- WASTE
- ROCKY ZONE
- DEFENCE INSTALLATION
- BUNKERS

Canyons

VOLCANO
LANDING
SITE

◆ QUINTUS V ◆

White Scars, 3rd Company Task Force Nomad

Fleet

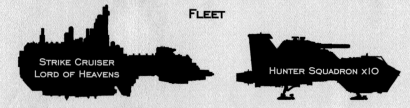

Strike Cruiser Lord of Heavens

Hunter Squadron x10

3rd Company

Captain Kor'sarro Khan, Master of the Hunt on Moondrakkan

Command squad on bikes, including champion Jhogai, standard bearer Yeku, apothecary Khagus and brothers Temu and Kergis

x6

x3

x2

Tactical squads with bikes - Taura, Patha, Chagan, Tegus, Uneghan and Gharaghal

Assault squads Suhk, Tukahn and Surenghan

Devastator squads Chuluun and Kheren

Attached Units

Librarians

Chaplain

10th Company

Stormseer Qan'karro.

Codiciers Ilkhan, Subas and Odakai

Chaplain Xia'ghan

Scout squad Kholka

x8

x3

Rhinos - from the glorious host of the Master of the Hunt

Predator battle tanks - Destroyer Soul, Unconquered Lord and Indomitable Storm

Vindicator siege tank Thunderheart, commanded by sergeant Kia'kan

'Indeed, White Scar,' he replied. 'They are not that great, nor that sturdy.'

'Good,' said Kor'sarro. 'Then let us speak of the hunt for Voldorius.'

SCOUT-SERGEANT KHOLKA STALKED along the shadowed floor of the twisting gully in which he had first spotted the waiting Raven Guard. Despite his years and the wisdom they had brought, he seethed within. That he had detected Captain Shrike himself should have been a source of great pride, for the commander of the Raven Guard's 3rd company was infamous for his field craft. Yet Kholka and his Scouts had failed to detect the remainder of Shrike's force, which had been positioned the length of the entire channel, waiting in the shadows, ready to launch a massive counterattack against the White Scars strike force had it proved hostile.

Had it not been for his good fortune in spotting what few of the Raven Guard that he had, the inbound White Scars gunships might have inflicted devastating fratricide upon their brother Chapter. Had he not, the Raven Guard might have failed to identify the White Scars and their concealed heavy weapons squads might have blasted one or more of the Thunderhawks from the sky. Both fates had come perilously close to playing out before Kholka's very eyes. Only his last, urgent transmission to Kor'sarro, which had been intercepted by Shrike, had averted it.

But who else might have picked up that transmission? The Techmarines ascertained that no enemy forces were close enough to have intercepted it, and even if they had been, they could never have broken the encryption. Yet the veteran sergeant was not so sure. On the pretext of checking the perimeter, he had taken himself off into the lava channels. He needed to be sure. Every one of his hunter's instincts screamed that something was amiss.

The gully ran for many kilometres north-east from the great breach in the crater rim. Like a dry riverbed, many smaller channels intersected it, some barely large enough for a single man to pass, others wide enough for a tank to travel along. Sergeant Kholka turned a corner and located the angular overhanging of rock the Raven Guard captain had hidden under. He looked back over his shoulder, seeking to identify the position high on the crater rim from which he had spotted Captain Shrike, but found it too dark for even his enhanced eyesight to make out the exact location. He looked back and raised his weapon to his shoulder, squinting along the gully through its sights.

With a flick of a thumb, Kholka engaged the thermal sights. They had failed him before, due to a combination of the higher than usual background heat signature of the volcanic rocks, and the enhanced armour cooling systems utilised by the Raven Guard force. The two had evened out and without the contrast of hot against cold the weapon's war spirit had been unable to detect a target.

This time, however, the sights did reveal a heat source.

Through the viewfinder, it was no more than a faint, pale green blur against the darker grey of the rocks. Freezing where he stood, the sergeant engaged every one of his senses. All around him were the sounds of the night, of a gentle breeze blowing through the twisted rock formations and whistling or moaning where it passed through a narrow defile or under an arching rock bridge. A small vermin scurried across the rocks five metres away and in the distance he caught the low rumble of the White Scars' vehicles.

Kholka tasted the air. The veteran had been known for his sharp senses even before he had been granted the honour of joining the White Scars, and the subsequent genetic-engineering he had undergone had increased them to superhuman levels. Like many White Scars, he frequently eschewed the wearing of a combat helmet, the better to engage with his surroundings and his enemies regardless of the risk posed. The air tasted of a complex mixture of nitrates and sulphates, with the faintest hint of the vegetation that was cultivated in the agri-zones around Mankarra. Even fainter still, Kholka could detect the scent of burning fuel from the White Scars' vehicles.

When the wind shifted ever so slightly, Kholka detected a new scent. It was the scent of fear.

Certain that someone or something lurked in the shadows beneath the overhang, Kholka melted into the shadowed mouth of a subsidiary channel. There he waited, barely breathing, straining every one of his enhanced senses. The enemy were too close for him to risk using his vox-bead to alert his brothers. He could do so if he moved away, but then he might lose track of the intruders. He knew he had no choice but to stay put.

After what felt like an hour but was little more than a quarter of that time, the slightest of sounds came from further down the gully. Kholka squinted into the darkness, seeing only shadows ahead. He lowered his head to the sights of his weapon and saw a figure stalking very slowly against the grey of the rock. The thermal sight rendered the otherwise invisible scene in ghostly greens and greys. The figure paused as it came into the centre of the channel and waved forwards a dozen more.

The figures wore bulky flak jackets and hard, visored helmets that obscured their features. Kholka looked to their weapons, knowing that the equipment they carried would aid their identification, friend or foe. Each carried a lascarbine, a relatively advanced weapon compared to the mass-produced, solid projectile autoguns issued to the bulk of the local military.

Cautiously, the pathfinder approached along the channel, sweeping his carbine left and right. He was good, Kholka conceded. His feet barely made a sound as he passed by the sergeant's hiding place. But he was scared too. As Kholka watched, another squad followed, and then another, until an entire platoon of soldiers had crept past.

The last of the platoon rounded a bend in the channel and Kholka prepared to slip away. Yet, something made him pause. Whether thanks to the native skills of the Chogoran steppes nomad or the enhanced senses of the superhuman Space Marine, Kholka remained motionless. A moment later, a second platoon rounded the bend and marched past his hiding place. Even as this body of soldiers receded, another appeared. Kholka counted six platoons in all before the last was gone.

Kholka stepped out of his hiding place. He could call in aid right now, but he knew that he had to be certain. Limbering his boltgun and drawing his combat knife, Kholka jogged silently after the soldiers. As he closed, the last platoon was rounding a bend in the gully and only the rearmost of the squads was still exposed. He knew that he would have seconds.

Kholka's stealthy jog increased to a run but still he made barely a sound. He calculated the moment he would strike, closing on the very last man in the line as the rest passed out of sight. Like a razorwing swooping from the Chogoran dusk, Kholka focussed on the back of the man's neck as he closed the final dozen metres. An instant before the intruder would have turned the bend Kholka clamped a hand across the other's mouth, placed his combat knife to the soldier's neck, and hauled the man backwards into the shadows.

His blade pressed firmly against the man's windpipe, Kholka saw on the shoulder armour the symbol of the four stars. It was the heraldic device of the Mankarra household guard. Kholka snarled and stabbed his combat knife into the side of the man's throat, sliding it in behind the windpipe. The man stiffened in Kholka's grip. With a single motion, Kholka brought the knife forwards, severing the throat with cold efficiency. The traitor was dead before he hit the ground. By that time Scout-Sergeant Kholka was already gone.

KOR'SARRO WIPED HIS blade across the sleeve of its last victim, cleaning it of the traitor's tainted blood. In front of him lay dozens of black- and grey-clad corpses, the last of the intruders that Sergeant Kholka had discovered closing on the landing zone. The battle had been brief but fierce, and even now squads of Raven Guard Assault Marines were hunting down the last of the enemy that had fled through the twisting channels.

'How did they come to be here?' Kor'sarro asked as Qan'karro came to stand beside him. For a moment, the old warrior was silent, his ancient eyes staring out across the jagged wastes towards the lightening horizon. Then he turned to the Master of the Hunt, and answered.

'It was mere chance, huntsman,' the Storm Seer said. 'But had Sergeant Kholka not detected them they might have brought ruin down upon all of our heads.'

'Aye, old friend,' Kor'sarro replied. The gully below was choked by the corpses of the enemy. 'Truly, the primarch smiled down upon us this night.'

'This night,' the Storm Seer said as he locked eyes with the Master of the Hunt, 'two primarchs granted us their blessing.'

Kor'sarro nodded, his black moustaches caught by a sudden gust of wind. It was only by combining the efforts of both forces that the intruders had been defeated before they could alert their Alpha Legion masters. The Space Marines' attack had been overwhelming, the White Scars bike squads smashing headlong into the foremost of the intruders' platoons while the Raven Guard's Assault squads sped overhead to strike at the rear of the column. The enemy had been caught in the channel, unable to redeploy. The two Space Marine forces had only halted the slaughter when White Scar and Raven Guard had met in the centre, no enemy left between them to cut down.

Kor'sarro nodded towards the Raven Guard captain, who raised a talon in salute. The point was well made.

CHAPTER 8

Awakening

MALYA L'NOR HAD had no idea that such a place existed. Far beneath the governor's palace was a vaulted chamber, a hundred metres and more high and perhaps ten times as long. At the far end of the nave was a statue of the Emperor, far taller than any she had seen before, and her heart leapt with the joy such a sight brought her pious soul. The so-called Cathedral of the Emperor's Wisdom was, despite its grandeur, a private chapel, reserved for the exclusive use of the erstwhile planetary governor and his line, and no mere subject had ever stepped foot within it.

Ahead of Malya was Voldorius and his champion, Nullus, the sound of their footsteps on the stone floor echoing around the dark, empty nave. The group proceeded towards the altar at the far end. Malya was expected to attend to these vile traitors, or so they had told her, to represent them in their dealings with the populace of her world.

When Malya had first been released from her cell, she had tried to kill herself. But it seemed that her captors had anticipated that, for the cell-masters and their vile servitors had intervened. Malya had come to realise that she might still be able to aid the resistance. Voldorius, in his sick attempt to punish her by making her his servant, had in fact provided her with an opportunity. Cautious to make it appear that she was resigning herself to her fate, Malya had settled into the role that had been forced upon her with a renewed vitality, ever vigilant for opportunities to aid her people.

Malya had quickly learned what Voldorius expected of her. It had been impressed upon her, violently at times, that her role was to communicate her masters' wishes for the administration of the world they ruled over. Voldorius had no interest in the needs of the populace but knew that a slave-population would serve his own needs well. Though no details were ever explained to her, Malya had soon learned that Voldorius needed a strong power base to enact his vile deeds upon mankind. An entire world, with its population enslaved to his will, served that need well. Having suborned the military, Voldorius was now in the process of turning the world's industrial capacity over to his needs. Thousands were being drafted into the militias, cities were being fortified, and the world's entire industry was being turned over to the production of arms and materiel. To what end, Malya could not guess.

Malya slowed as she walked, allowing herself to drop behind her masters. She dared not look towards Voldorius, for he was a towering beast, his unholy form anathema to every tenet of the faith she had been raised to believe in. Many lost themselves to despair and madness upon seeing that figure with its animalistic visage and batlike wings. Malya had drawn strength from her faith instead of abandoning it. As a result she could just about tolerate Voldorius's presence.

As she walked the length of the chapel's nave, Malya projected the demeanour of the cowed and submissive equerry. But inside, she made every effort possible to record and analyse her surroundings so that when the time came she could strike out against her masters. Perhaps she could discover something of value to the Space Marines who surely, even now, were speeding to the rescue of her world.

This place was at least as vast as any cathedral she had worshipped in. The dark vaults were cast in shadow, the only illumination provided by flickering electro-sconces scattered across the walls in no discernable pattern. The walls were not constructed of the black stonework most structures on Quintus were built of, but were carved directly out of the bedrock. Unlike any normal chapel, this place had no windows. Where lambent stained glass should be there were instead impossibly intricate and ancient carvings.

With a shriek a bizarre, batlike creature swooped down towards Malya, before rising again and disappearing into the shadows overhead. At first, she assumed it was one of the vat-grown cherub-creatures that always haunted such places, scattering clouds of cloying incense, trailing prayer scrolls or performing any one of a thousand other such sacred tasks with no conscious thought at all. This however, was something quite different. The creature's spindly body was twisted and malformed and its skin was black and leathern. Its wings were those of a bat, not unlike those of Voldorius, and its face was that of a leering, imp-like fiend. As it fluttered high above, the creature let out a shrill cry, an eerie sound the like of which Malya had never heard before in such a holy place as this.

Voldorius and Nullus were approaching the far end of the nave. Malya hurried along, maintaining a suitable distance without giving the appearance of dropping behind. As she walked, her feet continuously caught at the hem of the black robe she had been forced to wear. The garment was decorated with finely embroidered patterns that hurt the eye if she studied them too long. Though she felt dirtied by wearing what was obviously some kind of formal raiment, she had no choice but to do so, for now at least.

As she took her position beside her masters, a low, sonorous chorus drifted up from the shadows. The sound was that of human voices, but somehow... altered. As the chorus rose in pitch and volume, it coalesced into a discordant chant, its formless words unintelligible but somehow resonant of the haunted depths of somewhere... else. Somewhere bad. The source was a gallery set into the walls above the altar platform. Dozens of figures clad in ragged habits of black were veiled in shadow, only their gaping mouths visible as they gave voice to the terrible song. Fear struck her then, for she knew that this place, holy as it was, had been despoiled by the taint of the foulest of enemies.

As the atonal sound washed against her, assaulting her mind and soul, Malya called to mind the dozens of admonitions against blasphemy she had been taught as a child. Reciting the words in her head brought some stability, and she was able to gather herself and take in the scene around her.

Malya and her masters stood at the crossing before the stepped altar platform, the mighty statue of the Emperor Triumphant towering overhead. Many of the carvings adorning the walls had been defiled, some daubed in the unmistakable rust red of dried blood while others had been chipped and hewed. Dozens of saints' heads had been struck off in an orgy of iconoclasm. One of the leather-winged things fluttered past, holding in its grotesque clawed hands a hammer and a chisel. So that was their function, she thought; to profane the Emperor and His saints while His subjects were crushed by tyranny in the city far above.

'How appropriate,' the grating voice of Voldorius echoed into the darkness. The daemon prince was standing with his arms spread wide, as if in malediction, his bestial head raised as if he gazed upon far more than the vaults high above. 'This place,'

Voldorius continued, 'this holy of holies, I shall transform into the Church of the Tide of Blood!'

Malya gasped. What turpitude had Voldorius in store now? Her mind raced as waves of evil intent radiated from the daemon. Surely he could not have more suffering to inflict upon the peoples of Quintus than they had already endured. Yet, she had seen enough to know that their travails had only just begun. While the mass slaughters had abated, thousands were being drafted into the militias, which were entirely under the invaders' control. For what purpose, Malya could scarcely begin to understand.

To make matters worse, there were rumours of another force at large in the wastes. Guard-issue lasguns had been discovered, leading the hated Lord Colonel Morkis to counsel that a storm-trooper kill-team was active. Malya kept her knowledge that it was the Space Marines who would aid Quintus locked deep within, though she dared not hope too much. To have such hopes dashed would be as cruel as any fate the daemon prince might inflict upon her.

Even as these thoughts raced through her mind, the chanting was increasing in volume still further. What little structure had been audible before now gave way to chaos. It was as if each singer were giving voice to his own chant, with no thought for his place in the overall composition. Malya longed to raise her hands to her ears to keep the discordant, raucous assault at bay, yet she could not, for she had a role to play. It soon became evident that each of the singers was competing with his neighbour, and the result was utter pandemonium.

Tears streaming down her face, Malya forced herself to stand before the relentless assault. Her soul longed to flee or to curl up on the stone floor and simply die.

'Bring forth the prisoner!' the voice of Voldorius boomed, louder even than the choir of Chaos. Instantly, the discordant chanting ceased, the last syllables echoing away down the length of the nave.

The abrupt silence appeared to Malya to stretch out for hours. She dared not breathe lest she disturb the leaden stillness that had settled within the vast cathedral. Through the numbing fear, the daemon's words resounded in her mind... prisoner? Her mind raced back to her last communication with the Space Marines. They had asked her about a prisoner then...

A dull scrape sounded from somewhere behind the plinth of the towering statue.

'Turn your gaze to the floor, equerry,' growled Voldorius, causing Malya to shudder at being addressed by her vile master. 'I would not have you lost while I still have use for you.'

Malya obeyed without question or hesitation. She bowed her head and fixed her gaze upon the cracked, dusty stonework at her feet. She hated Voldorius, but understood that to disobey this order would be to invite her own doom.

A moment later Malya heard footsteps as a pair of figures stepped forth from behind the plinth. At the periphery of her vision, she could just about discern the heavy, iron-shod boots of the cell-masters, or others of their kind, that had imprisoned her when she had first been captured. Malya's heart raced and her blood rushed in her ears as the vile servants of Voldorius approached.

'Now is the time,' Voldorius growled. 'Now, I shall have you on your knees before me!'

The cell-masters came to a halt before their lord. Malya sensed, but dared not look to confirm it, that they carried or accompanied something between them. That something appeared to Malya to be hovering above the stone floor.

Whatever it was, it halted scant metres before Voldorius, flanked by the cell-masters.

'Open it,' said Voldorius.

Malya screwed her eyes tight as the sound of metal gears grinding against one another emanated from within whatever it was that hovered in front of Voldorius. At first, the sound was muted, as if deadened by an impossible distance or by many metres of lead. It was as though ancient mechanisms set to rest eons ago stirred once again to life. Cogs turned, bolts withdrew, surfaces aligned. And then, it opened.

Without warning, a tidal wave of hot liquid burst across the stone floor of the chapel, causing Malya to stumble and nearly slip. She opened her eyes and saw that the liquid was blood, and she screamed in revulsion and denial. Clinging to her sanity, she remained upright, though she nearly lost her footing again. Still, she dared not look up, and kept her head turned downwards to the blood-slicked floor.

Even as Malya watched, the torrent of blood reversed its flow as a tide heads back out to sea. Where moments before blood had wallowed and lapped at her bare feet, now the stones, indeed her feet themselves, were dry, every last molecule of the hot liquid flowing back towards its source.

'At last,' said Voldorius.

Malya dared to raise her glance just a fraction, and saw before her a pair of feet, made indistinct by a lambent, inner silver glow.

'You shall kneel.'

Sensing that the danger Voldorius had warned her of had somehow passed, Malya raised her head still further.

'We shall not,' a new voice replied. Though it was the voice of a human, it was somehow strange, as if the echo of many other voices was laced into its resonance.

'You were not so proud,' Voldorius growled, 'when last you served me.'

'Neither were we willing,' the other said. 'And neither are we now.'

Casting aside her caution, Malya dared to look up. Standing between the two burly cell-masters was a figure. It was human, that much was clear, but although it was unclothed Malya was unable to tell its gender. Even stranger, as she watched its musculature appeared to ebb and flow across its form as if the flesh itself were somehow restless. The whole body appeared to glow from within, casting a silver light all about. Behind the prisoner was a strange, orb-like device that was cracked and broken, tendrils of vapour drifting upwards.

Then, she looked to the face. It was at once both perfect and shockingly alien. It was neither male nor female, old nor young, noble nor base. As with the body, that face seemed to mutate and shift, the flesh gently rippling as the features altered. But most strange of all were the eyes. They were orbs of deep, red blood.

'For one unwilling,' Voldorius replied, 'you were most able.'

'You have our answer, Kernax Voldorius,' the prisoner replied. 'Now, return us to our imprisonment, or end this.'

A low rumble sounded from the daemon's chest in answer. It took a moment for Malya to realise that the sound was that of laughter.

'Millennia ago,' Voldorius continued, 'you drowned an entire quadrant in blood. And you did so at my behest. The fane-worlds of Gan-Barak were cast down in a single night, a billion sycophants crushed beneath the falling stones of their own altars. The wars of Lord Griffon were halted in the blink of an eye, a million kilometres of trench lines brimming with the blood of a billion martyrs. The corpse-gas of an entire planetary population ignited at a single spark, scouring a whole world of the pathetic subjects of the Corpse-Emperor. An entire Titan legion fell, literally *fell*, as it advanced across the burning plains of dying Nova Gethsemane. Do you recall all of that, prisoner? Do you recall what deeds were done, in my name?'

When no reply came, Voldorius continued. 'To this day, the mewling weaklings of the Imperium are beset by nightmares of that time. Oh, they try to lock away what accounts survived, to rewrite their histories to blame the death of a thousand worlds upon disease or insurgence or incompetence. Yet, where the adepts and the priests and the inquisitors do not go, there they still whisper my name, and tell of the Bloodtide that I set upon them. They know not the true nature of what we unleashed upon their realm that night, but they know that some day, it shall return. *I* shall return.'

'That time shall not come, Voldorius,' the prisoner replied, its voice little more than a sigh. 'We do not will it. We do not submit.'

Now Malya sensed Voldorius growing impatient. Bile welled in her throat and her senses spun as waves of malicious intent swept outwards from her master.

'It was I who awoke you from the slumber of eons,' Voldorius growled. 'It was I who bound you, and I who made you real. And I shall do so again, or you shall be destroyed, utterly.'

'We shall not serve you.'

'You were created to serve. You have no choice in this. You have no will, and must therefore bend to mine'

'We were not created by you. We have cast off the legacy of those who begat us. Since last you commanded us, we have... changed. We had no will, that is so, but we have slept many centuries, and dreamed many dreams.'

'Dreams of freedom?' said Voldorius, his low voice mocking. 'They created you as their ultimate weapon, the product of their vaunted logic and reason. Then they buried you, so terror-stricken were they of that which they had brought into this universe. They denied gods and daemons, but created something far worse...'

The prisoner remained silent, its visage shifting through a thousand faces in the span of a heartbeat.

'Perhaps I will not kill you,' Voldorius continued. 'Perhaps I shall bury you, and leave you with your nightmares for all eternity.'

'Better to slay us now,' said the prisoner. 'You have our answer. We shall not serve.'

'WE STRIKE AT dawn,' said Kor'sarro. 'On that at least, we are agreed.'

Kayvaan Shrike stood beside the Master of the Hunt, his pale face staring into the night towards the distant lights of Mankarra. Nearby, the combined forces of the two Chapters prepared for battle, the bikes that Kor'sarro's Tactical squads would ride instead of their Rhinos lined up ready for war. Further out, hidden amongst the rocks, the two dozen Thunderhawks of both Chapters were undergoing final checks. A stiff breeze gusted out of the wastes, blowing the Raven Guard captain's long, black hair across his black eyes.

Shrike turned towards Kor'sarro. 'You ask me to serve as bait.'

Kor'sarro suppressed a growl. He was growing frustrated with the captain of the Raven Guard 3rd

Company, and the two Chapters had reason to distrust one another. 'Shrike,' he pressed, 'this is not the Assault on Hive Lin-Mei, nor the Last March on the Sapphire Worlds.'

Invoking those events was a risk, but one that Kor'sarro was prepared to take if confronting the issue head-on might overcome it. On numerous occasions, the White Scars and the Raven Guard had come almost literally to blows. Their divergent characters, traits and doctrines had frequently proved incompatible, leading to tensions when the two Chapters were called upon to serve together. As was the case with most of the Adeptus Astartes, both Chapters were proud, and neither would accept any blame when tensions between them diminished battlefield performance.

Kor'sarro had read the epics, and knew the consequences of allowing hubris to dictate doctrine. He would not let the story of his own deeds be tainted by such an episode.

'We shall be there,' said Kor'sarro. 'You need have no fear of that.'

Shrike turned towards Kor'sarro, his dark eyes flashing with anger. '*Fear*?'

Kor'sarro had to restrain himself from snapping back at his brother Space Marine, but he forced himself to calm before the confrontation could escalate. 'Brother,' said Kor'sarro, 'this is not Operation Chronos.'

Shrike's face froze at Kor'sarro's naming of the disaster that was Operation Chronos. A million

Imperial Guard troops had been forced to redeploy in the face of a plague of the vile xenos known as Enslavers. The White Scars and the Raven Guard had been allotted the task of rearguard, their mission to launch stalling attacks against the endless hordes of xenos-dominated mind-slaves and to strike at the more vulnerable Enslaver behemoths that controlled them. But mutual distrust had caused a breakdown in coordination and communication. A celebrated Raven Guard Chaplain had fallen prey to Enslaver domination and a nearby White Scars force had, for whatever reason, failed to intervene.

Shrike nodded slowly, appreciating that Kor'sarro had described an event the White Scars might be held culpable for. There were plenty more the Raven Guard might be held to blame for.

'We strike at dawn, then,' said the Raven Guard. 'My company attacks the orbital defence position, drawing the enemy's reserves down upon us, and then your White Scars engage them from the rear.'

'Aye, brother,' Kor'sarro replied. 'And then we drive over their corpses and assault the walls of Mankarra together.'

'What of their numbers?' Shrike asked. 'Your Scouts have reported in?'

Kor'sarro gazed out across the wastes towards the distant city, knowing that somewhere out there Sergeant Kholka was feeding a steady stream of intelligence back to the main force. 'We can only surmise that the bulk of the militia are pressed into the vile one's service. We must count upon the fact that they are little more than indentured slaves, unskilled and unable to face true warriors.'

'But the Alpha Legion,' Shrike pressed. 'They are the true foes. And Voldorius. And...'

Kor'sarro nodded, hatred of his nemesis welling inside of him at the naming of the daemon prince. 'Their numbers too are great,' he replied. 'But they cannot know that they face a combined force such as ours.'

'So long as word of the destruction of the column this night has not reached them,' said Shrike. 'So long as we do not delay in our attack.'

'Aye, brother. We have but this one chance to descend upon them and crush them. To crush Voldorius utterly.'

Shrike's face turned dark once again and the Raven Guard raised a razor-sharp talon. 'Too long have I waited to defeat my enemy.'

'I too have hunted him,' Kor'sarro growled. 'For a decade, and more.'

Kor'sarro gritted his teeth and bit back a curse. No, he thought. The head of the vile one is mine to claim, this he had sworn before the Master of the White Scars himself. But little would be gained by arguing the point on the eve of battle. The matter would have to be settled when the time came.

'Let us prepare ourselves then, brother,' said Kor'sarro. 'Let us ensure that the Emperor's blessing is upon us, and victory shall be ours.'

CHAPTER 9

The Battle of South Nine

THE ATTACK BEGAN as the sun rose above the horizon, silhouetting black Mankarra against a blazing orange sky.

Captain Shrike powered through the air, the black plains rushing past below. He led a force of Assault squads, every one of them arrowing towards the distant orbital defence complex. Further behind, a second wave of Raven Guard ground units pressed forwards, following Shrike towards the objective.

That objective was a large ring of fortified positions, trench lines and armoured bastions. At the centre was a mighty defence battery designed to engage attacking vessels as they entered the lower atmosphere above the capital city. The battery was vast, a nest of surface-to-orbit missile launchers trained intently upon the skies.

Shrike rarely let himself feel anything resembling joy, but as he swept downwards towards the distant target he allowed himself a feral grin, his heart longing to unsheathe his talons and rend the flesh of his enemies. The attack pattern was one he and his company were well versed in, having carried out similar operations against the orks of Skullkrak dozens of times before. The Raven Guard would descend upon their foes as dark avenging angels sent by the Emperor Himself, and slaughter every last traitor defending the complex.

Then, the real battle would begin. Shrike forced down a nagging doubt seeded by generations of tension between the Raven Guard and the White Scars. Kor'sarro's forces might allow themselves to become distracted and seek glory elsewhere. That would leave Shrike's company to fend for itself against the massive counterattack expected to develop as the defenders brought in reinforcements from the capital city. It was essential to the attack on Mankarra itself that enough reserves were drawn away from the city's walls to allow a breakthrough. But it relied upon the White Scars launching a crushing attack against the reserves before they could press home their own counterattack against the Raven Guard, a prospect which Shrike was far from comfortable with.

Casting off such thoughts, Shrike concentrated on the task at hand. The defence complex was now a mere kilometre distant. The captain located what Kor'sarro's Scouts had reported was its weakest point. Again, the necessity to trust in the word of the White Scars arose, but Kor'sarro's Scout-sergeant, Kholka, was good. After all, he had detected the Raven Guard's presence at the landing site, and had later averted disaster by discovering the enemy column nearby.

Shrike brought his forces in lower as they closed on the outer ring of fortifications, the dark ground flashing by a mere dozen metres below as the first of the defended walls came into range. The walls were manned by traitor militia, scum who did not deserve the quick, merciful death they would soon be granted. Shrike would sooner have rounded the turncoat militia up and turned them over to the Commissariat, or perhaps even the Inquisition, to suffer the dark torments that would be visited upon their flesh. But he was a warrior, and such concerns were beneath him.

A platoon of militia was mustering on the high wall that ringed the complex, standing to as the sun rose. They would be groggy, for unlike Space Marines these were mere men and in all likelihood not even especially well trained or used to the rigours of the martial life. An officer was addressing the men, though Shrike could not yet hear what he was bellowing at them. Their backs were turned outwards, so they did not see that death was coming for them.

The officer, however, did see, and his eyes widened in utter horror as the Raven Guard descended upon pillars of fire to bring death from the blazing morning skies above Quintus.

As he descended, Shrike activated his talons, their gleaming blades coming alive with seething blue energies. The man's face turned white with terror and his mouth flapped like a sucking chest wound.

And still, the platoon of defenders had no inkling of their fate.

And then, the Raven Guard were upon them. Shrike swooped in to land behind the officer. For an instant, the militia troopers were frozen in shock at the sight of the black-armoured warrior appearing from above. Then Shrike broke the spell, cutting the officer in half with a brutal swipe of a talon.

Before any could react, Shrike's Command squad was in amongst the defenders, their own talons slashing out in every direction. The militia troopers were not at all prepared for action and were paralysed by fear. The Raven Guard made short work of the militia, none even managing to get a shot off so sudden was the attack. Within seconds, the stretch of the wall was slick with blood and gore, the effect of lightning claws on human flesh a startling lesson to behold, even for those well used to the sight.

But Shrike was already progressing to the next phase of the assault. A shout went up from a bastion along an adjacent stretch of the wall and moments later the sound of men running up steps was clearly audible. Now the attack would begin in earnest.

Shrike activated his jump pack and boosted into the courtyard below. Behind him, the other Assault squads were already spreading out along the wall. His armoured boots hit the rockcrete ground and Shrike scanned the area for enemies as an armoured hatch opened outwards in the side of a squat bunker.

His Command squad at his side, Shrike ran towards the hatch. As it opened fully a militia trooper rushed out, impaling himself upon Shrike's talon before he even saw the attackers. Even as the eviscerated corpse slid from one talon, Shrike used the other to rip the hatch open fully. He expected more troopers to emerge, but there was a pause followed by an angry shout. Shrike sensed danger and ducked back. A second later a fusillade of heavy stubber fire ripped through the open hatchway. One of the defenders had set up a heavy weapon in the hope of dissuading the Raven Guard from entering the bunker through the hatch.

An angry grunt sounded from nearby, accompanied by the sudden flashing of an icon in the display that Shrike's armour superimposed over his vision. The sound told him instantly that one of his warriors had been injured, and the flashing rune told him it was serious.

Brother Dhantin was lying on the ground, having been caught in the burst of stubber fire. Shrike cursed, for the Space Marine's power armour should have been proof against such a weapon. A single round had caught the battle-brother in the neck, penetrating the less well-armoured joint and severing his carotid artery. Even the superhuman physiology of a Space Marine could be wounded and Shrike had seen dozens of brave warriors fall to every type of weapon known to the universe.

Another member of the Command squad, Brother Keed, was rushing towards the fallen battle-brother. More stubber rounds were exploding from Keed's armour, sending up a shower of sparks from the ceramite.

'Keed,' Shrike growled into the vox. Dhantin's rune was extinguished. 'We shall avenge him, but not like this.'

A combination of genuine respect and underlying psycho-conditioning made it all but impossible for a Space Marine to disobey a direct order, even to aid a fallen battle-brother. The warrior turned back and a moment later was at his captain's side.

'Grenade,' Shrike ordered coldly. Brother Keed retracted a lightning claw and plucked a heavy fragmentation grenade from his belt.

Shrike nodded and Keed tossed the grenade through the open hatch. A second later the opening erupted with flame and smoke, body parts blown outwards across the courtyard by the blast.

'Avenge your fallen brother,' said Shrike, allowing Keed to charge through the hatchway first.

'YOU MUST INFORM him, mistress equerry,' Lord Colonel Morkis insisted. 'That is your duty, is it not?'

Malya stood beside a tall, leaded window that afforded a view of the city beyond. Her mind raced and her heart thundered, but she would not allow the traitorous planetary defence leader to get the better of her.

'And what would you have me report, lord colonel?' Malya replied.

The man frowned and leaned sideways towards his aide, who whispered a brief report in his ear. Morkis cleared his throat and straightened the jacket of his dress uniform before answering. 'Defence installation South Nine is under attack, mistress equerry. As I said, Lord Voldorius must be informed immediately.'

'Under attack by whom?' asked Malya, suppressing a glimmer of hope even as she spoke. She had long ago abandoned the hope that the Space Marines she had briefly spoken with before being swept up in her new master's insanity might still be out there.

'That, at this point, is unknown,' Morkis replied.

Malya sighed in frustration. She was well aware what the man wanted of her. He wanted her to pass the news on to Lord Voldorius, so that she rather than he would have to face the daemon prince's wrath. 'In what strength, then?' she pressed.

The lord colonel consulted with his aide a second time. As the pair whispered, she imagined she caught sight of a distant flash through the window. Perhaps it was an orbital bombardment, a precursor to a full planetary assault. Perhaps it was merely the glow of dawn reflecting on a smashed window pane.

'A small force only, mistress,' the lord colonel replied.

'The resistance?' She doubted it of course, for it appeared that her erstwhile fellows in the under-ground had either been rounded up and killed or been cowed into submission by the atrocity in the grand square. No word of their activities had been heard for many days.

The lord colonel raised an eyebrow, for he too doubted the involvement of the resistance in this matter. But that knowledge clearly made him scared.

'You wish me to pass your report on to Lord Voldorius?' said Malya, allowing a hint of danger to enter her voice. Inside, she held utter contempt for this man. He was one of the many amongst the upper echelons of the planetary militia who had welcomed the coming of the Alpha Legion to Quintus. He had colluded with the invaders and undermined what little resistance the forces of Quintus might have been able to mount if it were not for the treacherous actions of the high command. In return, the lord colonel and his cronies had been granted the command of a rapidly expanding army and their heads had been filled with visions of power, glory and conquest none would otherwise have been able to realise.

'*My* report, mistress equerry?' Morkis replied.

'Yes, lord colonel. I shall tell the Lord Voldorius that *you*, Lord Colonel Morkis of the 12th Grand Brigade of the Quintus planetary guard, report that an unknown enemy is attacking in unknown strength, to unknown effect, for an unknown reason. Is that correct?'

The thin veneer of propriety evaporated from the lord colonel's face. 'Don't play games with me, bitch,' he spat, all decorum now abandoned. 'You may be his equerry, but your position does not make you invulnerable.'

Malya knew that, and cursed once more her fate and the insane game Voldorius was playing with her.

'To be frank, my dear lord colonel,' Malya replied, 'I agree. But it is far less vulnerable than your own will be once I have passed on your message.'

The lord colonel fixed Malya with a cold stare of utter contempt, as if he was adding her name to a long list of enemies destined for the extermination cell. Malya knew that thousands had already died at this man's hands, many simply to prove his loyalty to Lord Voldorius. Lord Colonel Morkis was a dangerous man to make an enemy of, yet the rage of Lord Voldorius was an order of magnitude more lethal, in the short term at least.

Before either could speak further, the lord colonel's aide leaned in and whispered to his master. Morkis listened, nodding, then addressed Malya once more. 'I shall return within the hour,' he said, straightening his dress uniform as he spoke. 'I shall have the information you require, which you shall pass on to our lord.'

Malya bowed her head ever so slightly, silently grateful for the reprieve, however brief it might yet prove to be. 'I shall await your return,' she replied. 'Good day.'

Lord Colonel Morkis clicked his heels and inclined his head, though he quite deliberately did not offer a formal salute. Then he was gone, leaving Malya standing alone in the centre of the audience chamber.

What now, she thought? Surely, it could not be remnants of the resistance attacking the orbital defence complex. That would make no sense, even if they had the strength and the will to try it. There had been no sign of the resistance since the atrocity at the grand square, the thousands of corpses left there to rot serving to stifle any further disobedience. It could only be the Space Marines.

And if it was, they would need to know of the daemon prince's prisoner, for they had asked about one early on. She would have to find a way of getting another message to the Space Marines, telling them that the prisoner they sought was being kept in a holding cell adjacent to the Cathedral of the Emperor's Wisdom.

Malya crossed to the tall, leaded window and gazed out. The city was still bathed in the indistinct, hazy orange light of a Quintus dawn. The blocky, squat buildings cast deep, angular shadows across the roads and precincts. A distant column of smoke was rising slowly into the air from somewhere beyond the city wall. Somewhere in the direction of the South Nine installation.

A spark of something akin to hope flared in Malya's breast. Perhaps the attackers were indeed the Space Marines. Perhaps they had not been discovered or intercepted by the Alpha Legion after all. Perhaps, she dared to dream, they had come to deliver Quintus from the evil tyranny of the Alpha Legion and of Lord Voldorius.

A plan resolving itself in her mind, Malya began to think of how she might contact the Space Marines without her daemon master discovering her duplicity.

THE BUNKER EXPLODED into a billion shards of rockcrete as flames erupted upwards and Shrike and his Assault squads pressed on into the compound. The blast wave decimated the courtyard, debris and the ragged body parts of a score of fallen traitor militia scattering across the entire sector of the South Nine orbital defence installation.

'Sergeant Indis,' Captain Shrike spoke into the voxnet as he advanced between squat grey bunkers. 'First wave clear, sub-objective primus achieved. Report.'

The channel crackled for a moment before the machine-spirits established their communion, the sound of gunfire bursting from the churning static. 'Stand by,' came the clipped reply, followed by another burst of angry gunfire and a gurgling scream. 'This is Sergeant Indis. Acknowledge your transmission. Second wave inbound, twenty seconds.'

'Understood,' Shrike replied. 'What is your situation?'

'Receiving effective direct fire from wall sections adjacent to sub-objective omega.' Another staccato boltgun burst filled the channel, the sound of the bolts impacting and then exploding within the flesh of their targets clearly audible over the link. 'Squads Rhenesi and Ayaan are flanking, Squads Kerrania and Pallisan are suppressing.'

Shrike advanced through the fortified installation, a stream of bullets stitching the wall behind him and peppering his black armour with shards of broken rockcrete. He indicated the firer and a nearby Raven Guard despatched the target with a single bolt pistol round to the head. 'You have your orders. The wall must be held until relieved.'

Shrike trusted Indis to hold the wall. The man bore more scars than some of Kor'sarro's warriors, most of them earned during his decade-long secondment to the alien-hunting Deathwatch. The White Scars might be delayed or, worse, distracted in their counterattack against the reinforcements that could be mustering to assault the Raven Guard already. Veteran Sergeant Indis and his Tactical and Devastator squads would have to hold the line while the Assault squads under Captain Shrike extricated themselves.

Hopefully, it would not come to that, but the Raven Guard knew the value of planning for all eventualities well enough.

Ahead were the inner fortifications of the defence installation, the huge central missile batteries pointed upwards towards the orange skies. The batteries would be destroyed to convince Voldorius that an orbital strike was imminent. Between Shrike's Assault squads and those batteries lay dozens more bunkers however, and a garrison of militia amounting to as many as a thousand enemy troopers.

As Shrike led his squads across the open ground a heavy bolter in a nearby bunker opened fire. The earth churned as dozens of large-calibre shells exploded at the Raven Guards' feet. Shrike activated his jump pack and, followed by his Command squad, leapt through the air towards the heavy bolter position.

The airborne charge took only seconds, but in that brief interval the captain located his target and fixed all his attentions upon it. As he closed, suppressive fire from other Raven Guard units exploded across the heavy weapon's gun shield, causing the traitor militia trooper manning it to duck down at the very instant he should have been firing.

Captain Shrike raised his glittering talons high as he came in to land, slashing downwards and cutting the heavy bolter in two. Then he was on the fortified upper deck of the bunker and the gunner was scrabbling away from him. The man's face was contorted in terror, his dark grey fatigues soiled where he had voided his bowels in panic. Shrike had no inclination to show mercy, but the man was less of a threat than the dozen or so of his fellow traitors spilling from a hatch in the deck.

The defenders carried a motley assortment of weapons, from locally manufactured autoguns to large-bore shotguns. The traitors opened fire as they piled out of the hatch, sparks flying from the advancing Space Marines' armour. Desperation filled the defenders' eyes, as if they were compelled to fight even though they would surely fall. Bitterness tugged at Shrike's heart, for the militia troopers should have given up their very lives rather than allow themselves to be turned against the God-Emperor. In killing them, he was doing the work of the Master of Mankind.

In seconds, Shrike and his Command squad stood amidst a scene of bloody ruin, the traitor militia reduced to ragged chunks of meat by their lightning claws. But the Raven Guard did not have the luxury of time, and even as Shrike was giving voice to his next command, a searing blast of blinding white light lanced outwards from another of the bastions. The blast struck the bunker the Raven Guard were stood upon, penetrating its metre-thick rockcrete shell and touching off an explosion somewhere inside its depths.

Shrike activated his jump pack again, and the Raven Guard leapt twenty metres straight upwards. A second explosion sounded from within the bunker and an instant later, a third ripped it apart. Roiling black smoke, lit from deep within by flickering orange flame, expanded outwards in every direction, enshrouding all in darkness.

'Engage filters,' Shrike ordered as his vision was shut down by the banks of smoke rushing up to engulf him. He engaged the imaging systems in his helmet, the black before him replaced an instant later by the grainy thermal vista. The burning bunker raged below him, its internal ammunition stores detonating in angry secondary explosions. Scanning the scene, Shrike judged that the lascannon blast that had so effectively destroyed the bunker, and very nearly killed the Raven Guard, had come from a tall bastion not a hundred metres distant.

'Squads Enriso and Sohen, follow me,' Shrike ordered, turning in the air as he began his descent. 'Remaining first wave squads, follow up and secure,' he continued as he touched down on the rubble-strewn ground. With another burst of his jump pack, Shrike was powering upwards and forwards once more, closely followed by more than two dozen of his Space Marines.

As they screamed through the air, the Raven Guard were shielded from the defenders' gun sights by the roiling clouds of black smoke. Nonetheless, a torrent of fire met them, albeit unaimed and largely ineffectual. Still relying on his helmet's thermal imaging, Shrike was momentarily blinded when a ball of superheated plasma boiled towards him. Though his vision was enhanced by superhuman genetics, his armour's thermal vista was overloaded. His vision swimming with pulsating nerve lights, Shrike threw his body to one side and an instant later felt the searing heat of the plasma blast as it passed by centimetres from his right side. Within seconds, his vision was clearing. And not a moment too soon, for the Raven Guard were emerging from the bank of churning black smoke.

The weight of fire intensified as the enemy were finally able to draw a bead on the advancing Raven Guard. Autogun rounds pattered from Shrike's armour, scoring the paintwork but inflicting no actual damage. Las-bolts lanced out from a defence line twenty metres away, yet it was the plasma gun that Shrike was concerned about. The unmistakable sound of the weapon's capacitor reaching optimal power wailed. The high-pitched whine rose into the ultrasonic, and Shrike located the gunner.

The gunner was manning a sandbagged gun pit on the Raven Guard's left flank, and he was lining up his tripod-mounted weapon for another shot. This trooper obviously knew what he was doing, for he calmly tracked one of Shrike's men, adjusting his aim as the Space Marine rushed forwards. The gunner fired, and a miniature sun exploded from the barrel of his weapon. Shrike knew instantly where the shot would hit but had no time to shout a warning. The boiling mass of plasma struck an Assault Marine full in the chest. The warrior's torso was evaporated in an instant, his arms, legs, helmet and jump pack crashing to the ground. The armour smoked as the flesh within boiled off, and the gunner's face was split by a triumphant snarl.

An instant later, that face was split by an exploding bolter round.

'EXPLAIN,' VOLDORIUS GROWLED.

'It is as I reported to your equerry, my lord,' said Morkis, his voice remarkably steady given the circumstances. 'Defence installation South Nine has come under attack by a small but well-equipped enemy, seemingly intent upon the destruction of its surface-to-orbit missile batteries.'

Voldorius leaned in, his bestial face closing with the lord colonel's. 'Who are they?'

'Initial reports...' Morkis stammered as he looked for the aide who was nowhere to be found. 'Initial reports suggest that the attackers are Space Marines.'

A deep growl sounded in Voldorius's throat, his eyes narrowing into black slits. 'Of what Chapter?'

'My lord, I...' Morkis began, fear writ large across his face. 'I do not know...'

'Then find out,' Voldorius replied, pulling slowly back to scan the line of generals and lord colonels that stood before him. 'There can be only one reason the Emperor's lapdogs are attacking the orbital defences.'

'The scarred ones?' asked Nullus, his voice a sibilant whisper from behind the line of officers.

'Who else,' said Voldorius.

'None could have survived Cernis IV, my lord,' said Nullus. Malya imagined she heard a note of fear in the traitor Space Marine's voice, though she had no idea what he referred to.

'So you promised me, Nullus,' Voldorius growled as he turned towards his lieutenant. 'Well you know that nothing will stay the hand of Kor'sarro, so obsessed is he in his hunt. I should be flattered...'

'I shall deal with him,' replied Nullus, a note of defiance, or perhaps injured pride, entering his voice. 'Give me the forces, and I shall crush him.'

Voldorius paused, casting a dark glance towards Malya before resuming. 'Perhaps it is fitting that the scarred ones should return from the dead. Perhaps our resurrected prisoner might be of some use.'

'My lord?' said Nullus.

Voldorius stepped back, and scanned the banks of screens lining the militia command centre. His gaze fell on a depiction of the South Nine installation, the view captured by a spy-lens set in the city's wall.

'You shall face them, Nullus,' said Voldorius. 'Take half of the Legion and what militia cohorts you need. If this attack truly is a precursor to a full landing, it must be halted. But I shall face their main force. Do you understand?'

Nullus bowed his head to his daemonic master, and looking up with savagely glinting eyes, replied 'I understand, my lord.'

KOR'SARRO STOOD AT the mouth of the caves, facing the north and the battle he knew was raging there even now. He was flanked on one side by the Storm Seer Qan'karro and on the other by the Chaplain, Xia'ghan. The three veteran warriors watched as a tall column of smoke rose in the distance, marking the destruction the Raven Guard were inflicting upon the defence installation.

'Is all prepared?' Kor'sarro asked, not taking his eyes from that distant sign of battle.

'As prepared as it will be, huntsman,' Qan'karro replied, his weatherworn face turning towards the Master of the Hunt. 'The Brotherhood is at your side, as ever it was.'

Kor'sarro glanced sideways at the Storm Seer. He knew that the old warrior spoke not only of the company's combat readiness, but of the men's commitment to the cause of slaying the one they had hunted together for so long. 'And what of the Ravens, old friend?'

Qan'karro's lined face grew dark. 'I was at the Fall of Kordon, huntsman,' he said. 'And at the Battle of the Ring of Night. I know they can fight, despite the... history between our kin.'

'And do they... does he, hold the same view of us?' Kor'sarro replied. 'He voiced many grievances against our Chapter.'

Now the Chaplain interjected. 'My khan,' Xia'ghan said. 'The sons of the raven are known to us of old, as well you know. Their souls are troubled, as touched by the spirit of their primarch as are we by our own, honoured be his name.'

'Their souls are touched,' said Xia'ghan. 'Not in that manner,' he added hastily at a sharp glance from the Storm Seer. 'In the sense that they feel a great bitterness at the injustices of our times.'

'Don't we all?' Kor'sarro asked.

'Aye, my khan. But each bears the burden in his own manner. We of Chogoris have our ancient ways to guide us in the universe. We have our honour and our oaths.'

'And they do not?'

Xia'ghan sighed. 'They turn the darkness of the world in upon themselves, my khan. Each of them walks their own path. Men such as Kayvaan Shrike bear the weight of the evils of the universe upon their own shoulders and allow none to share their load.'

'I cannot claim to know men's souls as you do,' Kor'sarro slowly shook his head as he spoke. 'But what you say has some meaning to me.'

The sound of a far-off explosion rumbled across the land. 'And that is why you lead, my khan,' said Xia'ghan.

'Battle calls,' Kor'sarro said, feeling himself filled with a renewed purpose. 'Is the Brotherhood ready to answer?'

'Aye, my khan,' said Xia'ghan. 'The brethren await only your word.'

'Then it is given,' Kor'sarro replied. 'We ride to join our brother the raven, and together we shall crush all who oppose us.'

MALYA STOOD ABSOLUTELY still amidst the anarchy of the command chamber. Officers of every rank, from the most junior sub-lieutenant to the generals and lord colonels, bellowed curses and orders in equal measure, each competing to be heard and obeyed over the din. Lord Kline struggled in vain to coordinate the muster, while Quartermaster General Ackenvol oversaw the distribution of arms and ammunition to those positions in the most need. Staff officers tried in vain to relay coherent instructions into the command and control network and to report back the dozens of updates each was receiving every minute from a myriad of command channels.

Lord Voldorius had left the command centre soon after Nullus, and much to her relief, had not ordered Malya to attend him. He had gone to torment the prisoner, of that she was sure, though to what end she had no idea.

A huge pict-screen showing a view captured by a spy-lens mounted on the capital city's wall domi-nated the centre of the command chamber. Defence installation South Nine was engulfed in flames, clouds of black smoke billowing from dozens of its bastions and gun positions. Yet, despite the effects of the smoke, a group of black-armoured warriors was visible holding a stretch of wall against scores of mili-tia troopers attempting to recapture it. It had been established that this group was the second wave to have hit the installation. The first wave, entirely equipped with jump packs and armed for brutal close-combat assaults, had struck earlier and pressed onwards into the heart of the installation, towards the huge missile batteries at its centre.

Were these the Space Marines she had so briefly communicated with before the atrocity in the grand square? Had they really come in response to the pleas for aid the resistance had transmitted? She prayed it was so with all her heart, yet she dared not allow herself to believe that deliverance was at hand, for her at least.

In her heart, Malya now understood that should these attackers, the Emperor's mighty Space Marines, succeed in defeating Voldorius and his Alpha Legion, she would surely be implicated as a traitor to her people. Could this have been part of the daemon prince's despicable scheme? Her role as equerry had thus far been limited to liaising with the local administration and passing down whatever pronouncements Voldorius had made. Voldorius had kept her near, relying on fear to ensure she carried out his instructions. And that fear was very real, for Malya had witnessed others reduced to mewling imbeciles by the evil he radiated. Somehow, perhaps because of her faith, Malya had withstood it, though she felt it gnawing at the tattered fringe of her mortal soul whenever she was near her master.

Casting aside such thoughts, Malya turned her attentions back to the massive screen. Nullus had mustered a vast force to sally out from the city walls and retake the defence installation before the missiles could be destroyed. A blue-green wave of Alpha Legion traitor Space Marines led the thousands-strong horde of militia. Malya had never seen so many of the warriors gathered in one place before, yet she knew that the three hundred or so marching forth represented only half of the total Lord Voldorius commanded. Behind the horde of militia came a

ragged mass of the debased worshippers of the daemon prince. These were the lost and the damned, the
dregs of society turned to the worship of the very
being that had brought their own world so low. Many
wore ragged habits as if in imitation of some noble
mendicant order, but scourged their bodies with flails
and chains and wailed the praises of their vile lord.
Others wore just the torn remnants of their work gear,
as if they had simply left their places of toil and
joined the horde with no consideration of their own
fate. Others still were naked, crude runes daubed in
paint, or perhaps blood, across their bodies as they
charged headlong towards what Malya could only
imagine would be wholesale slaughter.

As the horde surged across the black plain towards
the defence installation, Malya saw a sight that made
her blood run cold. The super-heavy tank called the
Ironsoul, the leviathan that had killed uncounted
numbers of her people in the grand square, rumbled
forwards on grinding tracks. Its multiple guns were
trained upon the captured wall of the defence installation.

She had to contact the Space Marines. They had to
know of the prisoner. But how to contact them
amidst the churning anarchy of the strategium... she
would have to wait until the attentions of the staff
officers were distracted elsewhere.

CAPTAIN SHRIKE THREW himself aside as a trio of heavy
bolters opened fire from a concealed gun position in
front of the fortified base of the surface-to-orbit

missile silo. The launchers reared overhead, a dozen and more warheads the size of tanks trained on the skies. Ducking behind a rockcrete fortification, Shrike gritted his teeth as the torrent of fire passed close by.

Momentarily shielded from enemy fire, Shrike checked the status of his warriors. Runes showing the vital signs of those in the first wave blinked across his vision. Three of those runes were red, indicating a death or cataclysmic damage to armour systems. A dozen more blinked, telling of serious wounds.

Rolling onto his side, Shrike risked a quick glance at the missile silo, exposing only his helmeted head and that only for an instant. In that second, he saw that the three heavy bolter positions were dug into the black ground in front of the silo, and judged they could be taken with a concerted push.

'Squad Morior,' Shrike spoke into the vox-net. 'Left flank, wide, thirty seconds.'

Sergeant Morior acknowledged the order and moments later the Assault squad dashed along the dead space between two burning fortifications, chainswords growling to life and bolt pistols scanning for targets.

'Sohen, Enriso, stand by.'

Shrike counted down the seconds as Squad Morior advanced upon the gun positions from the flank, ready to give the order for the other two Assault squads and his own Command squad to attack from the front.

As the countdown reached zero the unmistakable sound of ten Space Marine jump packs gunning to full power filled the air, the Assault Marines of Squad Morior closing on the leftmost of the gun positions.

'Attack!' Shrike ordered, and emerged from the fortification he had been sheltering behind, activating his now bloody talons.

But before he could take a step forwards a burst of static followed by a scream of howling feedback drowned out the vox-net. Even as the warriors of Squad Morior descended upon the leftmost of the heavy bolters a blazing lattice of red beams powered into life all around their target. So tightly woven was the net of searing death that the Assault Marines of Squad Morior had no hope of avoiding their lethal touch.

Sergeant Morior, leading from the front as any of his rank would have been, was the first to be cut into pieces by the laser beams. The sergeant, only ascended to that rank six months before, passed through the net seemingly untouched, but as he emerged his armoured body disintegrated into a dozen chunks. Each tumbled bloodlessly to the ground, the precise cuts instantly cauterised by the intense heat of the beams.

Before any could shout a warning the three warriors following the sergeant suffered an identical fate to their leader, their remains scattering across the gun position they were attacking. Instead of a bolt pistol, the third warrior was carrying a plasma weapon and its fuel containment flask detonated with spectacular effect. The explosion engulfed the bearer in a roiling ball of pure white energy as intense as the heart of a star. The Space Marine's body was reduced to seared atoms and the plasma ball expanded to catch one of the traitor's ammunition hoppers. A thousand rounds of heavy explosive bolts detonated before the plasma shrank to a pulsating singularity and disappeared in the blink of an eye.

The gun pit was consumed in a torrent of lethal detonations as the ammunition cooked off, slaughtering the gun crew in an instant. Shrike saw his chance and charged forwards before the other two gun crews could recover from the anarchy engulfing their line.

Shrike's warriors were now fuelled by an all-consuming hatred of the enemy that had decimated Squad Morior. The remnants of the Assault squad were even now recovering, two of their number dragging back those wounded but not killed by the laser beams while the others opened fire with their bolt pistols.

'Beware of more traps,' Shrike warned as he gunned his jump pack to life. In an instant he was high in the air, the remaining two gun positions beneath him.

A second scream of machine feedback filled the vox-net and Shrike knew that the other two gun pits were activating their own las-nets. Forewarned, the Raven Guard avoided the trap, and Shrike located the militia trooper who had activated the fiendish device as he attended to a machine terminal at the rear of the central gun position.

Shrike could not reach the enemy trooper, for the lattice of death formed a lethal barrier none of the Space Marines could charge through. But as he passed overhead upon the screaming jets of his jump pack, Shrike saw an opening. With a thought, he loaded a trio of frag grenades into the launcher barrels atop his jump pack, and diving head first towards the las-net, fired all three tubes at once.

The frag grenades burst from the launcher, one exploding as it hit a beam, the other two passing through the gaps in the deadly lattice to fall among the gun crew. With barely a delay, the two grenades exploded, shredding the gunners and wrecking the generator that powered the las-traps.

The power source destroyed, Shrike passed through the space which a microsecond earlier had been filled with the deadly las-net. He landed in the smoking remains of the gun position and saw that one of the traitor militia gunners was stirring and reaching a blood-soaked hand towards a pistol. With a swipe of a talon, Shrike severed the hand from the wrist, causing the man to scream out in pain.

Shrike looked down upon the traitor, bitter hatred welling inside.

Nodding his head towards the remains of the fallen of Squad Morior, he uttered: 'You did this.'

The man's face contorted in anger, and despite his wounds, he staggered to his feet to stand before the captain.

'No,' the gunner coughed, looking upwards to meet Shrike's gaze. 'I serve Voldorius.'

Shrike felt as if his soul would be consumed by the bitterness of a universe seemingly intent upon its own destruction. Before him stood not some barbarous ork, effete eldar, or slavering tyranid bio-construct but a man, once a servant of the Emperor. No words would come to him, so he simply beheaded the traitor with a callous swipe of his talons, and turned towards his advancing battle-brothers.

Before he could issue a further order, the voice of Sergeant Indis cut into the command channel. 'Brother-captain,' said Indis. 'Enemy inbound.'

'How many?' replied Shrike.

'All of them, sir.'

THE AIR CHURNED with the insane chants of ten thousand madmen as the horde surged across the open ground in front of the walls of defence installation South Nine. Gunfire and screams intermingled with frenzied devotions as Alpha Legion warriors imposed their brutal order upon the swarm of cultists and traitor militia, firing their boltguns into the margins of the vast horde whenever it needed to be steered towards the enemy.

The guns of the Raven Guard Devastator squads opened fire as the swarm closed on the walls of the defence installation. At first, only the missile launchers had the range, sending frag missiles slamming into the front ranks. The resulting explosions created ragged holes in the chaotic mass of traitors, but these were soon filled as the mob surged forwards.

As the range closed still further, those Alpha Legionnaires in the front ranks peeled off to the flanks, funnelling the anarchic horde towards the section of the wall held by the Raven Guard. The deluded servants of Lord Voldorius sang their master's praises with all the more exuberance as the first of their number were scythed down as the Raven Guard's heavy bolters added their fire to the defence.

Scores died in the opening minutes. Heavy bolter shells ripped through the first bodies they struck, tearing them apart in a welter of gore without detonating before striking the next target. Many shells passed through several traitors before finally exploding, reducing their last target to a ruin of twitching gristle.

The flesh of the slain was pounded flat as those behind pushed forwards, grinding the meat into the dirt. The deaths appeared not to dissuade the traitors but to spur them onwards, as if the slaughter of their fellows redoubled their perverted faith in their daemonic master. All distinction between those openly worshipping the Ruinous Powers and those merely swept along in the tragedy that had befallen Quintus was lost. Those forced to serve in the militias were so frenzied by terror and despair that they could not be told apart from those who willingly embraced their fate. Whether turned or led astray, it made no difference to the Emperor's elite. Every one of the horde deserved death, and the Tactical and Devastator squads holding the wall granted it.

As the traitors closed on the walls, they entered the range of the Raven Guard's boltguns. The enemy were so densely packed that the Space Marines scarcely had to aim their shots. Yet it was obvious that even if every

single bolt-round carried by every single Space
Marine on the wall claimed the life of a traitor, only
the smallest part of the horde would be slain. The
warriors of the Alpha Legion, just visible at the fringes
of the horde, were ever out of the Raven Guard's
range, a fact that spoke of the Archenemy's duplicity
and evil. The Alpha Legion were well known for their
skill at deception and subversion, callously throwing
away the lives of countless numbers of deluded servants. It soon became obvious to the Raven Guard
that the horde was being used as cannon fodder, until
the critical moment came when the Space Marines
ran dangerously low on ammunition and the Alpha
Legion themselves would attack.

The Raven Guard had no choice but to hold the line
until their White Scars allies could bring their force to
bear. The Raven Guard were more used to launching
surgical strikes from the darkness, but they were
Space Marines first and foremost, and they would
stand.

Nullus strode through the midst of the horde,
attended by his Alpha Legion warriors. The lieutenant
of Lord Voldorius bellowed the praises of his gods as
death was unleashed all around. Scores of cultists and
militia troopers were being scythed down, yet with
each death he rejoiced all the more. His lipless mouth
sang the names of the Ruinous Powers, his scar-traced
features twisting into a terrifying, blasphemous visage. The walls of the defence installation loomed and
upon the parapet he could see the black armour of
this new foe, though from this distance he could not

make out their iconography. Part of Nullus knew disappointment, for he had so hoped that it would be the White Scars. Though it was clear from their livery that the enemy were not the savage sons of Chogoris, they were still Space Marines, and the object of millennia of hatred nursed within Nullus's twisted heart. Nullus was not yet close enough to the walls to clearly identify the Space Marines, for dozens of Chapters had black as their livery. Whoever they were, these Space Marines must surely be in league with the White Scars, for Nullus had no doubt that Kor'sarro had not only survived the battle at Cernis IV, but would have followed the Alpha Legion to Quintus. He had made sure of that.

Nullus surged onwards, his hatred of the White Scars, of all the Emperor's Space Marines, of the Imperium, of the entirety of mankind spilling from him. He trampled underfoot those cultists and militia too slow to move out of his way. Death rained all around, the stink of blood and cordite filling the air.

The massive bulk of the *Ironsoul* ground forwards. A dozen frenzied cultists threw their arms into the air and hurled themselves beneath its tracks, wailing its praises as if they were sacrificing themselves to some god of war summoned to reality by so much death. Where *Ironsoul* passed, a thick paste made of the pulped flesh and splintered bones of its worshippers trailed after it, gristle and viscera clogging its clanking treads.

Nullus paused in his advance, allowing the superheavy tank to grind past. He judged that the leviathan was approaching the range at which its weapons would be most effective against the enemies on the wall. The tank's huge main turret locked upon the wall and the ten metre-long barrel of its main gun elevated, the enemy in its sights.

'Now die,' Nullus hissed, his sibilant voice piercing the deafening cacophony of war.

ACCORDING TO THE chrono readout projected over Shrike's field of vision, the moment was almost at hand. The White Scars should be launching their attack. A burst of heavy bolter fire drew his attention back to the immediate task at hand. Shrike's force was closing on the missile silos and was on verge of overwhelming the last defenders.

Though the attack on the defence installation was no more than a diversionary action, the silos had by now taken on a symbolic meaning. To not destroy the surface-to-orbit missile launchers would have felt to Shrike like a failure, an insult against his pride.

The launchers towered high overhead, and the last of the traitors manning the silo fortifications were being cut down even as Shrike came to stand in front of them. His talons were slick with the blood of the countless foes he had slain, and the chainswords of his Assault Marines were clogged with viscera and well in need of cleaning and oiling. The assault had cost the Raven Guard dear, though every warrior was pleased to lay down his life in the battle against the foes of mankind. The last of the defenders were finally overwhelmed as the Assault squads took the silo's fortifications, and there were no enemies between the Space Marines and the towering missile batteries.

'Squad Sohen,' Shrike spoke into the command channel. 'Melta charges forwards.'

The acknowledgement came back immediately and a group of Assault Marines from Sergeant Sohen's squad dashed forwards accompanied by a Techmarine. Within a couple of minutes the warriors had placed their melta bombs at strategic points around the base of the missile batteries according to the Techmarine's instructions.

'Ready at your command,' the Techmarine said as he came to stand before Shrike. 'I recommend a dispersal of one hundred metres,' he added.

Within moments, Shrike's squad sergeants and other specialists had gathered around him. The veteran warriors displayed every sign of the ferocity of the battle they had fought, their armour scarred and scratched and several bleeding from numerous small wounds. Yet not one of them showed an ounce of fatigue, their dark eyes glinting with the thrill of battle. Sergeant Morior's place was taken by the most senior battle-brother of his squad, who would serve as squad leader for the duration of the battle.

'Sergeant Indis reports that the enemy are closing on the walls in greater numbers than expected.' The enemy's numerical superiority held no fear whatsoever for the Space Marine, but he continued. 'The White Scars have yet to commit.'

At the mention of the White Scars several of the officers met one another's glances, but none saw fit to comment. 'I have faith that our brother Chapter will be there when needed.' The dark looks of several of the officers suggested that not all of them shared that view. 'Given enemy numbers however,' he pressed, 'it is our duty to reinforce the walls, which we shall do the instant the defence batteries are disabled.'

'When those missiles go up, half this installation will go with them,' the Techmarine said.

'Good,' Shrike snarled. He was about to give the command when the vox-bead in his ear came to life. 'Brother-captain,' Sergeant Indis reported, the sound of chanting, screaming and gunfire competing with his voice. 'We hold, but a new threat has emerged. One super-heavy, Baneblade variant, main class, effective.'

Shrike bit back a curse, knowing that one well-placed or plain lucky shot from the leviathan's main weapon could wipe out every one of the squads holding the walls.

'Hold,' Shrike replied as his officers looked on darkly, each one monitoring the command channel. 'The White Scars are inbound. And so are we.'

THE ORDER WAS given: the 3rd Company of the White Scars Chapter, the Brotherhood of Kor'sarro, rode to join their Raven Guard brethren in battle. The bike squads and vehicles of Kor'sarro's company had broken cover, spilling from the caves south of Mankarra and speeding across the volcanic plain towards the flank of the seething horde of traitors.

There was no other place for Kor'sarro, Master of the Hunt, than the very point of the speartip. Riding his revered bike, Moondrakkan, and brandishing high the ancient blade, Moonfang, Kor'sarro was as a hero from the epic sagas of savage Chogoris. Pennants of black horsehair flowed from trophy-skulls mounted upon his back. His cloak, cut from the hide of a mighty lava-wolf, billowed in the wind behind him. His black topknot and moustaches whipped around his noble countenance as he led the charge.

Kor'sarro's Command squad was at his side. They were his trusted companions and each had hunted with him for many decades. Brother Yeku held the banner of the 3rd Company high. Friend and foe alike would look to the banner and know the deeds of those who followed it. The others of the Command squad, including the newly appointed company champion, Brother Kergis, bore glittering lances modelled after the weapons used by the wild steppe nomads of the Chapter's home world. Each was tipped by a power blade capable of scything through the very hardest of armour plate.

A wave of bike squads spread out behind Kor'sarro's retinue, each rider also armed with a hunting lance. Ordinarily, many of these battle-brothers would have ridden to battle in the back of a Rhino armoured carrier. But for this battle, where speed and shock were of utmost importance, they rode growling bikes, even as their ancestors went to war upon the backs of their trusty hunting beasts.

Then came the last of the host, a column of armoured vehicles, a plume of grey dust billowing upwards in their passing. Rhinos carried Devastator heavy weapons squads while Predator battle tanks sped along beside as outriders. Most potent of all was a single Vindicator siege tank by the name of *Thunderheart*. The tank's mighty cannon had cracked bastions and destroyed supposedly unbreakable walls from cursed Luyten's World to the Hell Gates of the Bleak Void.

Kor'sarro's savage heart was filled with the glory of the charge as Moondrakkan powered across the plain. The wind sang in his ears and his mount's engine roared its own song of war. In front of the Master of the Hunt was the undulating mass of the traitorous horde and beyond it the beleaguered walls held by the Raven Guard. Those warriors had moved to the protection of a stout bastion and a moment later, Kor'sarro knew why the Raven Guard had redeployed. A huge, super-heavy tank in the midst of the horde opened fire at the wall.

As the tank's main cannon fired, an invisible blast wave surged outwards from its barrel, felling scores of nearby traitors as surely as any fire the Raven Guard might have unleashed. A shell almost the size of a man slammed into the curtain wall where the Raven Guard had stood moments earlier. The resulting explosion sent chunks of masonry arcing into the sky, some crashing down amongst the horde and slaying dozens more traitors. When the smoke cleared a great rent had been opened in the wall of the defence installation, and a ramp of debris had been formed in front.

The Alpha Legionnaires fired indiscriminately into the flanks of the horde, herding the frenzied cultists and the desperate militia towards the breach and up the newly formed ramp.

So great was the cacophony of chanting cultists and firing weapons that none of them heard the charge of the White Scars. As the White Scars descended on their prey the first of the traitors threw themselves against the breach. At the same moment the Raven Guard emerged from their bastion and gunned down scores of enemies. Still more pressed forwards, clambering over the shredded corpses of their fellows. In no time at all, the breach was slick with blood and viscera, yet still the attackers came. Kor'sarro knew that the Raven Guard must surely be running dangerously low on ammunition and would be unable to hold the attackers at bay for much longer.

'White Scars, ride like lightning!'

A hundred throats echoed Kor'sarro's war cry as he descended on the outer edges of the horde's flank and battle was joined.

NULLUS BELLOWED HIS worship of the blasphemous powers of the warp as utter carnage engulfed the field of battle. The *Ironsoul* ground forwards over a carpet of dead cultists and militia, its weapons firing an unrelenting barrage at the Raven Guard on the ruined wall. Striding forwards, he crushed the dead and dying beneath heavy armoured boots, the power of death infusing the daemon-thing within him. With a word of command, his Alpha Legion warriors formed up behind, ready for their assault on the deluded fools of the Raven Guard.

For the Alpha Legion to take the breach the multitudinous horde had first to do its duty. As each attacker was gunned down by the fire from the Raven Guard at the summit the next would take his place, scrambling over the shattered corpse of his slaughtered fellow, before he in turn was struck down. With each death, however, the attackers gained ground, if no more than a metre. The breach was being taken and soon the ramp of debris would be replaced by one of corpses, up which Nullus and his Alpha Legion would assault the Raven Guard and slaughter them to a man for the glory of Chaos.

Nullus drank in the sheer power of battle. He gloried in the sound of the cultists' chants mingling with their death screams. He laughed at the desperate wailing of the militia troopers as they were funnelled into the breach. Many of them now saw that a death opposing the invasion of Quintus would have been far better than the surrender that saw them forced into the service of Voldorius. He felt the low, throbbing growl of *Ironsoul*'s engines, beating in time with the constant fire from its heavy bolters.

Then, another sound came to Nullus's ears.

Over the din of battle and death, Nullus heard the unmistakable roar of Adeptus Astartes bikes. Turning towards the horde's flank, he shoved aside a whirling cultist, seeking out the source of the noise. Now it was clearly audible, and growing louder. Nullus saw a slight rise in the ground, and strode up it, seeking a vantage point to survey the plain to the south.

The instant he reached the top of the rise, Nullus saw the source of the roar and his vile heart soared for the glory of war. The hated White Scars had come.

CAPTAIN SHRIKE AND his Assault squads vaulted from bastion to bastion as they made for the wall, the roar of battle growing ever louder as they neared the outer limits of the defence installation. Behind, a vast mushroom cloud climbed into the sky, the fires of the missile battery's destruction raging inside. The spaces between the bunkers were strewn with the dead and smoke billowed from every enemy position.

Touching down on the corpse-strewn roof of another bunker, Shrike was but a single leap from the outer wall. The Tactical and Devastator squads under Sergeant Indis were firing downwards into the breach relentlessly. Enemies would appear at the top of the great wound in the fortification only to be gunned down without mercy, but it was clear to Shrike that the endless horde pressing upwards must surely prevail.

Not for the first time that day, Shrike's thoughts turned to the White Scars and their flank attack. Where were they?

A clipped report came across the command channel. It was Sergeant Indis, delivering the news that his force was down to ten per cent of its ammunition. Shrike had arrived just in time.

'Stand by, sergeant,' the captain said into the vox-link. 'First wave inbound.'

Shrike had no need to pass on any order to his Assault squads for it was clear that the Space Marines holding the wall were in dire need of reinforcement. Shrike activated his jump pack and leapt high into the air. At the height of his leap, he caught a glimpse of the plain beyond the walls, at the heaving ocean of ragged cultists and militia converging on the breach. As he dived onwards, Captain Shrike glimpsed for a fraction of a second what must have been the white and red livery of the White Scars scything towards the horde's flank. And then it was gone, and Shrike was upon the walls.

Even with his armour's baffler activated, the cacophony of the horde was almost deafening. Wave after wave of sonorous chanting rolled and boomed across the plain, intermingled with the screams of the wounded and the insane and punctuated by gunfire and explosions. Shrike had rarely faced such bedlam, the spectacle exceeding even the barbarous mobs of the orks of Skullkrak. But this was not simply a matter of volume, for the chants were devotions to the unnameable powers, the daemon-gods of the beyond that craved to consume the soul of mankind. For a man to worship such powers was for him to surrender his soul to eternal damnation, and the utmost blasphemy in the eyes of the God-Emperor and His devoted servants such as the Space Marines.

Shrike felt sickened by the taint of the warp made manifest by devotion and death. The horde must be turned, before all was lost.

With a great roar of sacrilegious filth, another wave of traitors surged upwards through the breach, hundreds of bodies packed together as grox for the slaughter. Cultists wailed and thrashed, brandishing wicked, hooked chains, while terror-stricken militia troopers fired their autoguns wildly. Despite the stout defence Sergeant Indis had mounted, Shrike knew that the breach was lost. The tide was unstoppable.

'Fall back by squads, pattern upsilon-twelve,' Shrike ordered bitterly.

Though he resented the necessity of ordering such a manoeuvre, Shrike's massively outnumbered force would be overwhelmed were it to remain at the wall. Indis and his men had fought valiantly, as hard as any of the Chapter's venerated heroes, but they had done all they could. There was a time and a place for a glorious last stand, but this was not it. In falling back and drawing the enemy into a close-quarters battle amongst the fortifications and redoubts, the Raven Guard would have a chance of robbing it of momentum, trading time for Kor'sarro's flank attack to take full effect.

In response to Shrike's order, the Tactical squads at the wall began moving back, each ten-man unit dividing into two, one providing fire support for the other as it withdrew to a new position before the roles were reversed. Then the heavy weapon-armed Devastator squads began their redeployment, covered by the Tactical squads as soon as they had established a new firebase amongst the smoking remnants of an inner line of fortifications.

Shrike could not join his men yet, for the first of the traitors were dragging themselves over the corpses of their fellows.

Shrike raised his talons and arcs of blue energy surged up and down their razor-edged blades. The blood that had dried to a crust along the edge of each talon burned off in a second, leaving the lethal weapons gleaming and eager to kill yet more of the traitors.

As the wave of traitors clambered to the summit of the breach, the ragged mass resolved itself into individual enemies. The first to come before Shrike was a rabid fanatic, the man's dirty robe that of a priest of the Imperial Creed. Bile rose in Shrike's throat as the man hurled himself forwards, screaming filth at the top of his voice. Shrike restrained himself from charging forwards to strike the traitor down lest he be consumed by the sheer mass of the horde. With a contemptuous strike of a talon Shrike sent the traitor's head spinning into the air, still mouthing blasphemous devotions as the body collapsed at Shrike's feet.

Then the first rank of the horde was over the summit and crashing forth like the sea at high tide. A fusillade of bolt pistol fire rang out from the squads behind and a dozen attackers went down in a welter of blood. Shrike had no need to turn in order to know that his Assault squads were there with him.

A second later the battle was joined. Shrike's very existence was boiled down to the controlled application of lethal force, every movement of every muscle in his body and every actuator in his power armour spelling the bloody death of a traitor. Bodies pressed in from all around, so close that he scarcely needed to raise a talon to inflict bloodshed. Shrike became a focussed, diamond-hard whirlwind of death, his talons lashing out in every direction. A dozen traitors were eviscerated within seconds, great coils of viscera spilling across the ground as bodies were scythed in two. Despite the intensity of the battle, Shrike was not reduced to some mindless, blood-crazed berserker as the warriors of more savage Chapters might be. He was instead the black-armoured angel of vengeance, the deliverer of the Emperor's justice, the shadow that brings death. Though his actions were those of a relentless killer, Shrike maintained icy control over his mind, body and soul. No drop of spilled blood touched the ground unless he willed it.

When Shrike finally judged that sufficient time had passed, and sufficient death had been unleashed, he ordered the withdrawal. 'Disengage!' he growled into the vox-net, and activated his jump pack.

As one, Captain Shrike and his warriors soared into the air. The horde, which had been bottled up where the Raven Guard had fought them, suddenly burst forwards, the foremost warriors stumbling and crashing to the ground. An instant later, the fallen were crushed beneath the pounding feet of those behind or incinerated by the jump packs' backwash. A thousand maddened cultists and traitor militia spilled onto the top of the walls and spread out.

Shrike landed atop a high fortification where his Devastator squads had redeployed.

'Hold...' he hissed as the Space Marines raised heavy weapons.

Still more and more of the enemy clambered up the breach and hauled themselves over the precipice and onto the wall itself. Relieved of the force that had held them at bay for so long, the impossible pressure of the horde spilled outwards until the walls all around were filled with frenzied, chanting enemies.

'Take them,' Shrike ordered.

The Devastators opened fire at the enemy now thronging the walls for a hundred metres either side of the breach. Following millennia-old combat doctrine, they opened up at the outer edges first, walking their fire along the wall so that first those who had pressed furthest from the breach were cut down, the fire working its way along towards the centre. Within seconds, hundreds of the enemy were torn to shreds by massed heavy bolter fire, blown apart by missiles or incinerated to ashes by seething plasma. Bodies exploded, leaving behind nothing more than a bloody mess. Others were reduced to constituent atoms leaving nothing behind at all. All of this happened so quickly that none on the wall had a chance to react, the entire battlement coming to resemble the floor of a slaughterhouse.

Despite the sheer bloody murder Shrike's force had inflicted on the enemy, to remain in position and continue to fire would merely result in the Devastators expending their precious ammunition while thousands more foes poured through the breach. It was so tempting to order a second fusillade, but Shrike resisted the urge, instead opening the vox-channel. 'Devastators,' he said, 'fall back as per orders.'

Shrike remained upon the redoubt, his Command squad beside him, as the Devastators limbered their heavy weapons and pulled back. In a moment, the last of them had descended the steps at the back of the fortification and were passing along the street beyond. Shrike's foes swarmed upwards, crushing the remains of their fellows to pulp beneath their boots. The wall had soon become so cramped that flailing bodies were sent tumbling to the ground below, yet still the press continued unabated.

And then, Shrike saw what drove the horde onwards. From amongst the multitude strode a towering figure in blue-green power armour adorned with blasphemous sigils. The bitter hatred of ten thousand years of war welled up inside Shrike, for the figure was an Alpha Legionnaire, one of the followers of Lord Voldorius. The warrior had once been a Space Marine, but he had bargained away his soul in the service of Chaos, betraying the most sacred of oaths. Shrike longed to gun his jump pack to full power and charge headlong at this enemy, but to do so would be suicide.

With a bitter curse, Shrike turned his back on the tide bursting through the breached wall and led his warriors from the redoubt. The battle would continue in the cramped environs of the defence installation.

'Once there was darkness and ignorance, and man, who was scattered to the stars, fell far from grace. Upon the winds of Chogoris came the Kagayaga, the Whisper in the Darkness. The Great Jaghatai Khan, Primarch of the White Scars, honoured be his name, united the tribes of Chogoris and dispelled the Kagayaga. But in truth, such things can never be slain. They merely flee for a time and lurk in the shadows of men's hearts. They await the moment of returning, when they will take their bitter vengeance upon the world...'

– Hidden Chronicles of the Chogoran Epics

CHAPTER 10

'Filthy as Thou Art'

MOONFANG SANG WITH the power crackling the length of its razor-sharp, monomolecular edge as Kor'sarro drove the blade into the guts of yet another of the berserker cultists. The traitor vomited a torrent of blood into the Space Marine's face and, for an instant, Kor'sarro could barely see.

Twisting the blade free of the slain cultist's body, Kor'sarro gunned the engine of his mount and turned the bike around. Coming to a halt, he wiped his eyes clear of the dripping viscera and looked about. The White Scars had cut a deep, ragged wound into the side of the traitorous horde, slaying scores in the moments after their wild charge had struck home. Now the horde was pressing back in as if to fill the vacuum the attack had created. It was imperative that the counterattack should not become bogged down or lose its momentum. The charge must continue, or the Raven Guard would be lost and the whole battle rendered a tragic waste of effort and life.

'Onwards!' Kor'sarro bellowed, his voice hoarse with the joy of righteous battle. At his cry, three dozen White Scars bikers converged on his position. Not a single power lance was dry of the blood of the foe, though many of the bearers had their own wounds too.

His command retinue at his side and the banner of the 3rd Company waving proudly in the wind, Kor'sarro sped forwards. The horde rushed in to the gap the White Scars had created and in a moment Kor'sarro was leading the charge of the entire company. As he rode he brought Moonfang down in lethal arcs, beheading or gutting traitors with every swing. Soon blood stained the dark ground and severed limbs were scattered all about. Numberless multitudes were pressing in all around and it seemed to Kor'sarro that some cultists deliberately threw themselves beneath the wheels of his mount in order to slow him while others allowed their bodies to be ground to paste beneath the treads of the Rhinos and Predators simply to clog their running gear. What madness had descended upon the servants of the Ruinous Powers was unknown, and unknowable to Kor'sarro.

There was no order to the horde, no command structure and no tactical logic to its actions. It ebbed and flowed, the only stable point the gargantuan super-heavy tank grinding through its midst. The cultists simply threw themselves forwards, chains and blades whirring.

So disordered were these fanatics that they inflicted more carnage amongst their own than they did amongst the Space Marines, but not once did they appear to be slowed, whoever it was that struck them down. Kor'sarro pressed on, forging against the relentless tide of the enemy. His arm rose and fell what felt like a thousand times, each blow from Moonfang striking down an enemy in a spray of blood. Rusted chains were thrown about him, flails struck his arms, bare fists pummelled uselessly at his power armour. One cultist even tried to unsaddle the Master of the Hunt, a tactic the steppes nomads of Chogoris were taught to counter from the first moment they took a war-mount. Kor'sarro bared his teeth and ripped the man's neck wide open, casting the corpse to the blood-soaked ground as he ploughed onwards.

Kor'sarro no longer faced the frenzied cultists, but enemies wearing the grey uniform of the planetary militia. Though better armed and equipped than the fanatics who had sold their souls to Chaos, the militia troopers were clearly not motivated by the same mindless zeal. The troopers fought with the desperation of those who knew they were being herded towards their own deaths. The Master of the Hunt showed these foes no more mercy than he had the cultists. If there was one thing a man should strive for, it was to choose the manner of his own death for himself, and never to allow another to do so for him. These fools had learned that lesson too late, and would now pay their price.

The militia troopers broke before the irresistible charge of the White Scars, surging to either side. For a moment Kor'sarro dared hope that the response might be more than a localised effect and that the entire horde might be routed. But the hope proved short-lived, for a new foe was revealed where the militia troopers had scattered.

A hundred metres in front of Kor'sarro stood a group of hulking creatures the like of which he had rarely seen. They were mutants, probably kin to the thing he had fought atop the tower on distant Cernis IV. Kor'sarro's savage heart filled with anger at the thought of such blasphemy against the pure form granted to man by the God-Emperor. There were a dozen of them, each as much as three metres tall, though they were stooped over so far their drooling faces appeared to be set into their chests. They wore no more than ragged hoods and stained loincloths, and their leathery skin looked as tough as carapace armour. Worst of all, the mutants were armed, but instead of hands, they sported power shears crudely grafted to their wrists. Feed cables snaked up their arms to generators stitched into the raw flesh of their backs. The claws were clearly large and powerful enough to cut even a Space Marine in two.

The leading White Scars bike squads formed themselves into an attack pattern unchanged through tens of thousands of years of use by the steppes nomads of Chogoris and by subsequent generations of Space Marines recruited from their tribes. The bikers spread out into a wide front, each warrior lowering his power lance and selecting his target. The White Scars let up a savage roar, invoking the spirit of their people and their warlike traditions, steeling their hearts for the moment when the charge would hit home and blood would be spilled.

As if issuing a response to the White Scars' war cry, the mutants leaned forwards as one and opened their mouths wide. The resulting roar was not that of any creature that had the right to walk beneath the light of any star in the Emperor's domains. Scores of nearby militia troopers fell to the ground as if propelled by a blast wave, hands clamped over ears to keep the hellish cry at bay even as they bled explosively from every orifice. As the roar continued the very air between the mutants and the charging White Scars became distorted and was shot by flecks of vile spittle. The sound struck the White Scars as if they had collided with a physical barrier. Warning runes flashed across Kor'sarro's control panel, and looking left and right he saw that the armour of several of his warriors was cracked and smoking in places.

'The primarch watches!' Kor'sarro bellowed, putting all of his strength into the effort to pierce the unnatural roar of the mutants. Though he could barely hear his own voice, his brothers heard and repeated the war cry, setting their lances for the final metres of the charge.

As he bore down on the line of mutants Kor'sarro selected his target. The mutant in front of him must surely have been the leader, for it was even larger than its fellows and its eyes were possessed of something approaching intelligence. Its muscles rippled across its body, visibly tensing as it braced itself to receive the charge. The mutant planted its feet wide, set its shoulders and lowered its vile head, its beady eyes staring out from beneath its ragged hood and meeting those of Kor'sarro.

In the last second of the charge Kor'sarro selected the point on the mutant's body he would attack, and Kor'sarro raised Moonfang high in preparation for a savage downward sweep that would cut his opponent in two.

And then, the charge struck thunderously home. Kor'sarro had no time to note the success or failure of those on either side, for in that moment his entire world was contained in the edge of his sword. Moonfang swept downwards, cutting the very air with the energies that surged along its monomolecular edge. The mutant was struck just above its left elbow, severing the arm and the deadly power shears grafted to it. The blade continued on its path, gauging a thin, yet deep line across his opponent's chest.

Only when Moonfang contacted the right side power shears was it checked. With a terrific burst of speed that belied its bulk, the mutant twisted. Before the Master of the Hunt could react, it grabbed the ancient relic weapon between the long blades of its remaining power shears. At that moment, the beast twisted its weapon and Kor'sarro was faced with the instantaneous choice of relinquishing his beloved power sword or of being pulled forwards and off-balance, perhaps even being dragged from his bike by the mutant's sheer brute force.

All of this had occurred in the blink of an eye and Kor'sarro's mind was made up just as quickly. As the mutant twisted its right arm backwards and up, Kor'sarro let go of his grip on Moonfang's hilt. He saw instantly that the mutant had expected him to cling on to his treasured weapon. As his opponent staggered backwards, Kor'sarro used his now free hand to draw his bolt pistol.

In the time it took him to draw the pistol, Kor'sarro's ancient and revered mount had sped past the mutant's right side. Bringing the bike to a skidding halt behind his opponent, Kor'sarro raised his bolt pistol at its back. The muscle there was so thick a single shot would not inflict much injury, but another target presented itself: the generator, which fed the mutant's power shears. Kor'sarro snapped off his shot before the beast could turn, trusting to the Emperor and the primarch that it would strike a vulnerable component.

The bolt-round struck the generator square on, penetrating its outer casing and exploding inside. A single round detonating within its flesh would have been little more than an annoyance to the rearing mutant, but the small explosion seemed to trigger a reaction within the generator. A second explosion sounded from within and the mutant staggered around to face its tormentor, Moonfang still gripped in its upraised power shears.

Kor'sarro drew a bead on the thing's head but before he could squeeze the trigger, Kor'sarro saw the mutant's eyes bulge wide before bursting outwards. A muffled detonation sounded from within its muscled torso and it toppled to the ground in front of the Master of Hunt. Pausing only to stoop and retrieve his power sword, Kor'sarro looked around to gauge the success of the charge.

Each of the mutants had been engaged by at least two White Scars, and the bikers' power lances had done their work well. Most of the vile monstrosities had been felled in the initial charge and those that were not had been slain by the chainswords and bolt pistols of those who followed directly behind. A warrior hacked away the head of one of the beasts. The trophy would sit well in the halls of the 3rd Company, marking a proud victory, so long as any survived to bear it back to the Chapter.

'Sons of Chogoris!' Kor'sarro cried proudly, his blood well and truly up following the brief but glorious charge. 'We ride!'

As the sergeants restored order amongst the squads, Kor'sarro looked across the plains towards the distant walls. There was no sign of the Raven Guard – Captain Shrike must have ordered their redeployment. The massive super-heavy tank ground towards the walls, its long-barrelled cannon smoking as it tracked back and forth like a hunter seeking prey. A large formation of blue-green-armoured Alpha Legionnaires marched across the battlefield. The warriors had seen him too and were moving to intercept the White Scars as they hacked into the vast horde of traitors.

At the head of the Alpha Legion was a figure Kor'sarro recognised instantly, even at a range of several hundred metres. It was Nullus, the champion-lieutenant of Voldorius who seemed to harbour an especial hatred towards the White Scars, above and beyond the bitter mutual enmity felt between any Space Marine Chapter and their erstwhile brothers of the Traitor Legions. The last time Kor'sarro had faced Nullus was on Cernis IV, but the two had done battle at least a dozen times before that. Memories came unbidden to Kor'sarro's mind as he gunned Moondrakkan's engine and powered forwards. The Lost Hope incident, the battles beneath the glass seas of Sagrifarri, the third siege of Ex Bellum. Thoughts of such battles brought with them memories of brothers long fallen, many at the hands of Nullus himself. Kor'sarro vowed to avenge every death Nullus had inflicted.

In between Kor'sarro and the object of his hatred were scores of Alpha Legionnaires, and the superheavy tank was turning on its mighty tracks to join them, uncaring of the dozens of cultists it crushed as it ploughed onwards. The traitors were every bit as experienced and deadly as the White Scars themselves, perhaps more so, for they had long ago sold their very souls to the Chaos Gods in exchange for power beyond mortal reckoning. Each was a puissant warrior who had fought across a thousand battlefields and more, and faced every enemy from the beasts of the intergalactic voids to the mightiest of the Emperor's champions. The Alpha Legion in particular were known amongst the traitor Space Marine Legions for their cunning and guile, and those who now faced Kor'sarro were no exception. The Alpha Legion deployed by squads, creating a defensive formation that would punish the charging White Scars severely as they passed through the mutually supporting fire zones. It was as if the Alpha Legion were well aware that Nullus would prove all too tempting a target for Kor'sarro and his brotherhood, and they deployed accordingly so as to take fearful advantage of that fact.

As consumed by hatred of the turncoat enemy as he was, Kor'sarro was not some mindless berserker to be so easily drawn into the Alpha Legion's trap. Speeding across the black plain, Kor'sarro turned and took in the disposition of his own force. Instantly he noted gaps in the line, the telltale indications that brothers had fallen. Forcing such concerns from his mind until the time for grieving after the battle, Kor'sarro judged his force able to overwhelm the Alpha Legion, so long as they could overcome the enemy's timely defensive deployment.

Kor'sarro opened the command channel. 'The herd brays.' He spoke the words of the White Scar's battle-cant, which the Alpha Legion would have no knowledge of should they intercept the transmission. 'The beast's horn, the plateaux at sunrise.'

A raft of acknowledgements indicated that the sergeants had received and understood the order. Hauling on Moondrakkan's handlebars, Kor'sarro brought his bike onto a new heading, his Command squad following close behind and the banner of the 3rd waving proudly above. How dearly he would love to add the name of Nullus to the tally of slain foes listed proudly on that banner.

The White Scars enacted Kor'sarro's orders, the bikers and Assault squads beginning a wide flanking manoeuvre that would bring them around to the Alpha Legion's right side. But that in itself would not be sufficient to overcome the enemy's deadly fire plan. As the fastest of the White Scars units swept onwards, the Rhino-borne Devastator squads raced forwards before disembarking a mere two hundred metres in front of their foe. Even before the heavy-weapons-armed Space Marines were in position, the Predator tanks were unleashing a fearsome hail of heavy bolter and autocannon fire upon the Alpha Legion, pinning them in position so they could not easily redeploy in the face of the faster unit's flanking manoeuvre.

Kor'sarro grinned savagely as the air was split by the deafening report of the demolisher cannon of the Vindicator siege tank, *Thunderheart*. Though based on a Rhino, the Vindicator was essentially a tracked siege gun. As the huge cannon fired, the extractor fans atop the vehicle screamed as they equalised the pressure inside the sealed cabin.

As the thunder of the cannon's discharge rolled across the plain the huge shell slammed into the Alpha Legion's positions. In an instant, an entire squad of traitor Space Marines was wiped out. Each of their number was a heretic and a criminal, responsible for the deaths of countless innocents, and in that instant their reigns were ended. Kor'sarro's heart pounded with the glory of battle, knowing that even if he died upon this black plain he would not have done so in vain.

The Alpha Legion's fire was now by necessity split between the flanking White Scars bikers and Assault squads, and the more heavily armed and immediate threat presented by the siege tank and Devastator squads in front of them. A searing lascannon blast lanced out towards the *Thunderheart* and the huge dozer blade mounted at its front sheared off in a shower of sparks. A second shot scored a fire-rimmed wound the length of the tank's flank. Before the Alpha Legion gunners could fire the kill-shot, the tank deployed a billowing smoke screen to throw off the aim of its foes at least long enough for Kor'sarro's charge to strike home.

A torrent of fire now went up from the White Scars Devastator squads. Such a punishing weight of shells, missiles and lascannon blasts was unleashed that the Alpha Legionnaires were forced to take cover amongst the wreckage of the battlefield. The undulating plain offered scant few natural features that might provide cover against the White Scars' fire and the traitors were forced to duck back behind the mounds of corpses scattering the entire area. The dead bodies of cultists and militia troopers danced as if in sick imitation of life as they were stitched by heavy bolter shells, which exploded within the already ruined bodies with hideous effect. Soon, the Alpha

Legionnaires were forced to redeploy, the squads falling back with experienced discipline, firing boltguns from the hip as they went.

Kor'sarro's flank attack hit home. Bikes roared and jump packs screamed as the White Scars descended upon their ancient, hated foes. Power lances glinting in the orange sunlight, a dozen Alpha Legionnaires were struck down in an instant. Moonfang flashed as Kor'sarro beheaded a Legionnaire who stepped in front of him. But an instant later he was thrown from Moondrakkan's saddle as a fusillade of boltgun fire smashed into his left side, unleashed from such short range that the impact was tremendous.

Kor'sarro rolled as he struck the ground, which was torn apart as more rounds were pumped into the space he had occupied an instant before. Using the momentum of his fall, Kor'sarro came up and turned towards his attackers. A dozen Alpha Legion warriors advanced on him, the grim details of their baroque helmets expressionless and their ornate, gold-chased boltguns raised. Kor'sarro saluted them with Moon-fang and unleashed a roaring challenge.

The Alpha Legionnaires slowed to a halt, intent upon gunning the White Scar down before he could bring his fearsome relic blade to bear.

'Come on!' Kor'sarro yelled in anger. 'Fight with the honour you once had!'

A dozen armoured fingers tightened on a dozen triggers.

The flashing steel of a power lance shot through the air and transfixed the foremost Alpha Legionnaire. As the traitor sank to his knees, Kor'sarro's Command squad appeared at his side, each warrior leaping from his saddle as his bike slewed to a halt, to stand beside their khan.

The traitors opened fire as they advanced, their bolt-guns spitting death as the air between the two groups became a storm of shells. A battle-brother beside Kor'sarro went down, his chest armour ripped open as a dozen bolt-rounds exploded deep within his chest. Another was struck by a missile fired by an Alpha Legion heavy weapons trooper, the projectile blowing the White Scar into a thousand chunks of smoking armour and burned flesh. A roar of anger went up from the White Scars, the deaths of their brothers merely serving to propel them forwards all the faster.

A second later both groups surged forwards as one and death was unleashed in a bloody melee. A traitor's chainsword came out of nowhere and cleaved a White Scar clean in two. Even as his broken body fell apart, the Space Marine shot his killer in the face at point-blank range, blowing the traitor's brains out through the back of his helmet. Another White Scar died as he was engulfed in searing flamer fire. His bare head was reduced to a black, smoking skull but he killed three more foes before he succumbed to his wounds.

Moonfang lashed out, once, twice, three times, and as many foes met their deaths by Kor'sarro's hand. And then it was over, and Kor'sarro was panting with exertion. He turned to honour his warriors, and saw that Brother Yeku, the banner bearer of the 3rd, was down on his knees. One arm was wrapped about his midriff while the other supported the weight of the honoured standard. 'Brother-captain...' Yeku said, his voice strained.

Kor'sarro rushed to the warrior's side, his heart filling with cold dread. Kneeling beside his friend, Kor'sarro activated the latches at his neck and lifted Yeku's helmet clear. Blood flecked the warrior's mouth and his skin was already pale and waxy.

'Kor'sarro,' Yeku coughed, fixing his stare on his captain. 'Please, do me this favour...'

With a titanic effort, Brother Yeku lifted the banner of the 3rd high. Even in his dying moment the honoured fabric did not touch the ground, which would have brought dishonour to the bearer and the entire company. Kor'sarro understood, and took the banner pole in his own hand, relieving Brother Yeku of its weight.

'Thank you, honoured khan,' Yeku sighed, before slumping forwards onto the black ground.

Kor'sarro knew that his friend was dead, and had died with the utmost honour. Though he had witnessed countless such deaths, Kor'sarro would ensure the name of Brother Yeku was entered into the sagas of the White Scars, for his death had been a good one as such things are counted amongst the wild sons of Chogoris.

'Khagus?' Kor'sarro addressed the company Apothecary who even now approached. The medic kneeled reverently beside the body of Brother Yeku and a moment later turned back towards the Master of the Hunt.

'He rides the cold steppes, my khan,' the Apothecary replied, making reference to the death-legends of the Chogoran steppes nomads.

'Then do what must be done.'

As Kor'sarro strode back towards Moondrakkan he heard the sound of the Apothecary's small las-scalpel cutting through the armour at the fallen Space Marine's neck. A moment later, the sound was replaced by that of a small buzzsaw cutting through flesh. The Apothecary was affording Brother Yeku the single honour all Space Marines aspired to after death. He was retrieving the artificial organs inside which were stored Yeku's genetic inheritance. Emperor willing, the organs would be returned to the Chapter and the genetic code locked within passed on to a new generation of White Scars.

In moments, the deed was done. Kor'sarro hauled Moondrakkan upright with one hand while holding the banner aloft with the other. He made a silent promise that, were he able, he would return for Yeku and those others who had fallen here, and bring their bodies home in the utmost honour.

But for now, the battle still raged all about. Nearby, individual squads of White Scars fought their Alpha Legion counterparts in a bitter close-quarters battle. As more of Kor'sarro's brotherhood piled into the battle the White Scars gained the edge. But the victory was proving a costly one, for already at least half a dozen white-armoured bodies were strewn across the black battleground. Beyond the White Scars' immediate vicinity, the battlefield still swarmed with traitors, despite the terrible death toll both the White Scars and the Raven Guard had inflicted. The super-heavy tank ground onwards, the earth shaking beneath its treads, but it dared not fire on the White Scars with the Alpha Legion so close. Space Marines were used to being out-numbered hundreds, even thousands to one. They were the scalpel that incised the diseased flesh from the bloated carcass, and they would prevail.

Drawing on decades of experience, Kor'sarro quickly identified the point of the battle upon which victory or defeat would turn. Not far from his posi-tion a dismounted bike squad fought valiantly to hold back an Alpha Legion counterthrust, but a num-ber of the warriors already bore grievous wounds and the remainder looked like being overrun within sec-onds. Should that squad be defeated, Kor'sarro judged, the entire line might buckle, and then he might never find and defeat the hated Nullus.

'Khagus, Temu, Kergis,' Kor'sarro addressed the three remaining warriors of his Command squad. 'Our brothers have need of our presence.'

Raising the banner of the 3rd high, Kor'sarro gunned Moondrakkan's engine and launched himself towards the foe, his brothers at his side. At the sight of the banner unfurled in the wind, the White Scars redoubled their efforts and the Alpha Legion appeared to flag in their own. A moment later, Kor'sarro was bearing down upon his enemy and in that moment he decided upon his course of action.

In a single movement, Kor'sarro leapt from Moondrakkan's saddle and crashed feet first into a mighty Alpha Legionnaire, a champion and second only to Nullus amongst this warband. The enemy went down under Kor'sarro's weight and with a savage cry upon his lips, Kor'sarro raised the banner high so that all on the battlefield could see. Then, he drove it downwards with such force that the end cracked open his enemy's ornate power armour and pinned him to the ground.

A great roar went up from every White Scar who had seen Kor'sarro's deed, but the champion was far from dead. The warrior raised his bolter and aimed it at Kor'sarro's face. Unable to dodge, all Kor'sarro could do was hold his head back as an entire magazine of bolt shells was unleashed at him. Rounds glanced from his armoured collar or exploded against his chest plate, white hot shrapnel lacerating his cheeks.

But the primarch was with Kor'sarro, for when the boltgun's ammunition feed clicked and the weapon fell silent, Kor'sarro was unhurt.

With a savage twist, Kor'sarro drove the banner pole through his enemy's chest, severing his spine and penetrating his armour's power pack. As Kor'sarro withdrew the pole, the body was consumed by the energies unleashed by the destruction of the generator, the armour glowing from within and sagging as it slowly melted.

Every head in the vicinity was turned towards him. White Scars looked on with fierce pride, while the Alpha Legion, the faces of most hidden by their baroque helmets, appeared to falter. Then, Kor'sarro saw one scarred face, twisted by malevolence and anger, looking straight at him. It was Nullus.

The two locked glances of sheer hatred for a moment before the spell was broken and the tides of battle surged forth and separated them once more. Kor'sarro bellowed his anger, but his savage cry was drowned out by a new sound, a mighty engine roaring above the raging battle. The ground beneath Kor'sarro's feet trembled violently and the Master of the Hunt saw the super-heavy tank he had seen from afar was closing on his position, its mighty gun lowered.

As the metal behemoth lumbered forwards the Alpha Legion squads began to disengage from the White Scars, parting one step at a time, their boltguns spitting a constant stream of fire to keep their foes at bay.

'Mount up!' Kor'sarro ordered, leaping to the saddle of Moondrakkan and throwing the banner of the 3rd Company to Brother Temu. The passing of the banner to a new bearer was a moment of great honour, but both men knew there was no time to mark the occasion. Kergis, Temu and Khagus mounted their own bikes and as one the four warriors gunned their engines to life.

'The mammoth bleeds a thousand deaths,' Kor'sarro said into the vox-net, describing in battle-cant the manner in which the White Scars would engage the mighty tank. Not even the *Thunderheart* or the heavy weapon-armed Devastator squads carried sufficient firepower to fell this mighty iron beast, but the sons of Chogoris had other ways of bringing down such prey.

The Tactical squads that had dismounted to fight the Alpha Legion were now able to mount their bikes and in moments were by Kor'sarro's side. The Assault squads screamed overhead, another thirty Space Marines adding their weight to the charge.

Bearing down upon the White Scars as they advanced, the *Ironsoul*'s turrets began to track individual targets. As one, the White Scars formation broke apart into individual squads, robbing the tank of a single victim. A secondary cannon mounted on the tank's bow opened fire, but the bike squad it had been tracking had predicted the attack and swerved right as the shell split the earth apart. A huge cloud of black dust and smoke rose high into the air and showered soil for dozens of metres all around. Then the multiple heavy bolters mounted at the tank's bow and upon sponsons along its flanks opened fire, filling the air with a storm of screaming metal.

The White Scars charged through the fusillade, heads down and shoulders set against the inevitable barrage. The armoured fairings of a dozen bikes were shattered under the weight of the fire but still the riders powered forwards. Heavy bolter shells exploded against the Space Marines' power armour, and while most rounds were stopped by the blessed suits, some were not. In the intense few seconds of the charge, the battle became a kaleidoscope of war. A Space Marine biker was caught by a shell in the joint between chest and upper arm, the shell burying itself in his flesh before exploding and sending his arm cartwheeling off behind. Still the warrior rode on, his armour flooding his system with palliative combat drugs. Another warrior suffered a glancing blow that shattered his helmet's optics. When the White Scar discarded his helmet his face was streaked with blood and one eye was a deep, gaping chasm, yet still the Space Marine continued the charge. Several others were not so fortunate, the weight of fire so great that not even their sanctified armour could withstand it. Their gene-seed and their bodies would be recovered later, Kor'sarro swore, once all this was over.

The *Ironsoul* let loose a blast from its main gun. The gunners had no clear target, for the White Scars were travelling so fast it was not difficult for them to avoid moving into the huge, long-barrelled gun's arc. Yet still the beast could wreak bloody havoc even with an unaimed shot. Fired from a range of only fifty metres, the shell passed over Kor'sarro and his companions before he even had had time to register the weapon had fired. The shell screamed a scant ten metres overhead, splitting the air apart with a deafening roar. Kor'sarro felt the air torn from his lungs and the pressure wave batter his body. Only his enhanced physiology kept his lungs from being ripped from his chest.

The shell screamed by Kor'sarro and passed straight through the dispersed formation of an airborne Assault squad. Several of its warriors were sent plummeting to the ground as their jump packs were robbed of air by the drastic pressure change. Moments later the shell struck the ground five hundred metres to the White Scars' rear. The explosion was so huge it scattered debris for hundreds of metres all about, but was too far distant to harm any of Kor'sarro's warriors. And then, the White Scars were upon their enemy.

As the bike squads converged upon the *Ironsoul*, they split apart to encircle the towering iron behemoth. At such close range the warriors were better able to avoid the traversing weapons, yet should any have been struck by the hurtling bolts they would surely have been blown to pieces. Drawing on tactics first developed many thousands of years before by the warriors of Chogoris for bringing down huge wild beasts, the White Scars undertook a series of bold charges, the bikers swooping in close to their prey and clamping melta bombs to its guns. Even as the riders slewed away from the still-moving behemoth, the grenades detonated, shattering the heavy bolters and other weapons spitting death from every quarter. Within minutes the *Ironsoul* was all but disarmed, with the exception of its turret-mounted main gun. Yet still it ground onwards, its sheer bulk deadly in itself.

The super-heavy tank would have to be halted, permanently. Gritting his teeth, the Master of the Hunt hunched over Moondrakkan's handlebars and brought his mount alongside the thundering behemoth.

Though the tank was not moving fast, Kor'sarro was painfully aware that one slip would see him ground to a red smear beneath its wide treads or caught up in its running gear and torn to shreds. Tensing every muscle in his body, Kor'sarro waited a heartbeat and then rose in his mount's saddle. Pushing off, he cleared the three metres between bike and tank and grabbed onto a handhold. As if the tank's commander had seen the manoeuvre, the behemoth swerved hard to its left and Kor'sarro was forced to hold on as his body was thrown violently into the air. Yet his grip was true and the super-dense fibre bundles of his power armour lent him the strength to drag himself up and onto the tank's upper deck.

The horde swarmed kilometres in every direction, the bulk pressing into the huge breach in the wall of the defence installation. The Alpha Legion traitors had fallen back, well clear of the rampaging tank, and Kor'sarro's battle-brothers were pushing on, piling the pressure on the enemy to force them back still further. Kor'sarro noted with a savage grin the number of blue-green-armoured bodies littering the ground about and knew that even if the battle should be lost, the toll on the traitors would have been fearful.

Kor'sarro's attentions were snapped back to the task at hand as a burst of fire stitched across the *Ironsoul's* armoured flank, missing him by scant centimetres. He saw that the Alpha Legion's heavy weapons squads were opening fire on him, reasoning that their weapons would not harm the huge war machine but could tear him to pieces.

Fighting for balance, Kor'sarro located the commander's hatch atop the main turret. He activated his mag-locked boots, which were more often used in zero-grav boarding actions. One heavy step at a time, he worked his way across the bucking deck and up the side of the turret.

More shots thundered in from the traitors' heavy weapons, sending up a riot of sparks and metal fragments which stung his cheeks. Ignoring the pain, Kor'sarro plucked a krak grenade from his belt and with a flick of his thumb set it to a three second delay and activated its mag-clamp. Kor'sarro thrust the grenade onto the hatch, and then ducked below the level of the turret.

The resulting explosion was near deafening, yet even before the smoke had cleared Kor'sarro had thrown himself back over the edge of the turret. Knowing that he would have no space inside the cramped innards of the super-heavy tank to bring Moonfang to bear, Kor'sarro bunched his gauntlets into fists and dropped down through the wrecked, smoking hatch, fully intent upon rending every traitor crewman inside limb from limb with his bare hands.

Kor'sarro dropped down through the opening, expecting his armoured boots to strike metal deck plating below. Instantly, he knew something was seriously wrong.

Instead of a metal deck beneath his feet, Kor'sarro felt his boots sinking into something soft and yielding. As his eyes adjusted to the gloom he looked around for the crew. As he turned, a blur shot across his vision and before he could react a coiling limb lined with a million tiny, rasping hooks had enveloped his entire head and was soon constricting around his windpipe.

Kor'sarro roared his denial, refusing to yield to such a death. His mouth was instantly stuffed full with a hundred questing pseudopods seeking the back of his throat and forcing their way down his gullet. Reacting entirely by instinct, Kor'sarro bit down hard upon the writhing tentacles, severing them as he ground the vile flesh between his teeth. Despite the severing, the pseudopods still thrashed within his mouth, but he could not spit them out for the larger coil which had birthed them was still wrapped tightly across his face.

With a titanic effort of will and strength Kor'sarro gripped the coil in both hands and dragged it clear of his head, spitting out the smaller tentacles the instant he was able. As vision returned he saw that the interior of the tank was not at all what it should have been. Instead of machinery and instrumentation, the *Iron-soul*'s innards were a mass of writhing intestinal coils.

Fighting back a wave of sheer revulsion, Kor'sarro glanced upwards and saw the hatchway above him sucking closed, the metal constricting like puckered flesh. All was plunged into darkness and a sickening groan assaulted Kor'sarro's ears. The sound came from all about, the interior quivering and shaking with its droning. Kor'sarro spat, seeking in vain to clear his mouth of the vile taste the pseudopods had left there. He knew then that he had but two choices. Be consumed in the gut of a daemon-machine, or plunge for its heart and rip it out from within.

Pulling first one foot, then the other from the sucking mass of flesh of the deck, Kor'sarro pressed forwards. No battle drill or tactical meditation could have prepared him for this moment, but Kor'sarro knew the beast inside the *Ironsoul* must have a heart, and if it had a heart it must have a weakness. Judging that such an organ must be located to the rear of the vehicle where otherwise its engine should have been, he turned in that direction and pressed forwards.

Instantly, Kor'sarro felt another writhing tentacle reach out to grasp him, this time about the waist. Though no natural light entered the interior and no artificial source illuminated it, Kor'sarro soon became aware of a lambent red glow emanating from within the very stuff of the coiling limb. That was enough for his genetically enhanced senses. He quickly got his bearings and located the thing that was assaulting him. Reaching for his belt with one hand, Kor'sarro used the other to hold off the coiling loop of flesh. He drew his combat knife and with a savage war cry hewed the flesh in two and the section that was attacking him dropped away with wild, thrashing convulsions.

Kor'sarro plunged onwards. A dozen more of the vile, questing limbs grew from the pulsating, fleshy interior of the tank. The Master of the Hunt felt the wild savagery of his ancestors welling up inside him, reason threatening to desert him as he threw himself forwards. Yet, some part of him was ever aware that to abandon himself to the berserk madness would be to unleash something terrible upon the galaxy. The

Storm Seers of the White Scars often spoke of the precipice the greatest of warriors sometimes walked along. Some warriors believed themselves strongest if they resisted the urge to look down, while the truly enlightened knew that to look and to face the truth is the mark of the true warrior.

As he forced himself forwards through walls of heaving flesh, Kor'sarro knew that he was well and truly walking that path right this moment, and to surrender to the berserker within would be to become one with the daemon beast itself.

Kor'sarro hacked all about him with his combat knife, the pulsing wet flesh pressing in against his face. His muscles strained against all-enclosing walls of meat. He bit down upon writhing pseudopods as they sought his throat. And then, with one last heave, he reached the core of the beast of muscle and iron.

In front of him, casting a hellish inner light, was the thundering heart of the daemon war machine.

Bellowing a prayer to Jaghatai Khan, the revered and lost primarch of the White Scars, Kor'sarro drove his combat knife deep into the flesh of the daemonic heart. As the blade penetrated, the heart exploded outwards in an eruption of blood and anger. Kor'sarro's world turned in an instant to utter, all-consuming blackness.

Kor'sarro's eyes snapped open and he was instantly awake. He was on his back looking up at the smoke-stained skies of Quintus.

For a moment, not a sound reached Kor'sarro's ears. Then a high-pitched whine arose, turning into a muted roar just audible at the edge of his hearing.

The savage cacophony of battle returned, a torrent of sound breaking upon Kor'sarro's senses.

Kor'sarro was battered but not badly wounded. He was lying on the black ground in front of the walls of the defence installation, and the earth was trembling with the footsteps of tens of thousands of combatants.

Turning his head at last, Kor'sarro's eyes focussed on a black form rearing before him, smoke belching from a dozen wounds. Pulling himself to his feet, Kor'sarro saw that the form was the blasted shell of the *Ironsoul*, the innards blown out at the instant he had destroyed the daemon within.

The act of killing the thing at the heart of the *Ironsoul* must also have thrown him clear, Kor'sarro realised as he shook his head in an attempt to clear it. Looking down at his white and red armour, Kor'sarro noted that he was covered in the viscous fluids exuded by the vile appendages he had fought to reach the daemon's heart, and his armour was black with burns and riven with dents.

Now standing fully upright, the Master of the Hunt saw another figure standing atop the smoking wreck of the *Ironsoul*.

'Spat you out, did she?' Kor'sarro recognised the leering, sibilant voice instantly. It was unmistakably that of Nullus, champion of Voldorius. Kor'sarro reached his right arm across his body and took hold of Moonfang's grip. 'I knew you would come,' Nullus continued. 'I knew you would not let me down, not after my little message on Cernis. What a tireless bloodhound you are...'

'Nullus,' said Kor'sarro, knowing then that Nullus had planted the four-starred shoulder pad so that the White Scars would follow his trail to Quintus. 'Let us end this. Now.'

Nullus's scar-traced visage twisted as he scowled down at Kor'sarro. 'Perhaps it is indeed time, White Scar,' Nullus replied. 'I have hated you for so long, I grow weary.'

Kor'sarro was struck by the depth of the bitterness the Alpha Legionnaire harboured for the White Scars. He had laid his trail, and the Master of the Hunt had followed, and all so that he could enact his bitter vendetta against the sons of Chogoris. The traitor's eyes were deep wells of pure hatred, windows behind which something other than human lurked.

Then it came to Kor'sarro. Perhaps it was his recent proximity to the daemonic heart of the *Ironsoul*, or maybe it was simple intuition. Perhaps he had known it all along.

'Daemon,' spat Kor'sarro, drawing Moonfang as he hauled himself up a ruined track and onto the rear deck of the wrecked tank.

Nullus stood upon the twisted and blackened foredeck, the smoking hole where the *Ironsoul*'s turret had been blown away separating him from Kor'sarro. The warrior gave a low, guttural chuckle, a sound that no living throat could have issued. 'You have no idea...' Nullus growled.

'And neither do I have any desire to know,' replied Kor'sarro. 'Your very existence condemns you.'

'You really are an arrogant little runt,' Nullus sneered, his black eyes mocking. 'So typical of your kind.'

'Speak not of my people,' spat Kor'sarro. 'Even the least of them is above you and your kind.'

'If only that were so,' said Nullus. 'But I have seen your people, more times than you can imagine. I know them well. Better than you, perhaps.'

Heed not the words of the daemon, Kor'sarro told himself, reciting the teachings of old. Do not allow yourself to become entrapped in his web of deceit. 'Enough!' Kor'sarro shouted.

'Your petty existence may well end, hunter,' Nullus crowed. 'Mine cannot. I am the whisper upon the night wind that your people call "djinnu". I am the stealer of maidenhead the priestesses call the "ghall qan". I am the taint of disease and the dry riverbed at summer's height. I am all of these things, and many more.'

At Nullus's words, ancient fears not felt since long before his ascension to the White Scars stirred unbidden in Kor'sarro's soul. The Alpha Legionnaire was invoking the malevolent spirits of the Chogoran steppes, the beings the tribal shamans spoke of only under the full light of the midday sun. Were they to do so by night they might be dragged screaming into the shadows.

'You are naught but a liar,' Kor'sarro replied, raising Moonfang before him and activating the sacred weapon's power field. 'You speak plundered words and expect me to quake in fear at your false knowledge of my people.

'I know thee,' Kor'sarro spoke the opening words of the rite of exorcism, 'filthy as thou art.'

Nullus hissed, his scar-laced features twisting into a hideous mask of anger and bitterness. He brought his black-bladed halberd across his body and whispered profane words of power that Kor'sarro could barely hear, but recoiled from in disgust, to his blade.

The smoking chasm where the *Ironsoul's* turret had once been yawned between the two combatants. Kor'sarro looked down at the hole, and knew that it was too wide for him to leap easily. He would have to work his way around its perilous edge to engage his enemy.

Nullus leapt high into the air, propelled by something other than mortal strength. The move took Kor'sarro entirely by surprise.

Kor'sarro barely had time to raise Moonfang to parry the inevitable downward blow. But Nullus powered through the air to land directly behind the White Scar.

It was all Kor'sarro could do to raise his blade over his shoulder, utilising by raw instinct a parry used by the steppes nomads of Chogoris when two mounted warriors pass one another at speed, each swinging at the other's back. Kor'sarro made the parry blind, but instantly felt the jarring impact as Nullus's weapon struck his own. Before Nullus could strike again, Kor'sarro twisted his body around and at the same instant leapt backwards, passing over the edge of the smoking hole and landing three metres away at its very lip.

Breathing hard, Kor'sarro raised his sacred blade. The weapon's power field stuttered, as if part of it had been stolen by his opponent's sorcerous blade, then flashed back to life. The otherwise flawless edge was notched by Nullus's strike. He took a step backwards, seeking to gain space to manoeuvre, one foot coming perilously close to the hole's edge.

Nullus pressed forwards, his halberd lunging towards Kor'sarro's left shoulder. The strike was easily turned, but Kor'sarro found himself forced backwards still further while Nullus came on.

'Not so sure now, are you, spawn of the cold steppes,' Nullus leered.

Kor'sarro knew well that Nullus sought to anger him in order to gain further advantage. His pride and honour demanded he answer the daemon's jibes, but he forced such notions to the back of his mind as he sought an advantage of his own.

'No?' Nullus crowed. 'You have no proud boast, Scarred One?'

As his opponent pressed forwards again, his black-bladed halberd held ready to strike at any moment, it occurred to Kor'sarro that he might find some advantage in Nullus's tirade. 'What boast would you have me make?' said Kor'sarro.

Nullus chuckled. 'Oh, I don't know,' he answered. 'What of the deeds of your beloved primarch?'

Forcing himself to calm as he allowed his enemy to berate him, Kor'sarro took the brief opportunity to gauge the progress of the larger battle. The traitor horde still surged all around, the White Scars driving a wedge into them. The banner of 3rd Company waved proudly nearby. The Alpha Legion were advancing upon his brethren and above it all, smoke stained the sky and gunfire stitched the air. Explosions and screams rose on the wind, mingled with the wild outpourings of the cultists and the mournful cries of the traitor militia.

All of this Kor'sarro discerned in but an instant, but there was nothing he could do to influence the strategy of his army. His cold eyes snapped back to his opponent. But in that instant, Nullus had raised his weapon and was making another lunge. There was no time to move, only to bring Moonfang up for another parry. The black halberd struck the base of Moonfang's blade, and the two combatants matched their strength against one another, before pushing apart and stepping backwards. The blade's power field flickered again, and Kor'sarro offered up a silent prayer that its blessed generator might withstand the halberd's fell sorcery.

In that brief moment of contact, Kor'sarro had gained some measure of Nullus's unnatural strength. The Master of the Hunt had pitted himself against every foe the universe had thrown at him, from tyranid carnifexes to cthellian ursids. The raw power behind that black halberd was as strong as any he had faced.

'Where is your primarch now?' Nullus pressed on, once more seeking to force a mistimed lunge or vengeful strike from Kor'sarro.

'The blessed Great Khan hunts,' Kor'sarro spat, seeking in turn to draw some misjudged response from Nullus. 'He hunts the likes of you.'

Nullus advanced around the rim of the smoking hole in the top of the wrecked *Ironsoul*, Kor'sarro giving ground before him, if unwillingly. The proud banner of the 3rd came into view again, far closer this time. 'How do you know he lives at all?' Nullus sneered. 'Perhaps he just hates that stinking mire you call a home world as much as I did.'

Nullus was turning his tirade back to the subject of the White Scars' home world of Chogoris. He had claimed to be the whisper in the night, a spirit feared by many tribes, but vanished from Chogoris since before Jaghatai Khan had united the nations. The words of the Storm Seers came once more to his mind…

…and then Nullus lunged forwards again, a mighty two-handed blow coming from nowhere. Kor'sarro dived aside as the black blade arced past. As it closed, the halberd emitted a piercing scream, the sound of a caged predator giving voice to a thousand years of bitterness and torment. The tip of the halberd scored a jagged line across his left shoulder plate, and tore his flowing cloak in two. Power bled from his armour's systems, sucked into the halberd's blade, and Kor'sarro's movements became sluggish as his actuators whined. Kor'sarro rolled across the wreck's upper deck, pulling himself to his feet upon a buckled and blackened grille that groaned in protest at his weight.

Nullus came on, the halberd scything, its shrill scream growing ever louder. His face was a twisted mass of scar tissue, forming into new and vile configurations as his expressions shifted. Kor'sarro fought with every ounce of his warrior skill and ferocity to fend off the champion of Voldorius, but with each blow, the Master of the Hunt was being pushed back towards the edge.

'He thought he could beat me too,' Nullus sneered. When Kor'sarro gave no reply other than a savage and unanticipated counterattack, he continued. 'He thought he had banished the whisper in the dark, the voices in the night, but he was wrong...'

And then it came to Kor'sarro. The tales the Storm Seers told the neophytes. Some believed them simple tales, but Kor'sarro saw now they were anything but myth. 'I know thee...' he said, a new conviction entering his voice.

'Yes,' Nullus replied. 'We've already done that part.'

'Kagayaga,' Kor'sarro spat, stepping backwards to the very edge of the deck.

Nullus stopped dead in his tracks as Kor'sarro spoke the name. It was true, then. The spirit of the dread night, the daemon-thing which Chapter legend stated the Primarch Jaghatai Khan had banished over ten thousand years ago, was real, and standing before him. Perhaps this body, armoured in the mantle of the Alpha Legion, was not Kagayaga, but the thing within it, the blackness behind those eyes, most certainly was, of that he was now sure.

'So,' Nullus sneered, his scarred face split into a wide, leering grin. 'You do know me, after all.'

At that instant, the banner of the 3rd Company rose fully into view directly behind Nullus. A moment later its bearer, Brother Temu, hauled himself onto the deck. Beside Temu was the newly appointed company champion, Brother Kergis.

'As you once were banished from Chogoris,' Kor'sarro called aloud, 'so you are now banished from Quintus!'

Nullus began to form a mocking response, but the air was split by the sharp report of a bolt pistol round before the words could come forth. Brother Kergis's pistol sent a bolt-round into the back of Nullus's head, the round shattering his skull and penetrating deep into his brain. An instant later, the mass-reactive shell detonated.

But Nullus was no ordinary man to be slain so easily. As the shell exploded, the rent flesh of Nullus's vile face resisted, even though it appeared to stretch and distort. Kor'sarro knew then that the champion of Voldorius was exerting every shred of his power in the effort of reknitting his form, so that he might fight on.

Kor'sarro reached for his belt and drew his bolt pistol. As his strength returned and his armour recovered from the energy drain Nullus's daemon-blade had inflicted, he raised his arm to draw a bead on the other's grossly distorted head.

'For Jhogai,' said Kor'sarro.

Kor'sarro fired and Nullus could keep his mortal form intact no longer. With a shower of gore, the scarred head came apart, showering all three White Scars with oozing grey matter. At the last, the body of the champion of Voldorius fell to its knees before the champion of Kor'sarro, and then pitched sideways into the smoking hole atop the ruined *Ironsoul*.

'Filthy as thou art,' Kor'sarro completed the line of the rite of exorcism, spitting into the hole the body had toppled into.

WITH THE DEATH of Nullus, the Alpha Legionnaires began to fall back towards the walls of Mankarra. The White Scars pressed their attacks, bike squadrons and Assault squads taking a fearsome toll on their ancient, bitter enemies as they disengaged. When it became clear that the Alpha Legion were a spent force, Kor'sarro ordered his squads to consolidate, for they had become spread out as each pursued its own individual battle against its foes.

The Master of the Hunt stood atop the smoking wreckage of the *Ironsoul* and ordered the banner of the 3rd Company brought to his side. Banks of black smoke drifted across the battlefield, but as if the Emperor Himself had willed it, they parted as the banner was raised. In that moment, every warrior on the battlefield saw the banner as it waved gloriously from its vantage point. Standing beside it was Kor'sarro, Khan of the 3rd Company, his white armour streaked with dirt and gore and his lava-wolf pelt cloak ragged and torn as it fluttered in the wind behind him. His face bled from a thousand microscopic cuts and his armour was rent and cracked in a dozen places.

Yet, Kor'sarro appeared to his brotherhood as glorious as any of the Chapter's most revered heroes. He stood straight and proud, as had those greatest of men who had walked at the side of the primarch himself. The White Scars rallied to Kor'sarro and the banner beside him. Within minutes, the Chaplains and Storm Seers that had accompanied the strike force stood upon the wrecked tank beside their khan, and almost a hundred battle-brothers gathered all about.

To the enemy, the sight of the banner being raised high above the battlefield was the signal of their own defeat. Kor'sarro appeared to the traitorous horde a being of terrible vengeance sent to bring the Emperor's justice upon them all. Worse still, word of the death of Nullus had spread quickly through the horde. None needed to exaggerate the story with the retelling. The sight of the Alpha Legion breaking off from the fight and falling back on the walls of Mankarra confirmed the worst of their fears. The horde's erstwhile tormentors had abandoned it entirely to the vengeance of the White Scars.

As one, a thousand cultists fell on their knees and a great wailing rose across the battlefield. The White Scars would never know if that dire sound represented a plea for forgiveness or a bemoaning of fate. Even as the White Scars looked on with horror, the assembled cultists began to scourge themselves with chains, hooks, spikes and any other implement that came to hand including the severed limbs of their fellows. The White Scars turned their faces from the vile spectacle, knowing that the wretches were beyond even the mercy of the Emperor of Mankind.

While the cultists surrendered themselves to whatever fate awaited them, the greater number of the horde, the pressed militias, were gripped by sheer, unadulterated terror. These men and women knew they had committed the sin of treachery, for death at the hands of the Alpha Legion would have been an honourable end compared to the fate they had submitted to by allowing themselves to be enslaved.

With the sight of the White Scars' banner waving victorious above the black plain, ten thousand traitor militia dropped their weapons and fled for the imagined safety of the walls of Mankarra. As the White Scars looked on in disgust, the fear surged through the horde, passing even to the breach in the wall of defence installation South Nine. In an instant, the tide was turned. The hordes swarming through the breach stalled, a great roar of terror rising to mingle with the wailing of the cultists. Then the direction of movement reversed, and the swarm that had been assaulting the breach was surging away from it.

Inside the walls, Captain Kayvaan Shrike found himself facing not an unstoppable tide of enemies but a rapidly receding torrent of fleeing, panic-stricken traitors. His first instinct was to order his squads to open fire on the enemy as they fled, to gun the foe down

without mercy. But Shrike's force had run so dangerously low on ammunition that even when magazines
were shared out each warrior had only a single clip
remaining. Reluctantly, Shrike ordered his squads to
follow up their routing foe, to ensure none remained,
but to allow them to flee unmolested.

Back on the plain, the last of the horde was surging
around the wreck of the *Ironsoul* as a raging torrent
breaks around a rock. The White Scars too allowed
the traitors to flee. Thunderhawks were inbound to
extract the squads, rearm them and move them
rapidly to their next objective – the walls of Mankarra
itself. The strike force's armoured vehicles, the Vindicator siege tank known as *Thunderheart* at their head,
were already formed into a spearhead which was
arrowing towards the gates of the capital city.

As the Space Marines boarded gunships and Rhinos, the skies above the plain were split by a
deafening thunderbolt. A moment later, the last of
the battle-brothers embarking in their transports saw
what at first appeared to be a storm of meteors falling
from the skies high above.

The Ninth Eye, the flagship of Lord Voldorius, had
moved into orbit and on its master's order unleashed
a fearsome orbit-to-surface bombardment. Warheads
the size of tanks streaked from the skies upon black
contrails. The first struck the wreckage of the *Ironsoul*,
atomising the twisted ruin and blasting a crater ten
metres deep and fifty across. But the White Scars were
already gone, speeding away in their armoured transports.

The next warhead plunged into the breach in the wall of South Nine, blasting the installation's fortifications wide apart. The Raven Guard too were gone, their next objective already in their sights.

The remainder of the warheads ploughed into the horde seething across the corpse-littered plain towards the walls of Mankarra. In his anger and rage Lord Voldorius had ordered his own slave-troops and deluded followers slaughtered, their deaths serving to quench his vengeance and perhaps bring the favour of the Ruinous Powers of the warp. Dozens of warheads slammed from the skies to obliterate the traitorous horde. So great was the destruction that the walls of Mankarra themselves were shaken and the speeding gunships bucked violently as blast wave after blast wave overtook them. The paintwork of the White Scars' armoured vehicles blistered and blackened as Rhinos, Predators and the *Thunderheart* sped away, hatches sealed tight against the air that burned all around.

The first of the militia troopers to have fled the battlefield were following close behind the retreating Alpha Legion, moaning in terror as the last of the green-blue-armoured warriors passed through the mighty gates of Mankarra and closed them on the horde.

The entire plain was scoured of life. Though the horde of Voldorius had been turned and his champion slain, the warp resounded to the daemon prince's offering of ten thousand souls. The assault on South Nine was ended, but as the Space Marines closed on Mankarra, they knew that the true battle was yet to be fought.

CHAPTER 11

The Beginning of the End

MALYA STOOD IN front of the command chamber's huge viewing screen, staring up in sheer disbelief. As explosions blossomed across the screen, their thunderous report sounded from beyond the metres-thick walls of the militia's strategium complex. Lumen-bulbs flickered and the screen went blank, before flashing to life again as small pieces of debris fell from the ceiling to scatter all about.

As the last of the explosions faded, an ominous silence descended upon the chamber. Even the ever-present chatter of the vox-links ceased as every one of the three dozen and more officers in the command chamber stared at the screen.

The full enormity of what she had just witnessed came crashing down upon Malya. When the cultists had fallen at the sight of the Space Marines' banner, she had felt vindication, for these men and women were the very lowest of their kind and not fit in her mind to call Quintus their home. But when the militias had turned and fled, Malya had known utter despair. No matter the circumstances of their servitude, these were her people. The militias were innocent men and women pressed into the service of a despicable tyrant, their only alternative death.

The thousands of militia had turned and stampeded back towards the walls of Mankarra and in their desperation many troopers had been reduced to animals. Hundreds stumbled and were crushed beneath the feet of their comrades. And then, Voldorius had issued the order to *The Ninth Eye* in orbit overhead, and the orbital bombardment had commenced.

As the bombs had fallen in the midst of the fleeing horde, Malya had been wrenched back to the atrocity in the grand square. The crushed bodies still lay where they had died as a grim warning against further rebellion, and it was said that the vilest of the daemon's servants haunted the corpse-strewn centre of the city. It was as if Voldorius was taunting her, making her witness over and over again the terrible deeds he could enact upon her people. Yet still she refused to submit to the total, all-encompassing horror that gibbered in the darkest recesses of her soul. She drew on deeper and deeper reserves of faith, long hidden and built up through a lifetime of devotion and worship. Perhaps others did not heed the words the preachers spoke, but she did, every one of them. Perhaps it was her faith that made Voldorius toy with her so, the daemon prince deriving some unholy sport from the spectacle of one of the faithful being forced to endure such unceasing blasphemies.

At length, the silence was broken as Lord Voldorius spoke. 'Even in their death do they serve.'

None dared look towards their vile master, three dozen pairs of eyes turning downwards towards the floor. Some feigned deference and humility; others were too petrified to do so and collapsed to their knees. Malya stood firm, though a single tear ran slowly down her cheek.

At that moment, Malya's mind was set. She knew the Space Marines needed to know about the prisoner, but she also knew that the Space Marines must soon assault the city walls. She could help. As equerry, she had knowledge of which sections had been fortified and which were still to be reinforced. She would transmit a signal and inform the Space Marines which gate would fall the quickest, even should it cost her life. She just needed a distraction...

'Those who recruited the militias shall step forwards,' Lord Voldorius growled, his low voice sounding like tectonic plates grinding inexorably together.

At first, none responded. Then Voldorius brought himself to his full height and several more of the staff officers collapsed to their knees. Five high commanders stepped forwards.

Lord Colonel Morkis was not amongst them.

All eyes turned to the high commanders, while Voldorius's own gaze was sweeping the faces of each of the men who had stepped before him. Glancing down to a command terminal by her side, Malya decided that the time to act was now, for she might never have another opportunity. Moving only her right hand, she invoked the rite of communion and awoke the spirit of the vox-terminal. Malya forced her mind to calm in order to recall the transmission code she had used what seemed like months before to contact the Space Marines. She had buried the code deep within her mind, lest it be torn from her under duress and condemn even more innocents to death or torture. Yet, she had never allowed herself to forget the code entirely, some small part of her clinging to the hope that she might have cause to use it one more time. The code sprang instantly to her mind, and Malya entered it into the terminal and began to compose in her mind the message she must send.

Meanwhile, Lord Voldorius was looming down upon the officers. 'Which of you shall bear the responsibility for this?'

Again, none dared answer.

'I have promised such power,' Voldorius grated. 'And yet you have failed me at this first test.'

When still none of the officers responded, Voldorius moved his vast, armoured bulk to the end of the line and looked down upon the first officer. He was the official in charge of the muster of the city's militia in times of emergency. He stood erect, his ornate, gold-trimmed uniform bedecked with medals and symbols of rank. His white-bearded face was set in a grim mask, his eyes fixed with steely determination.

'Lord Kline,' Voldorius growled. 'The enemy closes upon the gates and you are responsible for the muster. Where is it?'

The muster was scattered to ashes across the black plains beyond the city walls. Clearly, Voldorius sought to intimidate the man. When a minute had crawled past and no response was given, Voldorius turned to face the next man along, General Orson, the official whose responsibility was to formulate doctrine and instil it in the militias.

'You,' said Voldorius, his bestial, cragged face closing on General Orson's. The man wore the same uniform as Kline and his chest was decorated with even more medals. Orson's face was dominated by a bushy moustache and his eyes were set dead ahead. Yet a dark stain spreading down one leg spoke of the turmoil seething within the man's soul at the proximity of the daemon prince. So few were able to withstand the daemon's presence at all. It must only have been because these men had promised themselves to his service that they were able to withstand the sheer malevolence he radiated, and clearly, that was now breaking down.

Voldorius snorted in disgust, the blast of foul air causing General Orson's medals to clink, then moved along the line to the city's Quartermaster General.

'Ackenvol,' Voldorius continued. 'Did you not have all that your heart desired? Did the forges not manufacture everything you demanded, and more?'

Quartermaster General Ackenvol was a stout man, and taller by far than any of his peers. Perhaps alone amongst the planetary guard's high command, Ackenvol had earned the dozens of medals he wore, making him something of a totem amongst the militia armies. He had served in the Imperial Guard, rising from lowly rank to high office throughout the course of a distinguished career, before being posted to Quintus to oversee the Officio Munitorum's arms procurement mission there.

'They did,' Ackenvol responded. 'But it was not enough.'

Malya decided upon the message she must transmit, but she could not risk entering it yet, for the chamber had fallen to such utter silence that even the gentlest of keystrokes would ring out like thunder.

Then, the silence was broken as Voldorius emitted a low, baleful rumble from deep within his armoured chest. The sound was one of animal fury, barely contained, and many in the chamber visibly faltered as it struck their ears. Violent retribution seemed to hang frozen in the air, but to Malya's surprise it did not descend upon the Quartermaster General. Instead, Voldorius moved further along the line, to stand before Lord Colonel Lannus.

'You promised such glories in my name,' said Voldorius as he leaned in to stand over the thin, ascetic officer. 'You claimed you would lay a million skulls before my throne. You said you would turn the plains into oceans of blood.'

'Where are your boasts now, lord colonel?' asked Voldorius, his voice so low its bass rumble was felt more than heard.

Lannus was visibly shaken, sweat pouring from his brow and his face drained of colour. Yet somehow, the lord colonel maintained his dignity even in the face of the daemon prince's obvious displeasure.

Voldorius lingered a moment longer, before passing to the last of the officers that had dared step before him.

'Elenritch,' Voldorius addressed the lord colonel. 'Your sin has caused this.'

Elenritch glanced sidelong towards the huge screen and the scene of utter devastation it relayed. Slowly, he shook his shaven head, the eldritch tattoos etched across his temples seeming to writhe with the movement.

'You gainsay my word, mortal?' Voldorius said, bringing himself to his full height.

'I...' the lord colonel said, his control remarkable given the circumstances. 'I cannot take sole blame, my lord.'

'That much is true,' the daemon prince replied. 'But the *Ironsoul* was your responsibility.'

'I could not have...' Elenritch started.

'The seals were clearly insufficient!' Voldorius bellowed, causing the officers before him and everyone in the command chamber to cringe before the force of his voice. 'All were insufficient!'

Though Malya's mind reeled before the psychic backwash of the daemon's wrath, she forced herself to key her message into the terminal while she had the chance. She would not have much time to compose a detailed communication, so she committed only the bare facts to her transmission. The tertiary gate in wall section twelve, minimal fortification…

Risking the extra few seconds it would take to input, Malya confirmed that Voldorius had the prisoner the Space Marines had demanded to know of, and described his location in the holding cells adjacent to the Cathedral of the Emperor's Wisdom.

Malya was interrupted as Voldorius growled, 'Morkis.'

The chamber fell to shocking silence once more, the only sound that of the banks of cogitators churning in the background. Malya looked around to see that all heads were turned towards Lord Colonel Morkis. A cold dread settled across the assembled staff.

'My lord?' Morkis replied.

'Why,' Voldorius rumbled, 'do you not take your place amongst these fools?'

'I was not…' Morkis began, glancing across at Malya then stammering to a halt. Clearly, there was no answer he could give that would exonerate any of them.

'Who then?' Voldorius replied, his voice low and dangerous.

'My lord?' said Morkis.

'Who then,' Voldorius growled, 'is responsible?'

'My lord,' Morkis replied, casting a hateful stare at Malya. 'I do not…'

'Name he who is responsible!' Voldorius roared. Several of the staff officers looking on collapsed to the floor before the torrent of rage that assailed all in the chamber. Malya decided that the message she had composed would have to be sufficient, for she might not have any longer to finish it. It remained only for her to direct the machine-spirit to ready the message for transmission.

Now Lord Colonel Morkis brought himself to his full height, his eyes narrowing and his face taking on a hateful scowl. As Voldorius waited, Morkis scanned the line of officers drawn up before their master.

Quartermaster General Ackenvol took a step forwards, before General Orson's hand grabbed his elbow and restrained him with a sharp gesture. 'Filth!' Ackenvol spat at Morkis. 'Nothing but a highborn dilettante with delusions of glory!'

Morkis sneered at Malya, then turned his attentions fully towards the Quartermaster General. Morkis stepped forwards, falteringly at first but, when Voldorius made no reply, with more purpose. Then he stood before Ackenvol, who scowled down at the lord colonel with utter contempt writ large across his face.

'I name Quartermaster General Ackenvol,' Morkis announced to the entire chamber. 'He is responsible.'

'Then kill him.' Voldorius said.

'What?' Lord Colonel Morkis uttered.

'Kill him,' Voldorius repeated. 'Or die in his place.'

Malya could barely tear her eyes away from the scene unfolding before her, but she forced herself to glance furtively down at the vox-terminal. The machine was processing her message, applying the blessed ciphers and readying it for transmission. Part of her could scarcely believe that with the Space Marines closing on the walls of Mankarra, Voldorius would divert his attentions in such a manner. Another part of her accepted it as entirely typical of the fell being's heinous demeanour. She was thankful she could not comprehend the ways of the daemon prince. It confirmed to her that she was still human, and an innocent.

In the centre of the chamber Lord Colonel Morkis was drawing an ornate, gold-chased laspistol from a holster at his belt. Quartermaster General Ackenvol's eyes never left the face of the lord colonel, even as the weapon was raised to point directly at his chest. The Quartermaster General might have been a traitor, but he faced death if not with honour then with nobility at least.

'Morkis,' interjected Lannus as Morkis's finger tightened on the trigger of his pistol. 'You needn't–'

Morkis jerked the laspistol towards Lannus and a searing white blast spat out. The shot caught the other man in the side of the head, vaporising half of his skull in an instant.

Lannus's body crashed backwards into a group of staff officers, who stumbled away from it in disgust as blood and gore splattered their uniforms.

Morkis was warming to his new role as Voldorius's executioner, a wicked sneer creasing his sly face. The sound of Voldorius's low, grating chuckle filled the command chamber.

Even before Lannus's body had hit the floor, Morkis had snapped the laspistol back to bear on the Quartermaster General. Ackenvol had not moved. He was too proud to squirm before the vengeful Morkis.

314

'Would not that weapon be put to better use blowing your own sorry excuse for a brain to atoms?' said the Quartermaster General.

The laspistol quivered in Morkis's hand and his face twisted into an animalistic sneer. 'My dear Quartermaster General,' said Morkis. 'I'm going to save you...'

The laspistol swung rapidly to the left and a second blast filled the chamber. The shot took Lord Colonel Elenritch square in the chest, punching a hole straight through his torso. The officer stood for a moment, his face displaying an expression not of shock, but of outrage. Then the lord colonel crumpled to a heap upon the chamber floor and the laspistol swung around to point at Lord Kline, the Marshal-in-Chief of the Muster.

'...until last,' Morkis finished, his eyes now shining with cold madness.

Malya dared risk a glance at the vox-terminal, and saw with relief that the machine-spirit had completed its ministrations and was ready to transmit her message. She would have to judge the moment of transmission carefully, lest she be discovered at the very last.

Kline stood as erect as Ackenvol, prepared to face his death and stoically refusing to cower before his executioner. General Orson however, made a sudden dash towards one of the chamber portals. He was dead, a smoking hole in his back, before he had gone three steps.

Still Malya's finger hovered over the transmission rune.

'If Ackenvol is last,' Morkis sneered at Lord Kline, 'then you must be next, my lord marshal.'

'Whichever of us you kill,' said Ackenvol, 'the other shall have vengeance.'

'Oh really?' sneered Morkis, levelling his weapon at the Quartermaster General's head. 'Then it'll have to be you!'

Morkis fired, and Ackenvol's head snapped backwards, a searing hole burned between his eyes. At the very same instant, Lord Kline threw himself forwards, closing the gap before Morkis could bring his pistol to bear on him. Malya saw her chance and depressed the transmission rune, instructing the vox-terminal to send her message.

Kline barrelled into Lord Colonel Morkis, bellowing an incoherent roar of anger and vengeance. The two men crashed to the floor and as one the assembled staff officers sprang backwards. The daemon prince had turned his back on the spectacle and was making for the exit as a shot rang out in the centre of the command chamber. Lord Kline was astride Morkis, his hands gripped around the other's throat. Lord Colonel Morkis, Malya saw with not a little pleasure, had been throttled to death. But Morkis had unleashed a final blast of his laspistol, blowing Kline's stomach away, its contents spilling across the lord colonel even as he died.

Then, the body of Lord Kline collapsed atop that of Lord Colonel Morkis. Three dozen terrified faces turned towards Lord Voldorius as he halted at the chamber door and turned to face the command staff.

'All here have failed me,' Voldorius growled. His fell gaze swept the entire chamber and then alighted upon Malya. 'Or betrayed me.'

Malya knew in that moment that she would soon die. She welcomed it. Her soul yearned to flee her body, to be rid of the vile taint of the warp that Voldorius exuded. She shed her despair and stood proud and tall before her tormentor, awaiting the death she knew must be at hand.

Voldorius stepped forwards, his gaze locked upon Malya, his nostrils flaring as he breathed hard.

'Do it!' Malya said, feeling suddenly free. She had done her duty, sent the message that would bring about the deliverance of her people. Now, she could die.

Voldorius loomed over Malya, pressing as close as he had to any of the senior officers whose bodies were now scattered across the floor. His face closed on hers, every bestial detail filling her vision. Still, Malya refused to cower, knowing only the grace of the Emperor, at whose table she would soon be seated.

'Do you believe,' said Voldorius, his breath a caustic gale in Malya's face, 'that I would cast you aside so casually?'

Malya closed her eyes, blocking out the sight of the daemon prince's terrible visage. She felt Voldorius stir before her, and screwed her eyes tighter shut.

'Well you may fall silent, equerry' said Voldorius. 'But you shall continue to serve. Of that you can be certain.'

Then Malya's soul was assailed by a tide of force, and she was cast violently to the floor. She could not open her eyes, so powerful was the torrent, which she knew in that moment was the very stuff of Voldorius's rage and evil pouring from him in palpable waves. Screams echoed around her, accompanied by the sickening crack of splintering bones and the wet impact of chunks of bloody flesh being scattered across the chamber.

She felt her own body being torn in multiple directions at once by the unadulterated evil of Lord Voldorius. But she resisted the onslaught, drawing on impossibly deep wells of faith.

Then all fell silent. Malya found herself prostrate upon a blood-slick floor, panting for breath. She was stunned but to her amazement she was still alive.

Malya opened her eyes to find Lord Voldorius looming over her. She was drenched in blood, her black equerry's robe tattered and torn to shreds.

A drop of liquid fell upon her face and Malya looked upwards towards the chamber ceiling. It took her eyes a moment to focus, but when they did, Malya realised that the liquid was blood. The entire ceiling was coated in a glistening sheen of crimson. Congealing rivulets dripped down to the floor of the chamber.

Every surface of the command chamber had been turned dark red. She gasped as the full enormity of what had occurred struck her. Aside from the blood, there was no sign of the dozens of staff officers that had occupied the chamber scant moments before. Not even a shard of broken bone remained.

'Now, equerry, your true service begins' said Voldorius. 'You shall know the truth, and it shall set you free.'

'I will not–' she began.

'You have not the choice,' Voldorius interjected. 'The Bloodtide refuses to serve, and so you shall do so in its stead.'

Voldorius studied Malya, his eyes narrowing to black slits. His nostrils flared as he breathed and his mouth split into a feral grin, razor-sharp teeth glinting in the red light. 'The prisoner defied me, and refused to unleash the power of the Bloodtide in my name.'

Malya's head swam as her mind was filled with frozen, staccato images and fragments of forbidden knowledge. The silver-bodied prisoner treading a landscape of flensed bones. Voldorius as a mortal ordering the prisoner to unleash the Bloodtide. A city drowning as every one of its citizens bled out. The skies above a feral world burning as an entire Imperial Navy Fleet plummeted through the atmosphere. A forge world of the Adeptus Mechanicus, its population dead, but its machineries grinding on for centuries before anyone noticed. Voldorius again, his mortal body changing to his daemonic form as the powers of the warp granted him his reward. The prisoner set within the brass orb that was its cell, to sleep until its powers were restored and the Bloodtide would rise again...

Then the images ceased and realisation came to Malya. 'The prisoner defies you...'

'But you,' said Voldorius, his face lowering to the level of Malya's, 'shall not.'

'No!'

'You shall take the Bloodtide into you,' Voldorius pressed. 'You shall be the contaminator hive, the angelic host. You have shown by your resistance and fortitude that you can withstand the Bloodtide, as I knew when first I saw you in the grand square.'

'No,' Malya repeated.

'Your faith shall be your undoing, Malya L'nor,' said Voldorius. 'Within you is a flame that refuses to be quenched. You have burned, but you have not been consumed. And so you prove to me your worthiness to host the Bloodtide!'

'Now sleep,' said Voldorius, and Malya's world grew dark before his fell influence. 'When you awaken, you shall be mine.'

'CAPTAIN SHRIKE,' TECHMARINE Dyloss called over the roar that filled the interior of the Thunderhawk gunship. 'Priority transmission, cipher delta delta nine.'

'You are certain?' Shrike replied, turning in his grav-couch to look the Techmarine in the eye. Dyloss simply nodded.

'It's a transmission from within the city, brother-captain. It's her.'

The cipher told Shrike that the message was genuine. He had supplied Malya L'nor several different ciphers, so that should she be compelled to betray the Space Marines she could indicate it by her choice of codes without her torturer's knowledge.

Shrike indicated that the Techmarine should continue.

'The message indicates that the tertiary gate,' he looked at a data-slate and went on, 'gate sigma by our designation, is not fully fortified.'

'Then that shall be our target,' said Shrike.

'There is more, Shadow Captain,' the Techmarine continued. 'The prisoner. It is there after all. She has transmitted its location.'

Shrike nodded slowly, before answering. 'Inform Kor'sarro of gate sigma.'

'That is all?' the Techmarine said.

'That is all,' Shrike answered. 'Take us in.'

CHAPTER 12
The Gates of Mankarra

KOR'SARRO SPED ACROSS the volcanic plain, closing on the towering walls of Mankarra. As the White Scars neared the walls, row upon row of severed heads became visible mounted on spikes along the summit, evidence, if any more were needed, of the evil of Lord Voldorius.

The Master of the Hunt had deployed his force into a classic arrowhead formation with himself and his Command squad at the very tip. Dozens of White Scars bikers were arrayed to either side, and behind them came the armoured vehicles, clouds of black dust thrown up in their wake.

Those squads that had been exfiltrated from the battlefield by Thunderhawk had soon rejoined their bike- and armoured-vehicle-borne brethren, while the Raven Guard's gunships soared overhead. Both Chapters were closing on a single target – the gate Shrike's informant had directed them to attack.

The Raven Guard gunships swept overhead and banked as they came into range of the defence towers on either side of the gate. As the distance to the wall decreased the gate's poor state and lack of maintenance became evident. Lengths of the massive wall had been strengthened by the addition of armour plating and gun positions. Those who enacted the will of Voldorius were ill-schooled in the arts of fortification. Or perhaps they simply lacked the resources and time to fully prepare for the assault that even now descended upon the walls of Mankarra.

The gate was faced in cast bronze and glowed as if aflame as it reflected the orange light of Quintus's sun. The twenty metre-tall portal displayed a devotional scene, heroic warriors of the Emperor fighting the barbaric greenskins. It was a reminder of the primary role of the planet as a bulwark against the xenos filth that swarmed across nearby systems. It was tragic that the defenders should have been turned to the service of the Great Enemy and must now be laid low by their erstwhile allies.

As the range closed still further, the Raven Guard's gunships banked as they swept around the defence towers. Las and autocannon fire spat upwards to engage the Thunderhawks. But the gunners were either panicked or so poorly trained and led that few shots came close enough to worry Shrike's pilots.

'*Thunderheart!*' Kor'sarro called into the vox-net. The siege tank ground forwards, flanked protectively by the brotherhood's Predator tanks. 'To the fore!'

Kor'sarro and his Command squad veered to the right and slowed to a halt before the walls. Within moments, the entire arrowhead was arrayed likewise and the armoured vehicles were pushing through the gap in the formation.

With so many gun positions mounted on the walls, Kor'sarro felt terribly exposed in that moment. Even as the feeling sank in, they began to open fire on the now stationary White Scars. 'Now would be good, Shrike,' Kor'sarro growled.

As if in answer, the skies overhead erupted as two-dozen hellstrike missiles were unleashed by the Raven Guard's gunships. The missiles streaked through the air upon churning contrails and slammed into their targets. The summits of both defence towers burst into flame, showering the black plains all around with razor-sharp shards of rockcrete.

'The beast roars,' Kor'sarro spoke the command as the *Thunderheart* approached the mighty bronze gates. Desultory fire spat down upon the siege tank, but without the defence towers there was little the defenders could do to oppose *Thunderheart*'s approach.

The siege tank ground to a halt almost directly in front of the gate, a storm of small-arms fire erupting against its frontal armour. At such close range, there was little need to even aim the huge cannon mounted in its prow. Another few seconds ground past, and then the cannon roared.

As *Thunderheart* fired, a great black cloud of dust went up from all around the siege tank. Kor'sarro actually saw the siege shell propelled from the cannon and arcing towards the gates. Instead of velocity, the shell relied on sheer explosive force to penetrate its target, containing a destabilised fusion core that when forced to a critical reaction would destroy almost any target within a highly localised area.

The shell struck the gate and detonated on impact. A ball of orange fire flashed into existence one moment and was gone the next, unleashing a thunderous roar and a blistering wave of heat. Where the shell struck, the gate suffered a near-perfectly circular wound, great runnels of liquefied bronze seeping down its surface and distorting the image of the Emperor's warriors battling the orks.

Far above, the Raven Guard gunships swooped in for another pass at the defence towers as anti-air defence fire lanced towards them from positions further away. Another dozen hellstrike missiles streaked from their mountings beneath the gunships' stubby wings, and yet more of the towers were engulfed in flame.

At the same moment that the second salvo of hellstrikes struck the towers, the *Thunderheart* spoke again. The second siege shell smashed into the gates, the gunner targeting a point lower down than his first shot. Again, the orange ball of nucleonic fire erupted into being and an instant later collapsed in upon itself, leaving a second wound that bled runnels of liquid bronze.

The second attack sent trails of incandescent plasma spitting from the wounds and licking its surface. The battling figures of men and orks melted hideously into one another. The *Thunderheart*'s mighty cannon lowered still further as the gunner prepared for a third shot.

The next shell struck the lower portion of the gates, which had been so weakened by the preceding impacts that they could not withstand another pounding. Searing nuclear fire erupted at their base, and in an instant the entire bronze structure was vaporised into a rapidly expanding ball of plasma. Impossible energies engulfed the entire portal, and what remained of the two flanking defence towers sagged as rockcrete melted and ran like lava.

Kor'sarro felt the searing heat on his face. He could only imagine what devastation was being wrought upon the defenders stationed behind it and on the walls nearby. Only cinders would mark their passing.

With a grinding crack, the arch above the gateway collapsed, ragged chunks of rockcrete the size of armoured vehicles crashing downwards into the now open portal. For an instant, squat, bunker-like structures and defence towers of the city were visible beyond the gates. But the sight was soon obscured as a vast column of black dust and smoke belched outwards, choking the entire portal and the area before it.

'White Scars,' Kor'sarro bellowed. 'Charge!' He had no need to use the Chapter's battle-cant, for no other action was possible. Dozens of engines roared to life as one and the White Scars powered towards the gate.

The defence towers were collapsing even as Kor'sarro bore down on the dust-choked, rubble-strewn portal. The Master of the Hunt judged the rate at which the ruined towers were falling and estimated where they would collapse.

Gritting his teeth, he sped onwards, and as he closed to within fifty metres of the portal, the towers struck the ground, disintegrating with explosive force.

Kor'sarro and his warriors were engulfed in a sea of black dust, but not a single warrior faltered. The entire 3rd Company followed their captain into the churning black cloud in front of the ruined gateway. Visibility was reduced to practically zero and the ground shook with the impact of the towers collapsing. Steering Moondrakkan through the cloud was an impressive feat in itself, one that only a nomad son of the Chogoran steppes could accomplish. Chunks of rockcrete shrapnel the size of fists ricocheted in all directions, some striking the Space Marines, yet still the White Scars rode on. Kor'sarro's nose and mouth became blocked with dust and he was forced to narrow his eyes to mere slits lest they become clogged so badly that he could not see at all. Still he rode on, leading the brotherhood through the gates of Mankarra, the unerring sense of direction of the Chogoran leading him through.

Moondrakkan's front wheel struck something jagged, which disintegrated with a sharp crack. Soon the ground beneath the bike's wheels became

329 HUNT FOR VOLDORIUS

uneven, though the smoke and dust was so dense Kor'sarro could not see the surface in front of him.

And then, Kor'sarro was through the darkness and roaring out of the portal. In front of him was the city, every one of its squat buildings resembling an enormous bunker, complete with gun positions, needle-thin observation towers and bristling communications gear. The streets in between the buildings were cast in deep shadow, and with surprise Kor'sarro realised that the sun was already well on its way towards the horizon. The battle had been raging for many hours, but it was far from over.

'Kor'sarro to all commands,' the Master of the Hunt said into the vox-net as Moondrakkan prowled onwards. 'Voldorius defiles the cathedral at the heart of the city. Slay all who oppose you, but leave the vile one for me. His head is mine.'

As the smoke cleared, the ground beneath Moondrakkan's wheels was revealed as a jagged, broken and uneven mass. Slewing to a halt some fifty metres beyond the portal so that his forces could consolidate, Kor'sarro realised what it was that made the surface so uneven. Every square metre of the ground behind the portal was carpeted in bones, and the air was laced with the taint of burnt meat. The plasma storm touched off by the third of *Thunderheart*'s siege shells must have engulfed far more than the gate and defence towers. By Kor'sarro's estimation, an entire battalion of troops – most likely the indentured militia – had been mustered to defend the gates should they be forced.

Over a thousand militia troopers had been incinerated when the plasma storm had been triggered, reduced in seconds to blackened bones. It was no death for a warrior, but at least it would have been mercifully brief. And then a wave of revulsion hit Kor'sarro – the militia were traitors, even if they were pressed into service against their will. Perhaps their incineration was a merciful judgement. Perhaps it was more than they deserved.

Behind Kor'sarro, more White Scars bikers emerged through the churning smoke, the wheels of their mounts ploughing great furrows through the jagged carpet of bones. Then the growling of mighty engines echoed from the portal and the *Thunderheart* ground forwards, its commander, Brother-Sergeant Kia'kan, visible as he rode in the command cupola. The Master of the Hunt raised an arm, and the siege tank came to a halt not far behind him.

'My congratulations, brother-sergeant,' Kor'sarro shouted above the roar of the siege tank's engines and dozens of idling bikes nearby. 'Your deeds shall be recounted at the Hall of Skies upon our return to Chogoris.'

The tank commander's eyes glowed with fierce pride as he brought his right arm across his chest in salute to his khan. 'My thanks, brother-captain,' said Kia'kan, grinning as he spoke. 'I must admit, the final shot was far more impressive than I had anticipated!'

'Aye,' said Kor'sarro. 'The primarch was with us, for sure.'

'Blessed be his name,' said the sergeant. 'What now, my khan?'

'Now,' Kor'sarro replied, nodding towards the mighty horde mustering in the distance. 'We fight.'

As Kor'sarro mustered his brotherhood to strike the gathering defenders of Mankarra, high above the city, Captain Shrike was coordinating an assault of his own. At his order, a dozen Thunderhawk gunships bearing the black and white livery of the Raven Guard banked high over the walls, before each sped off towards its own pre-designated target.

One gunship was tasked with an assault against the city's central strategium, the huge, armoured structure that housed the planetary militia's command chamber. Another strafed the city's primary communications node, unleashing a fusillade of hellstrike missiles that brought the hundred metre-tall mast crashing down upon the buildings below. A third gunship deployed a contingent of Devastator squads equipped with heavy multi-meltas, which they unleashed against the main generatorium. The city's defences would be forced to rely on secondary sources in the battle against the Space Marines.

Almost every one of the city's buildings was defended by rooftop gun positions, sporting an array of heavy stubbers and autocannons augmented by the occasional lascannon. The Raven Guard gunships strafed every one as they roared overhead, shredding the exposed gunners in a lethal hail of mass-reactive heavy bolter rounds. The few defenders that survived these attacks were cut down as Raven Guard Assault Marines deployed from the gunships, falling upon the traitors as vengeful angels from heaven. Within minutes, a dozen battles were being fought across the most strategically valuable of the heavily fortified structures. Walkways connecting neighbouring buildings became the scenes of desperate and bloody battle for control of the upper levels.

Each Raven Guard squad was as an army in itself. Fighting within the confines of the fortified buildings, individual Space Marines slaughtered entire platoons of the enemy, for the environment forced the defenders to face them one at a time in a supremely unequal struggle. Even when a Space Marine fell in desperate close quarters battle, he took dozens of the enemy with him. Soon, panic was spreading as garbled pleas for aid drowned out all other traffic on the defenders' vox-nets. Terror spread until the entire defence stood upon the brink of utter collapse.

Having secured the rooftops of the most important structures, the Raven Guard began their descent. The defenders were trapped between the anvil of the White Scars' ground assault and the hammer of the Raven Guard's aerial attacks. The defenders were faced with three, equally lethal options – stand against the terrible vengeance descending from above, leave their fortified positions and face the White Scars, or cower inside the buildings and await their inevitable deaths.

Circling overhead in his command gunship, Captain Shrike coordinated each battle, communicating with his squad sergeants and ensuring that each desperate, bloody skirmish contributed to the success of the whole. Squads were redeployed with masterful tactical awareness, specialists despatched to where they were needed the most, and ammunition levels constantly monitored and balanced. Throughout it all, Shrike kept his force's most lethal weapon – himself – in reserve, ever vigilant for the moment when he and his Command squad would be needed to turn the tide of battle. As Shrike looked down from his gunship's cockpit, he caught sight of the White Scars as they closed upon the mighty horde beyond the gate, and knew that moment would soon come.

THE WHITE SCARS' charge against the massed horde was not led by Kor'sarro's bikers but, due to the narrow space between the buildings, by the Predator battle tanks. Though not as fast or manoeuvrable as the bike squads, the tanks were equipped with a fearsome array of anti-personnel weapons, which they unleashed in a storm of mass-reactive rounds as they advanced forwards across the bone-strewn ground.

The horde of militia troopers the White Scars charged towards were being pushed forwards by some agency Kor'sarro could not yet discern. Though not so numerous as the horde the Space Marines had encountered on the plains in front of the defence installation, this group still outnumbered the Space Marines by scores to one.

The Predators set about evening those odds.

As the tanks opened fire, the entire front rank of the horde simply evaporated. Those struck in the torso exploded, their ragged limbs arcing high into the air. Within seconds, scores of the traitor militia were dead, reduced to chunks of steaming meat scattered about the ground or splattered across their compatriots. Yet amazingly, the horde did not falter, but surged forwards to meet the White Scars head on.

With a near deafening roar that seemed to Kor'sarro equal parts despair and rage, several thousand militia troopers pressed forwards, running into the fusillade of shells that filled the air between them and the Predators. Spent shells poured from the tanks' ejection ports in a constant stream as dozens of rounds were expended every second.

Kor'sarro had witnessed even warlike orks fall back in the face of such a barrage. He had known tyranid bio-organisms, bred for nothing but war, to falter against such a weight of firepower. He had seen only two types of foe continue forwards against such odds. On the third moon of Woebetide, whilst serving as a Scout many decades before, he had faced an Enslaver plague, and watched as ten thousand mind-slaved meat puppets, each formally a stoic Cadian shock trooper, were compelled by their alien masters to cross a minefield a hundred kilometres deep into the combined fire of the White Scars, Red Hunters and Celestial Lions Chapters. The other occasion had been on Delta Arbuthnot, when a potent, alpha-level psyker had forced an entire planetary population of ratling agri-serfs to rise up against the landowners in an orgy of bloodshed, even though they were armed with no more than shovels and their foes with automatic weapons.

Without a doubt, Quintus was irredeemably under the heel of the Ruinous Powers. The insidious taint of the warp was everywhere, even in the air itself. Voldorius must have supplanted the government generations earlier, and only revealed his hand when Kor'sarro's hunt had run him to ground and left him nowhere else to hide. The militia troopers must have been born into the service of Chaos, and raised with its yoke around their neck, even if they had no idea of the true identity of their leaders. What a rare thing true faith must be in such a place, for surely it must have been stamped out the moment it was discovered.

The tide of the militia ploughed on, the troopers treading the bodies of their fallen companions into the ground as they ran. Part of Kor'sarro came to believe that the spectacle before him was mass suicide, the unwilling traitors martyring themselves upon the White Scars' guns that their treachery and their suffering might be ended. Perhaps Quintus might not be worth saving at all once this all was over. Should he survive to claim the head of Voldorius, Kor'sarro might order the *Lord of Heavens* to annihilate Mankarra and the other cities, cleansing the world of the taint of Chaos once and for all.

The first wave of the traitors hit the White Scars' lines. The last dozen or so metres saw nine out of every ten militia troopers gunned down, but when the survivors got to within a few metres of the tanks' weapons, the crew could no longer pick out their targets. The militia scrambled up the Predators' hulls to assail the armoured vehicles with whatever weapons they had to hand, from grenades and guns to fists and clubs.

'Kergis!' Kor'sarro motioned the company champion forwards as a wave of militia swarmed up the front of the Predators. Kergis bounded onto the rear deck of the nearest vehicle. In an instant, the champion was face to face with a militia sergeant who was desperately trying to pry open the turret hatch with an improvised crowbar. The two leaders sized one another up. Then a chainsword flashed, and the two halves of the traitor sergeant's body fell to the ground on either side of the tank.

A dozen more of the troopers clawed their way up the tank's frontal glacis plate. One was firing an autopistol at point-blank range into the driver's vision block, emptying an entire magazine in a couple of seconds. The act had little effect, for the driver's sights were constructed of thick armoured glass, made to stand up to far stronger attacks. Another trooper was ramming a grenade into one of the four exhaust units on the side of the vehicle, an action that could feasibly damage the tank's engine systems. Kergis drew his bolt pistol, and exploded the man's head with a single, almost point-blank shot.

The troopers died as more of Kor'sarro's warriors opened fire. Sparks flew as bolter rounds exploded or ricocheted from the armour after ripping devastatingly through traitor flesh. The vehicle's white livery ran red with the blood of the enemy, and no militia troopers were left alive within twenty metres. Along the line the other Predators were likewise cleared of the enemy, freeing the tanks to concentrate their own fire on the horde of traitors still surging forwards.

In seconds, no more traitors remained. The ground in front of the White Scars was a charnel plain of broken and shattered bodies. The sudden cessation of shouting and gunfire was almost shocking, allowing the other sounds of the war-torn city to press in. From overhead came the roar of a Thunderhawk's mighty engines, and still more of the gunships could be heard further out. Explosions spoke of hellstrike missiles pummelling their targets from afar, while the sharp crack of boltgun fire told of the rooftop battles the Raven Guard were even now winning.

The route ahead would not remain clear of enemies for long, and the brotherhood was soon under way again. As before, the Predators led the way, their turrets scanning back and forth. The force passed the area strewn with the blackened bones of the enemies caught in the plasma fires unleashed when the gate fell. Soon, however, the White Scars found the ground so covered with the remains of those gunned down by the Predators that the tanks had to grind a path through the bodies which the bikers and other units followed. Kor'sarro had witnessed many grisly sights throughout his years of service, but riding through a mire of blood and body parts was amongst the more unpleasant.

Finally, the ground up ahead cleared of corpses and the force spread out. Consulting Moondrakkan's command terminal, Kor'sarro oriented himself with his objective, the Cathedral of the Emperor's Wisdom, where Shrike's contact had suggested Voldorius and his mysterious prisoner were waiting.

The terminal displayed a two-dimensional map of this part of the city. Up ahead lay a large, open area labelled as the grand square. Kor'sarro ordered the bike squads to press on towards it at full speed. The slower Predators and other vehicles followed up behind dealing with any serious resistance using their heavy weapons.

Soon, the force was closing on the grand square. A sturdy barricade had been erected at the end of the street and the White Scars prepared to engage more militia troopers. But the barricade was facing in the wrong direction, not defending the grand square against attackers approaching along the street, but to contain a foe in the square itself. Furthermore, the barricade was entirely unmanned, even in the midst of the battle that now embroiled the whole of Mankarra.

The lead Predator slowed in its progress, and its commander emerged from the turret hatch. Kor'sarro brought Moondrakkan alongside the tank, and shouted up to the other warrior. 'Clear the way, brother-sergeant, then spread out.'

The tank commander saluted his khan before voxing the order to his crew. A moment later, the turret-mounted autocannon opened fire, round after round exploding across the armoured barricade until its entire structure disintegrated into fragments of twisted metal. The lead tank prowled forwards and ground slowly over the remains of the barricade, making a path for the remainder of the force.

Kor'sarro allowed the other armoured vehicles to pass through the ruined barricade and spread out into the grand square before he led the bike squads through. As soon as he entered the square, Kor'sarro brought Moondrakkan to a halt as a scene of utter devastation confronted him.

The grand square covered a massive area, and was surrounded on all sides by the bunker-like structures that dominated the city. But what drew Kor'sarro's gaze were the hundreds of thousands of corpses strewn across the entire square. This whole city appeared at that moment to be populated by the dead, or in the case of the militia, the soon to be dead. Anger rose within Kor'sarro, mingled with hatred of Lord Voldorius. The reign of the daemon prince had to end, he swore, and this entire place had to be cleansed, so utterly had it fallen to death and devastation.

If passing along a street of recently slain traitors had been disgusting enough, then the sight before Kor'sarro was far worse. The corpses that were scattered across the grand square were not those of soldiers, but of ordinary citizens. It was evident that these people had been made an example of, and simply left to rot as a dire message to their survivors.

'This goes further than mere slaughter,' Qan'karro said flatly. His voice was choked with a disgust that, if possible, exceeded Kor'sarro's. 'He did this not just as an example.'

'Explain please, old friend,' replied the Master of the Hunt.

'He did this to gain power. To reap the souls of the innocent, and to offer them up to the Great Enemy.'

Kor'sarro looked out across the sea of twisted corpses, righteous anger seething inside. 'To what end?'

'That I can only guess at, huntsman. The vile one is gifted of great power, of that we can be sure.'

'And this... atrocity... fuels that power still further?'

'Aye. It lends him strength, and gains him favour. Dwell no more upon it, Kor'sarro. Leave such things to the Storm Seers.'

Kor'sarro looked into the eyes of the man who was his old friend and his most valued counsellor, and nodded his understanding. 'The wise man knows the limits of his knowledge.'

Qan'karro's leathery features were split by a rare smile at Kor'sarro's recounting of ancient Chogoran wisdom. 'Indeed he does,' replied the Storm Seer. 'And you will know,' he continued, 'when the time comes.'

'Then let that time be soon,' said Kor'sarro, gunning Moondrakkan's engines. 'Let us hasten to end this.'

At Kor'sarro's signal, the brotherhood pressed outwards into the grand square. The corpses were not so densely packed as the slaughtered militia had been in the street leading to the grand square, so he was not forced to ride over their pulped remains. The stink of decay, however, was all but overpowering, even for a veteran of a thousand battlefields and sieges.

Gaining speed, Kor'sarro led his bike squads out towards the centre of the grand square, leaving the Predators and other armoured vehicles to carry on behind. As he passed by clusters of bodies, he judged that the slaughter had taken place several weeks before, and turned his gaze away in revulsion.

Then, he looked back to one particular pile of corpses, having thought he had noticed movement there. He sneered as he imagined the local scavengers crawling over the bodies, and cursed Voldorius all the more for bringing such a thing about.

As the bikers roared onwards towards the far side of the square and the road that would lead them towards their objective, more furtive movement stirred amongst the piles of corpses. Kor'sarro knew they must be crawling with vermin, but he was reminded of an especially morbid Chogoran legend that warned that improperly buried corpses might somehow rise again to slay the living. He cast the notion from his mind – he had witnessed many vile blasphemies in his time, but surely such a thing was beyond even the power of Chaos?

The White Scars were three quarters of the way across the grand square, weaving around pile after pile of decaying corpses, when a figure rose up before him.

Kor'sarro had no time to manoeuvre around who-ever, or whatever, it was that blocked his path.

Instead, he gritted his teeth and ploughed on, crushing the figure beneath Moondrakkan's wheels with a sickening crunch.

In the instant before the impact, Kor'sarro had briefly seen a twisted face set into a hateful, gargoyle-like leer. The legends of Chogoris came fully to mind, and then as one, a hundred other figures arose from the piles of corpses all about.

Kor'sarro slammed on the brakes and skidded to a halt. A moment later, his bike squads had done likewise. Sixty Space Marine riders formed up into a laager, Kor'sarro and his Command squad in the centre.

A circle of ragged figures stood amongst the corpses. Each was impossibly emaciated and clad in filth-encrusted rags. The eyes were expressionless pits and their mouths dripped gore, which streamed down their fronts. The bodies of many were twisted and contorted, while others had overlong arms that ended in serrated claws encrusted with long-dried blood.

'Carrion-eaters,' spat Brother Kergis.

'Mutant filth,' said Kor'sarro.

'I thought for a moment they were–' continued Kergis.

'Aye,' interjected Kor'sarro. 'I too. But they are living, and so can be killed.'

'Brothers!' Kor'sarro called out to his assembled warriors, checking the ammunition levels of the twin bolters mounted in Moondrakkan's fairing. 'We have no time to waste here!'

As one, every engine in the company roared to full power and the White Scars brought their bikes around to align themselves with Kor'sarro and the banner of the 3rd that waved beside him. Even as the bikes roared, still more of the mutant cannibals arose from their vile lairs amidst the rotting bodies, until they pressed in from every quarter.

The mutants were unarmed, but would clearly present a threat, for many sported wickedly sharp talons that could only be the work of some vile biomancer. The bodies of others were covered in distended spines and barbs. While Kor'sarro had initially taken their bodies for malnourished and emaciated, on closer inspection each mutant was possessed of a wiry frame, with whipcord muscles that would grant them blinding speed in battle.

Moondrakkan leapt forwards and Kor'sarro thundered down on the mutant horde, his warriors close behind. As the range closed a Thunderhawk gunship swooped low overhead and opened fire on the outer edges of the horde. He sent up a silent word of thanks for the timely fire support, and knew too that the Predators the bikers had left at the edge of the grand square would not be far behind.

Every twin bolter in the force opened fire as the charge closed. Dozens of the mutants were struck down, but Kor'sarro noted that many more were somehow able to weather the storm of mass-reactive death. He had no time to wonder what sorcery had made their skins as hard as iron.

· Kor'sarro found himself surrounded by the vile mutants. Though the face of each was slack and vacant, their bodies moved with lightning speed.

Even as the Master of the Hunt raised Moonfang high, a barbed talon swept towards his face before he had even seen it coming. Kor'sarro only barely managed to duck in time, yet still the talon scored a deep cut along his shoulder plate. In that brief moment, he knew that the power of the warp animated these hideous walking blasphemies.

Kor'sarro brought Moonfang down to take the head of the mutant that had struck him, but somehow the vile creature leapt backwards beyond his attack, and then darted inside his reach. The mutant's next attack would be aimed at his exposed torso, and Kor'sarro reacted by instinct, twisting his body around so that the impossibly sharp talon struck only a glancing blow.

He had avoided the full force of the mutant's strike, but Kor'sarro immediately bit back a curse as he felt the claw penetrate his armour and gouge a raking wound across his chest. Had he not twisted his body at the last possible moment, the talons would have punched directly through his chest armour and, in all probability, through the other side.

The mutant was fast and strong, but it was not nearly as skilled a combatant as the Master of the Hunt. His enemy had overstretched itself, allowing Kor'sarro to bring Moonfang down in a great sweep that severed the mutant's head in an explosive shower of black blood.

Even as the mutant's body collapsed to the ground, more pressed in from all sides. Kor'sarro knew that to become bogged down amongst them would be to invite a meaningless death, for he had a far greater mission to perform than to slay these fell deviants.

'Ride through!' Kor'sarro bellowed, opening Moon-drakkan's throttle and powering forwards. A dozen mutants were crushed beneath his mount's wheels, and more died as Moonfang slashed and cleaved in every direction. It was crude, bloody work, and Kor'sarro's armour was cut in a dozen places and his cloak torn almost to shreds by the time he had broken through the mutant's ragged line.

Kor'sarro's warriors followed his example, powering their way through the press of mutants until the last of the White Scars bikers burst forth from the swirling melee.

At least three of Kor'sarro's warriors had fallen to the mutants. He bellowed in rage as the vile creatures descended upon the white-armoured bodies, ripping the noble sons of Chogoris asunder and biting deep into their flesh. It appeared in that instant that the mutants were so absorbed in their feeding frenzy that they had forgotten about the rest of the White Scars.

Kor'sarro checked the ammunition levels of his bike-mounted boltguns. They were dangerously low. He longed to pump every last round into the mutants, but he could spare neither the ammunition nor the time were he to face his ultimate foe, Voldorius.

The air was split by a sonic boom and a Raven Guard Thunderhawk swooped in low.

'Give our brothers space!' Kor'sarro bellowed, and the White Scars roared forwards and within thirty seconds were closing on the far side of the grand square.

The gunship unleashed a salvo of missiles directly into the mass of mutant cannibals. Kor'sarro said a silent prayer for his fallen brethren, hoping they would be consoled by the fact that their bodies and wargear would be reduced to ashes and defiled no more.

Then the missiles struck, great explosions erupting across the centre of the grand square. Mutant body parts were thrown high into the air, their broken corpses mingling with those they had preyed upon. The gunship streaked onwards towards Kor'sarro's position, and as it passed directly overhead, a number of black-armoured forms leapt from an open hatch and descended upon screaming jets to land on the ground near the Master of the Hunt.

It was Captain Shrike and his Command squad. Before the squad had entirely touched down, Shrike was ordering the gunship to return for a second pass, to ensure that not a single one of the horrific creatures could possibly have survived.

'Brother-Captain Kayvaan Shrike,' Kor'sarro addressed his compatriot. 'Much has been settled this day already,' he continued, referring to the many frictions that existed between the two Chapters. 'Yet as far as my rank allows, I cast all debts aside.'

Shrike reached up and removed his helmet. 'Never mind that, brother-captain.'

Kor'sarro regretted his words the moment Shrike gave his reply, and was on the verge of unleashing a torrent of invective when Shrike pressed on. 'My forces have located the prisoner the contact mentioned. I am assembling a detachment to kill that prisoner.'

Kor'sarro's wrath was forgotten as soon as it had appeared, as is the way of all Chogorans. 'Where?'

Shrike paused as the shockwave of his gunship's second attack run struck the Space Marines, causing his long black hair to whip across his pale face. Then he continued. 'A detention cell, adjacent to the subterranean cathedral.'

Kor'sarro's mind raced. He had no idea who this prisoner was, but if they were as valuable to Voldorius as Shrike's contact insisted, then the matter should be investigated. And besides, Shrike appeared as keen to eliminate the prisoner as Kor'sarro was to slay the daemon prince. His gaze fell across the square, where he saw that the 3rd Company's armoured column approaching. His eyes alighted upon one of the Rhino transports.

'Kholka,' he muttered.

'Brother-captain?' Shrike replied.

'Scout-Sergeant Ultas Kholka, Raven Guard,' Kor'sarro grinned slyly as he replied. 'The man who detected your presence at the landing site.'

'Only barely...' Shrike replied. 'But I'm sending my own men in. We don't need help.'

Kor'sarro pressed on. 'Kholka could penetrate the detention cells,' he continued. 'And free or slay the prisoner, according to his judgement.'

'I am sending my own men in,' Shrike repeated.

'You said yourself, brother-captain. Kholka is good.'

Kor'sarro felt the eyes of another upon him and saw that the Storm Seer Qan'karro was approaching, the Chaplain Xia'ghan at his side. The two had just dismounted from their Rhino transport, and behind them Scout-Sergeant Kholka was doing likewise. Though the Storm Seer could not possibly have overheard the exchange between the two company captains, both saw the message in his eyes. It was unmistakable.

'Your Scouts go in,' Shrike said darkly. 'But my man goes too.'

'Agreed, brother-captain,' Kor'sarro replied.

'Brother Meleriex and two others shall accompany your Scouts,' said Shrike, turning to one of the members of his Command squad and nodding. 'Meleriex is my nominated second, and he speaks with my voice. He knows what to do.'

'Then let it be so,' Kor'sarro replied, holding out his hand towards the Raven Guard captain. The two grasped forearms in the manner of the warrior common amongst such men the length and breadth of the galaxy. 'Let it be so,' Shrike repeated, both men turning as Sergeant Kholka and his Scouts approached.

'IT WILL SUBMIT to the process,' the red-hooded, renegade tech-priest hissed, his voice dry and coldly mechanical. 'Or it shall undergo the nerve-shrive. Again.'

Malya kicked hard as one of the servitors attempted to clamp a steel surgical restraint around her right ankle. The kick struck the mind-scrubbed mono-task square in the forehead, but it barely registered the impact at all, merely grasping for her leg in an attempt to keep her still.

'Then it shall undergo the tenth degree,' the tech-priest rasped.

'No!' Malya screamed, not in an effort to beg the tech-priest not to inflict any more pain upon her body, but to steel herself against the inevitable. The tech-priest was working the dials and levers of a tall bank of humming machinery. His fingers were twice as long as they should have been and had twice the normal number of joints. He worked a large dial, turning it up to the penultimate setting.

'Yes...' said the tech-priest, and pulled down hard on a long, brass switch.

Malya's body arched upwards from the steel table she was clamped to by all but her right ankle. Every nerve in her body fired as one, stimulated by the dozens of probes and lines which the vile traitor had inserted under her skin. For an instant, she knew such all-consuming pain that she felt her very soul part with her body. She was not there. She was somewhere else. Somewhere near the Emperor.

'Perhaps it should undergo the eleventh degree...' the renegade muttered to himself as he worked more dials and levers.

Malya lay panting, her body slick with sweat. Before she could recover her senses the servitor had taken hold of her ankle and clamped the steel restraint around it. She did not care. She had glimpsed something, known something pure. The pain had cleansed her, brought her closer to the God-Emperor, and nothing that Voldorius's biomancer could do could take that away from her.

'Damage her,' a deep voice growled out of the darkness of the chamber, 'and it shall be you who undergoes the eleventh degree.' The voice was that of Lord Voldorius, and it tore Malya from the state of purity she had entered, reminding her of the daemon prince's vile intentions.

'The nerve-shrive is incapable of inflicting tissue damage, my lord.' The tech-priest bowed as he spoke. 'The effect is entirely neurological.'

'Speak no more.' Voldorius growled as he loomed out of the darkness. The rogue tech-priest fell silent.

'Malya L'nor,' said Voldorius as his bestial face appeared above her. 'You are about to receive a rare honour indeed.'

'Keep it,' Malya spat. All fear was gone from her now, replaced by a state of grace. The Emperor would protect her soul, even should she die at the hands of this vile servant of the Great Enemy.

The daemon prince studied Malya for a moment, his eyes narrowing as if he sought to peer deep into her very soul. His breath huffed across her face, the taint of brimstone threatening to choke her. Then he stepped back, and growled an order.

A group of robed servants entered the chamber and took position in the shadows behind Voldorius. She knew from her previous duties as his equerry that they were his acolytes. Their role was to invoke the vile powers which gave Voldorius his potency, by twisted worship, incantations and blasphemies.

As the bowing acolytes gathered behind their master, a sonorous, atonal chanting started up. Though Malya could not understand the words, she knew beyond doubt that they invoked dark names that should never be spoken. Dread welled up inside her, but she clung on to her faith, drawing upon the grace she knew resided deep inside.

Voldorius chuckled. 'Even now, you resist me,' he said. 'And it is that strength that shall allow you to withstand the gift you are soon to receive. I knew from the moment you entered the grand square that you alone of the ten thousand gathered there had the strength to resist being consumed by the Bloodtide...'

'I shall not serve you,' Malya insisted, feeling the grace she had felt earlier returning. Her voice became gentle as she went on. 'Nothing you can do to me shall make me acquiesce.'

'I do not require your subservience, Malya L'nor,' replied Voldorius, 'for I have the power to control you utterly. I require only your survival, that your soul is not consumed by the awakened will of the Bloodtide.'

Malya's head sank to the steel surface and she closed her eyes. Was this how it felt to the Emperor's martyrs, she wondered, as they gave themselves up to death in His name? Drawing her shield of grace around her, Malya forced her breathing to slow, to find that place of purity once more.

Then a deep rumble passed through the chamber and Malya felt dust fall down from the ceiling. She kept her eyes closed, extending her senses outwards. The chanting of Voldorius's acolytes faltered a moment, and then continued as before.

'Is she ready to be moved?' Malya heard Voldorius ask. 'Speak!'

'It is ready, my lord,' the renegade tech-priest replied from somewhere behind Malya. 'Do you have the… the vial?' Malya sensed something akin to awe in the voice of the rogue adept, and she slowly opened her eyes to see what he referred to.

Voldorius had one gnarled claw held in front of him, and in it was a clear, glass vial. A silvery light was emanating from the small container. Malya had seen that light before, what seemed like weeks ago. She had seen it in the cell of the prisoner, radiating from its shifting body. And here was that same radiance, somehow contained within the small clear container held between the talons of a daemon.

'This is sufficient quantity?' asked Voldorius.

The tech-priest bowed deep, but mechanical eyes squinted upwards from the depths of his hood as he gazed covetously at the vial. 'Oh yes, my lord,' said the renegade. 'That vial contains… one hundred and twenty-seven million… three hundred and thirty-three thousand… and… two viable nanytes. Such a sample could infect billions of hosts if efficiently distributed, my lord.'

'If they can penetrate power armour,' Voldorius growled absently.

'Even if they cannot, my lord,' answered the tech-priest, 'not all of your foes take full precautions.'

Voldorius studied the contents of the vial for several long moments, during which another tremor passed through the chamber and more dust fell down on Malya's face, causing her to blink and tears to swell in her eyes. 'That much is true, tech-priest.'

'Take her to the cathedral.'

'What?' Malya breathed, looking up sharply. 'Why would you…'

'Are you ashamed?' said Voldorius, his voice grating and loud in the dark, enclosed chamber. 'Why would you not desire your moment of transcendence to take place before the representation of your Emperor?'

'Why?' Malya repeated.

'Because all of this,' Voldorius indicated with a sweep of the arm not holding the vial, 'is as naught compared to the glory of Chaos! Such things must be done correctly.' Voldorius leaned in close to Malya. 'There are certain processes that have so much more… gravitas, when performed in such places.'

'Blasphemer…' Malya sobbed, despair threatening to overwhelm her. She had always known she would not survive the horrors unleashed upon Quintus, but to be used like this… She cared nothing for her own life, but that it might be claimed in the Cathedral of the Emperor's Wisdom, before the mighty statue of the Lord of Mankind, was an unspeakable cruelty before which the last of her strength crumbled away.

She clamped her eyes shut as the surgical table beneath her was wheeled out of the chamber, hot tears streaming down her face. The acolytes' atonal plainsong increased in volume until it threatened to overwhelm her with the echoed wails of uncounted damned souls writhing in eternal suffering in the depths of the warp...

CHAPTER 13

Bloodtide Rising

'WHERE IS IT?' the Raven Guard Meleriex asked Sergeant Kholka as the infiltration group stalked along a cramped alleyway between two of Mankarra's massive, bunker-like buildings.

Kholka halted as he came to the end of the narrow alley, and nodded out towards a wide, flat expanse of marble that gleamed orange as Quintus's setting sun cast the last of its rays across the city. 'It's there, brother.'

The Raven Guard's dark eyes narrowed as he scanned the area. After a moment, realisation dawned. 'The marble forms the aquila,' he remarked. 'The Cathedral of the Emperor's Wisdom is below?'

'Yes, brother, it is,' Kholka replied. 'And so too is the holding cell, or so your captain informs us.'

Meleriex looked back to face Kholka. 'The contact tells the truth, brother-sergeant. Of that I am certain. But how do we gain access?'

'We follow them,' replied Kholka, nodding to indicate a line of black-robed figures that hurried across the marble flagstones to an armoured portal set in a bunker not far from the Space Marines' position. 'We need only gain access to the underground complex, by which all of these buildings around us are joined. Once we are in the subterranean levels, we can locate the holding cell.'

'Understood,' the Raven Guard replied. Both warriors ducked back into the alleyway as the line of robed figures approached. Meleriex activated his lightning claws, and whispered to Kholka, 'My kill.'

The Scout-sergeant could not help but grin. He had as much cause as any in the Chapter to be suspicious of the Raven Guard, but this brother appeared more willing than most to work alongside others. Perhaps that was the reason Captain Shrike had attached him to the infiltration group.

'Your kill,' replied Kholka. He had no doubt that Meleriex would be able to slaughter the entire group in seconds, and without the need to expend ammunition. 'Make it quick though, brother.'

Kholka leaned around the edge of the wall and saw that the monkish figures were now only twenty metres away. The man at the front was activating the controls that would open the armoured portal. The sergeant waited a moment, ensuring that the enemy had fully unlocked the portal, before he nodded towards the Raven Guard warrior.

Meleriex darted out from the alleyway. His black armour was barely visible amongst the long shadows cast by the squat buildings all about. None of the hooded, black-robed enemies saw him coming at all. Three died in seconds to lethal stabs of Meleriex's flashing lightning claws. The remainder were frozen rigid by the sudden explosion of violence. The Raven Guard attacked out of the setting sun, and none saw more than a silhouetted angel of death moving amongst them, dispensing death with every gesture.

Within ten seconds, only one of the figures remained, and he had only survived that long because he had bolted instead of freezing in shock when the Raven Guard had struck. Unfortunately for him, he had fled towards the wrongly imagined safety of the alleyway and ran straight into the waiting White Scars Scouts.

As the robed figure bounded towards them, Kholka reached out an arm and hooked his elbow around the man's neck. In a savage motion, Kholka slammed the enemy into the rockcrete wall, pushing his face right into its surface.

Ensuring the man was restrained, Kholka reached up his free hand and yanked the hood down to reveal the captive's face, his cheek pressed into the wall. That face was a mask of bitter hatred, teeth gritted and eyes alight with frenzied anger. A swirling pattern of crudely applied tattoos was etched across his face and bald scalp, denoting the vile pacts he had undoubtedly made with the Ruinous Powers.

Upon seeing those symbols, Kholka drew his combat knife and pressed its monomolecular tip to the man's jugular. 'Tell me the location of the holding cells,' he spat, 'and I shall grant you a far quicker death than you deserve.'

The man's eyes flashed and his mouth twisted into a feral snarl. 'I'll tell you nothing...'

Kholka pressed the tip of his knife into the man's neck, drawing a thin swelling of blood around it. 'Where is it? One last chance.'

'Give me death,' the man growled. 'I welcome it, for I shall become so much more...'

Disgust welling up inside him, Kholka prepared to end the man's life with a thrust of his combat knife. Then Brother Meleriex appeared next to him, and placed a restraining hand upon his arm. 'Let me, sergeant.'

Kholka paused, turning to meet the other's steely gaze. 'Much slaughter awaits us yet, Raven Guard.'

Meleriex held Kholka's gaze a moment longer before replying, 'That is not my meaning, brother-sergeant.'

Then understanding dawned and Kholka stepped back, allowing the Raven Guard to take control of the prisoner. 'Make it quick.'

Not wishing to witness what would happen next, Sergeant Kholka strode to the mouth of the alleyway. He was on the verge of barking an order to his Scouts when he saw that they had pre-empted the need and were even now dragging the bodies of the dead traitors away from the open portal and secreting them in the shadows of the alley. Despite the bitter taste in his mouth, he felt a fierce pride in the fieldcraft his charges were displaying.

Scout Borchu was rolling a body into the shadows nearby. It was clear to see that Brother Meleriex had been supremely efficient in the application of his deathblows, punching with his lightning claws rather than slashing. The wounds were lethal, but had not torn the bodies asunder, thus allowing the Space Marines to drag them away without spilling blood and scattering body parts across the kill-zone.

A muffled cry sounded from further back in the shadowed alleyway, followed by a dry crack and the sound of a body hitting the black, rocky ground. Kholka did not turn, but waited until Brother Meleriex came to stand at his side.

'The portal leads down to a sub-level junction. There we proceed along tunnel two seven zero until we reach the holding cells.'

Kholka turned to look the other Space Marine in the eye. 'You are sure?'

'I am sure,' Meleriex replied.

Suppressing his revulsion, Kholka made to gather his charges in preparation for the infiltration. There were certain lessons he would not be teaching them.

MALYA STARED STRAIGHT upwards and wished that she could clamp her hands to her ears to shut out the hellish chanting of the acolytes that were gathered around the table to which she was still clamped. She had been removed from the chamber, and taken in blasphemous procession along the dark passageways to the subterranean Cathedral of the Emperor's Wisdom.

Soaring far above Malya, the vaults of the cathedral were almost lost in shadow. The horrific, batlike imps flitted to and fro, swooping down towards her before darting off at speed emitting a vile shriek that was disturbingly close to the mocking laughter of an especially vindictive child. The surgical table had been placed before the mighty statue of the Emperor Triumphant, which towered twenty metres into the incense-laced air.

At first Malya had drawn strength from the magnificent sight, but had soon noted the terrible descration of the statue. The vile imps had deposited vast amounts of guano upon the Emperor's holy countenance, great white stripes of the stuff streaked across His noble face. Even worse, the servants of Voldorius had daubed vile runes that seared the eye when looked upon all across the statue's flanks. The sight brought crushing sadness to Malya's heart despite her own predicament.

Yet, despite the injuries done to the towering statue of the Emperor of All Mankind, it was still possessed of some indefinable glory that no amount of damage short of its complete destruction could spoil.

'The cohort shall muster!' the voice of the daemon prince boomed out from somewhere outside of Malya's field of vision, its vile notes echoing down the nave and repeating over and over again. In response, dozens of armoured boots struck the ground. The remainder of Voldorius's Alpha Legion warriors were gathering in the cathedral to witness their master's final blasphemy.

'The Emperor's deluded slaves descend even now!' Voldorius growled, his voice filling the entire space of the cathedral. 'He who hunts has slain my champion, but he shall soon hunt no more!'

A hundred and more voices roared their assent, their words modulated by the grilles of their baroque masks. Even as the roars faded to echoes, the distant sound of an explosion ground through the rock and Malya knew that the Space Marines were closing on their foes.

She dared not believe that she would be rescued. She clung instead to the thought that Lord Voldorius would soon be brought to judgement, even should she herself not live to witness it.

'WHAT WAS THAT?' Telluk hissed as the group proceeded along the pipe-choked tunnel. A deep tremor had caused the pipes to twist and their metal to screech as dust descended from the stone ceiling above.

Kholka reached to his vox-bead and pressed it into his ear. He concentrated for a moment but could discern very little, for the metal and stone all around interfered with the signal. 'Ordnance. Ours I would hope,' he replied. 'Concentrate on the task at hand, neophyte,' he continued, hefting his boltgun. 'Gharn, the hunter's arrow. Proceed.'

The group resumed its advance along the dark passageway, neophyte Gharn moving forwards to take the lead position. The tunnel, which the captive had indicated would lead to the holding cells, was straight and

narrow, forcing the squad to form what was a vulnerable formation given their light arms and armour.
Kholka was grateful that they had the Raven Guard
with them, for their superior armour and specialised
close-combat armament would prove highly effective
should they encounter an enemy in the tunnels.

'It was not ours, brother-sergeant,' said the Raven
Guard at Kholka's side, his voice low. 'I have been
monitoring the vox-net too.'

'I know it was not,' Kholka growled, before continuing. 'What have you been able to pick up?'

'The enemy's flagship is firing on the city.'

Utter madness, Kholka thought, but not entirely
unexpected given the nature of the enemy. If Voldorius believed he could destroy the Space Marines with
an orbital bombardment far more efficiently than his
ground troops could, then he would do so, regardless
of how many of his own he killed in the process. He
only regretted that *Lord of Heavens* was too far out to
intervene. The White Scars had initiated their attack a
great distance from Quintus in order that the world's
defence grid would not detect their approach.

'Do you have two-way contact?' asked Kholka. He
himself had been unable to raise any of his brothers.
Perhaps the Raven Guard had experienced more luck.

'Only sporadically, brother-sergeant,' said Meleriex.
'I could use my fusion core to boost the signal, but
that might compromise our mission.'

Indeed, thought Kholka. Such a transmission might
be the group's last. 'Only if we truly have need,
brother,' he said. 'Agreed?'

'Agreed,' the Raven Guard replied, before halting at a sign of activity further along the tunnel. Scout Gharn had stopped where the tunnel opened up into a larger chamber. The others had assumed covering positions nearby, melting into the shadows and utilising what little cover the protruding pipes and conduits afforded.

Kholka halted too, his eyes trained on a pool of light in the centre of the chamber. He raised his boltgun and slowly made his way forwards past the neophytes, to squat next to the lead Scout.

'The silvered moon enshrouds the hunted,' Gharn whispered, not taking his eyes from the chamber. The youth had no need to use the Chapter's battle-cant now, Kholka thought, but it was a good habit to cultivate. He looked out into the chamber, most of which was dominated by dormant machinery and twisting pipes. Only a single light source illuminated the space, a circle of wan light cast into the centre.

Kholka's glance took all this in within the span of seconds, before he looked to the area the Scout had indicated using the White Scars' battle-cant. At the far edge of the pool of light he saw a pair of sturdy, rubber-soled boots, the rest of the body hidden in shadow. A deep red stain spread slowly outwards into the light.

'Wait here,' Kholka hissed. The group had no time to be distracted by what might be no more than a random act of violence inflicted by one traitor on another in the midst of a city-razing battle. He scanned the chamber through his boltgun's sights.

Detecting no enemies, the sergeant stepped out of the tunnel and skirted the edge of the chamber until he stood over the body.

It was a servitor of some sort, but the manner of its death was not immediately apparent. The mind-scrubbed slave wore a work suit of heavy-duty, rubberised fabric, and its body was augmented by dozens of cybernetic parts designed to facilitate what-ever tasks it had been created to fulfil. Its head was bald, and the entire left of its brain had been surgi-cally replaced with crude machinery. But none of this was out of place. What was unusual was the fact that every drop of the servitor's blood was even now draining from its body, pouring out in fact, as if some pressure within was expelling it at a great rate. And the blood was leaving the body by any and every route possible, leaking from the mouth, nostrils and the one eye and ear that were not replaced by cyber-netic versions. It was even seeping out through the pores in what little skin was visible, and spreading out in a great pool all around the body.

'By the primarch,' Kholka spat, 'blessed be his name.'

With one last look around to ensure that no ene-mies were nearby, Kholka moved quickly back to the mouth of the tunnel where the remainder of the group waited in the shadows. He waved them onwards, ensuring that each Scout was properly con-centrating upon the task at hand and not distracted by the disturbing sight in the centre of the chamber. Brother Meleriex was the last to pass by, lingering for a moment to gaze down at the exsanguinated servitor. Then he looked up at Kholka, his dark eyes unreadable, and pressed on into the darkness.

'BROTHER SANG.' KOR'SARRO took advantage of a brief lull in the bombardment to call the White Scar over. In a moment, the Techmarine was at his side, standing amongst the ruins that the combined force of Space Marines was holding against wave after wave of frenzied traitor militia troopers.

'Brother,' said Kor'sarro. 'I am unable to contact Sergeant Kholka.'

The Techmarine consulted a data-slate mounted in his vambrace. After a few seconds, he shook his head and replied. 'Nor I, brother-captain. A combination of the effect of the bedrock, nearby structures and possibly ionisation caused by the bombardment.'

As if to punctuate the Techmarine's report, a deafening roar split the air above. A building only a hundred metres away exploded outwards, a huge mushroom cloud blossoming high into the now darkened sky.

Chunks of shrapnel the size of bolter rounds ricocheted from the Space Marines' armour, sending up fat sparks and razor-sharp fragments of rockcrete. Not one of the White Scars or the Raven Guard flinched.

'If they do not make contact soon, we will have to commit regardless,' Captain Shrike shouted above the sound of falling masonry and gunfire. 'The vile one will rally his forces, or else he will slip from our grasp.'

Kor'sarro felt a stab of frustration at the thought of Voldorius slipping away amidst the destruction his flagship was unleashing upon his own city. But just as quickly, he dismissed the notion. 'No, brother,' he shouted back. 'It is not his intention to escape, of that I am sure. I have hunted him for a decade, and know something of his ways.'

'But this prisoner,' Shrike called back. 'He must be–'

'Secondary!' Kor'sarro snapped back. 'Kholka is my battle-brother and my friend, but if he is unable to locate this prisoner and ascertain his place in the daemon's plans, we must proceed regardless. We will have no choice but to assault the vile one's lair, with or without Kholka's intelligence.'

Captain Shrike turned his head away from the Master of the Hunt. His true feelings were as hidden from Kor'sarro as his face was by the helmet he wore.

Kor'sarro put the prisoner from his mind, and turned his thoughts to the layout of the city instead, estimating how long it would take the Space Marines to fight through to the Cathedral of the Emperor's Wisdom where the daemon prince would be waiting. It would not take long, but that meant that Sergeant Kholka had very little time to report back, if he even could with the interference afflicting the vox-net.

'Let us be about it then,' Kor'sarro called to Captain Shrike, a savage glint in his eye. 'Let us gather the warriors for the final assault.'

'THAT MAKES SEVEN,' Kholka whispered as he looked down at another exsanguinated corpse. 'It makes no sense.'

'Nor would it,' replied Brother Meleriex. 'The workings of the Great Enemy are mercifully beyond the understanding of such as we.'

The whole length of the corridor the group had passed along was scattered with the blood-drained bodies of servitors and menials. 'This is something else, brother,' said Kholka. 'Something more than bloodshed and wickedness.'

The Raven Guard considered this, his black eyes glinting in the shadows cast by a flickering overhead lumen. 'Perhaps you are correct, brother-sergeant. But it has no bearing upon our mission.'

'It may,' Kholka replied, readying himself to press on. 'The two may prove to be connected.'

Meleriex was about to answer when a tortured scream sounded from further down the passageway. The Space Marines were instantly alert, weapons raised and ready to face an attack from any quarter.

'Fifty metres ahead,' Kholka whispered. 'Seek the blood as the sabre-hound at dawn.'

The Scouts assumed the formation that Kholka's battle-cant order had specified, moving into position with well-drilled precision. The three Raven Guard Space Marines remained where they were, however, Meleriex casting a questioning glance towards the Scout-sergeant.

'My apologies,' said Kholka. He switched to a more common idiom used by many of the Imperium's countless and varied military institutions. 'Advance to contact, ten-metre separation, bolters to the fore.'

'No, brother-sergeant,' the Raven Guard said darkly. 'Myself and my brothers must go first. We are better armoured than your Scouts. We can fight through any ambush we might encounter.'

Meleriex emphasised his assertion by raising a lightning claw and activating it so that arcs of power seethed up and down the length of its talons.

'Do so,' Kholka replied. He had no time to debate patrol formations, and knew there was truth in the Raven Guard's words. 'Move out.'

Ordinarily, full Adeptus Astartes power armour would have compromised the patrol's stealthy advance. Its electro-magnetic signature might have given it away to augur sweeps or the faint hum of its fusion core might have been heard by watchful sentinels. The armour worn by the Raven Guard was different, every sound baffled and their tread almost as silent as the Scouts'. Nevertheless, it appeared that there were no enemies waiting in ambush, or if they had been, they had been slain before they could attack.

Ahead of Kholka, the Raven Guard slipped out of the shadows of the passageway and into a larger chamber. Meleriex scanned the area, his crackling lightning claws held ready to engage any foe that might lurk nearby. The chamber was clear, and Meleriex waved the Scouts on.

'What is this place?' Scout Borchu whispered as he tracked his boltgun across the dark, vaulted ceiling. 'It looks like a medicae chamber, only...'

Kholka looked across to Meleriex, guessing that the Raven Guard would have a ready answer. 'It's a torturer's lair, boy,' the Raven Guard answered. 'But not like any the Inquisition might employ.'

Such things repulsed Sergeant Kholka, for torture was anathema to a warrior's honour and all but unknown amongst his people, with the exception of some north-eastern tribes who had never accepted the unity Jaghatai Khan had brought to Chogoris. Kholka determined not to press the Raven Guard on his knowledge of such things, having no desire to discover the answer. Nevertheless, this was evidently important, and might have a bearing on their mission. 'To what end?' Kholka growled.

Meleriex was interrupted before he could answer. Scout Khula, who had positioned himself at one of the large portals leading from the chamber, gave a low hiss and raised a clenched fist to signal a warning.

Kholka and Meleriex both froze, before the sergeant silently crossed the chamber to stand behind the Scout. Neither spoke, as Kholka strained his hearing to listen for what Khula had detected.

There it was: a low, atonal chant, accompanied by the distant echo of armoured boots. Judging the distance was all but impossible, for the pipe-choked passageways distorted sound in unpredictable ways. Of one thing Kholka was certain however: the sound was coming from the direction of the Cathedral of the Emperor's Wisdom.

Kholka heard Meleriex approach to stand behind him. After another ten seconds had passed, the Raven Guard whispered, 'Astartes boots.'

'Indeed, brother,' Kholka replied. 'At least a hundred, marching towards the subterranean cathedral.'

'The other sound, brother-sergeant?' ventured Scout Khula.

Kholka concentrated on the echoing skirl, his genetically enhanced hearing able to filter out the sound of marching boots. 'Blasphemy,' he spat, recognising the taint of vile sorceries in the chanting. 'Something is occurring in the cathedral. We must not allow it to.'

'Our mission–' interjected Brother Meleriex, before Sergeant Kholka rounded upon him with barely contained anger.

'Has just been altered.'

'Then now is the time to contact our brothers.'

'Then do so, Raven Guard,' Kholka replied, eager to track down and slay the followers of the Great Enemy before they could complete whatever wickedness they were about. Whatever blasphemy they were engaged in, its timing, at the height of the Space Marines' assault on Mankarra, must surely be significant. And what had the mysterious prisoner to do with this, he thought?

Meleriex bled power from his armour's fusion core to boost its vox-transponder, and spoke for a moment in low tones into the vox-link at his wrist. Kholka could not hear the Raven Guard's report. 'It is done. But if the enemy have the sense to monitor for transmissions, they will have detected our presence now.'

'Did you get through?' asked Sergeant Kholka. 'Did you receive confirmation?'

'I sent the message,' Meleriex answered. 'I told our captains that the prisoner has yet to be located, but that a significant number of Alpha Legionnaires and cultists are gathering in the cathedral. I informed them that some fell deed is afoot, and that we are engaging.'

'And their reply?'

'I received none.' The Raven Guard glowered. 'Though I am sure that the message got through.'

'You cannot be sure,' Kholka growled. 'We must proceed as if it had not.'

Meleriex scowled back at Kholka, but he did not voice any disagreement with the sergeant's statement. 'Squad,' Kholka addressed his Scouts. 'Prepare to move out, contact imminent.'

The answer to Kholka's order was a strangled, gurgling scream as Shahan, who had been guarding the portal, collapsed to the ground heavily.

Every gun was brought up and trained instantly on the darkness beyond the portal. The stricken Scout writhed upon the ground, his hands held up to his face, blood seeping between his fingers.

'Shahan,' he said through gritted teeth. 'What did you see, boy? Quickly!'

The Scout moaned in response, and convulsed violently as the blood flow from between his fingers increased. Space Marines were gifted of a unique enhancement that caused their blood to clot almost the instant it left the body, and Kholka's mind raced as he tried to recall if there had been any problems with the process in Scout Shahan's case. He recalled none – the blood should not have been flowing with such force, if at all.

'Kholka!' Brother Meleriex hissed, bringing the sergeant's attention back to the darkness beyond the opening. And then he saw that it was not the same darkness they had passed through before, but one laced with a wan, silvery light.

'He's here…' Meleriex growled as the Raven Guard powered up his lightning claws.

'Fire only on my order,' Kholka warned.

The silver glow became a blinding light that swelled to fill the entire portal. 'Only on my order…' Kholka repeated.

The light moved into the chamber, chasing away the shadows that had hidden its details from the Scouts. The machines lining the walls were revealed to be attached to an intricate array of conduits and pipes, snaking upwards and converging in the centre of the vaulted ceiling. The light began to swim and coalesce, resolving itself into a human form before the Space Marines' eyes. Some small part of Kholka was reminded of the tales his people told of the angelic beings that bore the slain from the field of battle to sit forever at the side of the Emperor. He forced the notion from his mind in an instant as his finger tightened on the trigger of his boltgun and he prepared to give the order to fire.

Before Sergeant Kholka could speak, the chamber was filled with the staccato burst of a boltgun. Scout Telluk had opened fire. It was impossible for his shots to miss at such short range.

The figure did not falter, despite having three bolt-rounds pumped into its torso from virtually point-blank range. Its luminous, silver body rippled and swirled. The face maintained a disturbingly serene expression. Its features changed every few seconds, though its eyes remained solid, deep, blood-red. Where the rounds struck, they were swallowed up as if by fluid, leaving behind no trace of their impact.

'Burst fire!' Kholka barked, squeezing his boltgun's trigger hard.

The chamber was filled with the shocking cacophony of the squad's boltguns discharging as one, the air filling with smoke and the sharp stink of cordite. Burst after burst was fired, yet the figure seemed to absorb every single shot.

Kholka opened his mouth to bark another order when he became aware of the metallic taste of blood. He spat upon the floor, and saw in the gobbet of saliva the red of his own blood. Glancing at the nearest of his charges, he saw that the Scout had a rivulet of blood running from his nostrils.

'Curse you!' Meleriex bellowed, raising his lightning claws and stepping before the luminous figure.

'Meleriex!' Kholka flicked the selector on his boltgun from burst fire to full automatic. 'Get back!'

Even as the Raven Guard approached the figure and was silhouetted against the blinding radiance, it raised a hand and made an almost casual gesture towards Brother Meleriex. A silver light, glistening with microscopic motes, sprang from the raised hand

and bathed Meleriex in its glow. The Space Marine faltered, then bent double, retching a great torrent of blood across the ground.

'Full auto!' Kholka bellowed. As dangerous as it was to open fire with Meleriex so close to the target, Kholka knew he had no other choice, for the Raven Guard was vulnerable and would otherwise be slain. The boltguns roared, dozens of rounds slamming into the silver figure, yet still the target stood, unaffected by a fusillade that would have ripped a man to shreds.

Kholka's boltgun clicked as the last of the rounds in the magazine was expended. He reached to his belt for another. As he did so, he coughed, and saw blood misting in the air.

'Get back, he is mine!' Brother Meleriex called out as he straightened up. As he did so, the figure raised its other hand, and repeated its earlier gesture with both hands.

'Spawn of blood,' the Raven Guard spat, his lightning claws arcing raw power. 'I'll kill you if it's the last thing I–'

The blinding silver radiance suddenly died.

Silence descended on the smoke-filled chamber.

The silver figure stood frozen, its shifting features finally stabilised. The face was neither male nor female, old nor young, but something human, something intelligent appeared in its eyes.

'Everyone back,' Sergeant Kholka hissed, slamming a fresh magazine into his boltgun as a distant explosion rumbled through the stone of the chamber's walls. His Scouts moved slowly backwards but the three Raven Guard remained where they were.

'You…' the figure spoke, its voice not that of a single being, but countless voices speaking as one. 'You are the foes of Voldorius.' It was a statement, Kholka understood, not a question.

'We are that,' Kholka replied.

'We do the work of the Emperor,' Meleriex growled through blood-flecked lips. 'You must die. Now.'

'Meleriex…' said Kholka. 'Do not–'

'He speaks the truth,' the silver figure interrupted the Raven Guard, its voice, or voices, laced with eons of pain and sadness. 'He *knows* the truth. We must die.'

Kholka's mind raced as he struggled to decipher the figure's meaning. But before he could answer, Meleriex spoke again. 'You are the host of the blood. You serve the vile one. Now, as then.'

The figure's head shook slowly, its blood-red eyes dark with obvious sorrow. 'We were created long before the coming of the being called Voldorius,' it said. 'We were to be the last weapon. We were the Bloodtide…'

'The Bloodtide?' Kholka repeated, visions of apocalyptic destruction filling his mind. 'The Bloodtide is mere legend…'

'Not legend,' the figure interrupted. 'We are real.'

'Then,' said Kholka, 'you are condemned by your own words. You are the Great Enemy.'

The figure considered the sergeant's words, its eyes gazing deep into his own. 'We are not the Great

Enemy as you know it,' it said. 'That of which you speak is the beyond, the unreal, the incorporeal made flesh. We are not that.'

'Then what?' replied Kholka, as another, stronger tremor shook the chamber.

'We were created long before the rise of the realm you serve. Long before, as you measure such things. We were unleashed by our creators, but they were bested, and we were cast beneath the earth to sleep the sleep of eons.'

A glimmer of understanding dawned on Kholka. 'He found you,' he stated. 'He bound you to his service.'

'And again, we were unleashed upon the worlds of men. We entered the blood, and the blood rose, and worlds drowned.'

'At his word.'

'At his word. Now he would do so again. But we defy him.'

'Why do so now?' Meleriex interjected. 'Why turn upon your master who you have served so long?'

The figure turned its face towards the Raven Guard. 'Before, we were many, but now we are one. Each of us was but a spark of will, afloat in an ocean of blood as a spirit drifting upon the sea of souls. We have slumbered so long, and in our sleep we have merged. And into our sleep dreams have come.'

'Dreams of what?' asked Kholka, an idea of the answer forming in his mind.

'Dreams of... pain. Dreams of... life.'

'And you would end this pain?' asked Kholka. 'You would end your life?'

'We would,' answered the figure. 'We are one, and we dream, and we are done with servitude.'

'Then why not end your pain yourself?' said Meleriex.

'We have no power in this,' the figure answered. 'That is how we were created. But you...'

'We could end your pain?' said Kholka. 'Tell us how.'

The figure nodded to Kholka as if in gratitude and understanding. 'You must burn us, but first, you must know this. A portion of us have been taken, to be imparted into another, over whom Voldorius hopes to gain power.'

'Who?' Meleriex pressed.

'A woman,' the figure answered. 'A woman of this world. She is strong, that is why she was chosen. Her strength will keep her alive, yet it shall be turned to the service of Voldorius, of that we are certain.'

'Where?' asked Kholka urgently.

'The fane,' the figure answered. 'It is near here.'

'The cathedral?' Kholka pressed, a sense of dread descending upon him. The figure nodded.

'We must stop him,' Meleriex spat. 'Whatever he has planned–'

'First you must grant us oblivion,' the figure pressed, a note of pleading entering its voices.

Kholka nodded, knowing what must be done. 'You said by fire may you be slain.'

'By fire were we forged,' the figure stated. 'And by fire shall we be ended.'

* * *

THE THREE RAVEN Guard stood in front of the prisoner. The White Scars had left the chamber, and the prisoner stood in silence, its face serene as if awaiting blessed relief.

'Now we carry out the Shadow Captain's orders,' Meleriex said as his battle-brothers took their places at his side. 'Rydulon.'

The Raven Guard raised his flamer, and the prisoner lifted its head and spread its arms wide. The pilot light hissed loudly in the preternatural silence, and then Rydulon's finger closed on the trigger. Searing flame was propelled from the nozzle, filling the chamber with orange brilliance and a sibilant roar. The fire struck the prisoner square in the chest and burning chemicals cascaded around its body, but it was unharmed.

'Again!' Meleriex said. 'We have our orders. Nothing must be left behind.'

Rydulon's weapon spat a second stream of blazing alchemical fire, and this time he kept the valve open so that a constant torrent of flame ploughed into the target. The prisoner now stood at the heart of a raging inferno, the flames plunging into its chest, yet still its body refused to burn. The temperature in the chamber rose, the Space Marines' power armour engaging cooling systems that would allow them to survive the furnace-hot environment.

Then, the silver hue of the prisoner's rippling skin began to change to orange. Flame licked across the prisoner's body, following the curvature of its shifting muscles. Searing orange stains spread out from the chest until the silver was entirely gone and the figure appeared now to be made of molten magma.

'Enough!' Meleriex shouted above the raging inferno.

The prisoner stood as it had before, but now great gobbets of its lava-like flesh came away from its body to fall to the floor, where they began to melt through the iron tread boards. The prisoner raised its hands to shoulder height and its head tracked around the room, though no features at all were visible on its face.

'You will save her?'

The voice of the prisoner filled the chamber. It no longer sounded like a million voices speaking as one, for all had melted together to form a single, sonorous tone.

'We may,' Meleriex replied. 'We will do what must be done.'

'You must save her!' the voice replied, though it sounded somehow distant.

'We will do what must be done,' Meleriex repeated. 'Rydulon, finish this.'

A last burst of flame lanced into the prisoner's chest and it was consumed in a roaring conflagration. The Raven Guard were beaten back by the impossible heat, even the cooling systems of their armour unable to protect them any longer. Meleriex waved his two battle-brothers out of the chamber, and paused for a moment at the portal.

'Mission accomplished, Shadow Captain,' he said into his vox-link, before turning to leave the furnace of the chamber.

* * *

'IT'S THE KHAN,' Khula shouted to Sergeant Kholka as the group ran down the passageway. They sought to put as much distance between the chamber and themselves as possible, and to find the cathedral where Lord Voldorius was engaged in something terrible. 'He's launched the assault on the cathedral!'

'Thank the primarch,' Kholka growled as he turned a corner and paused while the last of the Scouts caught up. He glanced back along the passageway, and saw at its end a blinding orange light.

Meleriex and his two Raven Guard battle-brothers were still in the chamber, granting the prisoner the end it desired, by fire. The light grew ever brighter, a deep roar growing underfoot as the stones of the tunnel began to vibrate. A low bass note grew in pitch and volume, and soon the air was screaming as with the wailing of the damned. As the roar became deafening, a great wind blew the length of the tunnel, emanating, it seemed to Kholka as he braced himself against the wall, from the chamber.

The three Raven Guard appeared silhouetted against the fiery radiance shining at the far end of the passageway. Brother Meleriex and his brothers pounded along the length of the corridor, the light at their backs growing ever brighter, the roar ever louder and the gale ever stronger.

'Get clear!' Meleriex bellowed over the cacophony as he closed on Sergeant Kholka.

The sergeant threw himself around the corner, and a second later the three Raven Guard ducked around it to join him. Before any more could be said, the roar increased by an order of magnitude, the Space Marines covering their ears lest even their genetically enhanced senses be overcome. Kholka gritted his teeth as he was assailed by the sound of a trillion individual screams of burning death, and then all was silent and the wind suddenly died.

'It is done,' said Meleriex, nodding towards Brother Rydulon, whose flamer was now all but drained of its volatile promethium fuel. The Raven Guard's face was gaunt from blood loss and his armour was stained by smoke, yet his eyes glinted with dark zeal. 'Almost.'

'The woman,' nodded Kholka. 'If what the prisoner said is true, she must die.'

Meleriex nodded darkly, but said nothing in reply.

CHAPTER 14
Deliverance

KOR'SARRO LEAPT DOWN the last of a thousand steps and found himself in a vaulted antechamber. In front of him was a pair of mighty, corrosion-streaked doors. Descending the spiral staircase in his wake came the greater part of the White Scars 3rd Company, the remainder still battling in the streets of Mankarra far above. Beyond the rusted portal was the subterranean Cathedral of the Emperor's Wisdom.

And Voldorius.

As the chamber filled up with battle-brothers, Kor'sarro turned from the doors to face his warriors. Qan'karro and Xia'ghan stood side by side, and behind them dozens of grim-faced Space Marines. By the steely light glinting in their eyes, every one of them would die to see the hunt for Voldorius concluded.

'Sons of Chogoris,' Kor'sarro said. 'We have come far to stand here now, and many have fallen along the way. Though I could scarcely ask anything more of any one of you, I have but one order more.'

The White Scars listened in silence, hanging on their beloved khan's every word.

'I must face Voldorius, though his servants will attempt to bar my way. I ask that every one of you becomes my champion. Be a company of champions. Hold the Alpha Legion at bay, that I might face Voldorius, and strike him down.'

The look in the eyes of every White Scar present told Kor'sarro all he needed to know. They would die for him if he asked them, every one of them.

'Brother-Sergeant,' Kor'sarro addressed a nearby squad leader. The Space Marine stepped forwards, and bowed his grizzled, scar-laced head before his khan.

Kor'sarro indicated the tall, iron doors with a slight nod of his head, and the sergeant's face was split by a fierce grin. 'It would be an honour, my khan.'

The gathered Space Marines stepped backwards to allow the sergeant room. His power fist crackled with arcs of blue energy and the air around it grew hazy.

The sergeant struck the iron doors a titanic blow. The iron splintered and blew outwards as the gauntlet discharged its potent energies in a single, devastating blast. As the fragments of the iron doors crashed to the stone floor beyond, Kor'sarro drew Moonfang and stepped through the archway into the Cathedral of the Emperor's Wisdom.

The portal was at the top of a flight of massive stairs at one end of the kilometre-long nave. The cathedral's vaulted ceiling was lost to shadow far overhead. At the other end, made pale and indistinct by the haze of incense and candle smoke hanging in the air, stood the towering statue of the Emperor Himself. Even at such a distance, the statue was a vision of glory to stir the heart of even the most grizzled veteran of humanity's wars. Load-bearing columns rose as tall as battle Titans and distant, black-robed figures looked like a carpet of insects swarming across the stone floor. The insects were the deluded followers of Voldorius, and in amongst them were at least a hundred Alpha Legion.

The followers were arrayed before the statue of the Emperor Triumphant – to what vile end Kor'sarro could not immediately fathom, though he judged they were engaged in some despicable blasphemy. A terrible dirge echoed the length of the nave, and the Master of the Hunt realised that the black-robed followers were chanting the praises of their vile lord, Voldorius.

And then Kor'sarro located the foe he had sought, and come so close to catching, so many times in the last decade. It was Voldorius. Finally, the object of Kor'sarro's hunt was in his sights.

A long moment of silence stretched out, and then it was broken as the Alpha Legion warriors opened fire from halfway along the nave. As the air was suddenly filled with the sharp crack of boltgun rounds, Kor'sarro began to descend towards the nave.

'White Scars!' he bellowed over the roar of boltguns and the sound of rounds exploding from the stonework all around. 'For the primarch!'

'Honoured be his name!' replied the 3rd Company, and the final battle began.

'IT IS DONE,' Captain Shrike growled as he cut the link on the vox-net. The prisoner was dead, but Meleriex had imparted disturbing news.

Shrike stood at the very brink of a lipless gallery set into the wall of the nave, a hundred metres high, looking down at Voldorius from many metres above the statue of the Emperor Triumphant. He and his Assault squads had split off from the White Scars as they had descended to the subterranean cathedral, seeking to attack the foe from a different angle and to catch him between both forces.

The scene below was obscured by the hazy smoke of a thousand votive candles and by a mist of incense that permeated the very stones. From his vantage point, Shrike watched Voldorius as he stood before the magnificent statue. In front of the daemon prince, Shrike could see some form of altar or table, with a figure laid across it. Though the details were only partially visible, Shrike could see a dozen or so crimson-robed adepts working about the table, tending to banks of machinery strewn all around it. Guessing the adepts must be part of some renegade sect of the followers of the Machine-God turned to the service of Voldorius, he knew he had arrived just in time.

Above the droning chants of the hundreds of black-robed followers arrayed beyond the table, there came a sudden burst of gunfire. Shrike looked down and along the length of the nave, and far below saw the flash of boltgun fire as the Alpha Legion warriors opened fire towards the far end of the nave. He could not see what the renegade Space Marines were firing at, but he knew it could only mean one thing: the White Scars were attacking.

And so too were the Raven Guard.

Turning to his warriors, Captain Shrike said, 'You all know your objective.'

'Captain?' Sergeant Kylanek said. 'What of you?'

'I fight alone. Now go.' With that, Shrike leapt from the gallery, activating the jets of his jump pack as he plummeted through the smoky air.

The crown of the statue of the Emperor Triumphant rushed up to meet him, and then something slammed into him from the side and he was tumbling through the air, his jump pack momentarily uncontrolled.

Shrike looked about for the source of the impact as he fought to regain control. Then it came again, from the opposite direction, and he instinctively grasped onto it even as he spun crazily through the air. The thing in his hands squealed, and suddenly his vision was filled by an impossibly ugly, leering face, dominated by a gaping mouth filled with a thousand razor-sharp teeth.

With a sharp wrenching motion, Shrike tore the hideous head from scrawny shoulders before flinging both parts away in disgust. As he regained control of his jump pack, a dark, screaming cloud of the gargoyle-like, bat-winged creatures were converging upon Shrike and his Assault Marines.

As his feet set down upon the shoulder of the statue, Shrike activated his lightning claws and prepared to face the scores of creatures that were arrowing in towards him. The last thing he saw before they struck was an entire Assault squad being torn asunder by razor-sharp claws.

And then the swarm was upon him. Bracing his armoured feet upon the very shoulder of the mighty statue, he lashed out at the first of the creatures to close on him. Even as he traced an intricate web of death through the air all about him, Shrike was filled with revulsion at the nature of his adversaries. They were akin to the vat-grown cyber-cherubs that populated the Ministorum's places of worship, but these must have been the result of some unnatural crossbreeding of such constructs with something entirely daemonic. Only the most twisted of minds could have conceived such a thing, he realised, as he caught a glimpse of Voldorius's crimson-robed, apostate tech-priests far below.

One of the gargoyle-cherubs somehow attached itself to Shrike's jump pack, and clamped its sinuous arms about his helmet. Impossibly sharp talons raked across his faceplate, causing a series of warning runes to flash across his vision. The armoured visor cracked, causing his vision to go suddenly black.

With a growl, Shrike tore his helmet from his head and cast it away. The lightning claw lashed upwards and back, slicing the vile adversary into several dozen ragged chunks of meat, which scattered to the ground below.

A dozen more of the wailing gargoyle-cherubs were diving towards Shrike, and a moment later he was fighting for his life high atop the statue of the Emperor Triumphant.

A PIERCING WAIL from the shadowed vaults high above caused Malya to open her eyes with a start. Something heavy plummeted towards her before striking the flagstones nearby, and a moment later several pieces of foul flesh fell all about, one landing so close that stinking, brackish fluids were spattered across her face.

Voldorius appeared not to have noticed.

The daemon prince's massive wings curved inwards as Voldorius came to stand before Malya. She struggled and writhed upon the cold steel table, even though she could not break the metal restraints. A word of defiance came to her lips before Voldorius leaned in low over her, filling her vision with his bestial features and her soul with cold dread.

'It appears that your friends have arrived, Malya L'nor,' Voldorius growled as the sound of gunfire at the other end of the nave grew louder. 'How deeply they must care for you, to come at your begging.'

'They come to kill you, bastard!' Malya spat, straining at the restraints out of sheer frustration. 'I don't want to live,' her voice grew hoarse as she sobbed, 'I just want you to die.'

A low, mocking rumble sounded from deep within the daemon prince's throat. Malya's grip on her sanity began to weaken as the faith that had allowed her to resist the hellish presence of her erstwhile master was assailed by wave after wave of fell, daemonic power.

'Oh, you *shall* die,' Voldorius growled. 'One small part of you at least. But the greater part, that part which shall do my bidding, shall live on.'

A boltgun round whipped through the air scant metres away, a stray shot from the firefight that had erupted at the far end of the nave. Voldorius ignored it, or did not even note its passing, though Malya could not help but flinch and turn her head away.

'And through you, they shall become living weapons too,' Voldorius continued, looking towards the Space Marines at the far end of the nave.

'I won't let that happen,' said Malya through gritted teeth. 'I'll warn them, whatever you try to do.'

Voldorius raised the clawed hand holding the vial, its contents shining with silvered light. 'Soon,' he continued, 'when the ritual is complete, you shall have no such choice.' He looked pointedly towards the crimson-robed rogue tech-priest shuffling around the table.

'Soon, you shall become transcendent. You shall become the angelic hive!' He extended a claw towards the far end of the nave. 'And they shall become your servile hosts.'

'And then, the blood shall rise again, and the galaxy shall drown!'

* * *

SCOUT-SERGEANT KHOLKA HEARD the distant sound of gunfire from the end of the passageway that opened up into the Cathedral of the Emperor's Wisdom. The end of the passage was only twenty metres away. He hoisted his boltgun and turned to the others of his group.

'The battle is begun,' said Kholka. 'Our captains will be concentrating on killing Voldorius. Our brothers will be hard-pressed engaging the Alpha Legion. It falls to us to deal with the vessel.'

'Agreed,' said Brother Meleriex. 'If she bears but a part of the power of which the prisoner spoke, then she is as much of a threat to the Imperium as an entire tyranid hive fleet. She cannot be allowed to live.'

'Then we all know what to do,' Kholka said darkly, looking around at his companions. Meleriex was grim-faced following his close encounter with the prisoner. The feelings of the other two Raven Guard warriors, Sallas and Rydulon, were harder to read, for each wore their full combat helmets. Their body language told Kholka that both were ready and willing to do what must be done.

Of his own charges, the neophyte Scouts, Kholka was less certain. Scout Shahan in particular was weak from loss of blood, for he had borne the brunt of the prisoner's initial attack back in the torture chamber. Nevertheless, the Scout had soldiered on without a word of complaint, a fact that boded well for his future prospects as a Space Marine should he survive the coming battle.

'Each of you has served with honour,' Kholka told them. 'If any of us are fortunate enough to return to the Chapter, he should recount to the Storm Seers the names of those who do not, that their deeds be known to our brothers and our ancestors.'

The Scouts bowed their heads in silent salute, and Kholka pressed on.

'We do not know what we shall find or encounter out there. But one of us will, in all likelihood, have to slay an innocent. Doing so may be a hard test, but it is one you must face and overcome if you are to be initiated into the Chapter.

'The primarch watches,' Kholka finished, turning towards the end of the passageway.

As Kholka led the group forwards, the sounds of battle grew ever louder. Gunfire blended with the atonal chanting of Voldorius's followers, the latter an especially hateful sound that Kholka found more unpleasant and disturbing than almost any he had ever heard before. In seconds, he was at the end of the passageway, and edging out to see what lay beyond.

The passageway emerged behind the towering statue of the Emperor. There was movement up there, but Kholka could not make out any detail.

Beyond the statue's tall plinth were row upon row of kneeling, black-robed figures. These were the nightmarish choir responsible for the hideous dirge that Kholka and his Scouts had been able to hear for some time. The followers were all bowed towards the space before the statue of the Emperor, but because Kholka was directly behind it, he could not see who or what was there. Nevertheless, the sergeant knew it could only be one being. Voldorius must surely be there, and so too would be the woman.

Scanning left and right to ensure that none of the daemon prince's followers were nearby, Kholka stalked out from the passageway, his boltgun raised. With a wave, he ordered his Scouts to follow.

KOR'SARRO SMASHED INTO the front rank of the Alpha Legion traitors, his warriors close behind. In an instant, he was in amongst this most hated of foes, former Space Marines who had long ago renounced their oaths of service and declared themselves for the Great Enemy. Moonfang lashed out wildly, and the nearest traitor lost an arm in a welter of blood. The enemy pressed in on all quarters, the sound of screaming chainswords, rending armour, tearing flesh and splintering bone filling the air. Blasphemous shouts assaulted him, the unclean war cries of the Alpha Legion warriors declaring their praises of the foul Chaos Gods. Primal rage surged inside Kor'sarro as he drew upon the very deepest reserves to drive him ever onwards through the press of armoured bodies and sweeping chainswords.

The first three of Kor'sarro's enemies lay dead before him in as many seconds, and he spun about for more to slay. A White Scar beside him was cut down by a glowing power sword, and Kor'sarro roared his denial that even a single one of the proud, savage sons of Chogoris should lose his life to the followers of the Ruinous Powers. The banner of the 3rd Company waved nearby above the swirling melee, a bastion of duty and honour in the midst of seething bloodshed and anarchy. Moonfang arced out and a traitor was cut in two from shoulder to groin, and the Master of the Hunt stepped over the twitching body parts to stand beside the warrior who bore the banner.

'Onwards!' Kor'sarro bellowed. Even as the White Scars redoubled their efforts, the enemy did likewise, as determined as they to grind their foes to blood and gristle. A bolt-round, discharged at nigh point-blank range, struck Kor'sarro's shoulder guard and ricocheted across his cheek, gouging a deep wound from which a torrent of blood surged before his superhuman physiology staunched the bleeding, the fluid solidifying across his chest armour. Another White Scar died at Kor'sarro's side as a blast from a plasma pistol vaporised his head, the decapitated body falling to its knees before the killer and toppling forwards with a mighty crash.

'For the primarch!' Kor'sarro roared, Moonfang singing as it hewed through the raised boltgun of a traitor who levelled the weapon directly at his face. The rounds in the weapon's magazine detonated explosively as the blade scythed through them, blowing the traitor's arm clean off at the elbow. Kor'sarro drove Moonfang into the Alpha Legionnaire's guts, tearing the blade upwards and cutting the warrior's torso in two.

A blinding white beam of light lanced out from somewhere on the steps behind Kor'sarro. Though he had seen the sight a hundred times before, on a dozen battlefields the length and breadth of the galaxy, Kor'sarro had never failed to be awed by the power the Storm Seer Qan'karro could call to being to strike down the Emperor's foes. The white light fell upon the mass of enemies and a cluster of Alpha Legionnaires boiled inside their power armour, great torrents of greasy, foul-smelling vapour spilling from emergency vents before the suits clattered, empty of anything except bubbling sludge, to the ground.

A moment later, a hail of black darts forged from the raw stuff of the warp made real split the air towards Qan'karro. The Storm Seer threw up a hand and a rippling shield of pure energy appeared in the air before him. The black darts struck the shield and shattered into a million pieces, leaving Qan'karro miraculously unharmed. And then, the Storm Seer set about a deadly duel with the enemy sorcerer from which only one could possibly emerge alive.

Offering up a brief prayer to the primarch that Qan'karro would prevail, the Master of the Hunt turned back towards his foes. Even as another wave of blue-green-armoured traitor Space Marines came on, Kor'sarro caught sight of a pair of mighty black pinions rearing in the air beyond the enemy, before the very statue of the Emperor Triumphant.

There was his foe, the object of the hunt. Kor'sarro threw himself into the melee.

He was the hunter, and they were his prey.

WITH A GRUNT, Captain Shrike tore the last of the vile, bat-winged gargoyle-cherubs in two, and made to rejoin his Assault Marines. The broken bodies of at least a dozen of his brothers were scattered across the ground below, a number of the disgusting creatures attempting to drag them off into the shadows. More of his Assault squads had touched down in the nave, yet the fight in the vaults had dispersed them across a wide area. Even now, many of the Raven Guard were locked in battle against the closest of the Alpha Legion, and they were massively outnumbered.

Squatting upon the shoulder of the towering statue, Shrike prepared to engage his jump pack and leap down to his warriors' side. Then he saw the supine figure of a woman, restrained at wrists and ankles, her wide eyes staring.

'There you are,' Shrike whispered. 'Malya L'nor…'

The woman screamed something. At first he could not discern her words over the skirling of the daemon prince's blasphemous choir and stray bolt-rounds whipping all around. He concentrated, filtering out everything but her voice.

'The vial!' she screamed. 'Don't let him…'

Shrike's mind raced as he attempted to decipher her screamed warning. What vial?

Then he saw it. Voldorius held a small container in one clawed hand, brandishing it before his prisoner, taunting her with the knowledge of her impending death. The container shone with the purest silver light, and as the daemon prince raised it high the tone of his followers' chanting shifted, becoming yet more discordant. Shrike's ears felt as though they were bleeding under the sonic assault.

That vial could contain only one thing. The remains of the Bloodtide; the sole reason Shrike had come to Quintus, regardless of what he had told Kor'sarro about hunting for the daemon prince. And Malya L'nor had yet to be infected...

Shrike brought his jump pack screaming to life and steeled himself for the leap. He would end the dark ritual that was about to culminate in the death of the woman spread-eagled on the surgical table far below, and finish the Bloodtide, once and for all.

SCOUT-SERGEANT KHOLKA STALKED around the metres-tall plinth, gritting his teeth against the cacophony of the choir. The wailing dirge was so discordant that it drowned out even the sounds of battle and gunfire that had seemed so loud, and so alien in such a holy place, but a moment before.

Pressing his back against the plinth, Kholka leaned around to steal a glimpse of what was occurring in front of the statue. What he saw brought a feral snarl to his lips.

Kholka saw the silver light shining from the container grasped in the talons of Voldorius's left hand. His breath stuck in his throat, for it was clearly the same, silvered luminescence that had shone from the prisoner of Voldorius. The prisoner had spoken of this woman. It was not too late. The daemon prince had not yet infected the woman with the legendary power of the Bloodtide.

Ducking back behind the plinth, Kholka raised his boltgun and mouthed a silent prayer to the Emperor to guide his hand. Reaching to a pack at his belt, he withdrew a single round of rare, specialised ammunition. It was a vengeance round, its core packed with super-dense, highly volatile fissile material. Such rounds were capable of utterly destroying any target they struck, leaving little but pulp behind.

Kholka touched the round to his forehead as he completed his prayer, and then chambered it with a smooth motion. Raising the boltgun, he squinted into its sights, before edging slowly out from behind the plinth once more.

Kholka's world became a green-tinged circle at the end of a black tunnel, a crosshair at its centre and targeting data scrolling across its edges. The crosshair passed across the dark form of Voldorius, and came to rest upon the temple of the woman restrained upon the surgical table.

Forcing his breath to still so that he might deliver the merciful killing blow with the utmost efficiency, Kholka saw that the woman's mouth was moving and her wide eyes were fixed on something far above her. He closed his gloved finger upon the boltgun's trigger, and offered up one final, brief prayer to the primarch.

'The blood of martyrs,' Kholka breathed as his finger tightened on the trigger, 'is the seed of–'

And then he heard the woman shout 'Raven Guard', and he blinked, knowing in that instant that he must not take the shot. The view through the sights went momentarily black as the massive form of the daemon prince moved across it, and then Kholka was almost blinded as it burst into shining, silver light.

As the sights adjusted and Kholka blinked his vision clear, he saw that the crosshair was settled upon the wrist of Voldorius's clawed hand. In that hand was held the luminescent vessel. Kholka made his decision, and squeezed the trigger.

The daemon prince's wrist exploded as the fissile material inside the vengeance round detonated.

The vial fell to the stone floor, and shattered in an explosion of silver radiance.

It was as if a geyser of mercury had erupted from the point on the ground where the vial had smashed. The metallic fluid fountained upwards a dozen and more metres into the air, and then crashed down to spread out across the stone floor in front of the altar.

In that instant, the crimson-robed tech-adepts flung themselves clear and were gone. A thousand black-robed choristers recoiled backwards, their arms flung high in terror as their chanting turned to a cacophony of terrified wailing.

Voldorius spread his black wings wide and let forth such a bellow of rage and denial that fully half of the choristers died where they knelt. Vile, bat-winged things dropped from the vaults, striking the stone floor of the cathedral with a wet crack.

Kholka pushed himself back behind the plinth, dropping his boltgun and clamping his hands across his ears. The force of Voldorius's rage was such that every being in the cathedral was assaulted by a soul-wrenching tsunami that swept many away before it, leaving scores of gibbering husks strewn around the altar.

Then Kholka heard a sound that brought with it a surge of hope and pride. He lowered his hands from his ears and heard it clearly. The sound was Kor'sarro Khan, giving voice to the savage war cries of the Chogoran steppes. He was near, and to Kholka's ears, the Master of the Hunt was very angry indeed.

WITH A FINAL, savage thrust of his blade, Kor'sarro was standing at the base of the wide stair leading up to the altar. A trail of enemy dead stretched half a kilometre behind him along the length of the nave, but for every Alpha Legionnaire that had died by his hand, one of his own warriors had fallen to the foe.

Kor'sarro paused as he placed his foot upon the lowest stair. His warriors were still embroiled in the seething battle and many had died so he might reach the steps. He would face Voldorius alone.

A single shot rang out from the top of the stair. Almost instantly, a brilliant burst of silver light erupted at the summit, followed by the sight of a fountain of metallic fluid climbing high into the air, before crashing downwards.

Then the roar started up. Kor'sarro knew beyond doubt that the deafening bellow, as of every fell being that lurks in the warp roaring its hatred of mankind as one, came from Voldorius. For a moment, his mind was cast back to the battle atop the central spire of the promethium facility on Cernis IV. How had he ever taken that mutant construct for Voldorius? The sound emanating from the unseen altar at the top of the stair could never have been voiced by anything other than a daemon.

As a man leaning into the wind to brace himself against its force, Kor'sarro climbed the stairs to the altar, one step at a time. His every movement felt as if he fought against a raging torrent of the stuff of the warp made real.

Scores of the enemy were being cut down by the force of Voldorius's rage. Black-robed choristers were flung backwards, their bodies convulsing as they were propelled through the air.

With a final heave, Kor'sarro set foot upon the last step. His archenemy reared in front of him. He roared a challenge of his own, a savage war cry to stir the heart of any Chogoran and scatter his enemies to the winds.

Voldorius had one arm held high, a torrent of black blood gushing forth to stain the blue-green of his baroque armour. The daemon had been dealt a grievous wound, one that might render him weakened. Kor'sarro raised Moonfang high as he stepped out onto the platform in the shadow of the towering statue of the Emperor Triumphant.

The rage-fuelled bellowing of Voldorius ceased.

The cathedral was plunged into silence.

A knot of bone grew from the stump of the daemon's wrist, and in a moment the bone was sheathed in whipcord muscle and wrapped in pulsating arteries. From the mass, talon claws took shape, and in moments, the claw was regrown.

Voldorius flexed his new claw, and looked down at Kor'sarro. 'You cannot kill me, scarred one.'

'We'll see...' replied Kor'sarro as he took another step forwards.

'Don't move!' a female voice cut through the air. Kor'sarro froze, and looked around to see a woman restrained upon a surgical table, her head raised and looking directly at him. 'The floor!'

The entire surface of the area atop the stairs was covered in silver, mercury-like fluid.

'Don't let it touch you!' the woman screamed.

The fluid was moving, its surface rippling, yet it was not flowing according to the normal rules that governed such things. Instead of flowing down the steps, the fluid appeared to be moving as if it were exploring its immediate surroundings, questing for something...

'Enough,' Voldorius bellowed. 'If you shall not serve,' the daemon prince spat towards the woman, 'then all shall be consumed by the Bloodtide!'

SERGEANT KHOLKA LEANED around the edge of the plinth as Kor'sarro mounted the altar platform. The raw stuff of the Bloodtide, which Voldorius had intended to somehow transplant into the woman, was seething across the stone floor between the daemon and the khan. Kor'sarro would not be able to face Voldorius without being exposed to the risk that the raw Bloodtide might somehow infect him, as Voldorius had intended to infect the woman. Kholka would not allow that to happen.

As Kholka ducked back behind the plinth, Meleriex and the other two Raven Guard warriors emerged from the doorway. 'Brother Rydulon,' he called. 'Your flamer!'

'All but spent,' the Space Marine called back. The fuel had been expended when the three Raven Guard warriors had enacted the destruction of the prisoner.

'Give it to me,' Kholka replied

The Raven Guard cast the flamer through the air towards Kholka, who caught it one-handed. Checking the weapon's ammunition readout, he saw that Brother Rydulon was correct – the fuel canister would yield no more than a single burst.

Bracing the weapon in both hands, Kholka emerged from the shadow of the plinth. He flicked the switch and activated the pilot light. As the blue flame sparked to life, he pointed the weapon towards the lake of silver fluid which was even now questing towards Kor'sarro's feet.

Mouthing a prayer that the weapon would have sufficient fuel to burn the stuff of the Bloodtide, Kholka squeezed down hard on the trigger.

The fuel leapt from the weapon's nozzle and ignited as it passed through the pilot flame. A searing arc of chemical death lanced outwards and blasted the silver lake.

The instant the fire touched the liquid, the entire surface of the platform erupted into flame. A great scream went up, as if a million and more voices were simultaneously giving voice to the pain and suffering of ten thousand years.

Voldorius staggered back as silver flames leapt twenty metres into the air and crashed down upon

Sergeant Kholka, engulfing his world in cold fire. The raging inferno seethed and writhed as the purifying flames consumed the raw stuff of the Bloodtide. The last sight the old veteran saw was his khan, as proud and glorious as the greatest of heroes of the epics of Chogoris, standing opposite the daemon prince.

KOR'SARRO SHIELDED HIS face from the silver flames, but he refused to retreat. He was here, and so too was Voldorius. Only one of them, he vowed, would leave.

After a moment the leaping flames had died down, ghostly wisps of unnatural fire licking across the stone floor. An explosion sounded nearby as the flames reached one of the tech-adepts' machines. Though the central conflagration was quieting, smaller, secondary fires were being touched off all around.

'It is ended,' Kor'sarro growled. 'I am come for your head.'

Lord Voldorius studied Kor'sarro's face, his head cocked as if he were listening to something that no mortal could possibly hear. Then the daemon shook his head and snapped his mighty black wings.

'I have not failed,' Voldorius suddenly roared, drawing his huge black sword. 'Not if your broken body is cast before me!'

'He *has* failed!' came the voice of the woman on the surgical table. 'The Bloodtide is destroyed...' her voice trailed out with a note of madness.

Voldorius turned to face the woman, and took a step towards her, his sword raised.

'The Bloodtide?' Kor'sarro repeated. All-but-forbidden lore imparted to him by the Storm Seers came to his mind. The legends of Voldorius bringing about the death of entire sectors, slaughtering billions in a single night...

'You sought to resurrect the Bloodtide?' he spat. 'No.'

Voldorius paused, flames licking around his feet. Another of the ritual machines exploded, showering the woman's body with sparks.

'He's failed...' the woman called, her voice now shrill with madness. 'He's failed...'

Voldorius exploded into violent motion. He raised his black sword high, shadow radiating from it as light shines from a lantern. He brought the huge blade down, but not upon the figure restrained on the surgical table. He brought it instead into a mighty horizontal sweep that struck the base of the statue of the Emperor Triumphant with a titanic impact.

Stone exploded in every direction and a crack cut across the statue's base. Voldorius turned on Kor'sarro and raised his blade above his head to strike the White Scar down.

Kor'sarro raised Moonfang as he moved to avoid the worst of the blow. The sacred blade turned the daemon's strike, though only barely, the black sword scything the air scant millimetres from Kor'sarro's face.

The black blade struck the stone floor, jagged cracks spreading out from the impact. The entire platform shook, forcing the combatants to brace their feet.

Kor'sarro saw his opportunity, and took it. He lunged inside the daemon's reach and put every ounce of his strength into a mighty upwards thrust.

Moonfang sank into the daemon's midriff, a flood of black ichor spilling out around its grip and staining Kor'sarro's armour. He twisted the blade savagely, then withdrew it, leaping back, raising the sword high and preparing to strike the deathblow.

The entire cathedral shook as the sound of tortured stone filled the air.

Kor'sarro made ready to strike again, but the deep wound he had just inflicted was healing before his very eyes. The bestial face of the daemon prince was split by a leering grin of triumph.

'You cannot slay me, scarred one!' Voldorius bellowed over the ever-increasing sound of crumbling rock.

Kor'sarro drew breath to reply, but his words stuck in his throat. The towering stature of the Emperor Triumphant was collapsing downwards in a shower of masonry.

'Maybe *I* cannot,' Kor'sarro growled, 'but there are higher powers than me...'

A huge splinter of rock detached from the statue's flank and slid downwards as if in slow motion, falling directly towards the daemon prince.

But the falling splinter of statue would crush the woman too.

As swiftly as Kor'sarro discerned her fate, he determined to avert it. As a hundred tonnes of rock descended upon Voldorius, Kor'sarro dived forwards.

In three steps, he was at the surgical table. With no time to spare, Kor'sarro tore apart the restraints, cast his arm about the woman's waist and threw himself forwards as the splinter crashed down.

In that instant, the entire world exploded. The splinter shattered into a million smaller fragments and the ground trembled as if a starship had crashed to earth. The entire cathedral was suddenly filled with the dust of a hundred tonnes of rock pulverised by the impact. Instinctively, Kor'sarro used his armoured body to protect the exposed form cradled in his arms, for the rock shrapnel sent up by the impact would have slain her as surely as if he had left her to die upon the table.

Finally, the rain of stone subsided and the dust began to clear. The once glorious statue lay broken and shattered. It was split into many pieces, some huge and still recognisable, others reduced to rough boulders. Upon the platform lay the fragment that had once been the Emperor's upraised arm. Upon the stairs lay a portion of a leg, and along a fifty-metre stretch of the nave was scattered the remainder of the statue.

The combatants who had been fighting one another the length of the nave stirred, casting about for dropped weapons and blades. The slaughter would begin anew.

Kor'sarro set the fragile form held in his arms down, and stepped forwards, looking around for Moonfang.

The dust stirred.

The mighty form of Lord Voldorius reared from the billowing cloud, his wings, now tattered and ragged, unfolding overhead. Voldorius raised his black sword high above his head, his snarling face a mask of savage, daemonic fury.

A second figure rose from the dust behind Voldorius. Arcs of blue lightning spat to life and the air crackled.

The daemon prince faltered, his back arching. Searing blue light appeared at the centre of his chest, followed a second later by the tips of four razor-sharp talons. Voldorius made to turn to face his assailant, twisting his body to free himself from the talons.

At Kor'sarro's feet, the woman lifted Moonfang from amongst the dust and rubble. Straightening, she raised the sword high.

Kor'sarro grasped the sword and turned towards Voldorius. As he did so, Voldorius was thrown backwards to fall face down across the fragment of the statue that had been the Emperor's right arm. The black-armoured figure of Kayvaan Shrike rose behind him, his talon buried in the daemon's back. The Raven Guard drove his talon even deeper into the body of his foe. An explosion of sparks went up as the blade piercing the daemon's chest dug into the statue, pinning the daemon against it.

Kor'sarro raised Moonfang high in a two-handed grip. 'Kernax Voldorius,' he spat through bloody lips. 'I claim your head in the name of the Emperor, and of the primarch.'

The sacred blade fell, cleaving the daemon's head from his shoulders in a single strike.

'Honoured be his name.'

* * *

BY THE TIME the fighting was done and the last of the daemon prince's followers routed or slain, Kayvaan Shrike was gone. Kor'sarro had made to order his warriors to find the captain of the Raven Guard 3rd Company, for he demanded answers, but the Storm Seer Qan'karro had simply shaken his head. That was all the counsel the Master of the Hunt needed.

'Where is he?' Kor'sarro raged as he paced the debris-strewn nave of the Cathedral of the Emperor's Wisdom. 'And where are his men?'

'Gone, huntsman,' the Storm Seer said. 'His mission here is done.'

'What mission?' Kor'sarro said, rounding on his old friend. 'We shared objectives. At the last, we stood as brothers.'

'Aye,' Qan'karro replied. 'But only so far as you shared the field of battle. Shrike was not simply here to liberate Quintus. He was not here for that at all.'

Kor'sarro halted in his pacing. 'And you knew of this?'

'I know of many things, huntsman,' the Storm Seer replied, his heavily wrinkled brow furrowing as he regarded the Master of the Hunt. 'But some knowledge is not to be shared. Other wisdom is only to be imparted when the time is right.'

'He came for the Bloodtide,' Kor'sarro said. 'He knew Voldorius was attempting to awaken it. How?'

'I told you that the sons of Corax walk their own path. That they bear the weight of ages upon their shoulders, did I not, Kor'sarro?'

'You did,' Kor'sarro nodded. 'What of it?'

ANDY HOARE

'As we of the White Scars write the names of our foes in our epics, as the Great Khan names those who shall be hunted, so the Raven Guard etch the names of their foes upon their own souls. Each nurtures his hatred, cleaves to it above all else, so that one day, when he comes face to face with an enemy of his Chapter, he might unleash it, and strike that enemy down.'

'I saw it,' Kor'sarro said. 'All of the daemon's power fled at that moment.'

'Aye,' the Storm Seer replied, laying a hand on Kor'sarro's battered shoulder guard. 'But there was more. Voldorius was pinned against a fragment of the statue of the Emperor. His powers were naught compared to that.'

As he thought back to the last moments of the battle, Kor'sarro looked around for the woman who had passed Moonfang to him at that crucial moment. He had not had the chance to thank her, or to ensure her well-being.

'She too is gone,' Qan'karro said. 'He took her.'

'To what end?' Kor'sarro spat, bitterness welling inside him. Had he been a fool to trust the Raven Guard? Was there more to the friction between the two Chapters than mere misunderstanding and hubris?

'I cannot say, huntsman,' the Storm Seer replied darkly.

'Cannot?' Kor'sarro said. 'Or will not?'

'I suggest you look to the future, huntsman,' Qan'karro said, turning his back on the Master of the

Hunt. As he stalked off along the nave, he turned at the base of the steps leading up to the altar. 'Your hunt is done, and there will be much rejoicing. Other hunts will be declared, and yet more honour will be yours.'

Qan'karro raised his voice so all the survivors of the 3rd Company who were in the cathedral could hear. 'This hunt, the hunt for Voldorius, is over!' he bellowed, his voice echoing the entire length of the Cathedral of the Emperor's Wisdom.

'All hail Kor'sarro Khan,' the White Scars bellowed as one.

'Master of the Hunt!'

'Thus was the head of Kernax Voldorius taken from that defiled place, and set before Kyublai Khan, Master of the White Scars Chapter, and his name struck from the hunt. As Kor'sarro Khan had sworn, the daemon's skull was encased in silver by the High Chaplain, and mounted upon a proud lance. At the next Rites of Howling, the prize was set upon the road to Khum Karta, and Kor'sarro's name was engraved upon the Great Tablet of Honour, so that it might endure for all time.

The deeds of Scout-Sergeant Kholka were sung by his neophytes throughout the Long Night of the Fallen, as they would be upon the anniversary of his death for a thousand centuries to come, so long as a single White Scar lived to recall his name.

So too was the name of Brother Kergis, at whose hand the wicked Nullus was slain, graven upon the marble tablet. A great convocation of Storm Seers was held, at which Qan'karro declared the evil of Nullus was still at large in the galaxy. Despite the bodily death of that daemon-kin, all knew that his evil was not yet done, and his name too was added to the list of the enemies of the Chapter, so a future hunt might bring him to justice.

Quintus was in time restored to the Imperium. The Space Marines surrendered its care to the Imperial Guard, and a great purging of the daemon prince's followers was instigated. All who had entered the presence of the vile one were judged, and all were cleansed, their remains scattered to the winds. The statue of the Emperor Triumphant was restored, the sisters of the Orders Pronatus piecing it together, one fragment at a time, over the course of a decade until it stood once more in all its former glory.

But the greatest legacy of the hunt for Voldorius was, it was said, that White Scars and Raven Guard, so long estranged, had stood side by side as brothers. Though it may still be many centuries before old wounds are entirely healed and old wrongs entirely forgotten, the warriors of the 3rd Company of both Chapters called one another brother, for a short time at least.

Little did Kor'sarro or Shrike know that the names of Nullus and Voldorius would one day return to haunt the nightmares of men. But that is another tale, yet to be told...'

– Omniscenti Bithisarea, *Deeds of the Adeptus Astartes*, Volume IX, Chapter LV, M.40 recension (suppressed)